The Burning City

The Burning City

Book Two of *The Spirit Binders*

Alaya Dawn Johnson

A Bolden Book

AGATE

CHICAGO

"Do Not Go Gentle Into That Good Night" By Dylan Thomas, from *The Poems Of Dylan Thomas*, copyright ©1952 by Dylan Thomas.
Reprinted by permission of New Directions Publishing Corp.

Printed in the United States.

Library of Congress Cataloging-in-Publication Data

    Johnson, Alaya Dawn, 1982-
    The burning city / Alaya Dawn Johnson.
       p. cm. -- (Spirit binders ; bk. 2)
    ISBN-13: 978-1-932841-45-9 (pbk.)
    ISBN-10: 1-932841-45-8 (pbk.)
    1. Young women--Fiction. 2. Islands--Fiction. I. Title.
    PS3610.O315B87 2010
    813'.6--dc22
                2009054036

9 8 7 6 5 4 3 2 1

Bolden Books is an imprint of Agate Publishing.
Agate books are available in bulk at discount prices.
Single copies are available prepaid direct from the publisher.
Agatepublishing.com

To my mother and my Aunt Vanessa,
the strong women in my life who helped inspire the strong women in this book.

Thou art slave to fate, chance, kings and desperate men...
— John Donne

Grave men, near death, who see with blinding sight
Blind eyes could blaze like meteors and be gay,
Rage, rage against the dying of the light.
— Dylan Thomas

What came before...

THE MORNING OF HER FIRST BLOOD, thirteen-year-old Lana is at once excited and terrified to perform her first dive alone. If successful, she will be initiated into the elite ranks of those who dive for the jewels created by the sacred mandagah fish. But two unusual jewels, given her by a dying fish, are destined to one day tear her from everything she has ever loved. In the islands, humans are engaged in a constant struggle with their environment—the countless volcanoes, floods, and divine winds that threaten their lives. And so, to control these natural forces and allow human civilization to flourish, a few brave individuals used the power of sacrifice to imprison the spirits of fire, water, and death that govern these acts of nature. Ever since that time, despite the continued worship by humans, these spirits have struggled to break free.

Soon after Lana's initiation, floods devastate the small rural island. Although Leilani, Lana's mother, is reluctant to leave, her father's desire to travel to the city prevails. Lana and Leilani stay in another, smaller city while Lana's father goes ahead to the metropolis of Essel—an urban center in the shadow of the smoking volcano, Nui'ahi, and home to the famed Kulanui, an ancient school.

Returning to the Kulanui is Lana's island teacher and youthful crush, Kohaku. There he is happy to be reunited with his deaf sister, Emea, someone whom he believes is very sheltered from the rest of the world because of her handicap. Unbeknownst to him, however, she is carrying on an affair with Nahe, the head of Kohaku's department at the Kulanui.

1

Meanwhile, Lana and her mother eke out a meager living in the dockside slums in Okika City. Lana's harsh work at a launderer's eventually makes her desperately ill, and Leilani turns to prostitution in order to pay for her daughter's medicine. A mysterious one-armed witch approaches Leilani and offers her a deal: enough money to travel to Essel and live comfortably with her husband in exchange for Lana's apprenticeship. Lana would learn how to harness the power of the spirits through sacrifice. Leilani must also wear a necklace with a bone charm carved in the shape of a key—the ancient symbol of the death spirit.

Lana generally enjoys her life with the witch Akua—although certain strange events sometimes make her question her mentor's intentions. Lana ignores oblique warnings from Ino, the water sprite who guards the nearby lake. When Lana is eighteen, Akua informs her that her apprenticeship is nearly at an end. As a final lesson, she promises to show Lana a technique that can be used to harness great power. Under Akua's watchful eye, Lana learns how to use the matched jewels she harvested during her initiation to trick another person into an unwitting sacrifice. What Lana doesn't know is that she will slowly kill the other person to whom she gives one of the jewels. She sells it to Pua, an older woman who has spent most of her life in the outer islands raising her nephew Kai, the half-human water guardian. Then, in a ceremony Lana doesn't understand, Akua binds Lana's fate inextricably with her own, tricking Lana into accepting this burden.

Soon after, Leilani collapses. Using her connection with Pua through the linked jewel necklaces, Lana recites a geas that will allow Leilani to live, but only with great sacrifice: Lana is doomed to be hounded by the specter of her own mother's untimely death until she herself dies. Akua, curiously unsurprised at Lana's predicament, gives her a powerful means to survive—a flute made from the hollowed bones of Akua's right arm.

In the days before Lana's fateful sacrifice, Kohaku's sister Emea dies—a victim of her lover's callous treatment after she becomes pregnant. Nahe expels Kohaku from the Kulanui to discredit his accusations. Destitute and bereft, Kohaku makes the pilgrimage to the inner fire shrine, where hundreds supplicate the fire spirit to become the new ruler of Essel. Kohaku merely intends an honorable death: of those hundreds who vie for rulership, only one succeeds—and the rest are all sacrificed. On the boat to the shrine, however, Kohaku meets Nahoa, a rough-edged but lovely sailor. The unexpected love he feels for her rekindles his desire for both life and revenge, leading him to do the unthinkable. For the price of his left hand, Kohaku deliberately weakens the bindings that hold the fire spirit—and thus becomes ruler of the most powerful city in the islands. He and Nahoa marry, but their happiness is tempered by his bloodthirsty need to avenge his sister—who appears to him as a ghost—and his growing paranoia about Nui'ahi, the great volcano.

While Kohaku becomes Mo'i, Lana spends her days engaged in a desperate battle of wits with the death spirit. She goes on a pilgrimage to the original wind shrine, destroyed five hundred years before, when that spirit broke free of its human-forged bindings. After she endures a three-day vigil, the wind spirit grants Lana its double-edged gift—she grows black wings that can help keep her from the clutches of the death spirit. Lana thus becomes the first "black angel," an ancient harbinger of destruction, in five hundred years.

Exhausted unto death, Lana flies away and collapses on the doorstep of a well-to-do country inn, wearing a cloak drawn over her shoulders. There, she is taken for a hunchback beggar and is about to be turned away before one of the richest guests demands that she be let in. The guest is in fact Kai, the water guardian, whose otherworldly features inspire more fear than respect. He takes her to his rooms and helps to nurse her back to health. Kai then offers her a gift she never could have hoped to receive: complete protection from the death spirit in his shrine on the outer islands. She accepts and begins a more peaceful existence with Kai in his home. However, despite their growing love for each other, he keeps his distance. Any woman who chooses to sleep with a guardian will kill him if she sleeps with another. Lana understands the risks, but gives herself to Kai anyway. As he teaches her more about the art of geas and binding, she discovers that Akua has left some vital gaps out of her education. This makes Lana suspicious, but she only fully understands the magnitude of Akua's treachery when Kai tells her of his beloved aunt Pua on the anniversary of her death. Lana immediately realizes that this is the same woman she had used as an unwitting sacrifice a year before. Kai's aunt died of a sudden illness one week after Lana cast the spell that saved her mother. Racked with guilt, Lana leaves the water shrine, determined to confront Akua and demand answers.

But Akua has abandoned the cottage, and the only information Ino can give Lana is a slim, ancient black book. And then, before she can look further, there is an explosion to the west. Nui'ahi, Essel's great volcano, dormant for a thousand years, has finally blown.

Just before the explosion, Akua appears in the city, where she kidnaps Leilani. The two women witness the destruction in silence, both equally shocked.

At that moment, Nahoa is sequestered in the fire shrine, having left Kohaku when she discovered the brutally mangled body of his sister's erstwhile lover. Nahoa gives birth to her and Kohaku's daughter amid the fiery carnage.

Lana arrives in the devastated city to find her parents' home razed. Her father tells her that her mother has gone missing, and the two grieve the only way they can, by playing a lament together in the smoking ashes of the great city.

Glossary

The black book

Characters

Aoi – Narrator of the black book.
Parech – Akane tribesman who served as a Maaram soldier.
Taak – A Maaram soldier.
Tulo – A Kawadiri princess.
Wolop – A Maaram soldier.
Yaela – First of the Great Binders, who bound the water spirit.

Nations/Tribes

Akane – A loosely grouped network of tribes conquered by the Kukichans a generation before.
Essel – The city that has become the dominant cultural and military power.
Kawadiri Archipelago – Home to tribes conquered by the Maaram but still fighting for their independence.
Kukicha – Large island known for its rice farming; the Kukichans are the conquerors of the Akane tribes.
Maaram – The chief rival of the Esselans. Their city is also called Maaram. Centuries later, the island of Maaram becomes known as Okika.

Lana's story

Characters

Ahi (full name Lei'ahi) – Nahoa and Kohaku's infant daughter.
Akua – A witch. Lana's former teacher.
Arai – Okikan general.
Edere – Mo'i soldier.

Elemake – Death guardian.
Eliki – Rebel leader.
Ino – Water sprite of the lake near Akua's house on Okika Island.
Kai (full name Kaleakai) – Water guardian and Lana's lover.
Kapa – Lana's father.
Kohaku – Mo'i of Essel.
Lana (full name Iolana) – The black angel.
Leilani – Lana's mother.
Leipaluka – Rebel soldier.
Lipa – Apothecary for the rebels.
Makaho – Head nun of the fire temple.
Malie – Nahoa's maid.
Nahe (deceased) – Kohaku's former superior at the Kulanui. Tortured in Kohaku's dungeon.
Nahoa – Kohaku's wife.
Pano – Rebel leader.
Sabolu – Stablehand for the fire temple.
Senona Ahi – Fire guardian.
Tope – Rebel soldier.
Uele'a – Stablehand for the fire temple.
Yechtak – Member of the wind tribes and ambassador of the wind spirit.

Landmarks in Essel
Essel has eight districts total, which spiral outward from the city's center.

Sea Street – The north–south road that bifurcates Essel and connects the two bays.

Greater Bay – The main harbor to the south. The Kulanui and the fire temple are both nearby.

Lesser Bay – The old, smaller harbor to the north. This has been in general disuse for centuries.

The Rushes – An ancient farming community on the far west coast of the seventh district.

Nui'ahi – Also known as the "sleeping sentinel," this is the volcano that has loomed over the great city of Essel for centuries.

Kulanui – The great center for learning in Essel; it has been in the city for nearly a thousand years. It is located in the third district, near the Greater Bay.

Mo'i's House – Another ancient structure, located more centrally in the third district.

Terms

Napulo – A philosophy of spirit binding. In the past, those who called themselves napulo were evenly split on its morality. In the present, only those who dispute the spirit bindings actively retain an association with the philosophy.

Mo'i – The ruler of all Essel, chosen once every fifteen years by the fire spirit itself. In the ceremony at the heart of the fire shrine, many will offer themselves, but only one will be selected—and all the others will die in the great flame.

Kai – An old word for water, used to invoke the water spirit.

Make'lai – An old word for death, used to invoke the death spirit.

Mandagah Fish (and Mandagah Jewels) – A type of fish native to the outer islands, where generations of divers harvest the brightly colored jewels that grow in their mouths. Recently, disasters have greatly reduced their numbers.

Outer Islands – The term for the warm, spirit-heavy islands that scatter the rim of the island world. The guardians of the three major spirits all have shrines in the outer islands.

Inner Islands – The term for the frozen heart of the island world, where the three major spirits remain imprisoned.

Spirit Bindings – The central tenet of island life. The spirits ruling fire, death, and water have been bound by humans for a thousand years, thus protecting humans from environmental extremes. Wind used to be bound, but it broke free five hundred years before Lana's time.

Prologue

THIS HOUSE HELD ANCIENT TREASURES—mats woven with long-extinct dune grass, walls of acacia wood turned burgundy with age, and notes slipped into its nooks and crannies like messages across time to the woman now trapped inside. Leilani could hardly have devised a more fascinating prison. The ocean was a constant presence, beating against a shore a few dozen yards away. Leilani could almost imagine throwing off her clothes and diving beneath the water—if it weren't for the winter cold and the sprites that ever so gently prevented her from exiting the door. She tried twice, and stopped. Leilani knew enough about power to recognize a superior force.

Her daughter was safe. Her husband...she would not think of her husband. Instead, she spent her days hunting for the notes. They were written in an ancient form of Essela and one could sometimes take her hours to struggle through. The words and grammar were largely the same, but the characters slightly, maddeningly different. The content of the notes would have been stiflingly banal in other circumstances, but fascinated her now.

"I would go to the Nui'ahi," read one in large, childish script. And another: "I would feed the big eel fish." She imagined a child a thousand years dead, exuberantly placing his or her wishes in the wall and hoping an indulgent parent would grant them. It reminded her of Lana at that age, though most of Lana's wishes had centered on diving. Some of the notes were in an older hand. "I wish to see Ile ride a wave," and "I would watch Ile dance." She showed these notes to Akua, but the witch would hardly look at them before going away again. Leilani learned to keep them out of sight if she hoped for conversation. Occasionally, the witch made Leilani sit in the middle of the room while she attempted a geas. It always failed, and given the witch in question, Leilani knew this was astonishing. Other than these eerie, aborted moments, Akua left Leilani largely alone. And Leilani, whose options were either brooding over her fractured family or exploring the ancient house, chose the latter.

But one month after the great eruption, she found a note very different from the others. The handwriting was recognizably that of the parent, but the characters seemed to form nonsense words. A different language? She stared at the brittle parchment. Almost everyone in the islands spoke the same language. They had for centuries. Somehow, she knew that this note would not convey the familiar wishes of a parent to a child. The characters were cramped and hurried. It felt like a confession. Like a secret. Like a hint of what had truly happened in this house centuries before.

Deliberately, she left it in the open and waited for Akua to return. The witch read it as though she could not look away. She bent down and picked it up. Her hand trembled. Leilani realized what should have been obvious from the first: Akua had loves and disappointments just like everyone else. It was her combination of extreme power and emotional detachment that made her seem inhuman.

"Where did you find this?" Akua asked.

"Beneath the mat closest to the door. What does it say?"

Akua was silent for a long time, long enough for Leilani to give up on an answer. Her words, when she spoke, rang with the natural intonation of poetry.

"Haven't I always loved you?
And yet you only see her,
Dancing by the fire."

The death had grown to know the girl, to feel comfortable in her shadow. It would trail her for hours, then days—a week, once—before recalling its geas. It attempted to kill her the way a master attempts to beat a skilled partner in a shell game, with more interest than conviction. It had been cast off like a splinter from a carving, a death not of death, and it had grown and changed. It recalled the sublime consciousness of the whole, but did not long to return there. The girl was complete and bright with the life it longed to quench. That time in the guardian's shrine, when she had nearly passed beyond the gate, she had tried to bind the death with words alone. She had noted the substance of its key, and it had stilled at the burning, frantic, hope in her eyes as she struggled for more, as she uncovered truth with desperation. "So long as it wields the key," she had said, "the death is bound to petty human emotion."

True. And its emotions were not merely petty. Of late, they had even been transcendent.

Oh, the dying souls it feasted on in the wake of the fires and ash. Oh, the thousand living flames, some as bright as hers, snuffed and snuffed and snuffed until it felt like a glutton at a banquet. The avatar had returned to the center to be subsumed by the ceaseless totality of the death godhead. But it had been forgotten, cast out again fully formed. The self-same splinter, sent to hound the water girl, the angel girl, once more. That had never happened before. The avatars are not of themselves. They are projections of the whole. Yet it seemed to be itself, to be a thing like she was a person, and the sensation stayed its hand, even when the old lady's geas seemed to burn with urgency.

The avatar is the death, but death is not its avatar.

Sixty days left, the geas said. *Fifty-nine days.* And still it trailed her and warmed its burgeoning selfhood with her own. They were much alike in that. New-molded clay being fired in the ashes of Essel's volcano. In the smoke from twenty thousand extinguished flames.

"Do you really think you'll find your mother?" it said to her, on day fifty-two.

Shadows looked like paint beneath her eyes, but she smiled. "Honestly? Probably only if Akua lets me."

She would not have known that a year or even a few months before. She was finally asking the right questions, at last getting closer to their answers. It wondered how long the old lady could continue her game.

And the lonely avatar, caught between selfhood and godhead? It bided. Day fifty-one, she realized she should visit the fire temple. The old lady's chosen player was quickly learning the stakes. Forming her own conclusions.

Which is the trouble with avatars, isn't it?

PART I
. . .

Fate

· 1 ·

THE WOMAN'S HAIR WAS THE FIRST part of her to catch fire—it was long, and streaked with gray, and for a horrified moment, Lana wondered if she'd finally found her mother. Her thin lips mouthed prayers that Lana couldn't hear over the thrumming whispers of the gathered crowd. The woman had wrapped her wrists in yards of sennit braid, the brown of the rough cordage blending with her skin so that from a distance it almost looked like lumping scar tissue. A breeze blew in off the great bay, bringing with it the familiar scent of ash and—far too redolently—burning flesh.

Beside her, an older man averted his head. "Napulo freaks," he said, almost spitting the words into the pounded ash at their feet.

Lana walked forward. The crowd might have been dense, but it receded like a tide at her approach, as if the splayed edges of her black wings might burn them.

The breeze picked up—the flames traveled down the woman's arms and caught on the sennit braid. Lana winced at the sudden flare. The woman threw her head back and collapsed to her knees. She let out a wordless wail, a high keening that made the skin on Lana's arms prickle and tears sting in her eyes. What possible reason could anyone have to burn herself alive?

"Someone stop her!" Lana shouted.

But two others—also napulo disciples, she guessed, judging by the rough cordage around their arms—stood in her way.

"We cannot let you pass, black angel," the oldest one said, almost gently.

The other frowned. "The great fire will be free. We know the black angel understands sacrifice."

Lana could have cursed, but she felt paralyzed with horror. This close, she could see the napulo woman's blackening skin, her agonized face as she waited for the fire to consume her. How could Lana have failed to recognize this as an exercise in power, however unusual? This fanatic was giving herself up in the ultimate self-sacrifice to her ideals.

The napulo fringe movement had, it was said, grown out of the philosophy of the very first spirit binders a thousand years ago. Even in those desperate times, not everyone had agreed upon the morality of binding the spirits. Some had thought the spirits should be revered and worshiped, and that all bindings were a perversion of the natural order. Lana had thought their kind had all but vanished, but since the great eruption, she had witnessed their growing presence in the city. It felt like an illness—after all that had happened, how could someone want to weaken the great bindings even further?

And yet a woman had set herself on fire in the bustling courtyard mere yards away from the great fire temple of Essel.

The woman pitched forward. If her moans had unnerved Lana, her sudden silence made her want to gag.

"The great fire can hardly use this sacrifice," the death said, suddenly beside her.

Lana regarded it, grateful to have something else to focus on. She had long ago grown used to the death spirit's unheralded comings and goings. Sometimes she felt lonely enough that its presence was even a comfort.

"She doesn't know the geas?" Lana asked.

The two women blocking her path thought she had addressed them. The older one shook her head. "We offer only prayers. *All* bindings are immoral, black angel," she said.

But the power of binding is also the power of unbinding, Lana thought. She didn't say it. Nui'ahi had erupted in a cataclysm of fire and scalding ash just two months before. Lana suspected that someone had manipulated a geas to weaken the great binding of the fire spirit, because how else could the volcano that had slept for a millennium awaken with such fury? The last thing anyone in this suffering city needed was for some misguided napulo fanatic to learn how to invoke a proper geas. She doubted anyone would survive if the volcano erupted again.

"She's gone," the death said. Lana looked up and saw that the woman had become a pyre. What had looked moments before like a person was rapidly collapsing upon itself, like rotting fruit.

Someone fell against her wings and Lana stumbled forward. The sight of the woman's gruesome death had distracted her from the growing commotion in the crowd behind her. They had watched the woman's self-immolation in relative silence, but now the several hundred gathered men and women were shouting and hurling invective—not at the napulo fanatics, but at the armed guards even now pushing through the crowd. Lana had just a stunned moment to realize that the Mo'i himself had come to witness this gruesome protest before his guards broke through to the front.

"Stop her!" a guard shouted, grabbing one of the two napulo by her arm. She struggled to shake him off.

"It's too late," the other said, and then the guard took a good look at the pile of smoldering char that had once been a woman and relaxed his grip.

"If you zealots have weakened the binding…"

"I think Bloody One-hand's already taken care of that!" someone shouted from the crowd. Lana couldn't quite tell whom.

"Maybe our great Mo'i should just drown himself for penance."

There were a few shouts of agreement. Lana looked for a way to escape. The Mo'i—referred to derisively by most residents of Essel as "Bloody One-hand"—was justifiably famous for his temper and his penchant for violence. Lana didn't want to be caught in a crowd that might as well have marked themselves for death.

But when the Mo'i finally reached the front of the crowd, Lana's terror vanished, replaced by something closer to awe.

She had known that the Mo'i was called Kohaku, but she had never once suspected that he could be the same person who had been her teacher all those years ago on her home island. *That* Kohaku had been a student at the Kulanui, and had urged her to return with him and learn at the great school. She had refused him; she had become a black angel and a witch. And he...

...he had become Bloody One-hand.

"Lana?" Kohaku said. His voice was hoarse, his face too pale. His shoulders shook.

"Great Kai," she whispered. "It's...Kohaku, how..." She couldn't finish. *How did we come to this place? How did we travel so far off course?*

He shook his head and offered her a rueful smile. Involuntarily, her eyes slipped down to his left arm. It ended just at the wrist. Everyone knew the tale of how the most recent Mo'i had lost his hand when the great fire had chosen him as Essel's next ruler. At first, Esselans had considered it evidence of his unusual devotion to the city. Then Nui'ahi had erupted, and people had other thoughts.

Kohaku took a few jerky steps forward and embraced her. "I'd never thought to see you again," he said. She thought she heard tears in his voice. Lana bit her tongue to stop her own. She had loved him, all those years ago. A childhood devotion, but it had felt powerful enough at the time. It had nearly torn her apart to refuse his offer, but as always her loyalty to her family came first. And now he had come back again, just as the world seemed to be falling apart.

"I'm glad," she said. "I wondered what had happened to you. Mo'i..."

"Black angel."

They regarded each other for a moment, and then smiled. Then he looked beyond her shoulder and frowned.

"Arrest those two," he said. "And throw the bones in the bay." He raised his voice. "Hear me: all practices of the napulo heresy are hereby expressly forbidden and punishable by death. This city has suffered enough—"

"Thanks to you!" someone shouted.

Kohaku paused. Lana almost backed away at the senseless fury that twisted his face for a moment. He nodded at one of his guards. The man who had spoken tried to escape, but the crowd blocked his way. He screamed for mercy until a guard smashed a fist into his face.

"The great fire will stay bound," Kohaku said. His voice was not loud, but it carried. He turned again to Lana. "I must go now. But come visit, Lana. It will be good to talk."

Lana nodded, torn between remembered affection and immediate horror. She knew what would happen to the prisoners taken today. Kohaku climbed into his palanquin. The crowd dispersed, muttering among themselves, but softly.

Lana took a shaky breath. Bloody One-hand, indeed.

Essel had become a city of the lost. Search parties regularly combed the impromptu shantytowns and the only slightly less ramshackle infirmaries. The Mo'i had installed the latter to help ease the suffering of the countless injured. Lana herself had witnessed many teary reunions—a father finally discovering both of his daughters in a shantytown, two weeks after the disaster; a wife locating her husband in a dockside infirmary, covered in burns but still recognizable. And she'd seen still more bitter disappointments, someone loved and dead, without even a body to mourn her by. Two months after Nui'ahi had erupted in the greatest explosion since the spirit bindings, the hand-lettered missing posters began to fall off the sides of buildings, tattered and forlorn. No one replaced them. The evening after her unexpected meeting with Kohaku, Lana walked past one wall plastered with at least a thousand missing faces. She wondered if, in twenty years, anyone would be alive to remember these names.

She turned to the death now, which had faded into near-invisibility beside her.

"How long do I have left?" she asked. It turned to her too quickly, as though startled by her question.

"How can I tell you that?" it said, its voice oddly expressionless.

Lana frowned. "I shouldn't even ask?" she said. "It's been two months since you tried to take me. I know my mother is still alive, so the geas still holds. Shouldn't you have tried to kill me by now?"

The corners of its mask-mouth drew up in a smile that had once intimidated her. "Is that an invitation, black angel?"

Lana clamped her lips shut, aware that sometimes what she said to the death went beyond mere conversation. Sometimes even the most casual statement could be rendered as a geas. She shook her head, slowly. "It was when I played 'Yaela's Lament' with my father, wasn't it? It's kept you bound all this time."

It inclined its head. "What else did you think? As for how much longer...we'll see, won't we?"

Lana smiled, a little sourly. "So not much longer."

It fell silent. Lana didn't press.

A few people had gathered at the other end of the street, staring silently at her. She no longer minded speaking to the death in public. It could hardly draw more attention than her great black wings. They all knew that the black angel had been reborn to witness the destruction of the world. Her companion was the death itself, her benefactor the wild wind spirit.

"Do you really think you'll find your mother?" the death said to her, observing the crowd of people.

She smiled. "Honestly? Probably only if Akua lets me."

Lana had learned a great deal in the months since her sacrifice to the wind spirit and her transformation. She had learned to trust no one—except perhaps the death, and only as far as its unchanging desire to kill her. Even from her father she hid her growing awareness of the tangled plot her mother had sold her into so many years ago in Okika. Leilani had been desperate and alone when a witch had offered her the answer to her prayers. Salvation for a sick daughter, reunion with her destitute husband—and all she had to do was let Lana become the witch's apprentice.

Akua, it turned out, had wanted Lana for far more than that. But how could Lana blame her mother? Even Lana hadn't understood, and she'd had far more access to the truth than Leilani. Yet she couldn't shake the treacherous sentiment that Leilani should have guessed. Had she asked any questions at all when Akua offered a solution to all her problems? Leilani had been the adult, not Lana. Why, out of all the impoverished women in the city, had Akua found Leilani and demanded her daughter? Had her mother ever suspected that Lana was marked by the spirits?

At this point in her thoughts, Lana would shake her head in the manner of a dog frustrated by a persistent flea. Of course Leilani hadn't known. The day of Lana's initiation, when the sacred mandagah fish had given her the red jewel that marked her as one for the spirits, she had hidden it from everyone. And even after the floods came and they'd been forced to flee their beloved island, she had never quite had the nerve to tell her parents about it. Why bother? she'd thought. It was not as though she could become an elder now anyway.

But the payment had merely been deferred: Lana had become the first black angel in half a millennium, a witness to the greatest natural disaster since the wind spirit broke free of its binding.

On far corner of the street, a man draped in ragged barkcloth knelt and bobbed his head. In his fingers he held a length of sennit braid, worn in the manner of the napulo, who used it for prayer. Most of those who passed him by averted their gazes, but Lana paused. She threw a kala at his feet. He didn't pause in his prayers, and she didn't mind. She knew better than to believe a word of the napulo philosophy, but at least those who followed it were attempting, in their misguided way, to help.

Even she, a black angel, couldn't do more than that.

Ahi had cried all night, refusing both Nahoa's breast and the sweet carrot juice she normally loved, and only exhausted herself after dawn. Malie had offered to take her down the hall so Nahoa could rest, but Nahoa still didn't quite trust her maid. Not enough to let her take her daughter. Nahoa had found it useful to pretend a great ignorance of politics. It was easy enough—she emphasized the broad vowels of her sailor's accent, and she stared wide-eyed whenever some messenger from her mad husband, the Mo'i of Essel, came to the fire temple. She pretended she didn't understand the nature of her stay here, and the significance of her tiny, fire-birthed baby to the struggles in the streets. The Mo'i had aligned himself with the forces of the fire temple because they had his wife and his child. Nahoa understood that. And for now, she was a willing pawn. Despite everything, Malie and the horrible head nun had helped her when she needed it most. Nahoa might understand more than they gave her credit for, but she was still a novice at the intrigues they played.

She fell asleep with Ahi on the floor by her pallet, and awoke to the sound of her daughter's gurgling laughter. As she struggled against her body's insistent need to sleep more *now*, she became gradually aware of another presence in the room.

A stranger, she thought, peering up through misted eyes in dim light. A man in the street clothes of a laborer, his face grimy. No surprise there—the ash fall had still not stopped a full two months after the eruption. Still, most visitors to the fire temple took great care to appear well attired and respectful.

"Here, I brought something for you," whispered the stranger, and he dangled a bit of ginger candy in Ahi's mouth while she laughed and suckled. His voice tickled a memory in the back of Nahoa's mind, but she couldn't place it. And yet, she felt no alarm at his presence in this chamber. His eyes were warm and kind; they crinkled at the edges, like the eyes of a man used to smiling. His skin was dark, baked like a farmer's or a sailor's. His hands, so close to her baby's head, smelled like just-turned earth, and she finally remembered where she had met this man.

"The pamphlet," she said, her voice a whisper. "That night at the cook's party, you were the one who dropped the pamphlet in my lap. You wanted to chuck out the Mo'i."

He sat back on his heels and looked at her curiously. Then his face broke into a grin. Ahi laughed, too, as though she longed to be in on the joke, and he stroked the sable curls on her forehead.

"Name's Pano," he said. "I didn't think you'd remember that."

"Your hands still smell like dirt." She recalled that his pamphlet had declared the fire spirit powerless, the old traditions mere superstitions. "I guess you were wrong about the fire spirit," Nahoa said, wariness edging into her voice as she considered the implications of this man's presence.

He shrugged. "Wrong, and not wrong. The fire spirit has power. Twenty thousand dead to prove that. But the Mo'i doesn't keep it at bay. Oh no, my lady. Your husband helped make this happen."

Nahoa didn't deny it. She, too, had spent long nights brooding over the implications of Kohaku's missing hand. "You're going to ransom us?"

The man fell silent. Ahi flailed for the half-dissolved candy lying on the edge of her pallet and then began to cry.

"Shh, Lei'ahi," Nahoa said, hauling herself to one elbow. She uncovered her breast and now, finally, Ahi was ready to drink. She rocked Ahi back and forth, whispering to her and growing less and less aware of the man in the room. Pano. She knew she should be afraid, but she couldn't find the energy. He seemed too kind to be cruel.

"No," Pano said firmly, as though coming to a decision. "Not against your will."

Nahoa regarded him impassively, and he met her gaze. Still kind. That was good. Her daughter had proved to be an excellent judge of character.

"My will is to go back to Kukicha, tell my mother she was right and I should've never left. But there you go, that ain't happening, and I have choices to make. What's yours?"

His eyes crinkled, but his lips stayed solemn. An odd expression—it reminded her of an old temple officiant back in her hometown. Something about age and joy and disappointment. He reached into a pocket in his vest and pulled out a folded sheet of paper, soft with overuse. She opened it with the hand not supporting Ahi. A list of names, none of which she recognized.

"Lipa the apothecary, Rololo the carpenter—" She looked up at him. "Who the hell are these people?"

"Men and women your husband has tossed in his dungeons."

"Couldn't they have died in the fire?"

"They were known to be alive after the eruption."

Nahoa put the list down carefully. Maybe this man wasn't as safe as she'd thought. Ahi smacked Nahoa's chest, as though wondering what was wrong.

"Well, so what if you're right? What can I do about it? I'm stuck here, and you know I can't go back to him." Just the thought made her throat tight.

Pano shook his head. "Nothing like that, lady. But we know the Mo'i asks you to see him every day. And we know you have always refused. All I ask is that you agree to see him if he agrees to free these people."

Nahoa stared at him, but it appeared he was deadly serious. "How...why the hell would he agree? If he put them in jail, wouldn't he want to keep them there?"

His smile reached his mouth now. "I think, lady, that you underestimate how much he wants you."

Her stomach twisted. "What would you know about it?"

"His cook tells me he orders two meals every night. Just in case you come back."

"I'm not coming back!"

He shrugged. "He doesn't know that. Will you help us? Every person on that list is innocent. And you know what might happen to them if they stay."

Nahoa looked away. He was too polite to rub her face in it, but somehow he had an idea of what she had discovered in her husband's secret dungeons. She still had nightmares about Nahe's wordless grunts, his panicked signing over and over, begging her to kill him. She could smell the blood, and it wouldn't leave her nostrils until she buried her face in Ahi's hair.

She pulled Ahi from her breast abruptly and set her down on the pallet. She felt nauseous.

"Okay," she said, still avoiding Pano's gaze. "I'll try."

"Thank you," he said, so sincerely that she looked back up at him. He stood.

"How did you get inside?" Nahoa asked, belatedly realizing the unlikeliness of his presence here.

"There's many paths inside the temple," he said, and winked to acknowledge that he had not answered her. He walked to the door and then paused.

"Why weren't you afraid when you first woke up and saw me?"

"Ahi liked you."

He smiled again, and left.

· 2 ·

The next morning, in the apartments she now shared with her father—on the coast of the fourth district, far away from Nui'ahi's carnage—Lana took a knife and a bowl of water and attempted a scrying. Her left wrist was marked with an orderly row of scars and scabs from her previous efforts. She'd taken to wearing long-sleeved shirts after she noticed her father's bleak, silent appraisal. But he knew she was trying to find her mother, and they both wanted her back too much to comment on the cost.

Her father would still be asleep at this hour. When she was younger, he'd been an early riser. Was it grief over her mother that led him to stay in bed hours past sunup? Or had he slept this late for years, and she had been too distant to know it? It depressed Lana that her life had been so removed from her parents that she didn't even know these simple details. But then, her father had only just now learned of her red mandagah jewel. They all kept secrets from each other, large and small, and no one could ever completely know another person. Not even Kai. Not even the death.

The death was not allowed over the threshold without an invitation, so it hovered outside the window. It faced the ocean, but she knew it was as carefully aware of her as she was of it. She had performed this ritual in its presence many times now. She lifted the knife above her ridged wrist and looked into the bowl of water.

"I call on the spirits of earth and fire. Show me my mother, Leilani. Show me what has become of her and the witch Akua."

Lana cut her wrist. A sure stroke, just deep enough, with no hesitation. She barely noticed the pain, only the sudden rush of power in the room. Heady, as though she had just smoked a bowl of amant, or spent a minute too long on a dive. She kept her breathing shallow.

The water in the bowl turned cloudy with blood and power. She focused on it, unblinking, willing the glassy smooth surface to reveal what had every other time remained hidden from her.

A ship? Or at least something that creaked in bad weather, with wind and a spray of seawater. She pushed on her arm, dripping a little more blood into the water. The image resolved itself for a moment more: her mother's hair, grayer than she remembered, but unmistakable as it blew in the wind. The turn of her mother's cheek, a curious light in her eye, as though something had just amused her.

"How long ago were you young?" asked Leilani, and Lana's heart seemed to leap into her mouth, so strong was her sudden longing. But to whom did her mother speak?

The image dissolved then, as it had every other time, into a cacophony of fire and bright lights and screaming death. And then, all other senses deadened, Lana heard Akua's voice, dry as tinder: "Your daughter is listening."

Lana seemed to go blind for a moment. The images vanished like a candle flame snuffed. Lana groaned and accidentally knocked over the scrying bowl as she fell. Bloody water puddled around her, and the power leaked from the room as though through a sieve. She shuddered on the floor and gripped her throbbing wrist. She felt as though one spirit had frozen her bones and another had melted her skin. She could hardly move after the effort to push through Akua's barriers. But this time she'd had enough skill, or used enough power, or just—finally—had a stroke of dumb luck. Because this time she had seen Akua. She had finally scryed more than the screaming jumble of impressions that had tormented her every time before. A smile began to curve her lips, and it quickly spilled into a laugh. Her mother was alive and Akua had taken her. Presumably against her will, though Lana wondered at the hint of easy companionship she had seen in her mother's expression, and in Akua's reply.

Lana shook her head and sat up slowly. So Akua had kidnapped Leilani, but this time Lana had finally discovered a clue. They were somewhere on the water—not very specific, but still, that ruled out the inland towns. More importantly, the geas that guarded Akua from Lana's scrying was clearly fire-born. Strange, since Lana had reason to be familiar with Akua's affinity for the death. She considered that Leilani had vanished just an hour before the great eruption, and that the fire spirit had found a way to break some of its bonds. Akua—whatever her ultimate goal—was clearly meddling with the great spirits.

"Lana, are you..."

Her father stood in the doorway to the sleeping room they shared, his face exhausted and concerned. He glanced at her wrist and then away, pursing his lips.

"It's okay, Papa," she said, hastily rolling down her sleeves. "I just needed a little blood for the scrying. And guess what? I found something this time!"

She stood up hastily, folding her wings behind her with barely a thought. Kapa stayed where he was, but some of the worry left his expression.

"You mean...Leilani?" He almost choked on her name and Lana's heart twisted a little. Her mother would have known whether Kapa liked to wake up early or sleep late. She would have known how to reconcile him to the red jewel around Lana's neck and the wings on her back. But now they only had each other.

She nodded. "I saw her. Just for a moment, but I did see her, Papa. She seems okay. She's with Akua—"

"Don't tell me you still trust that witch!"

Lana winced at her father's emphasis. "Of course not. But Akua doesn't do anything without a purpose. If Mama's still alive, that means Akua has some use for her. And I'm going to find out what it is, I promise."

She walked closer to her father, as though she might embrace him, but he held himself so carefully still that she gave up and went instead to the kitchen.

"I'm going out," she said, taking some leftover spicy red beans and breadfruit mash. "I'll be back by this evening. And you, Papa?"

"They need me at the shelters."

Lana nodded. The shelters for those most affected by the eruption always needed aid, but spending every day tending to the wounded and homeless had worn at Kapa. No wonder he could hardly bear to look at her. If Lana herself heard vicious whispers about her responsibility for the disaster, then what must her father hear? She could barely hope that he didn't believe them.

She bolted down the food and left the apartment quickly. The death appeared by her side the moment her sandals hit the seashell-paved street. "And where do you go today?" it asked, its normally sepulchral voice almost eager.

She smiled. "To the fire temple," she said.

"You've been there twice already. Or do you like the head nun's company?"

Lana grimaced. "She's enough to make me wish the temple hadn't been spared. But my scrying worked this morning. I have some more questions."

The death fell in stride with her. Though the sun had barely cleared the horizon, the streets were still busy with people. Most of them were used to her presence in the neighborhood, and drew back at her passage with a murmured "Ana" and a warding sign. Every once in a great while, someone would stare at the death as though it were a shadow he couldn't quite account for.

She finally understood what Kai must feel like when he ventures from his shrine. The water guardian might not be a creature so fantastical and terrible as a black angel, but people had good reason to be wary of anyone who had grown too close to the spirits. And Kai looked so alien, with his pale skin, reflective hair, and ever-changing eyes. Lana paused as the road turned away from the docks to watch the red dawn sun rise over the ocean. The citizens of Essel had grown used to violent sunsets and sunrises since the eruption— it had something to do with the haze of ash that even now rained down in bad weather. Where was Kai now? Fighting his own battle with the spirits in the outer water shrine? Or had events forced him to leave, to track down the other guardians, or even travel to the inner temples? Whatever his duty, he obviously had no intention of finding her. It had been two months since she left him. Since he had forced her to leave. And even now she couldn't think of that separation, or the reasons for it, without lingering grief.

Lana had killed Kai's aunt. Or, more accurately, she had trusted Akua when she should have known better, and used Kai's aunt Pua as an unwitting sacrifice. Lana had avoided calling on the power of Pua's matched mandagah necklace until her mother fell deathly ill, but then she had used it to save Leilani's life. Lana had doomed herself to be eternally hounded by her mother's death—and she had taken Pua's life in exchange. She'd been horrified when she learned of what she had done, but she couldn't bring herself to re-gret it. When Kai asked her if she would do it again—if she would trade his aunt's life for her own mother's, knowing everything she did—she had been forced to answer truthfully:

Yes.

There was not much purchase for love, she supposed, after that sort of betrayal. So she had left, and he must still think he was better off without her. She turned away from the ocean, wiped her eyes, and continued on her way. The fire temple was in the third district, a long enough walk from the eastern edge of the fourth that she should have hired a rickshaw or flown, but she did neither. She was afraid her flight over the city might cause a riot, and she hated the expressions on the faces of those forced to serve her. Better to see the city and breathe its sooty air.

The third and fourth districts were still strictly under the Mo'i's control, but rebels had managed to turn whole neighborhoods of the first district into a battlefield. There were three checkpoints on her walk to the fire temple, manned by stone-faced types from the Mo'i's own personal guard as well as new conscripts drawn from throughout the city. Their uniforms were the bright orange of ground turmeric, which made them easy to identify—and easy targets. Their faces barely flickered as they waved her through, as though she were just another Esselan. She had seen them harass and search the other pedestrians in a way they would never dare with her. There were some benefits to being a black angel.

She came upon the fire temple sooner than she would have liked. Neither of her previous visits had yielded anything more than an abiding frustration with the head nun and a conviction that everyone she spoke with hid secrets from her. Not that these necessarily had anything to do with her mother or Akua, but everything she learned pointed back, in some way, to the fire spirit.

That woman was there again, sitting out front in one of the gardens with her baby, when Lana walked up to the main entrance. The baby gurgled and laughed, but the woman had left her shirt off so the child could find her way back to the breast if she so chose. It was a large, beautiful baby with olive skin and dark red hair—the color of cooling lava, Lana thought unexpectedly, and then nearly made the sign of warding.

The woman caught Lana staring and nodded coolly. Her arms were stiff, as though she were afraid, but she didn't grip the child to her breast or call out.

"What's her name?" Lana asked, just to set the woman at ease.

"Lei'ahi," she said. The baby, apparently sensing its mother's distress, stopped gurgling and looked at Lana. Her expression—curiously, if such a young child could even be said to have an expression—was nearly as quiet and wary as her mother's.

"I'm not sure if she likes you, black angel."

Lana felt a sad smile curving her lips. "And no reason why she should." That baby couldn't be much older than the eruption itself.

Lana looked at the woman more closely, startled. Of course. That accent, her constant presence at the fire temple. Her identity should have been obvious, just from the rumors. The Mo'i's child, it was whispered, had been birthed in the flames of his folly. Lei'ahi. Daughter of fire.

"Good day, Nahoa," Lana said, and walked into the temple.

Makaho, the head nun, was waiting to greet her. "Ana," she said, bowing low, so that her breasts lightly smacked against each other. "To what do we owe this honor?"

The woman was old, and her face seemed to have grown crueler with age. Lana could deal with bad temper alone, but Makaho set her teeth on edge with an obsequiousness that barely masked her unscrupulous cunning.

"I'd like to ask you more questions about that woman I'm searching for."

"But, Ana," she said, "as I told you before, neither I nor anyone at my temple has ever seen a one-armed woman of that description. You would be the first to know if our paths should ever cross..."

Lana pursed her lips against a sharp reply. "Perhaps you never saw her, but it's possible someone else at the temple did. I have it on strong authority that Akua did have some contact with the fire temple just before the eruption, and that she might bargain with it still."

Makaho narrowed her eyes. "On what authority, if I may be so bold?"

"A geas."

"A witch, too? And I'd taken that for idle gossip."

Well. Lana could play that game as well. She kept her voice pleasant. "You mean to tell me you have never spilled a little blood for power?"

"It defiles Konani's sacrifice for his officiants to spill for any other." Her frown reflected perfect piety.

"Perhaps his other servants are not so dogmatic."

"Ah, yes. Perhaps not. May I assist you with anything else?"

Lana forcibly stopped herself from gnashing her teeth. This woman! Lana knew that her mother's trail started here. She knew that Akua and this horrible woman had met. And yet she could prove none of it. What was she to do? Don a disguise and follow her around? That would have been unlikely even before she'd received the wind's gift, and it was impossible now.

"Yes," Lana said stiffly. "Perhaps you could show me to your stables? I understand that you wouldn't sully yourself to speak to your laborers, but they might have seen Akua."

Lana had the deep satisfaction of seeing the head nun's eyes widen with the shock of a point scored. But then she was all solicitousness.

"Oh, of course. But perhaps it would be best for me to inquire myself and report back to you? The servants, I'm sure you understand, have less of an understanding than I of your...peculiar situation. They might panic."

Oh, she was good. She'd barely spoken to Lana, and yet had managed to ferret out her singular vulnerability. Everyone was afraid of her, from the baby in the courtyard to old women in the streets. And she hated to force her presence on people who despised her. But in this case, she would.

"I don't care if I start a riot," Lana said. "They'll speak to me."

Makaho paused and then inclined her head. The stables were secreted to the side of the temple, hidden by dense foliage and cracking garden walls. The fire temple had four carriages and several mounts—not half as many as a rich family in Okika, but more than enough for the densely populated Essel. The streets were so narrow that if the rich didn't want to dirty their feet they made better use of rickshaws or palanquins than horses and carriages. A young girl was shoveling manure while another about Lana's age was on her back in the packed dirt, adjusting an axle. Both of them scrambled to their knees when they saw Lana and Makaho.

"Get up," the nun snapped. "The black angel has some questions for you. For all the good it will do her."

They stood up, but the only one who darted a look at her face was the youngest.

"I'm sorry to interrupt your work," Lana said, "but I'm looking for someone you might have seen a few days before the great eruption. An older woman, with olive skin and graying hair. Her right arm is missing."

The older girl shook her head slowly. "I apologize, Ana. I never saw anyone like that."

The nun smirked, but Lana wondered if she detected the faintest hint of relief. "There. You see? I suggest you try another corner of this city for your search, Ana. There are many other places fire is worshiped besides this humble temple."

Lana was about to concede defeat as gracefully as possible, when a slight movement from the younger girl caught her eye. She hadn't answered, had she? And yet Lana thought it likely that the presence of the head nun would stifle any information the girl might have to give.

"Then I'd appreciate if you could spare a carriage to send me home."

Her smirk turned into a full grin. "Of course. Uele'a will see to it. Now, if you'll excuse me. My duties are numerous in these trying times. I trust you won't hesitate to ask if you require anything else."

After the nun left, Lana tried to think of a discreet way of taking the young girl aside, but it turned out she had no need. The girl approached her after the older one led the harnessed carriage outside.

"You wanna know about that lady?" the girl said softly.

"Have you seen her?"

The girl clucked her tongue. "Great black angel like you's gotta have a lot of kala."

Lana would have admired her cunning, if not for her frustration over this added delay. She fished into her pocket, pulled out the handful of half-kala coins she had left, and tossed them in the girl's outstretched palm. "You want more," she whispered, "come to the fourth district and find me later. But tell me now what you know."

The girl stared boldly at Lana's wings, then straight into her face. Lana bore it. Even this awed scrutiny was better than fear. "The woman with one arm? Yeah, I seen her. She came late at night, a few days before the blow. The old bag met her, but I woke up because Sweetstraw was nervous. The day of the blow, Uele'a was supposed to drive her carriage, but I had to do it because she got sick. Your woman picked up someone else down at the market and I took them to the docks. They went on some merchant ship. That's where I saw Nui'ahi. Right there, by the water. And I thought, you know, how could something like that be so pretty? That's what you're like, isn't it? Just like that."

Something the girl said resonated. "She picked up someone in the market? Who? What did this person look like?"

"A woman. I didn't see her real well. But she was younger than the one-armed lady. And darker, like you. She was buying some pomegranates, I know, cause they fell out of her bag."

Lana realized she was trembling and bit her lip to stop. It was suspicious enough, interrogating the girl like this. She couldn't let her know she'd learned something important. "Find me this evening," she said again. "Fourth district, near the docks. Ask anyone. They'll know where to find me."

The carriage was ready, and the older one looked at the two of them anxiously. Lana shook her head and made a show of seeming disappointed. "I suppose that couldn't be the one I'm looking for, then," she said loudly as she climbed into the carriage. "It's too bad."

The older girl relaxed her shoulders. Lana closed the door before her face could reveal any of the triumph she felt.

Lana dozed on the roof of the boarding house, only waking when the sun gave way to the nearly full moon. She stretched and looked blearily at the streets below. Even this far from the volcano, the marks of its eruption were unmistakable. Aside from the omnipresent ash, there were simply more people visible everywhere. Those made homeless by the disaster huddled in makeshift shantytowns near the docks. They begged and worked for what money they could, and their haggard, dirty faces had become as much a backdrop of the ravaged city as its blackened buildings and piles of cooled lava. Lana shivered—she knew how lucky she and her father had been. They had money and a place to live far from the center of destruction. If not for her black wings, if not for the constant ache of her missing mother, Lana thought they might well have been able to pretend that nothing much was wrong at all.

The air was chill on her skin, but it was so lovely out here with the stars for company. She was blissfully alone. Even the death had faded away entirely, as it had done occasionally ever since the eruption. Her current protective geas was steady enough for now, but she knew that wouldn't last much longer. She would have to think of some other way to bind it. She could do so easily enough with Akua's bone flute, but felt terrified at even the thought. She shook her head. Her father wasn't going to like the new scars that a death binding would likely require.

She had finally gathered the energy to climb down when a rattling sound, too close, startled her. She nearly stumbled over her wings before she could peer over the edge of the roof. A tiny figure was hurling something. Pebbles.

"Black angel," the figure called. "I came like you asked." A girl's voice, and not very hard to place, at that. Lana smiled.

"Then I'll come down for you," she said. Why not give the girl a show? She looked to be about eleven, young enough to be awed by her power but not cowed by it.

Lana unfurled her wings and launched herself into a lazy updraft blowing in off the ocean. It felt so good to fly after so long, to stretch out the muscles that had gone stiff from disuse. She found herself climbing higher and laughing. Her back ached and burned, but even that felt perversely marvelous. She always forgot the simple joy of flying. Like diving in some ways, though it replaced the silence and teeming life of the ocean with the wind's shrieking voice and endless distance. She spiraled as though she could reach the moon and then turned and plummeted. She caught a current just in time, spreading her end feathers as wide as they could splay, and letting her sore muscles take the brunt of her sudden descent. She landed with barely a noise in front of the girl, who was grinning in unmitigated delight.

"How'd you get those wings, black angel?" she asked. "Can anyone have them?"

"No," she said, and something in her face made the girl take a step back.

The girl swallowed. "So, you promised me a reward."

Lana gave a rueful smile. If only she'd been half as bold as this girl when she was that age. She took her back inside the apartment. Kapa seemed surprised to see Lana's young guest, but smiled gamely.

"What's your name?" Lana asked the girl.

"Sabolu," she said. "You gonna give me the money?"

Lana looked up at her father and shrugged. "Could you give Sabolu some kala, Papa? I promised her for helping me."

He took a few stone coins from his pockets and handed them to her. "Where are you from, Sabolu?" he asked.

Sabolu shrugged. "Dunno. Here, I guess. My parents never said and they died ages ago. You eating catfish?"

Lana looked and saw, indeed, that her father had brought back a meal of fish and taro mash. Kapa spread his arms. "Would you like to join us?"

Sabolu grinned and dashed over to the table. Lana looked at her father fondly. "Soft heart," she whispered. He just shrugged.

"I see lots, black angel," Sabolu said, when she'd stuffed herself. "You want, I can come back here and tell you if I hear more about that one-arm witch and the old bag."

Well, she could certainly use an unobtrusive ear in that den of secrets. "If you hear anything else interesting, we'll pay you for it. But I don't want you to get yourself in trouble. Don't do anything too dangerous."

She shook her head. "No one notices the stablegirl." She left soon after, and Kapa sat silently before the remains of their meal, frowning.

"What is it, Papa?"

"That girl...she's so young. Are you sure you should use her like this?"

"She practically begged me, you saw."

"Still..."

"Papa." She made her voice hard. "Do you want me to find Mama or not? Sabolu is the only one who's seen her."

Her father didn't argue, but he didn't meet her eyes the rest of the night.

Nahoa sent for Kohaku the afternoon after she spoke with the black angel. Her daughter's reactions mirrored her own feelings for the infamous woman quite accurately, as it turned out. Ambivalence, but perhaps a glimpse of someone she might like. She certainly liked how the black angel had left Makaho in a lather after their encounter. Why, the head nun had been so distracted and frenzied that Nahoa nearly had a delivery boy send the black angel some mandagah jewels in gratitude.

"The stablegirls, indeed!" she heard Makaho mutter as she stalked to the privy.

And so fortified, she sent word to the Mo'i that she would be willing to meet him on the grounds of the fire temple in a private room an hour before sundown. She came armed with the list Pano had given her the previous morning. He had claimed they were all innocent, but she wasn't as naive as all that. Pano and his people were fighting an armed resistance, and she knew civilians numbered among its casualties. Though she had firsthand knowledge of her husband's cruelty, she wasn't sure how she felt about the costs of resisting it.

Makaho seemed quite ambivalent herself that afternoon, when one of her servants finally deigned to mention what Nahoa had conveniently forgotten to tell her: that after two months of begging, the Mo'i would be allowed to see his estranged wife and daughter.

"It was very irresponsible of you not to tell me, dear," Makaho said, with that syrupy tone and fake smile that turned her face into a death's head of wrinkles.

Nahoa grimaced and contrived to sound both stupid and contrite. "I'm sorry, Makaho. I didn't know you'd care."

Makaho's smile grew even wider. "I care about your welfare, dear." Nahoa heard the subtext: *I care about your powerful husband.* "I hope you're not considering going back to him." *I hope you're not thinking of removing yourself from our power.*

Nahoa shook her head and did not have to feign her frightened earnestness. "No, of course not. I only thought...it's been two months, and he hasn't even seen his daughter. At least I could do that for him?"

Makaho sighed, apparently satisfied that Nahoa was firmly hers. "I suppose. And it will be good for him to see that you are well." *It will solidify our hold over him.* "Yes," Makaho said, visibly warming to the idea. "I think it will do quite well. Only you must keep someone in the room with you the whole time. For your own safety. Malie perhaps?"

Nahoa clenched her teeth but managed to blush. She had grown used to the servants constantly monitoring her behavior in the temple, but for this she had to be alone. Perhaps Malie herself was involved with the rebels, but she couldn't be sure. "I'm sure I will be safe enough, Makaho. I don't intend to go back to him, of course not, but he is my husband and it has been quite a long time..."

The head nun stared at her for so long Nahoa thought she could feel sweat beading on her forehead. Playing stupid was flaming exhausting. Only Ahi's sleeping weight reminded her why she was doing this.

Then Makaho grinned and Nahoa knew she'd won. "Well, that's understandable, my dear. Perfectly understandable. We'll just leave a guard stationed outside the room for your...privacy. Just call out if you need anything."

Nahoa knew that these guards would be listening quite carefully through the bamboo-reed walls, but so long as no one was physically in the room with her she ought to be able to contrive to send Kohaku the message.

She was so giddy with her victory, and Ahi so perfectly content against her breasts, that she forgot to be nervous until the temple guards led her to the meeting room. Then, her heart began to pound so loudly that Ahi wiggled uncomfortably against her chest. What would Kohaku say? When he tried to convince her to return, would she be tempted? Because—despite everything—Nahoa missed her husband. She remembered how he had been on the ship when they returned to Essel, and the gentleness with which he had always treated her. Her ma would say this mess was all her fault for falling in love too quickly, and Nahoa was inclined to agree with her. What had she known of Kohaku before she had married him? Only that he was educated, and some tragedy had befallen him that led him to offer himself as a sacrifice to the fire spirit.

She hadn't known about his sister, who died trying to rid herself of a baby. Her married lover, a famous Kulanui professor named Nahe, hadn't much cared about the safety of the potion he procured to get rid of it. She hadn't known of Kohaku's expulsion from the Kulanui after he attempted to confront Nahe. Would she have fallen for him if she had? He had a kind smile, but his earnestness had masked an implacable, even paranoid need for revenge. But maybe she still would have wanted him. He was so unlike anyone else she had courted, so learned and sure of himself, despite the tragedies in his life.

And if she had not loved him, she wouldn't have Ahi.

Kohaku entered the room before Nahoa was ready, when she had relaxed just a bit and offered Ahi her breast for the third time that hour. She could have sworn her heart stopped when he stepped through the door. He froze a few feet away from her, as though similarly stricken. He looked much thinner than the last time she had seen him, older and more careworn. And yet he had a new air of maturity that she didn't remember. It made her want to study his eyes and run her fingers through his russet hair to comfort him.

"Nahoa," he said, his voice rough, and Ahi tore herself from her mother's breast as though startled.

Nahoa flushed and turned her daughter around so she could see her father. She seemed immediately delighted with him, which made something twist deep in Nahoa's belly.

"You can go," she said to the guard, who merely nodded and backed out of the room, sliding the screen door shut behind him. They had the appearance of privacy at least.

Kohaku repeated Nahoa's name and then, moving as jerkily as a gasping fish, knelt on the cushions across the table from her.

"I've missed you," he said.

She bit her tongue and looked away, dangerously close to tears. She had been afraid that this would happen.

"Lei'ahi," she said softly, lifting her daughter onto the low table. "Here's your father. Would you like to greet him?"

Ahi was too young to crawl, so she sprawled with evident happiness on her belly, oblivious to the tension taut as a rope between her parents. Kohaku looked at his daughter for the first time in either of their lives and smiled at her with a tenderness that made Nahoa rub her eyes furiously. Why had she fallen in love with a doomed man who had sold his soul for survival? Why couldn't they have met earlier, before his sister died, before he became destitute and homeless, before he became Mo'i? Maybe then they could have been a normal couple, with normal problems and normal loves. Instead, she'd become a willing pawn in desperate intrigues in order to hide from him. Instead, her daughter was growing without a father.

Kohaku caressed Ahi's hair, only a shade darker than his own, and let her grab one of his fingers with her chubby hands.

"She's beautiful," he said, and Nahoa only nodded because she could not trust herself to speak. He played with Ahi for a few moments more, and then looked at Nahoa until she was forced to meet his eyes.

"Will you come back? Please, tell me you'll come back."

"I can't. You know I can't, Kohaku. You shouldn't even ask."

He looked devastated, although she didn't know what other answer he could have expected. "Why? Is it because of Nahe? You *know* what he did to me. He used my sister and left her to die, and yet you think I should have let him go free and get old—"

"I don't think you should've..." *Tortured him.* "...done what you did to him. It was cruel. Pointless. If you want justice, give them a trial. Don't toss them in a secret dungeon and string them up. That makes you just as bad."

His eyes narrowed. "Something tells me we're not just talking about Nahe."

"How do I know what you've done to the others? Sometimes I don't think I know you at all. How you could do..." *Blood everywhere, and that stench.* She choked. "...that."

He was furious, but just as aware of the guards on the other side of the door as she, and so kept his voice low. "I love you, Nahoa. I want us to be a family. And you won't come back because of *politics*?"

"It's not politics. It's torture. It's treating humans the way you wouldn't treat a dog, that's what."

Kohaku laughed, and Ahi made a hiccupping sound like she was about to cry. Nahoa picked her up again. "Politics," he said again. "You won't come back because you disapprove of my policy decisions." He shook his head.

"Chopping people up while they're still alive is not a policy decision, damn it!"

"And I thought the fire temple was just manipulating you. But here you are, plotting right with them."

"Will you stop that? You know I'm not plotting anything. You don't have to be a rebel to think that you're hurting everyone with these disappearances. With torture."

"Well," he said, his voice a strangled whisper, "what would a barely literate sailor know, anyway?"

Ahi began to cry in earnest, breaking into the argument and defusing it. "Shh," Nahoa whispered, knowing that her daughter could hardly fail to respond to their angry voices.

"Here," she whispered, letting Ahi's plaintive wails cover her own voice. She pushed the worn piece of paper Pano had given her across the table. "I may be barely literate, but I can read this well enough. I want you to free these people. All of them."

He picked up the list and looked it over quickly. "*Not* about politics? Half of these people are known rebels. Or do you think it's good for the city to fight a civil war two months after 20,000 died in the disaster?"

"No, of course not," she whispered, and almost wished Ahi would cry louder so she could be sure the guard outside wouldn't hear. "But don't you see, Kohaku? This list is half the reason *why* the people are fighting. Act less like a tyrant and maybe they won't fight you like one. You have judges, you have a court—"

Kohaku slammed his hand on the table, and Nahoa got her wish. Ahi began to wail so loudly that they both winced. "You will *not* lecture me about this. You couldn't possibly understand. I'm doing all I can to help these people and—"

"Would you like to hold her?" she interrupted. Kohaku looked shocked, but he didn't object. Nahoa stood and walked around the table so they were seated with barely an inch between them. She handed him the screaming infant, and he managed well enough even with one hand. Ahi began to quiet almost immediately. Perhaps she liked Kohaku's smell as much as her mother did.

"Nahoa..." he whispered.

"Free those people," she said, even more quietly. "Or I swear you'll never see your daughter again."

"One of them...the apothecary, Lipa. She helped murder my sister..."

Nahoa stared, for she remembered his halting tale of Emea's death, and even six months ago he had credited the apothecary with doing all she could to save his sister's life. Now he blamed Lipa for Emea's death? She'd known he was succumbing to paranoia, but she hadn't realized how firmly it held him in his grip. Perhaps he truly was insane, like they all said. But all she said was, "Even she. Do you understand?"

And Pano must have understood something about her husband that she didn't. Kohaku had just called her an illiterate sailor, but now he looked at her mutely and nodded. She had that power over him. "All right," he said.

She let him hold Ahi for a minute longer and then called the guard back in the room. Kohaku didn't try to touch her before he left. Nahoa found herself, treacherously, wishing that he had.

Lana woke up the next morning with a headache and a knot of dread in her stomach. It took her a moment to place its source. Of course; she had promised Kohaku that she would see him, and she had planned to do so this afternoon. Only she realized now that much as she valued her memories of him, she was terrified of the man he seemed to have become. After leaving the fire temple yesterday, she'd made discreet inquiries into the fates of the napulo women and the heckler who had been taken away by Kohaku's guards when she first reencountered him. The answers were unsurprising, but depressed her all the same—no one had heard from the two napulo, but the heckler had turned up dead and bloody just that afternoon. No one had any doubt that Bloody One-hand was responsible. But she had to see Kohaku. Even without her past connection with him, he was the most powerful person in the city. And that meant he might have heard something about Akua or her mother, and she needed any information she could get.

Still, she thought, she could wait a day or two. An ash rain was blanketing the city in its bleak gray sludge, and she had no desire to travel in that. Instead, she found the strange little black book that Ino had given her just before Nui'ahi had erupted. Ino was the water sprite who inhabited the lake beside Akua's house. They had, quite improbably, established a wary friendship over the course of her years under Akua's tutelage. And though Ino was geas-bound not to say, he knew more than anyone (other than Akua herself) of

Akua's ultimate plan. In the months that had followed the eruption, Lana had hardly had a moment to spare for rest, let alone the task of deciphering the cramped and ancient handwriting in the black book. She couldn't see any way the knowledge in the book would bring her any closer to finding her mother. It was a curious narrative—an account, like the other book she had found in Akua's collection, written a millennium ago, before the spirit bindings. But as every other method she had used to find Akua and her mother had failed, Lana hoped that perhaps something in the black book would prove worth the struggle of deciphering it.

The writing was at times so archaic that she needed to spend hours researching the long-disused characters. Spoken Essela had not changed much in a millennium, but the means of writing it certainly had. And the political situation in the islands at the time was complicated enough to make her head spin. She recalled Kohaku attempting to teach her something about the wars between the Esselans and the Maaram, but those long-ago lessons had vanished in a barely recollected haze. Lana knew Okika, the large island where she and her mother had first lived when they left their home, had once been called Maaram, and that they'd spoken a different language in the days before the spirit bindings. Even then, however, Essela had been the dominant language and culture. There had been a great war between the Esselans and the Maaram (they only became Okikan later), and eventually the Esselans had prevailed. Then the great spirit bindings had occurred, making all thoughts of further war and conquest untenable. The Esselan peace had been part of island life for so long that she had a difficult time understanding war as anything other than an abstract concept.

She studied the book for perhaps an hour, carefully copying in a separate notebook all the characters and phrases she didn't recognize. Thankfully, each paragraph went by more easily than the last.

Ino had defied the geas of an astonishingly powerful witch to give this black book to her. Lana only hoped it would provide answers worth the struggle.

The black book

I met Tulo and Parech on a battlefield, and if that seems prescient I came to understand that it would have been impossible for the three of us to come together any other way. It was the third battle I'd found that week, a fact I was grateful for, because I could use some of what I lifted from the dead bodies and sell the rest. The Maaram might have conquered the Kawadiri archipelago a generation before, but the native tribes still didn't seem to know it. There was always some skirmish being fought, some territory to be regained or defended. The forests, I'd learned, were best for finding the odd dead soldier abandoned in haste. Most passersby refused to scavenge, afraid of vengeful ghosts, afraid of what spirits might have fed on the death. I had starved for a month after I landed on the largest island in the archipelago, and I'd learned to fear hunger far more than I feared a dead soldier's wrath.

I did not know much about spirits, then. I didn't fear them either.

She was the only other girl I'd seen in months, and she knelt among a field of corpses. Her chest was bare, a custom of many of the Kawadiri tribes, and she bent her head forward. She rubbed a length of sennit braid between her fingers; her lips moved in silent supplication. The battlefield was pungent with the stench of blood and spilled intestines, but not too ripe—this battle was only a few hours over. She was praying over a body, another young soldier fallen and abandoned. Her lover? Was she trying to release his ghost? Or was she a dark witch, trying to bind it?

"If you mean to kill me," she said, her deep voice carrying easily in the post-battle quiet, "you had best do it fast. But I'm no threat to you." She spoke in lightly accented Essela, though Maaram was the language of this island. As though there was something about my footfalls that proclaimed me a foreigner. But an Esselan? Even now the specter of war loomed between the two empires. On the other hand, a century of Esselan dominance in trading had made knowledge of their tongue fairly common on every island I knew. Perhaps she merely wanted to make sure I understood her words.

I hesitated, my heart pounding with a fear I thought the last few months had beaten out of me. I was directly behind her, far out of her line of sight. I had moved quietly among the corpses, and whatever sounds my sandals might have made were easily covered by the wind even now rustling the treetops.

"I'm just here to take what I can from the soldiers. I'll leave yours alone."

Her shoulders shook, as though she was laughing. "He's not mine. So you're a scavenger? Do you steal from the heroes or the Maaram devils?"

I walked closer to her. Her hair was thick and wild, with tight corkscrews that bounced near her shoulders. She was younger than I'd guessed at first—my age, or maybe a few years older. I wondered how she had ended up among this grove of the dead. Was she like me? A lone girl, a refugee of floods and famine and plague, driven to the Maaram because of their wealth and power?

"Does it matter?" I said. "Light fingers make no difference to the dead."

She turned from the fallen soldier, her face tight with fury. "You disrespect the dead! It's a sin before the ancestors, and may they punish you if I can't."

Her words barely registered; I was too curious about the direction of her gaze. Or rather, the lack of it. She stared past my shoulder, her eyes sliding up and down in some sort of ceaseless questing. I looked behind me, and saw nothing but trees and corpses.

My damp skin felt suddenly chilled, despite the steam rising from the soil. "You're blind," I said.

She clenched her teeth. "And you're an ignorant Kukichan. May the ancestors flay your traitorous skin."

I had to laugh. "I think we have different ancestors."

The soldier groaned, and then exhaled in hiccupping bursts. The girl bent once again over her prayer braid and began furiously chanting.

"He's alive!" I said, running toward them and kneeling by his side. Only now did I notice the brown wrap and leather braces of a Maaram soldier. "Why would they leave one of their wounded behind?"

"Because the Maaram are the children of tree snakes. This one was hurt too badly, so they went on without him. And now I must beg the ancestors to prolong his sorry life."

"And here I wondered why you hadn't just slit his throat already."

The soldier made that same noise again, the aborted exhale, only this time the corners of his mouth quirked up. I stared.

"Are you laughing?" I asked the soldier.

He opened his eyes and squinted at me. "She is," he said—and it took me a moment to realize he wasn't speaking Essela, but my own native Kukichan—"exuberant in her hatred. Ask her why..." He coughed and his face contorted with pain. "Ask her why she's here. Why she won't leave me to die."

Blood and mud smeared across his face had hidden what I ought to have recognized immediately. His skin was too dark to be Maaram. Its earth-red undertones marked him as an Akane, the barbarian tribe my Kukichan people had forced onto the smaller islands surrounding Kukicha generations ago. His arms and chest bore the beautifully intricate tattoos of a warrior of his people. How strange for us both to have traveled so far from our homes, only to meet on a Maaram battlefield. Most people from our corner of the world had probably never even met a Maaram, let alone fought in their wars or scavenged on their land.

"He tells me to ask why you're here," I said in Essela. "Though I'm not sure why, as he clearly knows Essela."

The girl's hands clenched the worn prayer braid so tightly she was in danger of snapping it in half. "He has stolen my birthright. A thing of power from my ancestors." She turned her head to gaze unerringly at the soldier's face. "And if you won't tell me where you've hidden it, *they'll* make you!"

"It's gone, Princess," he said in perfect Essela. "I destroyed it."

She moved so quickly I had no time to stop her. The blade she took from a sheath by her waist was obsidian and intricately carved. Expensive for some blind tribal girl begging on a battlefield, but perhaps that's why the soldier had called her "Princess." She screamed so loudly as she raised the blade that the vultures circling overhead scattered. But she missed the soldier's body entirely—biting instead into the earth. I moved to touch the soldier's forehead; her head shot up. I shuddered again at her disjointed gaze.

"He's already dying," I said. "No need to speed him there."

"How would you know what I need? Maybe I could sacrifice him to get my eyes back, since he's taken them from me."

The soldier gave that painful laugh again, and I wondered what kind of person was so driven to mirth on his deathbed. It made me like him. "How did you know this Kukichan girl was in the grove?" he asked the girl. "How did you find me here among all the dead? How can you sense my face, yet miss my chest?"

The girl's face was frozen in a revelation that I struggled to piece together. "You're blind," I said, "but...not just blind. You have some other way of seeing?"

"He took it from me. He stole the power of my ancestors and destroyed it! You heard him. He's taken my sight."

"And yet you can see," he said, very softly.

The girl sat back on her heels, knife forgotten in the mud. She didn't seem inclined to grab it again, so I turned my attention back to the soldier.

"What is your name, Akane?" I asked him in Kukichan.

"Parech," he said. "And yours, wetlander?" That's what they called us—because of our rice farming, I suppose.

"Aoi," I said.

He gripped my hand, and I wondered how long it would be before this strange soldier became another battlefield corpse. I thought of the ceremony I had once seen as I waited in the shadows of an earlier skirmish. An Ana—the Maaram honorific for one who wields great power over the spirits—had lit a pipe and begun to dance among the bodies. He moved as though the spirits were lifting him—making his jumps higher, his twirls faster. And as the Ana passed my hiding place, I breathed in his acrid ceremonial smoke, and I felt, just on the edge of my consciousness, that I could see the spirits he supplicated. I felt the power he called, and the force of the death he expiated from that place. The event had stayed with me, and I brooded on it often. Later, I learned that all Maaram soldiers carry a bit of that herb on them. I'd never dared take it. I had that much reverence, I suppose.

"Will you let me blow your spirit to the gate?" I asked. In Essela, so the girl could understand.

She looked up from where she huddled, and I saw that she'd been crying. "You use their ceremonies, too?"

"Why not?" Well, I never had before, but her scorn made me loath to admit it.

"That's how the Maaram and Esselans will get us in the end, isn't it? We'll just agree to their tyranny for the sake of comfort."

I had to roll my eyes. "A blind girl, a scavenger, and a dying soldier are hardly in any position to worry about tyranny. Please. At least the Maaram Anas help save the local harvests. That's more than I can say for anyone on Kukicha. Or the Kawadiri ancestors."

"The old ways have power, scavenger."

"And the new ways have evidence."

To emphasize my point, I plucked the square of resin-saturated herb from Parech's satchel along with some flint and a small clay bowl. His eyes had fallen shut, and his breathing was at once shallower and more labored. How long before he passed from the herb's reach?

"Parech," I said. "Are you still with us? It won't be much longer now."

"Oh, he's still here. That one is bright as a lightning bug. Death will have to drag him past the gate."

Whatever Parech had taken from her hadn't impeded her strange sight. How different the world must look to her. I struck the flint over the resin; it caught easily, releasing a lazy swirl of pungent smoke. I inhaled, and after a moment, so did the girl.

Parech opened his eyes, and I had the curious sense that I could see the whites glowing as though from a hidden ember. *His dying makes him burn even brighter,* I thought, and then wondered if the smoke was letting me glimpse what the blind girl saw.

I took another deep breath of the smoke. It tickled going down my throat, seemed to cling to the insides of my lungs. And then, everything flipped. What had been a dying man on the grass became a torch surrounded by seething spirits. The girl was still herself, but more terrible and beautiful. Her eyes were not merely blind, but black holes that shut out all light. And yet the rest of her was suffused with it—an ethereal silver that reminded me of river nits after moonrise. If I looked at her askance, some creature seemed to be hidden within the folds of her light. A spirit of a fundamentally different nature from those that even now were attempting to feed off of Parech.

"Ze's flight," I whispered. I had undertaken this duty too lightly. The Maaram Ana had made this ritual look simple, routine. And yet, staring at this impossible profusion of spirits, all feeding on the undirected sacrifices of dozens of battlefield dead, I realized that the Ana were, in fact, warriors. The spirits waited to see if my untested power would blow them away and release Parech's ghost. And if I failed?

"You can see them, can't you?" said the girl. She reached across Parech's body to grip my hand. I returned the gesture with fervor.

"What will they do...what if I'm not strong enough?"

"They will devour you as a sacrifice. The Maaram Ana sometimes discuss it. I saw it happen once, when I was very little, to a boy who wanted to be shaman."

One spirit—a giant yellow frog with a great tadpole tail—edged nearer to Parech and flicked its tongue at his guttering flame. Parech groaned.

"Hurry, wetlander," he said.

Words. I had to muster the words the Maaram Ana had chanted to blow the dead souls to the gate.

"Mask, heart, and key," I began. The feeding spirits paused and turned toward me, and I saw their tense attention like ribbons of gray light reaching out to bind me. Fear trapped my voice in my chest and emptied my mind. What next? What came next? I wondered how it would feel to be devoured by a spirit.

Parech's flame flared and then guttered. The spirits crept closer. The girl whispered, "Overpower them. Quickly."

I closed my eyes and bit my lip until it bled, hard enough to push aside the fear and focus. *Mask, heart, and key*, the Maaram Ana would chant, wafting the thick resin smoke over countless battlefields. And next? *Great hunter, make'lai, take these ones beyond the gate. Water, wind, and fire begone and leave the death to its business.*

I prepared to begin again and spat on the ground beside me. But the spirits surrounding me recoiled, and my strange herb-sight rendered my innocuous bloody saliva green as the trees and bright as Parech. And there, if I looked closely, I saw strange ribbons wafting from me toward the spirits, shifting in an unseen wind. I took another breath, and all paused, as though what I had to say had now gained utmost importance.

"A sacrifice," the girl whispered.

But I hardly knew what a sacrifice was, let alone how to manipulate spirits with one. "Mask, heart, and key" I repeated, and then continued, "Great hunter, make'lai..."

Where a moment before there had been nothing in front of me but a few greedy spirits and the glowing auras of the trees, I now saw a tall figure dressed in white robes and wearing a crude mask. Two parallel red lines, like unknown tribal marks, slashed its cheeks diagonally. Its eyes were black as two bogs, much like the girl's in this dream world. A rope was lashed around its waist, with a single key attached. *Mask, heart, and key.* I knew upon whom I looked.

Parech knew as well, for I could feel his fear like burlap on my skin. The death itself. The lesser spirits slunk away from us, fading and slithering as though they might escape its notice.

"Would you bind me with that?" the death said, nodding its head toward the still-glowing mess of my saliva and blood. The wan strands of power that emanated from it were so clearly unequal to the death's power that I found myself, unexpectedly, laughing.

"I'm not so foolish," I said. "I beg you to clear this battlefield. To take this one's spirit."

Its mask turned to Parech. "That one has not yet given up. Time enough and he will come to me. What do you sacrifice to make me take him so soon?"

A sacrifice? Surely I'd never seen the Maaram Ana make a sacrifice on the battlefield. I didn't understand what I'd done wrong, how I'd summoned so great a power. I wanted to tell it to leave, that all I knew of spirits and sacrifice was what I'd overheard in towns and trade boats. But Parech was lying there in agony. I had to do something.

And then, the solution came clear.

I reached into Parech's belt and withdrew his fighting adze—sharp and crusted with someone else's blood. The death looked at me, and though its mask remained impassive, I could have sworn it looked curious.

"And what is that for, girl?" it said.

"I...he won't be needing you after all," I said, strangely giddy with the audacity of my plan.

"Won't he?" The death paused, and then inclined its head. "I think we will meet again, wetlander."

The spirits began to creep back once the death disappeared. I didn't mind. It would only make my task easier. I took the adze and swiftly slit my left wrist.

My blood soaked the earth; I was suddenly suffused with power and light. The spirits stared at me, as though transfixed.

"I bind you, spirit of earth," I said, and as the words left my mouth, bands of my light encircled a stout root that waved its shoots about like antennae. I had it. Its power was my power—my joy was sharp and sweet and clear, like the juice from a grapefruit. The girl whimpered, but gripped my hand more tightly.

"What are you—"

"Save his life," I commanded the spirit, minor though it was. "Heal him as far as you are able. Stanch his blood, save his soul, and then you shall be free of me."

Parech lived, as I had known he would. Tulo—the girl's name was offered to me grimly in the first silent minutes after—bound my arm and then helped me move him away from the battlefield. We never discussed staying together. We never discussed leaving. We simply knew.

We had seen death.

I had conquered it and tasted the purest power, the dominance of humans over spirits.

Parech had burned hot as the heart of a volcano and laughed even as he lay dying. And Tulo was fierce and loyal and half-hated us for being foreign and somehow complicit in the decimation of her people. But she followed us. Later, Tulo told me it was because we both burned bright as torches, and we dazzled her eyes.

For a while we lived in the forest. It was fruiting season and easier to stay there, despite the occasional bands of roaming soldiers, than to scavenge in towns. None of us had any goods to trade in a town, and Parech was still too weak to work. Tulo liked it better in the forest. She said it was easier to see there. I thought this was curious, but she said that there were more spirits in the ancient forests than in the new towns—and fewer people to cast their bright lights. The subject of her blindness, and of the ancestor's gift that Parech had destroyed, was still raw between them. It took several weeks before I learned the full story of what had happened before we met.

Tulo and I built a crude shelter of branches lashed together with bark, dug half into the earth for warmth. We covered the ground with moss and covered our heads with the largest leaves we could find to keep out the rain. When he was well enough to walk, Parech helped us craft spears for fishing. He knew better than either Tulo or I which fruits and ground roots were good for eating. I was surprised he knew this land so well, but I suppose I should have expected it.

I'd only traveled from town to town. He had lived in this forest for at least a year as a soldier fighting off tribal incursions. The Maaram paid their soldiers haphazardly, and supplied them with even less frequency, so he'd needed those skills to survive. I wondered if he would go off and join the army again once he recovered, but he made no mention of it. I think maybe he was tired of war, or perhaps saw in us an even brighter adventure. I know he smiled often, even when his wounds surely hurt him greatly. He took the unexpected gift of his life with a resigned cheer strikingly similar to how he had anticipated his death. It bound both Tulo and me closer to him, I suppose, though I doubt either of us realized it at the time.

He still called her Princess, and me he called Ana, always mocking. I called him a barbarian Akane and let my hands linger on his chest when I changed his bandages.

One evening, three weeks after we met, he sat beside me before the fire and declared, "We should go to Okika." That's how the Maaram now styled their new capital city, after the name of a beautiful flower their enemy Esselans prized. It was fashionable to speak Essela, for all that the Maaram were at war with them.

Tulo and I stared at him. "But," I said, "we have no sennit braid save that bit of Tulo's, and no mats, or anything at all."

"I heard the Maaram devils enslave anyone without passes in the streets after dark," said Tulo.

"And you're still hurt," I said.

Parech smiled indulgently at these objections. "Are we to live in the forest forever? Become monkeys and climb the trees?"

Tulo stuck out her chin, a sure sign that she'd once again found another reason to take offense. "My people have always lived close to the forest."

Parech flexed his hand. I knew his wound pained him, which perhaps made him respond more harshly than he would have otherwise. "Well, *your people* struck you blind and then left you to die in the 'life-giving forest,' so you think you'd be a little more curious about how civilized people do things."

Tulo was on him in a moment. Parech was still too weak to do more than roll away before the fire scorched them both. He started to laugh as she smacked his face, but stopped abruptly when she kneed him in the side.

I cursed in Kukichan and moved to haul Tulo away.

"Bastard!" she yelled as I drew her arms into a lock and we fell onto the ground. "Scum of a slug! How dare you insult my people? How dare you, you craven peasant! You Akane never tried to fight back. And now you're vermin, less than human. We Kawadiri will die before we become like you!"

Parech's face had gone oddly pale and tight, and I saw fresh blood staining his bandages. And yet, he had laughed off worse.

"You don't know anything, Princess." His voice sounded as though it were being scraped from his chest. I wanted to punch Tulo myself, but didn't dare release her arms.

"I know you Akane do whatever your Kukichan masters tell you."

He had his breath back now, and the hard stare he leveled at Tulo was tempered by a certain gentleness in the set of his lips. "Are you so sure of that? No one likes to be another's slave."

"And yet you happily help the Maaram enslave my people."

"No. I happily *eat*." Then he laughed abruptly and shrugged. "And maybe enjoy being on the other side, too. Who wouldn't rather be the master?"

Tulo swatted at me and I reluctantly released her. She probably wouldn't attack him again. "I would never," she said, her voice so stiff with pride that even I nearly laughed.

Parech eased himself carefully upright and raised his eyebrows. "Wouldn't you? And yet you were a princess of your tribe, and you possessed more than anyone else. And I'm sure you had servants who worked harder than you and received barely a fraction of what you wasted in the evenings just by virtue of your birth. And I'm sure there were others even lower than that, who ground your corn and dug your privy holes, and you never once thought of how much your life differed from theirs. Now tell me, Princess, how was their lot any different from yours now? How are they any more conquered under a Maaram slave master than under a Kawadiri princess?"

To my surprise, Tulo started to weep. She trembled with the force of it and Parech shot me a worried glance. I shook my head. Tulo's shoulders were still rigid with righteous fury. She wouldn't appreciate any comfort from me. "It is not the same," she said, barely able to choke out the words.

Parech moved toward her slowly and reached out to touch a coil of her wild, springy hair. "No," he said, with such resigned tenderness that my heart seemed to wring itself like a rag. "Not quite the same. And I'm too much of a hypocrite to rail for justice. My parents did, you know. The Akane might be meek now, but perhaps only because there are so few of us. We rebelled thirty years ago. And the Kukichans slaughtered every adult they could find until the only ones left were squalling babies."

Tulo, of course, couldn't see the look he gave me as he said this. Parech could not be completely serious about his own death, and yet now he could pose as a spirit of implacable fury. Tears stung my own eyes. I hadn't been alive, I wanted to say. But my parents had been. Had they taken part in this massacre?

"I didn't know," I said, but I could hardly hear my own voice.

"I'm sorry, Parech," Tulo said, as his fingers traced her jaw. She tipped her head onto his palm.

"I'm sorry, too, Princess."

We prepared to leave the forest. Parech recovered faster every day. We wove baskets from drying breadfruit tree bark to carry our supplies. We washed our worn clothing in the river, though I'd taken to leaving off my shirt in the Kawadiri manner. It was much too hot and wet in the forests at this time of year to behave like I was still on Kukicha. I was not used to eating meat, but Parech caught one of the pygmy boars that rooted around the undergrowth and roasted haunches of its flesh over the fire. The smell revolted me, but he assured me that we might have need of it in our trek. I thought, but kept to myself, that surely the fruit and fish would be plenty. Parech found a tree with green salo fruit, the juice so sour it could stop your tasting for a week, and went off to the river. When he came back, his wavy hair was close-shorn, and bleached the same shade of pale yellow favored by the upper castes in rural Maaram. And, indeed, when he cocked his head just so, and spoke with the right accent, the effect was fairly convincing.

"But what about your tattoos?" I asked. "Maaram yeomen aren't covered like warriors."

He laughed and stretched his arms high above his head, for he had somehow divined that I found this ensemble attractive. "And I doubt most Maaram yeomen have battle scars. People see what they want to see, Ana. Most aren't as perceptive as you. Also, you're a wetlander. A Maaram couldn't tell a warrior mark from an ink stain. Don't worry."

"What are you two speaking of?" Tulo said, not bothering to look up from her weaving. I realized that I had spoken to him in Kukichan.

"Of his brilliant plan to play a Maaram farmer in the city," I explained in Essela. "But what about us? I don't speak Maaram very well."

Tulo gave a wicked little smile and said, "Then we should *only* speak Maaram, Parech, so Aoi can practice."

I stuck my tongue out at her—a petty pleasure, since she couldn't see it. "Is that really necessary? Kukicha isn't at war with anybody."

But, oh no, there was Parech grinning like it was the fire festival, and I knew that Tulo had gotten her revenge. She probably thought that I spoke to Parech in Kukichan to share something with him that she couldn't. She probably thought I was jealous of whatever was weaving between them, leaving me as the onlooker, and she was probably right. Tulo was far prettier than I, and far more compelling in her harsh, proud way. I had thought I was willing to concede the competition, but maybe not entirely.

"When we get to the city," Parech said in Maaram, "I think Aoi should work as a road sweeper, don't you?"

Tulo laughed. "Yes, and I'll weave baskets you can sell in market."

"I have no intention of sweeping anything," I said in Essela.

"Hmm?" Parech said, touching my hand. "What's that? You love the idea?"

I ground my teeth. "Want...don't," I said, forgetting the proper Maaram word order and making Tulo and Parech break into laughter.

After a moment I joined them. Parech grabbed me and we fell to the ground beside Tulo, giggling and dirtying our clothes again in the soil.

"We're almost ready," Tulo said. "Why don't we just enjoy ourselves today? We can leave at dawn tomorrow."

This seemed like a marvelous plan, even in hideous Maaram, and we all decided, as though we could read each other's minds, to strip and race to the gully a few minutes upriver and swim.

Even Tulo jumped in from the ledge, though I saw Parech's tension in the water below and the careful way he made sure she surfaced. In many ways, she could see far more than either Parech or I. But in everyday, practical ways she was as blind as any ancient soothsayer. I wasn't only jealous when I saw them together. Or even mostly. The way my heart squeezed, I thought, sometimes, was just love.

We played in the water until the sun reddened and dipped below the trees. Then Parech went upriver and came back with two plump catfish so quickly I'd have thought he'd used a geas, if I wasn't already familiar with his skill at fishing. We ate them under the waning rays of the sun, giggling, delighted by the salty-sweet taste, the languor in our muscles, and the drowsy beauty of the late-summer forest.

"I think," said Tulo, her head on Parech's chest and her hand splayed across my bare stomach, "that it is impossible for life to be any better."

"Here?" Parech said, gesturing toward the forest like a Maaram lord would at his peasant's hovel. But the laughter, as always, lurked just beneath his words. "Scavenging in the woods like buzzards?"

"No!" I said. "We're like the gods in the legends, the ones that lived before the age of the spirits. This forest is our perpetual garden, filled with all the bounty we need to be happy."

I said this in Essela, but they were too punch-drunk to chastise me for it.

"So what is it?" Tulo said. "Are we buzzards or gods?"

"Is there much difference, Princess?"

"There's all the difference. It's between the highest and the meanest. A peasant like you and a royal like myself."

"Squint at it another way and it all comes back around again. The buzzard and the god, eating catfish together by a pool."

"And what does that make me?" I said.

Parech rolled on his side to look at me more directly. "The great spirit, tempting us outside."

I could not breathe. His nose was an inch from mine. What did that mean? That I tempted him? That I had power? How was the spirit bound with the gods in the garden? Didn't it push them away? Banish them to another garden and await the coming of people? I wished I remembered the story more clearly.

Then Tulo smacked Parech playfully, and the moment ended. "Aoi luring us outside? You're the one who insisted we go to Okika, Parech! Having second thoughts?"

Parech smiled his monkey smile, full of sly knowledge. "Oh no," he said. "I predict good times for us in the Maaram city."

We were silent for a while after that, watching the sunset burn into night, and no one was eager to take the necessary steps back to our tiny shelter. Besides, what need had we of it on this warm night? Tulo was right. I'd never been happier than I was here, with these unexpected people.

"What spirits are here, Tulo?" I asked, when it seemed the starlight was tricking me with glinting objects just outside of my field of vision.

"There's a water sprite in the pool who looks like a million tiny fishes all in one. And two creatures of the earth lumbering past. They always look like animals or plants, or both at once. And a death sprite is watching you, Aoi. I can always tell those by the little keys they wear."

I was too tired, too happy, for this fact to properly worry me. "Will I die tonight, then?"

"Oh no. They're often around you. You and Parech are like torches in a swamp—you draw all the creatures closer. But I think the death finds you curious. They do something else when they're going to take someone. Something with their keys, but I can never quite see it."

I thought again to that glimpse I'd had of Tulo's world when I had smoked the Maaram Ana's herb. How strange to have to interact with this world when you could only see the other. And that reminded me of what Parech had said, of how the people Tulo so proudly defended had taken her sight and left her to die.

"Why did they blind you?" I whispered, though there was no one to hear but Parech, and he breathed as though asleep.

She moved closer to me, sliding her hand further across my belly. "For the warriors," she said, her voice as low as mine. "We were losing too many battles, spilling too much of our blood. Our shaman—our Ana—thought to bind the spirits to make the warriors see farther, move faster. They needed a powerful sacrifice. So my father offered me."

"When? Were you young?"

She shook her head. "My fourteenth year. I did...I was proud of my people, proud of our resistance. But I didn't want to lose my sight. I wasn't trading it for anything I'd get in return, you understand, like the shamans did in other tribes. I'd be sacrificing it in truth. And I was young and pretty and a princess, and now everything that made my life so perfect was making it...was ruining it. I thought about running, but they say that it matters if the sacrifice is willing. And I loved a boy who was fighting and didn't want him to die because I was a coward. So the shaman let the spirits guide him and smacked me very hard in the back of my head. I fainted. And when I woke up I couldn't see."

I laced my fingers through her own and squeezed. She had grown resigned to the horror, I suppose, but for me it was fresh. And yet, even so, I found my curiosity seizing on another part of the story. "And did it work?" I asked. "Did the sacrifice of your eyes make your warriors see farther? Did they win?"

"Yes. For a while, it was everything we could have hoped for. We thought to rid them from our island for good. And then the power ran out, and the Maaram brought their Anas and their hundreds of sacrifices and made us regret our success in a thousand ways. The boy I loved died, and he had rejected me anyway for my eyes. I was a princess, but I was blind and touched by the spirits and they all avoided me—even my own father. And then...well, the Maaram were hitting us too hard. We had to move quickly. They left behind what they couldn't carry and those too old to walk."

"And you, too?"

I knew she said "yes," but her voice was so quiet and dry I heard it as only a rustle in the dark. "The Maaram captured us very easily."

"Then when did you get the spirit sight?"

"Paka'paka gave it to me, a year after the sacrifice. She was an old witch. In her own way, she knew more than our shaman did about spirits and sacrifice. She stole the ancient hand and told me the spirit inside was mine now, and could help me see."

"But you can still see," I said. "And Parech destroyed the hand."

"I don't know. I don't understand it. I couldn't see, and now I can."

"You were blinded in sacrifice," Parech said, startling us both. How long had he been awake? "And then they gave you your ancestor's sacrifice. The spirits can't fully hide from you, and so you see what they see. There are shamans of my tribe who made the same bargain."

"Yes," I said, thinking aloud. "Once the witch gave you the old sacrifice, the spirits bound to the hand were bound to you. I saw something clinging to you when I healed Parech. Perhaps that's what it was."

"But how could you know that, Parech?" Tulo asked. "When you destroyed the hand, how could you know I would still see?"

Parech was silent for a moment. "I didn't. But the Anas told me the hand was lighting a beacon for the enemy shamans. So I got rid of it. Lot of good it did us...turns out the beacon was *you*."

"I should hate you forever for what you risked."

"I'd never have done it if I'd known you."

"Why is it better if I were a stranger? I'd still be just as blind."

Parech shrugged and kissed her forehead. "I don't know. That's just how it works. I can't afford to care for those I don't know. Too many people in the world for that. Too much suffering. How else could I be a soldier?"

We thought about that for a while in surprisingly companionable silence. Frogs burped and night birds trilled and monkeys slapped sleepily at each other high in the branches. I nearly fell asleep listening to the cacophony of the forest and the quiet breathing of my companions.

"Princess," Parech said quite softly. "You said this was the happiest you've ever been. Truly? Even when you had your sight, and your privilege?"

"I've never been grateful for what the shaman did to me. And I'm still not. But I am happy."

Okika lay at the mouth of the great river, on the far southwestern side of this island. The main Maaram island was massive, even larger than Kukicha. Our forest idyll was not very far north, but it took us nearly two weeks of traveling on foot to reach the city. I had landed there nearly half a year before, determined that Maaram would offer me opportunities Kukicha couldn't. I'd been disappointed, of course. I had no resources, no status, and as Parech would say, a slave didn't become a master by changing owners.

My parents were rice farmers who died in a flash flood when I was ten. An old priest in a ramshackle water temple took me in. I loved him more than my own parents, for he had achieved a sort of tranquility they never had. He was a member of the fringe napulo sect, though at the time I didn't understand the ways in which his observance of the spirits differed from the rest of the world's. He prized knowledge, but he enshrined unknowing. Instead of tales of capricious gods and caring ancestors, he described a world where death was the ultimate end, a gate beyond which no knowing could return. Spirits and humans fed off each other, he taught me. A binding doesn't just invoke power, he would say, it establishes a trust.

The priest taught me Essela and the basic script, though I couldn't imagine why I would ever need to read. I was hardly scribe material, but he told me that no knowledge was ever wasted. He died of a flux in his chest when I was fifteen. A great windstorm destroyed his decrepit temple a few days later. I took it as a sign from the spirits and left as soon as I could burn him and salvage my things from the wreckage.

There are no great cities in Kukicha, but there are a few towns, and so I went to those, trading my knowledge of Essela to traders in exchange for food and shelter. I would translate and write simple bills of sale with the few characters I knew, and if no one needed that, I'd fetch and carry with the boys. It was boring work and there were long stretches with none at all. I spent more than a few nights huddled against a tree and longing for my old priest's fire, or even the sunken hut my parents had called home.

I had long heard of the Maaram and their slow war with Essel. I had heard of Essel's glittering capital, of the great school recently founded there and the thousand different wonders I'd never see on Kukicha. I'd heard Esselan canoes were as long as ten men and their sails so large they had to climb ladders to unfurl them. And though Maaram was far larger and had more people to defend it, they were afraid of Essel's army. The Esselans used weapons of metal, not wood and bone and hard stone like the rest of us. I wondered at first how they could make something so soft and yielding as copper or tin into a cutting weapon, but one of the merchants showed me a knife he had purchased in the great city. Its blade was made from no substance I'd seen before—it was dark gray and shiny and so hard it held an edge that could slice a soursop rind with only the slightest pressure. The metal was made from combining two others at a precise temperature, he told me, and then shaping the blade in a fire. One of these metals, iron, could only be mined on the scattered islands off the coast of Essel. I thought of what the blade could do to flesh and knew that the Maaram were right to be afraid.

I was of an age to marry, but I did not want to marry. I even had an offer from a farmer on his way back to the countryside. He was ten years older than I, but handsome enough, and not cruel. I thought that a solid life like that, with a hut of my own and a harvest to trade, was probably the best I could hope for. But then I thought of my parents, who had died without ever leaving their village, who had never learned any language but their own, who had never read a book or written a phrase, and who had died as they lived—in muddy water. And I thought, "I'd rather die now than live like that." And so I refused him. I found a leering merchant who would take me on his canoe if I worked for him. I left when he tried to rape me, and I found another boat. And so it went until I arrived in Okika for the first time, nearly starved and so used to the rocking of the water that land seemed treacherously unsteady.

There were more people in just the area around the docks than I'd seen in my entire life. Sailors clad in nothing but wrap-cloths and straw sandals, women in divided skirts and women baring their breasts, wealthy citizens with cloth over their noses and adorned head to toe in opulent fabric. I thought I would find something exciting there. But instead I found my prospects much the same as they had been on Kukicha. It didn't help that my Maaram was terrible, and I had little opportunity to improve it. I looked longingly at the rich houses—the first I'd ever seen built all of wood and not thatched straw. I thought that I'd like to be rich, but I didn't know how to begin. I realized that perhaps it hadn't been very clever of me to blithely give up what I knew on Kukicha. Perhaps farming wasn't glamorous, but it was a life. And suddenly, I'd felt more like a spirit than a girl, rudderless and in need of binding.

I left for the countryside in winter, when the canoes stopped coming and even the little work I used to find had disappeared. I'd meant to just stay in a village, perhaps fish in the river, but a new bout of fighting broke out between the Maaram and the Kawadiri natives who refused to submit peacefully to the yoke of their conquerors. All the roads became unsafe. I took to the forest. And there I discovered the untold benefits of battlefield looting. I was too hungry to refrain, once I saw how well I could live.

I followed the roaming bands of warriors for weeks, hardly noticing how far they traveled. So I was surprised, when the three of us started for Okika, to find us so far north. Tulo and Parech and I encountered no other soldiers on our way down. Perhaps some kind of temporary truce had been achieved.

Parech used the long days of our journey to grill me in Maaram, so that by the time we arrived I had finally grasped the inverted nature of their sentences and could make simple phrases with relative ease. I didn't think I'd ever understand their thousand different tenses. Parech declared that I'd never pass for a native, but I'd do well enough for our purposes.

"And what purposes are those?" I asked, when we were just a day or two from the city.

He grinned that monkey grin. "You'll see, my young Ana. You'll see. But it won't be street sweeping, I promise you!"

PART II

. . .

Chance

· 3 ·

KAPA SMILED AT Lana the next morning and ate a few bites of pan bread before he left for the apothecary tent. Even that slight gesture, that hint that the distance between them might be bridged, left her oddly enthusiastic about the day. He still loved her, she knew that, but her father had never found it easy to adjust to new situations. The last time he'd been forced to live without her mother for months at a time, he'd ended up homeless on the streets. Leilani was his anchor, and since her transformation Lana had grown too strange for her presence to do anything other than unsettle him.

As soon as he left, however, she contemplated the day with growing unease. Lana knew she could put it off no longer—today she would have to confront Kohaku. She'd been too surprised when she'd seen him before, caught so off guard by his impossible presence that none of what she *knew* about the Mo'i had seemed relevant. Now, unfortunately, she didn't know if she could bear to look at him. But even without their shared history, she would have had to confront the Mo'i eventually. He might know something about her mother.

Still, she lingered on her walk to his house. Like most of the third district, the streets near the Mo'i's house bore little evidence of the eruption. Even the ubiquitous ash had been swept from the boulevard leading up to the grand wooden edifice. And yet, it looked nothing like she remembered. There were so many fewer people, for one. The large, laughing, gawking crowds that used to clog the avenue had dwindled to a few hunched, hurried figures. Perhaps one could blame the lack on the unseasonably frigid weather—persistent in the city since the eruption—but then she noted the stone-faced guards and the fear in the faces of those who passed them. She could hear the distant crash of the ocean, a sound that should never have been audible this far from the shore. Lana knew how much she should hate Bloody One-hand.

These thoughts occupied her so thoroughly that she didn't notice the whispers and hisses of a few people on the street until something wet cracked against her shoulder. She looked down: an egg, the yolk smearing into the white all down her arm. The woman who tossed it had readied another.

"Go away!" she said, her voice loud enough to carry to every staring person on the street. "Don't you think you've done enough damage? Leave us be!"

Lana was reminded, forcefully, of the time she and Kai had been chased out of that village on the rice islands. She recognized the hate in their faces. And though she had seen it countless times since then, the woman's unthinking fury still gave her a frisson of primal fear, as though *this* time the mob truly would crush her beneath their feet. Lana shook her head and tried to walk away without meeting anyone else's eyes, but the people pressed closer to her, their murmurs grew less hushed and more indignant. How dare she, they asked each other. How dare she pretend to be one of them, as though she hadn't brought this all upon the city?

"I'm just a witness," Lana said, but not loud enough for anyone but the egg-thrower and a few others to hear her. She had thought the streets unusually barren, but she realized there were still more than enough people nearby to threaten her safety. The egg-thrower raised her arm, and Lana winced in anticipation of the hit, but someone stepped up and gripped the woman's wrist.

"You shouldn't do that," her unexpected savior said, gently shaking the woman's wrist so the erstwhile missile cracked harmlessly on the cobblestones. He was dressed in laborer's clothing, ash-gray like almost everyone else's, with already dark skin darkened further by the sun. He had laugh lines around his eyes.

"You all have better things to do," the man said, pitching his voice so the whole block could hear, but somehow without ever seeming to strain. "I expect you should go to them. The black angel has nothing to do with Nui'ahi. We got here through superstitions, and we'll not get out with them."

Several members of the gathered crowd still eyed her resentfully, but more nodded with a thoughtful sort of respect and started walking past. Lana wondered what kind of laborer could defuse a mob with a few carefully chosen words.

The woman who started it all looked angrily up at him and then spat at his feet. "I don't care what you say, or who you pretend to fight for. That woman caused all this. And if that doesn't matter to you, then I hope One-hand wins."

And then she left. Lana was virtually alone on the street with the strange man.

"Thank you," Lana said. "If that had lasted much longer I might have had to fly away."

His eyes crinkled. "I suspect that would hardly have helped your cause. I've heard no reports of the black angel using her wings."

Lana smiled a little. *Except for last night, to put on a show for Sabolu.* But Lana was fairly confident that no one but the girl had seen her. "I can't hide in the city, but I don't want to disturb people."

"And yet you're still here. If you don't mind my asking, why is that?"

It was funny how no one had thought to question her presence here but this man. "I'm looking for my mother. She went missing right before the explosion."

He nodded slowly. "I see. You truly are one of us, then. One-hand even took someone away from the black angel."

"And who are you?"

"Pano," he said. "And if you ever need anything, black angel, you can ask for me at the barricades on Sea Street."

He wiped the drying smear of egg from her shirt sleeve and then walked away, hands deep in his pockets. Sea Street. The oldest and busiest street in Essel neatly bisected the island, running from the lesser bay and the old docks in the north to the greater bay and main harbor in the south. It also marked the division between the ravaged first and seventh districts and the comparatively well-off second and third districts. It had become, in the months since the eruption, the front line of the sort of conflict the islands hadn't seen in five centuries. The rebels controlled much of the territory west of Sea Street in the first district, which meant that her unlikely savior was probably one of them. Lana shook her head, then shot a worried glance at the stone-faced guards. They hadn't moved an inch since the confrontation began, but they must have noticed. Did they also know Pano? Would they report it back to Bloody One-hand? Would he…

Lana shook her head, forcefully. No. She'd heard Kohaku's voice when he saw her. She couldn't believe he'd betray her like that.

The death appeared moments later. It had vanished early this morning, and Lana was oddly jolted to see its familiar mask again. On the other hand, that the death still chased her meant that Leilani stayed safe. Akua had meant to kill her mother once before, using a linked necklace of a key made of bone. To save Leilani's life, Lana had invoked the ancient geas that now bound her to the death. If Akua had meant to kill Leilani, she'd be dead by now. But though Lana thought her mother was most likely safe, she'd learned not to trust the witch for anything.

"Where's Akua?" she asked the death, though she knew well enough not to expect an answer.

The death shrugged. "And why would the avatar know?"

"Because Akua and death are obviously—" She stopped abruptly, just now snagging on the peculiar word the death had just used. "Who's the avatar?"

"Myself," it said.

"But...you're the death."

"I'm death's avatar. I am of, but not one. The avatar is the death, but death is not its avatar."

It occurred to her that she had never before heard her death refer to itself in such concrete terms. She had never known it considered itself somehow separate from the great death.

"And the godhead might know where Akua is, but you don't?"

The death leapt up and a nearby rickshaw driver stumbled and nearly fell on his face. Lana glowered at the death—she'd so far avoided causing anyone else grievous bodily injury due to their proximity to the spirit. *The avatar.*

"Clever," it said from directly over her head. "But you'll need to understand more than that to beat the witch."

She wanted to yell that she understood that perfectly well, but people on the street were already giving her wary glances. So instead she hugged her elbows and wished she could be smarter, braver, more talented. She wished that *she* were the greatest witch on the islands, instead of the novice pitted against her. But how could she possibly beat Akua if she didn't even understand what game the witch was playing?

The Mo'i's house was as grand as she'd always heard—with large panes of clear glass windows, floors of patterned red acacia wood, and countless pieces of fine art and furniture. The fire temple, where Kohaku's wife had hidden herself, paled in comparison. And yet, there was something chilling about the place, in the way the servants who passed her so quickly kept their heads down, in the utter absence of conversation and banter. Not that anyone in the city had been very cheery after the disaster, but it wasn't hard to imagine Kohaku terrorizing his servants the same way he terrorized the city.

As a servant led her to the garden, she wondered what he would say to her in this more controlled setting. She wondered if she should mention what she had learned from Sabolu the previous evening. The precocious stablegirl had found her to say that she'd seen the Mo'i and the "old bag" speaking in one of the pagodas near the stables. This wasn't terribly shocking news—the old bag had his wife and child, after all—but it put Lana in mind of an angle she hadn't before considered. Surely the fire temple must know more than it was saying of how their own spirit had loosened some of its bindings. And if the head of that temple was meeting with the one who had enabled it? Indeed, it was bizarre that the fire temple had not repudiated Kohaku entirely. Maybe they were pleased that the fire spirit had become more powerful. The eruption certainly had increased attendance at temple services. She considered who she could approach for more information. The rebels clearly hated Kohaku and the fire temple enough to have gleaned some intelligence about them, but she wasn't sure how much she trusted Pano and the ones who had brought edged weapons onto the streets. But their old friendship might make Kohaku disclose more than he would otherwise. Lana had to learn more about the nature of the fire temple's relationship with Akua.

She found Kohaku sitting beside a decorative pool filled with fire eels. The trees arching above him had lost their flowers, but a few were heavy with end-of-season fruit.

She could only see his back as the servant hurriedly departed. His voice was low, but animated in what appeared to be heated conversation. She froze, wondering if she should wait for his other guest to leave. Why had the servant led her here if he was indisposed?

"What possible harm could they cause me?" he said. His voice was thready and high, like he was pleading. "Is it so untenable to just…"

He paused. Lana strained, but couldn't hear the other person's voice. A stark suspicion began to worm its way through her gut. She swallowed and started to move, ever so carefully, to her left.

"Yes," Kohaku said. "Yes, of course." He laughed bitterly. "Don't I always do as you say, Emea?"

But he was alone in the garden. His gaze rested on an empty chair, and beyond that, a decorative persimmon tree. His head snapped up, and he turned around. His initial look of startled terror quickly morphed into a carefully pleasant smile. Lana did her best to keep her own expression steady. He had been speaking to thin air.

"Lana!" he said, standing as she approached. "I'm so glad you came. I wondered if you would."

"It's good to see you again," she said. Strangely enough, she meant it. He reminded her of the time before the disasters, before Kali's death, when the sum of her problems were a mother who sometimes demanded too much and a girlhood crush on her schoolteacher.

Though she'd meant to speak immediately of Makaho and Akua, Lana found herself reminiscing with Kohaku. She told him what had happened to the island after he left and their desperate efforts to save the remaining mandagah fish from the salt water.

"I don't know if it will ever be safe for them again," she said. She drew out the red jewel that always lay beneath her shirt, though she had no reason to wear it now but sentiment.

Kohaku leaned forward slightly and touched her hand in sympathy. "Sometimes I think of how the scholars will look back on this time. This is a dark age. We're so close to the brink, of everything going back to the days before the spirit bindings. There is a man in the tinkers' guild who can make clockwork solstice dolls that walk and jump, and there are other men a few streets away who sharpen kitchen knives into swords and plot to start the first Esselan war since the spirit bindings." He sighed and tucked the ginger hair she remembered so well behind one ear. "Who's to say which side will win out? The creators or the destroyers?"

Destroyers? That didn't seem to describe Pano, quietly dispelling the angry crowd. She'd read much of the rebel literature passed furtively in the streets. The tracts displayed a shocking level of ignorance about the mechanics of binding, but she doubted that their endless lists of abuses and atrocities attributed to the Mo'i were entirely false. Perhaps something had to be destroyed before something good could be created. Or perhaps the destruction could go too far.

"I think that violence always leaves the control of those who start it."

He nodded enthusiastically. "Yes, that's precisely it! Why else do we have the taboos against war, Lana? Because our blood feeds the spirits. Before the great bindings, that was bad enough. But now? A war in Essel could unleash far worse than even the disaster of Nui'ahi."

Just the thought made Lana's stomach clench and her eyes dart involuntarily to Kohaku's missing left hand. War might unleash the fire spirit? And wouldn't he know? The disaster had destabilized everything, not the least of which was the death spirit. She didn't even want to contemplate what would happen if death broke free. A dark age, Kohaku had said. And here she was, a black angel, at the center of it.

She shook her head. "I need to ask you about the fire temple, Kohaku," she said. "It's said you're close to them now—especially Makaho, the head nun. Do you know what they were doing prior to the disaster? Surely the spirit's restlessness must have made itself known there at least."

She had carefully phrased her question to avoid any reference to his own wrongdoing, but he still stiffened imperceptibly and looked away from her. She felt a pang of regret. But they were so far from her first home. They could never again share the camaraderie of teacher and student.

"Makaho?" His mouth twisted. "She stole my wife. I keep relations with her in the hope of getting Nahoa back."

Lana didn't think that the wary girl with the baby would let anyone steal her, but didn't say so. She was here to find Akua, not antagonize the Mo'i.

"But still, you must know more than I do of what the fire temple is scheming."

"If you're asking if I think Makaho had a hand in the disaster, of course not. She was as surprised as all of us. *All* of us."

He glared, as though daring her to contradict him. She raised her eyebrows. "Kohaku. I'm just looking for my mother."

This seemed to blunt his righteous anger. He blinked. "Your mother?"

"She lived—lives here. She disappeared right before the eruption."

For a moment he looked genuinely grieved. "Oh, Lana. I'm so sorry. But, have you looked...I mean, it's been months. I'm about to add all the missing to the rolls of the dead."

It only made sense, but she remembered those tattered missing posters, those forlorn hopes. "You're right," she said. "But they'll hate you for it."

He laughed. "They already hate me. It's quite liberating, the scorn of public opinion. But, Lana, your mother—"

"*Isn't* dead. Don't ask how I know. But she disappeared right before, and I know that the fire temple is involved."

"I've never seen your mother here, Lana. The city is huge. I doubt I'd even recognize her after so many years."

She sighed. "But I believe another woman was with her. An older woman with a gravelly voice and graying hair. Missing her right arm."

She watched his expression carefully as she said this, but she needn't have bothered. He blanched so pale even young Sabolu could have determined the news perturbed him.

"Have you seen her?" Lana prompted.

"No!" he nearly spat out the word as he leapt from his chair. "No, I've never seen any one-armed woman. Someone else who nefariously sacrificed herself for the spirits, right?"

No wonder everyone suspected him of helping the fire spirit. He wore his guilt like a habit. And yet she wasn't sure if he was lying. Perhaps Akua had plotted something with him, but she rather doubted it. Akua liked her associates either more clueless or more cunning. Kohaku was too helpless a mixture of both.

"I meant nothing at all, Kohaku," Lana said as gently as possible. "It's just her distinguishing characteristic. Are you sure you never saw her? Or heard anyone else speak of her?"

He relaxed slightly, but his mouth still turned down in an oddly familiar scowl of derision. "No, I've never heard of anyone, anyone at all, matching that description." His pause was small, but his eyes had widened as though he remembered something.

She stood herself, so she didn't have to tilt her neck quite so far back to meet his eyes. "Are you sure, Kohaku? It's terribly important. I must find my mother."

He fiddled with his left sleeve. "Of course I am. I'd help you if I could, Lana."

It was this pretense of concern when he was so clearly concealing important information that broke her self-control. How dare he murder so many in the ashes of Nui'ahi and then compound the crime by arresting and torturing scores more? How dare he pretend that he hadn't been involved? That he was some innocent victim protecting the city from the—what had he called them— *destroyers*? It was a sick joke.

She took a step toward him, shaking out her wings so that they trailed briefly in the pond and splattered the stones around them. He flinched, but didn't retreat. "I'm quite familiar with sacrifice, Kohaku. Yes, *that* kind of sacrifice. I sat vigil on the mesa at the heart of the ancient wind shrine to get these wings. I have spoken with two of the great spirits and tested their geas. I know more about the spirits and sacrifice than you ever will, and I know what you did in the fire temple. You can no more accidentally burn yourself in the primeval fire than you can accidentally kill yourself in the heart of the death. You sacrificed, and you got something in return. And so did the fire spirit, didn't it?"

His shoulders trembled, but his voice was strident in its panicked dissembling. "Rumors! Nothing but rumors, Lana. What would you know? You're barely a sapling. No one will believe you. They're about ready to string you up already. They think the black angel brought this destruction. And how do I know they're wrong? Maybe you did, maybe—"

She cut him off with a disgusted wave of her hand. "Don't be a fool. They can blame us both if they please, but you and I both know who is responsible."

She turned to leave, struggling to calm her pounding heart, her rapid breathing. "They'll never believe you," he said again when she reached the door. "You can't say anything. I'll—"

"I loved you back then, you know," she said more quietly. "I almost came back with you."

Kohaku stilled, then shook his head. "You should have."

Choices, Lana thought. Bad and good and indifferent, and so often impossible to tell which was which at the time. She could only move forward.

Now Lana had only one viable choice left. She would go to the source of all the rumors and the turmoil: Sea Street.

· 4 ·

THE FIRST DISTRICT HAD BEEN hard hit by the lava flows. Much of Sea Street was now riddled with crevasses exposed by the molten rock, and improbable mountains where it had settled and hardened. Its buildings had almost all been destroyed in the fires that swept through the district. The first district was a ruin, a burned-out cinder of the teeming neighborhood it had been just a few months ago. And it served as a perfect, defendable barrier for the rebels, a no-man's–land where the Mo'i's forces feared to venture and the rebels scared away anyone who didn't belong. Lana flew there, because she was too furious to care about prudence and the exertion calmed her. If anyone pointed or shrieked as she passed overhead, she took no notice.

"You made an enemy today, Lana," the death said, placidly soaring along beside her.

She grimaced. "Witness how little I care. He did all this. He killed all these people." She paused, and then looked again at it. "Why did you call me Lana?"

"Isn't that your name?" it said, and then faded to near-complete transparency.

She of all people knew how dangerous mass violence could be at this time, but she still found her sympathy for the rebel cause growing by the hour. The destruction of the city was far easier to see from up here—perhaps another, unvoiced, reason for why she had avoided flying the last few months. Tents and impromptu shanties had sprung up in the ash-beds of the destroyed buildings, like a sallow reef slowly blooming on the carcass of a sunken boat. The path the lava had taken down the slope of Nui'ahi cut across the eastern half of the city like a sinuous scar and emptied, eventually, into the sea, where it had created several new miles of island. She wondered how Essel would rebuild, how it might accommodate itself to this violent, sudden reshaping. Though she could have flown straight past the rebel barrier, she landed in the middle of Sea Street. It was safe enough—no one to see her here but rebel soldiers. One approached her as soon as she touched down, a war adze tucked into a sash. He was young, one side of his face and neck covered in such broad swaths of still-healing burns that she wondered how he'd even survived. Did the rebels have witches who could manipulate geas well enough for healing?

"What do you want?" the rebel guard asked. His tone was brusque, but not unkind. And honestly, such directness was a relief after her meeting with Kohaku.

"I'd like to speak with Pano."

His hand tightened on the haft of his adze. "What do you know of Pano? What do you want with him, black angel? I won't have you hurting him."

"Stand down, Tope. It's all right. I asked her to come, and here she is." Pano climbed the lava slag they were standing upon and touched the boy lightly on the shoulder. Then he gestured to Lana. "Follow me," and Lana was left to awkwardly balance herself as they climbed across the dried lava flows, deeper into the first district. Rebel territory, Lana thought, but the frisson of danger she expected to feel was undone by the utter normalcy of the scene behind the lines. She saw the same destruction, the same fire and ash, but perhaps slightly less desperation. It appeared the rebels took care of their people at least as well as the Mo'i. And they hadn't caused the devastation in the first place.

There were no undamaged buildings within sight of Sea Street, but Pano led her into one that was still mostly standing. It looked like an ancient tree nearby had borne the brunt of the fire, sparing the meeting house. Everyone they passed nodded to Pano, which confirmed her suspicion that he was an important member of the rebel movement, perhaps even its leader. But when they finally entered the main room—roughly patched with scavenged wood and heated by a smoky fire—someone else was seated before a short table piled with papers. She was an older woman with skin so unusually pale it reminded Lana of Ino, the water sprite. Her hair was thick and frizzy, the color of dirty sand, and held back from her face with a blue headband. Her eyes were the oddest shade Lana had ever seen—pink, like a washed-out sunrise. She'd never met anyone with this sort of coloring before, and even the air in the room seemed to heat when the woman leveled that uncanny gaze at her. No question, Lana thought, of who had led here.

"Eliki," Pano said lightly, pushing Lana ahead of him. "Look what just flew in."

The woman—Eliki—gave her such a thorough look that Lana fidgeted. "Fascinating, as usual, Pano," she said. Her voice was clear and firm. It carried much the way Pano's had on the street the other day. She sounded, Lana realized, like one of the elders back on her island. Like Okilani, who perhaps had always known, it occurred to Lana for the first time, about the second jewel Lana had found on the morning of her initiation.

"You're very young," Eliki said, addressing Lana.

Lana shrugged. Eliki gave the barest of smiles. "And yet I suspect you've seen things I can't even imagine. These are not times when one has the luxury of youth. My daughter was about your age when she died."

"What happened to her?" Lana asked, though she wondered if she should have just nodded politely.

"She drowned. Her ship capsized in a storm. Almost everyone was lost." Eliki said this so brusquely Lana didn't dare offer condolences, and Pano forestalled them anyway by offering her a stool.

"So, I didn't think you'd take me up on my offer so soon," Pano said, once they'd all settled. "What brings you here?"

Eliki raised her pale eyebrows. "He means, what do you want?"

Lana swallowed. She was obviously a curiosity to them, but she didn't want to think of what they would do if they perceived her as a threat. "I'm trying to find my mother."

Lana expected this to surprise Eliki the way it did everyone else—as though just because she was the black angel she must have sprung from the earth fully formed—but Eliki just nodded.

"And you think we can help?" she said.

Lana explained her search for Akua and her suspicions of Kohaku. "I think he saw something, but he won't say. I know Makaho is involved, but she'll never give anything away."

Pano stroked his chin thoughtfully. "A one-armed witch? I haven't heard of anyone like that, but I could poke around. Ask some questions."

"I'd be incredibly grateful."

Eliki rapped Pano's thigh with the edge of a book. "Don't get ahead of yourself," she said. "And what are you going to do in return, if we help you?"

"I have some money. It's not much—"

"We don't want your money. It isn't much use out here, anyway. We prefer barter."

Lana hardened her expression. It wouldn't do to let this woman see how much she intimidated her. "I don't know what else to offer you."

She laughed. "You're the black angel! There's a thousand things you could offer."

"I don't have any power here. Sometimes I think I'm a hairbreadth away from being thrown out of the city!" Pano nodded. "It's true, Eliki. We met when I saved her from a mob."

"I know how you met, Pano. But listen to her. She waltzed up to the Mo'i's house and they took her in to see him just like that. *That* is power. Now, the question is, what can it do for us?"

Lana didn't like the direction this was heading at all. She shook her head. "No, you don't understand, I doubt Kohaku will want to see me again anyway. We had an argument before I left."

This seemed to interest Eliki even more. "An argument? With Bloody One-hand? Explain."

Lana felt her cheeks get warm. This wasn't going very well. She started to regret her impulsive decision to come here. Why had she thought they would help her when Kohaku wouldn't? Because Pano had seemed kind when he saved her on the street? But still, she'd already come.

"I told him I knew what he'd done," she said. "I mean, that I knew how he'd lost his hand. And he tried to deny it, but great Kai, he was talking to someone who's made geas with two of the great spirits. As though I wouldn't know exactly what bargain he made? I was furious. I stormed out."

Eliki and Pano shared a shocked look. "You are sure?" Pano said after a moment. "There's no doubt in your mind that he traded his hand to become Mo'i?"

"And weaken the binding in exchange. But everyone knows that. I can't go down the street without hearing someone say it."

"People say many things they don't really believe," Eliki said carefully. "They curse the spirits, and then bring extra large wreaths for the solstice fires. Just because some people suspect doesn't mean they believe."

Lana's skin prickled. They seemed so surprised. "Well," she said uncomfortably. "They should, because Kohaku is responsible for all of this. I mean, he might not have known....I'm sure the fire spirit misled him, minimized the danger. It isn't as though he went into the chamber vowing to burn 20,000 people to death, but..."

"He's responsible, nevertheless." Eliki's tone was hollow and clipped, like when she'd described her daughter's death.

Pano stood and walked to one of the windows covered in fresh oil paper. "This is amazing," he said, running a hand through his salty hair. "Amazing." He whirled on Lana. "Explain everything. Step by step. I'll write it down so I don't miss anything." He took a few long strides and knelt before her. "The trouble was we all thought he must have, but it didn't make sense. Everyone gets burned to death in the great fire. That's the whole point of the ritual. To sacrifice the penitents and keep the fire spirit bound. In return, we get a leader. So, how was One-hand's sacrifice different from all the others? Why did it go the other way?"

Lana suddenly understood. The mechanisms of the spirits and their bindings were as natural to her as the tides, as the phases of the moon. Her mother had explained it many times as she was growing up. In the outer islands, the spirits were very close, and life wasn't stable or easy enough to forget what must seem like a rustic superstition here in this city. And then all of her time with Akua had ground it deeper into her bones. But most Esselans didn't understand how *anything* worked, no matter that it had become central to their very existence.

"The power of the geas depends on your desire, what you invoke, which spirit you invoke it for. A geas is a binding, but that power is in the unbinding as well. A black angel's sacrifice released the wind spirit, remember?"

Eliki gasped. "Of course! How could we have forgotten that story?"

Pano shook his head. "I never heard it told like that. I heard she killed herself over the grief of loving it."

"This goes in the next pamphlet," Eliki said. "All of it. The details about how spirit bindings work, all confirmed by our very own black angel."

Lana bolted to her feet and backed away. "Oh no," she said. "You can't use me like this. I need to find my mother, not get stoned on a street corner."

"Why would they blame you when they can blame the Mo'i?"

Lana grimaced. "You can't. I need Kohaku. Yelling at him is one thing. If you print this, I may never find her."

Eliki stood, her erect carriage radiating every bit as much anger as Lana felt. "So, is this the thanks we get for helping you?"

"You've done nothing for me yet!"

"You doubt our word?"

"Of course!"

Pano put a hand on Eliki's shoulder. "She's right," he said softly.

"We need to give her something. Earn her trust. This news can wait."

Eliki glared at Lana with those disconcerting eyes for a moment longer and then nodded to Pano. "Fine. You see if you can find the one-armed witch. And this one should pray Kohaku doesn't find some way to take her like he has all the others. You may be the black angel, child, but anyone who cares to look can see you're still just flesh and blood."

Ahi was dying. Nahoa couldn't think of any other way to say it. The infant had started to lose her appetite at noon the day before. By that evening she cried in agony at the slightest touch and was so hot Nahoa had to bathe her in ice water. Ahi grew weaker by the hour, no matter what she and Malie did to ease her suffering. She knew children died all the time. Illness took them harder and carried them away faster. Nahoa's own mother had lost her first child to a wasting sickness. But Lei'ahi had always been so strong and healthy—Nahoa had never even thought to worry over the danger.

Nahoa had screamed at Makaho, begging and demanding the horrible, useless woman to do something to save her child. The nun had sent for several apothecaries, but they'd prescribed tinctures of herbs that Ahi had quickly vomited back up. Then Makaho had merely shaken her head and said, "It will be as the spirits will it." Which was the worst sort of hypocritical piety, Nahoa knew, since the whole reason for the fire temple's *existence* was humans taking the spirits into their own bloody hands. But what did Nahoa know of bindings? How would a spirit stop the horror that was even now sucking her daughter's life away?

It was midnight again, and Ahi had finally fallen into a fitful sleep. Her breathing was like iron rasping against stone, and her skin was so hot that Nahoa wrapped another damp cloth over them both.

"Ahi, sweet Ahi," she whispered. "Come on, girl. You can make it. You were born in the fire, weren't you? A little fever can't hurt."

Ahi sighed with a painful wheeze and hiccupped. Nahoa kissed the crown of her head, too exhausted to even cry.

"Would you like me to take her?" Malie said.

Nahoa shook her head. Malie looked as tired as she felt. The two of them had taken turns caring for Ahi since she fell ill, but neither had gotten more than a few minutes of sleep. She still might resent Malie's role in bringing her to the fire temple, but now she couldn't imagine anyone she'd rather have with her. Malie had borne the endless misery without complaining. If she hadn't been there, Nahoa might have let grief claim her hours ago.

Malie slumped against the wall beside her, eyes lidded but not quite shut.

"I think you should contact him," Malie said.

"Who?"

"The Mo'i. If Makaho won't help..."

Nahoa clamped her teeth down on a sob. Malie was right. Kohaku would do anything to save his daughter. He loved as fiercely as he hated. If anyone could find a witch, someone to wrest her daughter from the death's grip, it would be him. And yet, the moment she asked for his help, she would once again be entirely in his power. How could she do that after she'd given so much to be free? And yet how could she deny her daughter this one last chance?

"Oh crap," she said, feeling a tear slide down her warm cheek, and then another. "Crap, crap, crap. Malie, I don't know if I can bear it—"

The maid put her arm around Nahoa's shoulder. "Shh," she whispered. "It'll be all right. I'll go with you. It'll be all right."

The three of them fell asleep like that, exhausted and hurting, and Nahoa only awoke when Ahi did. She was coughing again. Nahoa adjusted her arms to relieve some of the pressure and glanced up.

Pano was in the room, staring at her like he'd seen a spirit.

"Nahoa," he said, his voice so low she could hardly hear it. "What's the matter with Ahi?"

She was so tired that it did not seem very odd to find Pano here again, though she had not expected it. She figured he'd leave her alone after she helped him free those people. "She's sick. She's very sick. Pano—I think she might..."

Pano took a few quiet steps across the floor and knelt before her. His bushy, dark eyebrows drew together, deepening the lines on his forehead. He touched Ahi's head with his large, gentle hands, and the child relaxed beneath them. His eyes grew tight as he met hers. He nodded slowly.

"You must come with me now," he whispered. "If we move quickly, it may be a few hours before Makaho notices."

"Come with you?" Nahoa repeated. This was an option she hadn't considered—putting herself in the rebel's power instead of her husband's. But would it be an improvement? "Can you save her?"

"I don't know. But there's someone we can ask."

"A witch?" she asked, for she knew her child was beyond the skills of a mere apothecary.

He nodded. "An Ana."

"What are you doing here?" Malie's voice was rough with sleep, but alert and distrustful. She had known Pano from before the eruption, in those long-ago months in the Mo'i's house.

He acknowledged her with a nod. "I came to ask your lady for a favor, but now..."

"Now you just want to kidnap her?"

Nahoa gave Malie a sour look. "Not so different from how you got me here, is it?"

"The Mo'i is insane," said Malie defensively.

"So's Makaho. He says he knows an Ana who can help."

"We have to leave now," Pano said. "Just trust me enough for this, Nahoa. I promise. I'd never let any harm come to you or Ahi."

It was strange, because the last year had taught her that everyone played politics, even the girls who emptied her chamber pot. Yet she trusted Pano. She trusted the crinkles around his eyes, the smell of dirt that never seemed to wash off his hands. She trusted the terror in his voice when he said Ahi's name—as though it meant nearly as much to him as it did to her. She knew that he would help her, and though his help might come with strings, they wouldn't bind as tightly as her husband's.

"I'm going, Malie. Stay here."

"But Naho—"

"No," she whispered fiercely, as Ahi started to whimper. "If anyone comes, they have to find you here. You have to make sure they don't know I've gone."

"You're going to the rebels without me?" she asked.

"I'm coming back," Nahoa whispered. "I need you here for me when I do. Makaho has to think you're still loyal."

Malie nodded slowly, and despite everything, Nahoa felt an odd sort of pride. It had taken some time, but she was learning this game. If life forced her to be a player, she wouldn't be the first piece scuttled off the board.

When Nahoa had slipped on her sandals and wrapped Ahi in a shawl, Pano nodded curtly and held out his hand. She took it. He led her down the silent hall and then up another flight of stairs, pausing occasionally to check for guards or any nocturnal wanderers. He stopped before an open window overlooking an overgrown part of the temple grounds. The pagodas here had been given up to the creeping vines that made quick work of the ancient stone carvings. It was a sad, disturbingly beautiful sort of destruction. He looked out over the edge and touched the sturdy vines that crept up the temple walls.

"Take your shawl," he whispered, his mouth close to her ear. "Tie Ahi to my chest. I'll climb down with her. You follow."

Nahoa did this without objecting. She was too exhausted to trust herself with Ahi's weight if she had to climb down the side of the temple. Pano went first, and she waited until he was halfway to the ground. Then she heard a faint scuffling on the stairs nearby—so light it could have just been a rat or a mongoose—and she scrambled onto the vine outside with hardly a thought. A shadow fell on the sill a few moments later. Her breathing caught in her throat. That had been too close. She went down carefully, but the vine here was sturdy and old, with plenty of places for her feet and hands. She wondered why no one had thought to cut it down, but perhaps no one but a gardener would know to trust its hold on the crumbling stones.

"Come," Pano said, when her feet touched the ground. She thought to ask for Ahi again, but her daughter was sleeping so soundly against Pano's chest she thought it better to leave her. It didn't even occur to her that Pano could run off with Ahi, putting her permanently in his control. They walked until they reached the water and Pano hired someone to take them to a small local dock in the fourth district. She fell asleep on the tiny canoe, her head on Pano's shoulder and her hand resting against Ahi's foot. His shoulder smelled nearly as nice as his hands—of lye soap and sweat and ashes. She dreamed the two of them were the points of light floating on the waves and Ahi was laughing at the moon. He woke her what seemed like a year later, though it couldn't have taken very long. She found she barely had the energy to walk when they climbed back on land, but thankfully the building where they stopped was close to the docks.

The front door was locked, but Pano just pounded until someone opened it. It was an older man, gaunt like so many others these days, and glaring at the two of them through tired eyes.

"Do you know how late it is?" the man said.

"I apologize," Pano said. "But we need to see the black angel. It's urgent."

"The black angel?" The man tilted his head in sleepy befuddlement. Then some sort of horrified awareness gripped him and his shoulders slumped. "Oh," he said. "You mean Lana. Yes. Follow me."

The black angel had a name? But of course she did. The girl who had stared at her so frankly across the courtyard that day hadn't been belched from the ruins on the wind island. She was a person, with a home and a lover.

"Papa?" the black angel said when they entered the apartment. She was wearing nothing but a pair of short pants, holding a lamp that partially illuminated her sleepy face.

Not a lover. A father.

"You have visitors," the father said.

The black angel peered at Pano and Nahoa and then brought the lamp closer. Her eyes widened. "What are..." she trailed off and then looked at them more closely. "What happened?"

"Nahoa's daughter is sick," Pano said, gesturing to Ahi who had started coughing feebly against his chest.

Nahoa thought he might have to explain more, but the black angel looked so immediately grim and competent that Nahoa knew she must have done this many times before.

"You can go back to bed, Papa," she said, her voice far gentler than her expression. "I'll take care of this."

"But, the child...shouldn't I fetch an apothecary?" He caught his daughter's look and stopped. "Of course. I'll see you in the morning, Lana."

He avoided Lana's eyes and shuffled into the other room in the apartment, closing the door behind him. Nahoa took in Lana's dark skin, her broad accent, and realized what should have been obvious from the first: she was an outer islander. A rustic outer islander, of all people, had become the black angel? It certainly explained her utter lack of self-consciousness at meeting them shirtless. On the outer islands, women only covered their breasts for ceremonies. It was too hot otherwise.

Once her father had left, the black angel cleared the low kitchen table of utensils and told Pano to rest Ahi in the center. Even an hour ago, Ahi would have cried at the lack of human contact, but now she just twisted weakly and struggled to breathe. Nahoa knelt beside the table. How much longer did Ahi have? Would the only worthwhile thing in Nahoa's life vanish forever?

"You don't have much time," Pano said to the black angel.

"I can see that," the black angel snapped, and Nahoa wondered, distantly, how these two knew each other.

The black angel knelt and lifted one of Ahi's limp hands. "How long has she been like this?" she asked gently. "What part of the body does it most affect?"

Nahoa rushed through the nightmare of the past two days, but she didn't know how to answer Lana's second question. "It's everywhere! None of the apothecaries knew what to make of it. She coughs, she can't keep food down, her stools are liquid, she shivers..."

Lana nodded and carefully rested her hands on Ahi's chest. Lana hissed and drew them away immediately.

"Her skin is boiling. How can she be so hot?" She paused for a moment. "But she was born in the fire. Of course."

The black angel stood with a rustle of wings and moved purposefully about her kitchen. She took a rough cloth and a knife with an edge so sharp Nahoa could see it glint from where she sat.

"This will be messy," Lana said. "I don't think there's enough time for more preparations."

Pano glanced at Nahoa, his worried expression conveying volumes. He knew about witches and sacrifice and was wary about what the black angel might be asking. Nahoa wasn't sure she cared so long as it saved her daughter.

"I offer myself!" he said. "If you need a sacrifice. It will be willing."

Lana flinched as though struck. Then, slowly, she walked to the table and sat beside it. Her shoulders shook as though she were furious or frightened.

"I need no sacrifices but my own," she said, harsh as Ahi's breathing. "And I never will." She stared at Pano until he looked down.

"I apologize, Ana," he said, though Nahoa didn't quite understand why. She slipped her hand inside his. It was dry and warm. She was gratified that he would offer himself for the sacrifice, though she supposed it was good for them both that the black angel was not *that* kind of witch.

Lana laid out the cloth, placed her arm on the table, and lifted the knife. With her wrist exposed, Nahoa finally noticed what Pano must have seen before: the row of barely healed scars inching up her forearm. She had done this many times before. Always at cost to herself. It had insulted her that Pano would have assumed otherwise. The black angel didn't hesitate when she brought the blade down. Blood welled over the blade and stained the cloth beneath. Nahoa turned away and stared at Ahi. This was for her. For her. But she had to swallow bile at the thought of Lana's deliberate self-destruction. She'd always thought it best to give the spirits a wide berth before, but she'd never had such a clear demonstration of *why*.

"Fire, who so recently broke its bounds," said the black angel.

The hairs rose on Nahoa's arms. Pano gripped her hand more tightly. The air seemed charged, like on the ocean before a thunderstorm. And Lana was utterly, imperturbably calm in the face of it. She might be incongruously young, but she really was an Ana.

"I bind you with blood. I bind you with my knowledge of fire. Show me the cause of this child's illness. She burns with your flame."

Lana's pupils had dilated until her eyes seemed black in the lamplight. She gazed at something neither Nahoa nor Pano could see. Her mouth moved, but the only sounds they could hear were indistinct glottal stops unconnected to any vowels.

"Yes," she breathed, after several long minutes. She lifted her still-bleeding arm from the table and reached behind her. Again, without the slightest hesitation, she plucked a large feather from above her shoulder.

"The wind's sacrifice to brush it clear, to erase the other binding." She dusted Ahi with the feather, starting at her feet and ending with the crown of her head. Nahoa fought the urge to slap the black angel's hand away. The action looked primitive and sinister, but she had no choice but to trust her now. The air had grown stifling, making it a struggle to even breathe. Ahi's body crackled and sparked. Lana's hair floated in an eerie nimbus around her face, but she didn't seem to notice. And then Lana released the feather above

Ahi's chest. It hung for an impossible moment, trembling, and then burst into flames.

Nahoa shrieked and Pano gripped her arm before she could scramble forward. But it was all right. The feather was consumed and the ashes floated gently down, dusting the table. The heat dissipated and Lana slumped toward the ground, as though exhausted.

"Is that—what happened?" Nahoa said. Lana gestured silently to Ahi, and Nahoa took this as permission to touch her daughter. As soon as she did, she realized that Lana had succeeded. Her daughter's skin was cool, her breathing clear and easy. She slept peacefully, but when Nahoa tentatively pulled her to her breast, Ahi awoke enough to drink.

Nahoa looked back up. Lana was smiling at them both, and Nahoa wondered why she had been so ambivalent about the black angel before. She'd love her forever for saving her daughter. "Thank you so much," Nahoa said. "I don't know what I can do—"

"Keep her safe," the black angel said. "That wasn't a natural illness. It was a geas. I couldn't tell who laid it—it was clumsy, so probably not someone very familiar with binding. But they bound your daughter with fire."

Pano released her hand and leaned in closer to the black angel.

"You're saying...this means that someone in the fire temple tried to assassinate an infant."

"It could have been anyone. I'm no politician, but I don't see what advantage the fire temple gains by killing the one thing that gives them a hold over the Mo'i."

"They'd still have me," Nahoa said quietly.

But Pano was shaking his head. "And if your husband thought you and your daughter weren't safe there, he'd start a war with them to get you out. The only reason he hasn't already is because he thinks he can still convince you."

Nahoa stared at him. "Start a war? *Another* one? You're crazy."

"No, he is. And whoever tried to kill Ahi knows it."

Ahi, as though objecting to the topic of conversation, stopped drinking and started to wail. Nahoa lifted her up and started rocking her back and forth, making meaningless noises and struggling to hold back sudden tears. She had come so close...it had come too close.

"How do I stop it from happening again? How can I protect her if I don't even know who wants her dead?"

Lana held a clean edge of the bloody cloth to her wrist. She winced now, though she hadn't given any indication that she felt the pain before. "Someone might have spent enough time with her to recite a geas. You would have noticed if you'd been in the room. Or they touched her with an object already bound to a spirit."

Pano caught her eyes, and she was again startled by how serious he looked, how worried. "If you must go back there, Nahoa, then you can't let anyone else touch her but you. You can't accept any gifts."

"What about Malie? I can't do this all myself."

"Do you trust her?"

After a moment, Nahoa nodded. "I'd never have made it without her. I think she's loyal. She'd never hurt Ahi."

"And send word to me if you think that anything is wrong," Lana said.

Nahoa realized then that they had to get back or risk Makaho discovering she'd left. Pano thanked Lana and tried to give her some coins, but the black angel refused. Nahoa thought she might have accepted them if Pano hadn't insulted her earlier. Which was stupid, Nahoa thought. As if pride should stop this girl from taking care of herself.

Lana walked with them as far as the docks, and the air was warm enough that she didn't seem to notice she'd forgotten to don a shirt. Nahoa bound the sleeping Ahi to her back with a shawl, and wrapped another around her head. Pano didn't want anyone to recognize her out here. Nahoa hadn't realized she was so famous.

The same canoe was waiting for them when they arrived. Pano stepped into the boat and held out his arms to help Nahoa inside. She had gripped his hands when she noticed an oddly furtive movement at the other end of the darkened street. She shook free of Pano and peered closer—it was a man, and he was raising some sort of strange object shaped like a crescent moon and he was pointing it straight at the black angel, whose back was still turned to him.

Nahoa gave a wordless cry and yanked hard on a clump of Lana's loosened hair. Nahoa stumbled to her knees and Lana's shriek of surprise turned to a gasp far more ominous. Lana tumbled sideways. Pano was already out of the boat and sprinting down the road, but Nahoa didn't think he'd catch the attacker: the man was fast and too far ahead.

What was that strange weapon? Nahoa had never actually seen a bow and arrow before, but she guessed that's what the assassin had been using.

Lana groaned at her feet, but at first Nahoa couldn't see any injury.

"It's her wings, miss." Nahoa looked up, startled. The boatman had climbed up to the docks and was kneeling beside her. He was right: an arrow, like a tiny spear, had pierced Lana's left wing dangerously close to where it met her back.

"What...what happened?" Lana gasped. She attempted to turn over and stopped, trembling. The cobbled street beneath her wings was running with her blood. Quickly, Nahoa unwrapped the shawl from her head and held it to the wound. She prayed that the boatman wasn't one of those who would recognize her.

"A bow, I think," Nahoa said.

"Who was he aiming for?" Lana said. "Which one of us?"

Nahoa thought back to the confused glimpse she'd had of him aiming the weapon. She hadn't been afraid for herself, though now she realized she should have been. But his aim had been steady, not following her progress. He'd been focusing on an obvious target.

"You," she whispered.

Lana closed her eyes—in either pain or shock, Nahoa didn't know. She looked back down the street and saw Pano returning, panting and empty-handed.

"He was too far ahead. I couldn't get a good look at him. How is she?"

Nahoa adjusted the pressure on the shawl she held pressed

against the wound. Lana groaned and then went completely limp, her head lolling against Nahoa's shoulder. She and Pano shared a worried glance.

"We have to get her off the street. Someplace safe," he said.

"Her father?" she asked.

He thought for a moment, then shook his head. "There's too much blood. I don't think he knows...there's nothing for it. You go. I'll take her."

"Take her where?"

"Sea Street. Rebel territory."

The black book

Tulo hated the city. She'd never been to one before, but even I had to admit that the smell of accumulated shit on the packed dirt roads—not to mention some of the people walking on them—could be fairly unpleasant. She hated the crowds, too, and the bustle and the noise. What she hated most of all, though it took Parech and I nearly a day to understand, was how much more of a handicap her blindness was in the city. The humans cast too much light, she said. Trying to see the spirit paths was like holding a torch close to your eyes and then trying to see the stars. Everything had turned to a featureless haze. She cried herself to sleep for three nights after we arrived, and the other travelers who shared the cramped room with us would huff loudly until she fell silent. Parech would stare at me after she slept and I knew what he was asking, *Should we go back? Should we stay in the forest for her?* But I didn't want to go back. I liked this city. I liked its laughably abundant food, sold by people from all over the islands. They made a kind of fried bread with spices that made me cry the first time I tried it. I'd never tasted anything better in my life.

I wanted to be selfish, but Tulo's misery dragged at me, too. I didn't know how I would have survived in her situation. It seemed cruel to make her suffer more. Finally, I told Parech that we could leave, and I almost winced at the relief in his face. He cared for her more than me, I thought. Well, I could manage. But it still hurt.

We told Tulo together while we sat on a hill of pampas grass that overlooked the bay. We'd thought she'd be overjoyed, but instead her shoulders went up just like they always did when we offended her.

"I agreed to come here, didn't I? What am I, some baby for you to indulge and discuss in the middle of the night? Yes, I like the forest better. I know the forest. But I lived for a year without the spirit sight, and I can make do here. I will. And don't you two dare tell me I can't just because I'm blind!"

I glanced at Parech and was rewarded with his surprised laughter. "Tulo," I said, "we never..."

"You thought it!" she said, glaring at me.

And I had. It didn't really seem fair for her to be mad for my thoughts, but she was right. Perhaps we should have just talked to her instead of assuming she'd want to deprive us of this adventure.

"I'm sorry," I said. Her expression softened, but her carriage was still haughty.

Parech reached out and took her hand. "I forgot for a moment you're a princess." Which was the precisely right thing to say, because she suddenly gave both of us a bright grin and leaned against his shoulder.

"See, now, everything will be all right. We'll all find something to do. And it's getting better, the longer I'm in the city. I got so used to the spirit roads being so clear it was like I couldn't see them at all when they got fainter. I'll use a stick and we'll stay. It'll be all right."

I hugged her. "You're sure?"

She laughed. "Of course I am. You think I haven't noticed how fat you've been getting on those spice cakes?"

"The princess is very observant," Parech said. "Our Ana may turn into a real beauty yet. She was too skinny to see before."

I blushed so furiously at this that Parech laughed again.

"I know you had some reason to bring us here, you fool soldier," I said, when the wind from the ocean had grown chilly. "It can't just be to sweep streets and weave baskets."

Tulo seemed surprised at this. "Does he?" she asked. "You have a plan, Parech? What is it?"

Parech tossed me a wry expression. "You really are a witch."

"You're cute when you think you're being mysterious."

"'Think?' I *am* mysterious, I assure you. You two will just have to be curious a little while longer. It's not quite ready yet. But I promise, this plan will make our fortunes."

Parech's plan, as it turned out, involved deceit, fraud, theft, and a serious possibility of violence. It started with Tulo, who would pretend to be a blind soothsayer ("I know you're the Ana, but she looks the part," Parech explained). Since she was obviously Kawadiri, she would play on what Parech called "people's preconceived notions." I gathered this meant speaking halting Maaram with a heavy accent, baring her chest, and wearing some absurd costume Parech cobbled together out of feathers and straw and ragged monkey pelts.

"It doesn't feel like anything Kawadiri," Tulo had said doubtfully, and I'd glared at Parech and informed Tulo that as little as I knew of her people, she could be assured that not one of them had ever worn anything at all like it.

"That doesn't matter," Parech said airily. "It's only important to make them believe you're Kawadiri."

"I *am* Kawadiri," she said indignantly. "Why can't I wear my own clothes and speak Maaram like a properly educated person?" And then Parech was off again about his "preconceived notions." I stormed off to get some food.

As for me, I was to play the wealthy daughter of an Esselan chief whose canoe had capsized somewhere off the coast. Only by the grace of the ancestors had I washed ashore in Maaram. I had struggled to reach the city. ("That explains why a rich woman would be as skinny as you, Ana," Parech said, and I nearly punched him in the stomach.) Now that I was here, I needed some "kind soul" (Parech for "rich fool") to help me get back to my people, whereupon I would send him a generous reward for his aid, and perhaps some information about the Esselan army. Parech would play a middling Maaram merchant, just returned from Essel, who just happens to recognize me and verify my tale of woe. And how did Tulo fit into this master plan? Well, Parech had one particular "rich fool" in mind: A soldier named Taak, whom he'd encountered several months ago while on leave in Okika. This man was the spoiled youngest brother of the Maaram war canoe chieftain. And according to Parech, this wastrel had a peculiar weakness for prognosticators and omens. Once, apparently, he'd forced all the soldiers out of the city house and made them sleep in the street because some soothsayer had told him he'd have better luck if the spirits had their privacy.

"Maybe he's repented of that foolishness," Tulo said.

Parech grinned. "Oh no, not that one. A spirit talker could tell him there'd be high tide at midnight in a quarter moon and he'd take out his canoe."

It took a few extra days while our store of scavenged salt and sennit braid dwindled and Parech wore down our resistance with wild yarns of all we could do with a fortune—"a house in Essel all to ourselves, and coconuts and eels every night. We'll make you fat yet, Ana!" Despite ourselves, we started to see the possibilities. And what was the harm? The fool wouldn't be harmed for parting from his wealth, and the three of us could go on to the glittering city of Essel. Early the next morning I awoke to find Tulo asleep in my arms and Parech gone. I covered her with the blanket and wrapped a shawl around my shoulders before I went outside. Parech was perched on the low wall of mud bricks that overlooked the boarding house's pond. The fish seemed as drowsy as I felt as they nipped at the crumbs of stale panbread that Parech was tossing on the water.

His face was uncharacteristically solemn, and I caught myself observing him while he still hadn't noticed my presence. He'd changed from his soldier's wrap as soon as we'd entered the city. Now he wore a knee-length skirt of red-dyed barkcloth and a vest he'd left undone this morning. From my viewpoint I could see his swirling black tattoos, which seemed etched into his muscled flesh like chisel marks into sandstone. The wound that had nearly killed him had scarred into a pale welt than ran from his navel around to his back. I thought it might still hurt him, but he always laughed too much to let it show. I watched him there, with his salo-lightened hair and downturned mouth. Right there, I decided that I'd agree to his mad scheme and convince Tulo to do the same.

"Why are you up so early?" he asked. He said this with a smile, but it fell too quickly. "You and Tulo slept like the dead."

I shrugged. "Parech, I've been thinking, it's not such a bad idea. Dishonest, sure, but I'll do it."

"There's something else. Another reason."

He didn't even look at me as he said this and so I teased, "What, something even more compelling than an endless feast of sour fry-cakes?"

This forced a laugh out of him, and he held my shoulder as he leaned against the wall. He left his hand there so long my breath came short and I could hardly think through a torrent of wordless confusion and longing. Had I been wrong about everything I saw growing between him and Tulo? Was it possible? But no, he lowered his hand and I could see nothing like what I felt in his enigmatic expression.

"I haven't told you much about my time as a soldier," Parech said.

"Was it bad?" I managed, after a moment. I was proud of how unaffected my voice sounded.

He met my gaze again and laughed. "Bad? You have a way with understatement, Ana. But I fought with the Akane, back on Kukicha. That was worse. I knew some of the men I killed. My chief gave me these warrior marks for slaying my cousins. Here...everyone was all the same. You can get used to death. And when it comes to you, well, you've killed too much to really resent it."

I was shocked. This was the first time Parech had ever even hinted at his experiences as a soldier. And yet this helped me understand how he had managed to laugh at his death when I first met him. Parech wasn't terribly fierce, but he had a clean core of bravery that sprang from his sense of the absurd.

"But something happened? Something that's making you sit by the fish pond like some moody poet?"

Parech put his arm around my shoulders and pulled me close. "Truly," he said, "it was a spirit path that led me to you two. I wonder what they'll demand in payment."

I relaxed into him. "So what's this thing you haven't told us?"

He sighed. "The Maaram are going to launch a new attack on Essel at the start of the cold. Everything they have. The Esselans have the advantage of weapons, so the Maaram want to take them by surprise and overwhelm them with superior numbers."

I recalled the numbing horrors of the battlefields I'd stumbled upon during my months in the forest. And those were just minor skirmishes with a few rebellious tribes. I couldn't even grasp the scale of death and suffering that would be unleashed if the Maaram brought a war like that to Essel. And I had a sensation that I did not quite know how to articulate that such death—with no true dedication or purpose—could do terrible things to the powers of the spirits.

"What does that mean for us?" I finally asked, since there seemed to be no point in going over the probable effects of the invasion. Parech understood the horrors far better than I.

"We need to get to Essel. Soon. Before cold sets in. We need to get Taak's wealth, because I don't know how else we'll afford passage."

"But I thought you said the Maaram were going to invade!"

He looked so grim that I tugged on a lock of his hair until he looked at me. "They will," he said softly, in Kukichan. "And they're going to lose. You do not want to be in Maaram when the Esselans land, Ana. None of us do."

We spoke to Tulo a few hours later, once she had dragged herself awake, up the latest as usual. She made no further objections once Parech explained the real source of his urgency. She didn't ask him why he hadn't told us earlier. And why would she? She had been inured to war with the Maaram for her entire life. She understood what this meant.

"I hope they rot," she said in hushed Essela. "I hope the Maaram clog the oceans so Esselan fishermen dine on their entrails for weeks."

"It might go worse with your people, Tulo, under the Esselans."

"What could be worse? Slavery? Butchering our children?"

Parech gave her a sidelong glance at this but just shook his head and refused to say any more.

And so we played our parts. Tulo started first, setting herself up across from the great lodge where all the important Maaram chiefs slept. I had wondered why so much of the army crowded Okika City, jostling the locals with their loud manners and ready weapons, but Parech's revelations made everything comprehensible.

As Parech predicted, Tulo was an immediate hit with her absurd headdress of tatty pheasant feathers and cape of draped monkey pelts. He'd even attempted to paint her arms, but Tulo had kicked his kneecap and threatened to let the two of us go on without her help. It didn't hurt her popularity, I realized, that Tulo exuded youth and unconscious beauty. Her hair was wild as ever, and accentuated by the red and blue feathers. By the second day, men had started to line up to have the bones cast and their fortunes read by the blind Kawadiri girl in the square. Parech perched in a nearby tree to keep watch. I stayed with him, though the duty grew tedious. Parech wanted to make sure none of these men took advantage of Tulo. I had to stay here because otherwise the commander's brother might see me before the appointed time and our whole plan would be ruined.

At the end of the second day, a group of men stumbled from the officer's lodge and headed straight for Tulo.

"Look," I whispered. "Is he one of them?"

Parech shaded his eyes. "I'm not sure, maybe the tall one—"

"Wait, that one on the left, is he...wearing a bear?"

He started to laugh. "A pelt! Well, isn't Taak one to boast? I suppose he'd have us believe he slayed it himself. Probably for some spirit boon."

The man in the bear pelt—head and all—turned to speak to one of his friends, and I saw that what would have been a pleasant face was slashed by three wide, deep scars that ruined his left eye.

"Maybe he did slay it," I said softly.

Parech glanced at me. "He always was an idiot."

His friends all took their turns with Tulo, but I could tell from here that she'd focused on Taak and his bear pelt. She took her time with him, closing her eyes and rocking back and forth, as though deep in the throes of some trance. I had to cover my mouth to keep from laughing. Finally, she slumped on her stool and waved off the rest of the crowd. Taak, I thought, was suitably impressed.

That evening, Tulo told us the whole story. She'd given him a portentously vague reading about destiny and danger and his wise soul and suggested that he needed to return to her once she had "regained her strength" to hear more.

"I swear, I could tell him to give me a farm because the spirits said so. He's more gullible than even you thought, Parech. Did you know that he killed a bear because some charlatan told him he'd be invincible in its pelt?"

We all laughed, though I felt guilty for doing so. It seemed a shame to take advantage of him when he'd already lost so much. But we needed to leave Okika, and I wasn't going to be picky about how it happened.

Parech squatted by Tulo's feet, and she put a hand on his shoulder. I saw the gentleness of the smile he briefly turned up to her. And how sad, I thought, that she would never see him. And that I, who could see Parech smile whenever I wished, would never receive a smile from him like that one.

Taak found Tulo late the next evening. She roped him expertly, as though she had been running grifts her entire life. Parech wouldn't let me close enough to overhear, but afterward she told us everything. She had stared deep at Taak (who was, she said, so untuned to the spirit world that he looked as dim as a dying firefly) and declared that he was at a crossroads of fate. She insinuated that he had money problems. That his family didn't appreciate his ingenuity and give him enough freedom. That he had bravely fought against a great spirit, and the eye he had lost was a sacrifice to guarantee his safety in battle (he had gasped at this revelation, she said, to my discomfort). But he wanted more ("Yes!" he had said, "That's it exactly!"). He wanted the glory he deserved ("You know my every thought!"). And, as he should well know, the fastest path to that glory was wealth ("It is? Yes, it is!"). Well, from there it was easy work to convince poor Taak that the crossroads in his fate would soon bring him an opportunity to receive this wealth, "if only you're brave enough to take it!" What was the nature of this opportunity? Tulo was very coy, but she implied it had to do with foreigners and women, and that he must not speak a word to anyone about it, or the spirits might grow angry and twist his opportunity to evil purposes. At which point she began to tremble and fell into a dead swoon, from which he gallantly caught her.

From our vantage in the tree, Parech laughed so hard he had tears in his eyes. I had to cover his mouth with my hand when the few people nearby started to glance up, but I was having difficulty keeping laughter back myself. I could imagine what Tulo was really thinking behind that demure facade. Tulo recovered quickly and allowed Taak to buy her a stick of cane sugar and some restorative tea. He left only after he had presented her with a pile of sennit braid and a basket of salt—far more than her requested payment—and begged her to return the next day. She smiled mysteriously and he left. She read a few more fortunes, just so as to not raise suspicions, and then signaled with a rattle of the beads around her wrists that she would meet us by the main irrigation ditch in the farms a safe distance from the city's edge.

Parech lingered when I would have left, silently watching Tulo's contained, quiet movements. She had grown skilled at moving about the city in the two weeks since our argument. Her blindness was obvious as the feathers in her hair, but her grip on her stick was sure, not desperate. She held it before her as she walked, and that seemed to be all the aid she needed. She hardly ever stumbled anymore; in fact, she moved far more gracefully than most of Okika's residents. I asked her how she did it, for I knew her spirit sight was useless here. She shrugged and said it was easy, once she paid attention. Packed dirt felt different from loose; cobbles felt different from grass. She could smell people before they passed her; she could feel their heat beside her. The air itself felt different by the water, or before a set of stairs. And anything she could not determine with her four senses, well, that was the stick's job. Once we explained a place to her, she said, once she had oriented herself in her own mind, moving through it wasn't very different from seeing. I held her in quiet awe. I would never have been able to live as she did. I knew it, and it humbled me.

Finally, Parech responded to my preemptive tugging on his arm, and we made our way through the fields to the irrigation ditch. Follow it long enough and it led straight through the heart of Okika to the mouth of the river.

"I'm up next," Parech said, bunching his hands under his arms for warmth as a brisk breeze blew in from the west. We'd made it to the meeting place before Tulo, so I moved closer to him. He gave me a wry look and then wrapped both arms around me. The warm weather had vanished completely, and I wasn't used to this kind of cold.

"I'll settle for less food in Essel if we can have a chimney," I said.

Parech's chuckle tickled my scalp. "I'll see what we can work out. But first you and I have to make ourselves worthy of Tulo's performance."

I sighed. "She was marvelous wasn't she? The look on his face when she fell into his arms!"

"He'll dream of her breasts for weeks, I'm sure. That's our princess."

Our princess. I smiled. "When will you start with Taak?"

"Tonight, I think. Best that he gets used to me for a few days before he runs into our distressed chieftain's daughter."

"Will you ask to stay in their lodge?"

He shook his head. "Too expensive for us, and conveniently also for the role I'm playing. No, the commanding officers like going to cockfights. I'll go there, gamble and lose to him, and make a few friendly gestures. Nothing that intrusive. I only need to be a presence in his mind. A disinterested third party who happens to know you. It might be suspicious if I try to get too friendly."

I thought of Taak fighting a bear single-handedly on the advice of a street-corner charlatan. "Suspicious? Taak? You could tell him the spirits didn't like the cut of his kilt and he'd fight the Esselans bare-assed."

Parech shifted and I could hear his laugh deep in his chest. I closed my eyes. But instead of some comical image of Taak leading the Maaram charge, dangle flying, I saw a graphic flash of a furious bear raking one giant claw across Taak's head, ripping his eye apart in a gout of blood and gore. And then Taak's club as it bludgeons the beast to death. Blood matted on fur. Taak almost dying and then recovering, determined to wear the skin of that bear into battle.

All because of a street-corner charlatan. Like Tulo.

I pushed Parech away because I was afraid I might vomit on him. I shivered and stared at the muddy trickle of the irrigation ditch that fed these fields. What were we doing? It was one thing to plan a con game on some faceless soldier, an agent of so much destruction in the islands. It was quite another to take advantage of a gullible fool who'd almost died because someone just like us gave him advice she never expected him to take.

"Aoi?" Parech said. He was staring at me. He looked strangely tentative. Worried in a way I'd thought he reserved for Tulo.

I looked away. "I don't think...we shouldn't do this. I know he's just another Maaram soldier, I know, but..."

"Oh, don't tell me you like him now?"

"Of course not! He's a fool, a water-carrier, but Parech, *did you see his face?*"

He winced, and I realized that Taak's disfigurement must have been as much of a surprise to Parech as it had been to me. "We're not planning to maim him, Ana. Just relieve a fool of his wealth."

"We're manipulating him."

"I thought that was the point."

"He's Maaram," Tulo said. Both of us looked up, startled, as she stepped from the surrounding fields of taro flowers, silent as a ghost. "A Maaram soldier." She could have called him a shit-eater and conveyed more respect for his occupation. "He deserves whatever we give him."

She squatted beside us and carefully removed the pheasant-feather headdress from her tangled hair. Parech threw a shawl over her bare, goose-pimpled shoulders. I could only imagine how her skin must ache from so many hours uncovered in this chill, but she didn't seem unduly uncomfortable. Perhaps her people had gone bare-chested longer into the cold season.

"Not all Maaram are bad people, Tulo," I said.

Parech and Tulo shared tight, knowing smiles. "She's a wet-lander," Parech said, as though in apology.

"What's that supposed to mean?"

He shrugged. "Just that you wouldn't understand. To be a Maaram soldier is to be guilty. Just like on Kukicha. You think a single soul who fought for you wetlanders was innocent of Akane blood? Of course not."

"*You* were a Maaram soldier!"

His mouth quirked. "And I've never claimed innocence."

Tulo had shimmied out of the pelts and replaced them with a split skirt. "Don't worry about the soldier, Aoi," she said. "You'll be happy for his money when we're in Essel."

I stood up, furious, though I'd been perfectly fine with this scheme less than an hour ago. "How can you two be so callous? We're about to ruin the life of another human being!"

Tulo's lips thinned. "Another human being? I suppose he'd think of me as another human being, then, if he found my brothers and uncles and cousins defending our homes? Perhaps he'd speak to us, negotiate with us, respect our rights to our ancestors' land? Or maybe he'd just murder us, every last one, and then find the nearest villages and murder everyone there, too. Maybe he'd even rape the women before murdering them. Perhaps we should treat the soldier like the Maaram do the Kawadiri. Like human beings!"

I sat down again. I felt myself reeling with horror for the second time in an hour. I looked at Parech. "Is it true?" I asked in Kukichan. "Did you do that?"

"The other soldiers did," Parech said in the same language. "I hid until it was done. Taak would have done it many times."

They were right. No one was innocent, let alone a Maaram soldier. A part of me was still disgusted at the manipulation necessary, especially when juxtaposed against Taak's gullible joy. But we needed to get to Essel, and this soldier's money would get us there.

I stopped arguing. The three of us followed the irrigation ditch until we reached the beach. As usual, crowds of Okikans had gathered there under the flickering light of torches to watch the rising tide and gamble and drink and smoke. The three of us traded salt for a thumb of amant and a jug of kava and sat down to enjoy the evening. A group of drummers pounded an intricate rhythm nearby, accompanied by an occasional drunken-sounding flute. At one point Tulo stood up to general approval and began gently, then more violently, swaying to the beat. She shook off her sandals and stomped her bare feet in the wet sand—smack, smack as she moved her arms and head in a traditional Kawadiri dance, silhouetted against the torchlight. She was so beautiful it took my breath away. Parech stared at her, entranced, and we moved closer together while we watched. She came back to us when she was drenched in sweat, though the crowd that had formed bellowed and cheered for more. She moved with an old assurance, without need of her stick. In the flickering torchlight, she seemed to glow like a spirit.

"How can you move like that?" I asked her, my heart still racing from the sight of her dance.

She laughed and flicked her hair over her shoulder. "I was born to dance for the ancestors."

Parech ran a finger down her arm and then offered her our half-drunk jug of spirits. "Like a true princess of her people," he said.

She beamed at him and then at me. I felt as though a slow fire was consuming me as I met both of their gazes. Joy and passion and desire. I sometimes thought I didn't understand anything anymore.

"The spirits are so clear here on the beach," she whispered. "Maybe it's you two. You're like a homing beacon."

I leaned against her. Parech polished off the spirits, and I shared the amant with Tulo. The air at this time of night, so close to the ocean, had gone from brisk to frigid, but someone had built a bonfire, and so we crowded around it with the others who were too reluctant or too intoxicated to go home.

"I don't think," I whispered to Tulo late that night, "that he is a bad man."

She put her arm around my shoulders and frowned thoughtfully. Somehow she knew who I meant. "You heard what Parech said. You heard what he did."

"But so did all the others. Can you truly hate every Maaram soldier?"

"Yes. Maybe. It doesn't matter, Aoi." She hesitated and then flung the ashes of our amant into the bonfire.

"If he is not a bad man, then there are no bad men."

For the next two nights, a young and swarthily handsome, but otherwise nondescript, Maaram trader spent and lost some modest sums in the gaming pens. The cocks he bet on were not obviously infirm, but a sound judge could have told him to bet more wisely. He chatted with the soldiers who had come there to gamble, trading innocuous stories about the sea routes and troubles in Essel. The second night, after his third loss in so many hours, the trader asked a nearby officer for advice on his next choice. The officer was happy to oblige, and their chosen cock dispatched the other with a savage swipe across its stomach that sprayed intestines and entrails all over the sand-covered pen. The officer bought the trader a cup of cane spirits in mutual celebration, and the two parted on friendly terms.

Parech was sure that Taak thought nothing of him, but would remember him clearly when the time came. And, more importantly, so would the other commanding officers who attended the cockfights with Taak. And then, finally, it was my turn. Parech had spent several days combing the city for the perfect clothes. He said it mattered more for me than he or Tulo because so much of my story depended on Taak's perception of my station. No matter that I was some Kukichan country bumpkin—a bit of Parech's magic, and I'd become a highborn Esselan lady in temporarily dire straits. In the end, the man selling the clothes that Parech wanted demanded an inordinate length of sennit braid and would not take salt, so Tulo had to reprise her role as street-corner spirit talker to earn the rest. Parech bound my hair in braids and pinned it like ropes to my scalp. He tied a shimmering rope of clamshells around my ankle and draped me in a tunic of patterned purple barkcloth in the Esselan style. This was a marvel of ingenuity, because the cloth he found was stained and distressed in precisely the way you'd expect of someone who had been nearly drowned in the ocean. Though I spoke Esselan with perfect fluency, I'd never been there and had not the slightest idea of how their ruling class dressed. Parech assured me that Taak had even less of an idea than I did, but a few details would help to make my case more convincing. He met Tulo and me in our room carrying a vial of green ink made from the crushed skin of a salo fruit and a row of bamboo needles.

"Parech, I don't know how to make Akane warrior marks. You know that, right?"

Tulo looked at me sharply. "What's he doing?"

"He has ink and a tattoo needle."

Parech grinned. "Ana, you mistake me. It's for you."

Tulo looked confused. "You want warrior tattoos, Aoi? Are you going to fight?"

"Of course I'm not going to fight! And I'm not going to mark my skin like some ignorant Akane either!"

He just laughed and drew me down next to him. "I've seen the way your eyes trace my 'barbarian' marks, Ana. I don't think you object to them very much at all."

And I blushed so deep and hot I thought even Tulo could tell. "What do I need tattoos for, though?"

"Highborn ladies wear their family marks on their upper arms. Come, are you afraid of the pain? It doesn't hurt too badly."

I looked down at the ink and then back to his laughing eyes. I *was* a little leery of the mallet and the needle. I'd seen others getting their marks and the experience had never looked less than agonizing.

"Is this necessary?" I asked.

"It's all about confidence, Ana. The more you look the part, the more confidence he'll have in your story, and the faster we'll be able to leave this benighted city."

Tulo frowned. "I thought you said we should go to the city because we shouldn't live in the forest like monkeys."

"And we shouldn't. That doesn't mean we should live in *this* city. Maaram is headed for a fall."

"They have the larger army," I said. "And the element of surprise."

He leaned back on his elbows, so his bleached hair brushed Tulo's belly and his shoulders rested against her thighs. "You reveal your ignorance of politics, Ana," he said. "Maaram is to Essel what a drizzle is to a hurricane. I'd be very surprised if the Esselan chieftains are not already quite aware of what is surely the worst-kept secret in the country. And remember, they have the trick of the metal edge."

I found myself shivering and looked abruptly away from them both. Tulo had laid out our sleeping pallets, which took up most of the small room not already occupied by the low table. The scene was familiar, yet for a moment it seemed superimposed with something more grisly and frightening: the bodies of dead soldiers and civilians sprawled in their own blood on the dirt streets of Okika. Buildings burning and people running for their lives from the long blades that sparkle like water in the harsh sun. Taak bleeding to death on his bearskin cloak.

"...seems rather extreme," Tulo was saying, oblivious to my mood.

But Parech watched me carefully. "Well, I can't make her do something she doesn't want to. You know my feelings on the matter, Ana. What do you say?"

I forced a smile and shrugged. A little pain now might be enough to help us avoid disaster in the future. "Why not? But try not to make it too hideous, Parech. You can't wash off skin-needle ink."

I thought he would respond with more teasing but he merely levered himself up and squeezed my shoulder. I bit my lip.

The pain was entirely as bad as I had expected, though Parech tapped the needle and filled the well with such assurance I gathered he had performed this service many times before. I had to raise my arm so he could make the mark all around its circumference several times over. I bit my tongue until I tasted blood and then just ground my teeth. Tulo held my other hand in silent support. I thought Parech would tease me, but he was intent on his design, and I was not inclined to disturb his work with anything other than the occasional grunt.

Eventually he leaned back and let the empty needle and inkwell fall to the floor. "There you go, Ana."

"How is it?" Tulo asked.

I didn't have the energy to lift my head, so I was grateful when Parech answered, "Impressive, though I suppose I would think so." He paused. "It suits her."

There was a certain quality of admiration in his tone that infiltrated my weariness and made me sit up and examine his handiwork. The mark moved from near my shoulder halfway down my upper arm. It was a complicated pattern, similar to Parech's warrior marks, but more intertwined, with a distinctive knot near my shoulder. My skin was now red and raw, but even I could see how soon the marks would meld with my skin. It made me look sophisticated. I imagined myself in the purple tunic and realized I might even, in a certain light, be held to look beautiful.

"It's...it's good," I said. My voice was uncharacteristically husky.

"Of course it is," Parech said.

I went to sleep soon after, stunned for reasons I couldn't articulate. I was seventeen years old, I remember. Seventeen, and I'd lived on my own for the past two years, but the night Parech marked me was the first time I felt like a woman.

"Please, tell me what I can do!" the foreign girl begged. She had dropped to her knees before the wild-haired fortune-teller and the bystanders who waited their turn peered curiously at the scene. "I have nothing left," she cried, the tears on her cheeks obvious even from a distance. "My father doesn't know where I am! It seems so hopeless." She bent her head and heaved sobs so great the men gambling on the other side of the square paused and looked up.

I didn't see any of that. Parech told me later. I was too focused on the tears pouring down my cheeks while Tulo placed a gentle hand on my shoulder. I found that it was easiest to work up a good torrent if I thought about Kukicha. First my parents' deaths, then my old priest's, and finally, when it seemed like my distress might exhaust itself, I forced myself to remember the foul-smelling trader who had tried to rape me. None of us had the luxury for mistakes now. The game had been engaged in earnest, and we had to see it through. I saw how eyes snagged on my family marks, as though evaluating my station.

We three had planned this scene carefully. This was the second market day, and Tulo had set herself up on a relatively busy street not very far from the officer's lodge. Taak would be sure to hear of her presence, and in the absence of any obvious workings of fate would be eager to consult with her again. But it being a market day, and with Tulo's newfound reputation, the crowd surrounding her was far larger than it had been the week prior. Taak was waiting behind several other people when I approached Tulo and began my performance. He would have been able to hear my anguished cries, but not Tulo's responses.

"If you show patience, my lady," Tulo was saying in that gentle, almost musical tone she affected for this work, "the spirits will lead one to you who can help restore you to your family and proper position. You need only be prepared to receive."

She lifted my face from her skirt with her finger and I nodded earnestly.

"But I don't know how much longer I can stand this wretched existence away from my people!"

Tulo bent over and began expelling great seismic coughs. A moment later Taak pushed his way through the crowd and knelt before her. A few of the people in the line grumbled, but I thought they noticed his uniform and didn't dare raise too much of a fuss.

"My lady," Taak said, placing a hand on Tulo's trembling shoulders, "Are you well?" Before she could compose herself and respond, he turned to me with an expression so fierce I flinched. "What have you done to her?" he said.

"She has done nothing, young soldier," Tulo said, no matter that Taak was at least five years older than she. "Indeed, perhaps it is I who have wronged her."

Taak looked puzzled at this. "But she's one of the miserable Esselans. What harm could you have done to someone like her?"

"The worst harm in the world: I might have given her false hope. When I read the spirit paths for her five days ago, I thought I surely saw a fortuitous meeting in her future, some heretofore unseen method of returning her to her prior station. But she now says she has no more options and is close to begging on the streets. Perhaps the spirits led even me wrong this once."

I kept my dry eyes on the ground, deliberately not even looking at Taak in my assumed pose of abject misery. I released a muffled sob, as though I was too overwhelmed to even pay attention to the crowd surrounding us and the soldier by my elbow. In reality, I could tell the number of breaths he took in a minute. Would he take our bait?

"Indeed, lady," Taak said after a moment. "I cannot doubt your skill. I can almost feel the spirits when you're nearby! But I too haven't..." he trailed off and looked around nervously. The waiting crowd seemed to have grown a little too quiet for privacy. He lowered his voice. "I too haven't met the one you saw in my future. The crossroads of the spirits. The method by which I can achieve my destiny."

Tulo looked up to the sky, her hands raised dramatically. She could not have known it, but she stared directly at the bright afternoon sun. Its light seemed to set fire to her hair. Even knowing all I did, I shivered. Tulo truly *was* uncanny, just not in the way all these people thought.

"And yet," she said, her voice colored with the slightest tint of otherworldly mistiness, "I see both your roads so clearly. An opportunity and a destiny."

Taak glanced at me. His curiosity was clearly piqued, but not enough to inquire who I was. I played an Esselan, after all, and he was part of an army about to lead a war against them. I'd need to be more explicit.

"I don't believe you!" I shouted. "What destiny is this? My father is the high chief of all Essel and here I am, stuck in this backwater drainage hole with nothing and no way to ever get back to him!"

There, that ought to do it. I glanced surreptitiously at Taak, worried that I might have been a little too transparent in my desire to transmit this information to him. But a deep line creased his forehead, and his expression was one of such furious speculation that I knew he only suspected what we'd arranged for him to know.

Tulo couldn't see his expression, but she had other ways of sensing people's moods. She smoothed the back of my hand in a way that reassured me.

"My dears," she said in the gentle manner of a mother coaxing her children to stop playing and weed the garden, "I regret that I cannot help you more. But there are others waiting their turn for me to peer into the spirit realm, and even one such as I must eat."

Taak stammered out an apology and signaled to one of the other soldiers who had been waiting behind. He paid her with a bushel of breadfruit. I nearly drooled onto it: we'd eat well by the fire tonight!

Taak backed away with his friend and after a moment, making sure I had composed myself, I stood and wandered dejectedly away, toward the coop of green and red plumed jungle fowl clucking complacently on the road. Perhaps a dozen other stalls filled the clearing, making up all of Maaram's fabled market day. At the time this had seemed like an unbelievable cornucopia of worldly goods. But Parech was right: Maaram is to Essel like a drizzle is to a hurricane. I loitered by the chickens so I could keep a surreptitious eye on Taak. He was talking in low tones with his friend on the other side of the square. My stomach knotted. I certainly hoped this friend had no great knowledge of Essel or its customs. Taak I knew well enough by now to feel safe about our prospects. But it would be hard for me to fool anyone even slightly less gullible or more intelligent.

Finally, just when I was wondering if I should break the plan entirely and approach Taak myself, he started walking toward me. His friend stayed behind, frowning and crossing his arms over his chest.

My hands were trembling entirely of their own accord—no need to feign nervousness.

"You," he said, peremptorily enough that the woman minding the chicken coop gave him a speculative glance. I took a step back. He had begun in Maaram, but now he switched to heavily accented Essela. "You're the daughter of the Esselan chief? Truly?"

"Yes, s-sir," I stammered, pitching my voice so it sounded high and innocent.

His eyes widened and a smile trembled at the corners of his lips. "Just as I thought," he said, his voice strained with tamped-down glee. "Perhaps this is the lady's sign of destiny."

I contrived to look even more timid and confused than before and said simply, "Sir?"

He gave a curt nod to the overcurious chicken farmer and grabbed me by my elbow before I could do much more than squawk. I had a moment of genuine panic—had Tulo and I misread him this badly? Would he try to force me? Then I realized that Parech would almost certainly kill him before he got very far, and so stumbled along behind him. He took me inside an open-air hut with a cockfighting sandpit that doubled as a kava hole during the day.

"Who are you, sir?" I asked, as the proprietor poured two bowls of scummy kava. I stared down and wondered if I saw drowned ants in the brew. The light was too low to be sure.

"An o—" He swallowed down the real answer and regarded me with an expression he fancied guarded. "Just a soldier," he said. "How did you come to our city? It's an unlikely place for a high-born Esselan. And you seem to be in trouble."

I attempted to make my bottom lip quiver, but when I realized I more likely resembled a gawping fish, I stared at the table and gripped the edge. I told him my carefully rehearsed tale of woe. How I had been on my father's own ocean canoe, traveling toward the fire shrine on Holoholo, when the water and wind had risen and swirled into a storm so great that the proud ocean canoe had been reduced to kindling. All of my companions had drowned, and I was only saved by clinging to the splintered mast. I floated for two days before I washed ashore on the mainland. I went to Okika to see if there was anyone who could help me reach my father, but the world was a cruel place and now I would surely die before I saw my homeland again.

I actually managed to work up a few tears to cap the end of this speech. Honestly, I'd cried more in the last few hours than I had in the past five years. But the tears were well worth it, because by the end he grew florid with a crude, avaricious joy. I pitied him. I'd never met a mind more ill-suited for scheming, but that very quality made our game possible.

"Indeed," he said. "I'm sorry you've suffered such great misfortune. And I think...yes...yes, it's just as the spirit talker told me it would be. And you, too, I gather. Together we can each find our destiny!"

"Destiny?"

He put his hand over mine and for a moment I saw a spark of something, a certain tilt to his head, that made me blush and wonder if I might not be a little pretty, after all.

"My dear," he said, "I have a proposal for you."

It went just as Parech said it would. I, a helpless chieftain's daughter, would be given resources sufficient enough to travel back to Essel in some style and comfort. When I arrived there, I would simply contrive to send Taak a "few simple notes" regarding army size, naval capabilities—and the infamous edged weapons. I pretended not to understand their import. I even pretended not to know that the two powers were approaching confrontation, though that was increasingly obvious by the day. As a guarantee of my delivery of these notes, Taak would send a soldier friend of his to escort me back home. Parech looked slightly discomfited that Taak had already suggested someone else for the role he had meant to play, but there were many methods of discouraging a soldier from making a long sea voyage, and he quickly set about applying them. A powder slipped into the surly friend's palm wine gave him the runs right before he was to leave for the cock pens with Taak.

Left without a companion, Taak looked around and recognized the amant-smoking trader from previous nights of gambling. The trader was a good gaming companion, and soon they'd nearly doubled their stakes and become too drunk to walk a straight line. The trader said something offhand about leaving for Essel soon to finish some business there. Taak, thinking again about his friend with the runs, conceived of a brilliant plan. Did the trader know of a great chief of the Esselan army with a pretty young daughter? ("Did he use that exact word?" I demanded of Parech later. "What, *daughter*?" Parech teased.) Tattoos right there? Parech made a great show of drunkenly attempting to recall. Oh, yes! Of course. That one. The second highest in the Esselan army and he doted on his daughter, it was said, more than was seemly. He described me in a roundabout way that left no doubt as to my identity.

Taak proposed a deal. In exchange for a fee, would Parech convey the girl safely to Essel and see that she gave him a sealed missive before he returned to Okika? The full sum was larger than I'd ever imagined it could be, though we'd only see half. The other was to be payable upon Parech's return. All told, in motley payment we would be leaving Okika with enough resources for both the journey and to secure a place of our own in the great city.

To celebrate, the three of us went to the beach again, though by now the fingers of chill had turned to an angry, icy fist. We huddled around the bonfire with the other itinerants and revelers, singing songs in twenty different languages and sharing our food with each other. I roasted the breadfruit Taak had given Tulo, and we three gorged on what we could and then shared the rest with the others huddled beside us. There were some divers from the outer islands here, their necks adorned with the shining blue and white jewels of their trade. Their skin was dark and kissed by the sun, and they huddled so close to the fire I was afraid their voluminous cloaks might catch flame. The older one started a droning chant and was soon joined by the younger, so that their voices twined in a dissonant yet eerie harmony.

"What does the song mean?" I asked them, deep into the night, when the moon had set and those remaining on the beach were either copulating quietly or having low-voiced conversations.

The older one looked at the younger and then raised her eyes to the sky, as though reaching back for an answer. "*Death guards the gate*," she said finally. In Esselan, for we both spoke that language better. "*Its key unlocks our souls. Its key unlocks the gate.* It's an old poem. My ancestors have dived with mandagah for generations. There is much death all around us. We understand the great water spirit, Kai. We worship make'lai."

I stared at them both, fascinated. There had been only one death shrine in all of Kukicha. These deep island customs had never reached us. I knew nothing of this conception of death: a key to unlock a soul, a key to unlock a gate.

"And what of afterward? What happens once death opens the gate?"

The younger one laughed. "Oh, you are young! Beyond the gate? No one knows."

"No one?" I echoed. "Not even death?"

She paused, bemused. "Well, but when will it get a chance to tell us, eh?"

We all three laughed and then the older one caressed the younger one's shoulder. "Come, Yaela," she said. "We'll be warmer lying together."

And so the one called Yaela smiled and kissed her friend in that particular way and I was left feeling utterly alone. Tulo and Parech were speaking to each other in soft, throaty whispers, and I thought it would not be very long now before there was another couple sharing warmth on this winter beach.

We nearly lost everything. I came to the inn to meet Taak and the Maaram trader he wished me to travel with. I had thought, given Taak's utter lack of suspicion, that Parech's entire twisted scheme would conclude easily. But we had not counted on his friend, well acquainted with Taak's ruinous gullibility, being quite so observant. As soon as I saw the scowling man—the same one to whom Parech had given a generous case of the runs—I felt my stomach knot. The friend moved with a certain deliberateness that made me think the effects of Parech's potion still lingered. Please, I thought, let him desperately need the back trench for the next half hour! But he sat down across from me. His expression was grim, though Taak grinned.

"Well, there she is, Wolop, and now you can surely stop scowling because her tale is perfectly true."

Wolop didn't even acknowledge his friend. "Your brother made me promise to look after you, Taak. And no offense to the lady, but this does seem like another one of your disasters."

I bit my lip, since that fit both my persona and my own desires, and contrived to look both hopeful and confused. "Pardon, sirs, but could you speak in Essela? Maaram is hard for me..."

Wolop nodded, but otherwise didn't seem inclined to believe me. So I hurried on, "Taak, is this the trader who is to take me back to my father?" I asked, smiling at the scowling man.

Taak gave Wolop a speaking look and shook his head. "No. I'm sure he'll be here shortly."

Ze's flight, I hoped so. I didn't know how much longer I could stand this man's scrutiny alone. I tried a different tack. "I cannot begin to tell you how grateful I am for your generous, selfless aid, sir Taak," I said. "If only I could pay you back in some greater way than the paltry figures you requested."

I almost pushed my breasts against the table so they'd swell against my tunic, but realized that Taak's suspicious friend would see through this quickly. Taak smiled and waved away my gratitude. "Well," he said to his friend. "Satisfied? She's who she says she is. What more evidence do you need?"

Wolop cocked his head and offered me a drink from his half-drunk cup. Sensing some sort of test, I demurred. This seemed to satisfy him, though I was by now so nervous I could feel the sweat trickling from my armpits. "The family crest on your arm," he said. "What spirit does it represent?"

Inside, I cursed in every language I knew and attempted, desperately, to think of what Parech had said of the marks. Family crests, he'd said, but they were symbolic like clan and warrior tattoos, not pictographic like some religious tattoos.

"Spirits?" I ventured, wide-eyed. "Why, I'm sure I don't know sir. My father never said anything about our family knot representing spirits. I'd think we sacrificed enough for them already!"

It took all my effort to meet his narrowed gaze. Finally he shrugged and leaned back. "True, I've never heard the head families speak of their symbols as such."

I could have cried when Parech finally walked inside, making a great show of looking for Taak. Neither of us could know that his arrival would only make our problems worse.

"*You're* the trader?" Wolop said, not bothering to disguise his incredulity.

Parech smiled, like an uncle indulging a strange child. "And is that so surprising, officer? Perhaps I seem young to you? But I was raised into the profession by my father, so I have much experience."

"Yet you seem so familiar," said Wolop.

Taak looked exasperated. "Of course he is. We've seen him often at the cockfights this past week. He's waiting for favorable winds to head for Essel."

"No," Wolop said, shaking his head. "I never got a good enough look before. The light was too low. I've seen him somewhere else."

I didn't dare meet Parech's eyes, and his posture remained entirely as relaxed and faintly amused as before. Yet I wondered: had Parech known Wolop in his prior life? He'd been a soldier, and it wasn't impossible that this man had commanded him.

"Perhaps here in Okika?" Parech suggested, as though they were determining if they shared a kin relation. "I often trade from here."

"And what do you trade?"

"Cloth, mostly. And the Esselans have the most violent passion for Maaram spirit dolls, so I usually carry a few of those. But if you have need of a trader, officer, you'll have to look elsewhere. My berth is full."

Wolop pursed his lips and refused to say any more to either of them. Taak seemed to take this as acquiescence, and I was happy to believe him. Parech and I were formally introduced, and I struggled to maintain my role in the face of his sardonic gaze. We arranged for my passage on Parech's vessel tomorrow. He'd stood and was bidding us all good day when Wolop sat bolt upright.

"The northern division!" he said. "The bands fighting the Kawadiri. There was a soldier there—commended to me—and you look remarkably like him, trader."

I felt Wolop's words like a giant wave crashing over my body, but Parech only looked mildly confused. After a moment his face cleared, as though he understood; his mouth turned down in what even I would have taken for genuine grief. How had I never known Parech was so skilled at these games?

"My brother fought in your army, officer. But I got word not two weeks ago that he perished deep in the forest on one of your battlefields, and I'm sure the boars are even now trampling his bones. It's good to know you'd remember one such as him, though. It's a great honor."

Even Wolop looked contrite in the face of this revelation. He mumbled vague condolences and an apology, and Parech sauntered out. I left soon after, once I'd collected the baskets of fungible goods from Taak. Wolop made no more suggestions.

We had done it! Or at least I thought so. But Parech sensed something amiss, even if I didn't, and insisted Tulo board the boat before the two of us and made us both wear our costumes. He had reserved passage on another trader's sea canoe and paid an extra bag of salt for the trader to insist the boat was Parech's in case someone asked. We had boarded, and the trader was just about to cast off, when a furious commotion of pounding feet and raised voices sounded from down the street. Parech and I gave each other a single, wary glance, and he had a quick word with the trader.

"Stop! Stop! In the name of the great Maaram king, stop!"

We were drifting out to sea, but it would be easy enough to turn around. The trader, crouched low to hide, looked as though he was considering the option. If they recognized his canoe, after all, he might never be allowed back into the city.

On the dock, the approaching figures became clear: Taak, looking confused and hurt, Wolop, red with righteous fury, and a third man, more finely dressed than the others, who looked as though he wanted to spill someone's blood. I guessed that this must be Taak's famous brother.

"What on earth is all this?" Parech asked.

"That soldier, the one who died on the field? He was Akane, not Maaram. And no one in his family was ever notified."

"And so I spoke to his spirit? I assure you, sir, my brother died on that field. If I resemble another dead soldier, then you'll have to forgive me, because last I checked resemblance is not a crime."

This speech, masterfully delivered, made Taak look at his brother triumphantly and Wolop hesitate. But the brother shook his head. "Pretty words won't save you now, soldier. You're a deserter and subject to water's mercy. Turn around now and perhaps we'll show leniency."

Parech gave me a soft kick on the ankle, and I realized that my silence was beginning to look suspicious. "No!" I wailed obediently. "No, I must get back to my father! Taak, sir, don't you see this man can't be the soldier? It's his ship!"

The brother smiled thinly. "Actually, this ship is registered to another trader altogether. But perhaps the records are out of date. Just turn around and we'll settle the matter."

Only now did I notice that several soldiers had arrayed themselves behind the three officers, and they were holding the bows and arrows that had so decimated the Kawadiri. I looked at Parech in utter panic. His expression was grimmer than I'd ever seen it, and I remembered Tulo, hiding in the hold with the supplies. What would they do to her once they realized she'd been part of the grift? Suddenly Parech grabbed me by my hair and dragged me in front of him. He held a flint dagger to my throat and my scream was only partly fake.

"Will you kill her, then?" he said. "This innocent girl? A chief's daughter?" And I realized how Parech had gambled. Apparently, they suspected him without guessing my role. And if he could convincingly play the villain, we might all get out of this alive.

The real trader leapt up. "Oh no!" he said. "I'll have no part of this." The wind puffed into the untended sails, and we drifted a little further into the bay. Parech took one look at the trader, muttered an apology, and planted his sandaled foot neatly into the small of the other man's back. He tumbled over the side with a satisfying splash, and the soldiers on shore, thrown into utter disarray at this turn of events, scrambled to rescue him.

"I suggest you scream," Parech whispered into my ear. It didn't take much effort to wail and moan. "Please don't shoot," I shouted. The wind was picking up and I realized we were soon going to be out of reach of their arrows.

"But their boats can still catch up with us," Parech said, finishing my thought.

I closed my eyes. We were going to die. Surely there was no way out of this now. And this plan had seemed so clever when Parech first conceived it. Amoral, but clever.

I felt him tense behind me. "I'm going to toss you over the edge," he hissed. "They don't know your part in this. Tulo will claim she booked passage and then hid when the soldiers came. Act innocent. They won't want to harm you even if they have suspicions."

"No," I said angrily, "No, I won't leave—"

"There's no time—"

He gestured with his head. The soldiers had hastily commandeered another sea canoe. It was larger and more unwieldy than ours, but then again, they probably knew how to sail it.

"Tulo," I called out, "what spirits are near?"

I heard her crawl out from the hold cautiously. "Water and death," she said quietly, adding after a brief pause, "Death is always near you, Aoi."

That should have frightened me, but at this moment, it made me feel powerful. Like a true Ana. "Cut me," I told Parech. "On my arm. Deep."

I could feel his shock, but he said nothing. We had come this far. And unless I did something drastic, he might die.

"I call on you, death," I said softly. Parech kissed the back of my neck, and my head swam so much from the gesture I hardly noticed the bloom of pain and blood from my arm. I sensed the power like a tide, like a dam inside me had been breached. I saw death as I had seen it on the battlefield beside Parech. It was less substantial this time—I did not have the Maaram Ana resin to aid my sight into the spirit world, and there were no dying for it to feed on. Still, its mask seemed to regard me with curiosity.

"And what do you call me to do, Aoi?" said the death.

"As you are out of the world's sight, so make us. Let us travel in the spirit world for a time, so we are invisible to the real one."

Tulo gasped. The death inclined its head. It vanished, but then, so did the boats in the harbor and the city beyond. The ocean itself seemed made of light and not water. The vision of the world was now as deep and confusing as anything I'd witnessed back on the battlefield. Only the three of us looked the same, and the boat we still sailed.

"Ana," Parech said, his voice stretched so taut with awe it cracked on the last syllable. Tulo staunched the wound on my arm with a strip of barkcloth.

"Aoi?" she said, her voice hoarse.

"What is it?"

"I can see you."

PART III

. . .

Kings

· 5 ·

K
AI HAD ALWAYS INTENDED TO FIND HER. His conscience wouldn't let him rest otherwise, though when he thought of what she'd done, what she'd said, he felt an overpowering urge to weep, and let all of his power ebb through his tears into the vast ocean. He found himself in a peculiar situation: in love with a woman he sometimes hated, and only death would free them of their obligation to each other. He knew what chased her. He was beginning to have some idea of the deep game she was embroiled in with the great spirits. And he worried about her. The witch Akua had taught her so little about the true mechanisms of geas. She'd survived on her own until now, but how much longer? She could travel beyond the gate, out of his reach forever, and he might not even know for months.

That week after she had left, Kai had loitered in his solitary palace, alone save for the sprites that had been his friends and enemies his whole life. He had dissolved into the water and experimented with his new powers. Deep on the ocean floor, he had been seared by vents that pushed boiling, sulfurous water into the ocean like smoke from a chimney. He had lost his eyes and maneuvered through a world he could breathe through his skin, his smell a kaleidoscope of colors for which he'd never know the words. He saw as the spirits did, the ancient roads and connections that his ancestors had always navigated. He saw the gate it was his duty to guard as a towering wall of black that pushed up from the sea floor and made the spirits cry out in fright. Having deliberately abandoned so much of his human side, he felt the same primal fear, the same confusion at this great wall encircling the world. He understood something that had made only a vague impression on him before: *every* spirit and sprite, in some way, had been bound during the age of the spirit bindings, not just the great ones in their frigid prisons on the inner islands. Humanity had devised a method of controlling them all, because otherwise they could control nothing.

No one could tell him how, but the fact remained: the fire and death spirits were trying to break free. And somehow Lana, a bumpkin mandagah diver turned black angel, had become instrumental in their struggle. He tried to forget her that week, but her memory chased him. He missed her. He thought, perhaps, he had judged her too harshly. They were living in times when it seemed everyone had to make impossible decisions. Her mother's life or that of a woman she didn't know? Pua had raised him and loved him in a world otherwise devoid of companionship or affection. He had loved Pua the way Lana loved her mother. But Lana was the one who had made the choice.

And maybe that explained his resentment and rage far better than his grief could. So he had risen from the depths and reassumed his half-caste humanity; he had decided to find her. But Kai had not been on the surface a day when he felt the first tremors, the first hint of violence unleashed, greater than anything the islands had seen for more than a millennium. The first wave came hours later, when the sun had dipped below the horizon. It swelled like a mountain; it bore down like an avalanche. He had known it was coming, and so sped his boat to the nearest islands he could help: the rural outer archipelago near the water shrine, where divers much like Lana's people still harvested jewels from the dwindling populations of mandagah fish. The islanders knew him, though he had never traveled there before. They held him in silent awe and obeyed when he told them to take their boats from the water and move to the center of the island. It took a greater geas than any he had ever used to channel that titanic wave. The water receded before it like a crowd drawing back in the presence of a king. For a moment, the ancient land channels between the islands lay exposed, the seaweed and coral limp and helpless in open air. They seemed to shrink in the deep gray shadow of the wave. But the water that should have by rights crushed the island paused as though in thought. The wind blew mist from its crest that fell like rain. Slowly, the wave began to melt back into the ocean. And then, when the great wave had become nothing more than a series of whitecaps, Kai collapsed and allowed the water to wash him ashore.

He didn't forget Lana. He couldn't. But the world had realigned itself again, and his obligations dragged at him. Floods from the waves he couldn't stop had destroyed countless communities and killed countless people. And on every island, human lips passed the rumors. There was a black angel loose in the world once again. It was an age of disasters, an age of the spirits. And this black angel was odd, living in Essel as though she was just some girl and not a spirit incarnate, a creature of legends.

But she *is* just a girl, he wanted to tell them. And she's stronger than any of you could know.

Months passed. Sometimes he felt more like death's guardian than water's, so great was the misery he witnessed. So many bodies in the sea, not all of them human. The war between spirits and humans had made casualties of innumerable other creatures: whales, dolphins, sharks, octopods, and enough fish to feed every human for a year. Even the sprites ached at the destruction. A few faded out of existence, absorbed into some other power or perhaps just dissipated. His father, Kai thought, had been wise to die before this. Perhaps he had believed his son's warnings after all.

And now he had arrived in Essel, months after he had first set out. His need to see Lana had disturbed his sleep. But now, so close, he found that his feet wanted to stick on the surface of the water. The approaching shore lurched with the sudden fury of his heart. What would she say? Would she even want him anymore after so much time apart? After the harsh way he had treated her? Would the sight of her remind him of the rage he had largely forgotten? Would they be driven apart much the way they had been before, or could this greater disaster help bring them together again?

But he couldn't find her. He went to the house they said was hers, but her father regarded him with barely concealed horror.

"She left last night, guardian," he said. "I don't know where she is now."

Kai wondered at the clear exhaustion on his face, at the wince he didn't quite suppress when he mentioned his daughter.

"Do you know when she'll return?" Kai asked.

Her father shrugged. "I don't know much about Lana these days. She was with that man, that gardener who's with the rebels." He laughed and his fingers tightened on the doorway. "Who knows. Maybe *she's* with the rebels now." He looked up at Kai, the last vestiges of sleep giving way to suspicion. "And what does the water guardian want with my daughter?"

Kai felt his eyes turn to water, felt his skin pale and his tongue grow large and unwieldy in his mouth. But if Lana had not told her father of their history, what right did he have? "She's the black angel," Kai said, and her father's face closed like a shuttered window.

So Kai asked and found that the whole city knew precisely where to find the rebels and the gardener who helped them. He walked to the lava-slagged, burned-out ruin that was Sea Street. He asked after the gardener and the guards nearly collided in their haste to find him.

The gardener's shirt was dark with ash and a stain that Kai recognized as blood. "Are you all right?" he asked the man.

"It's not mine," said the gardener. And for the first time, Kai became scared.

She was unconscious when they led him to her. He felt it all again: the rush like the ocean, the gentle easing in a place that had grown hard in her absence. An older woman was grimly yanking splinters from the torn flesh in her wings. The blood matted her feathers and made them glint in the lamplight.

"What happened?"

"Assassination attempt. Had to be Bloody One-hand—no one else can make arrows that go farther than that doorway."

Someone had shot her with that ancient weapon, the bow and arrow, developed a millennium ago by the Esselans in their wars of conquest. He'd seen a rotting example somewhere in one of the hundreds of rooms of the water temple, but never thought to use it. How had the situation in this city deteriorated to the point where there could be assassination attempts made with long-range weapons?

Kai could barely force the next words from his throat. There was a great deal of blood. She wasn't moving. "Will she..."

The older woman shrugged. "She's lost some blood, but this one is tough. She'll be fine."

So Kai sat. He watched as the apothecary bound the wound. He watched as Lana stirred and grimaced, though she did not wake. The room was chill, but he made no move to light a fire. He watched her. Eventually, when sunlight peeked through the ever-present ash haze in the sky, she shifted, and groaned, and opened her eyes. They stared at each other for a very long time.

"Why are you here?" Lana asked.

"I meant to come sooner."

"I thought you hated me."

"You never thought that, keika."

Lana smiled, an expression of such incongruous joy that he had to match it. "No. What does this mean?"

He pulled a strand of hair from between her lips; he touched the softness of her under-feathers. "I forgive you."

Lana had dreamed of Kai—ocean eyes and sky hair and tentative, kind smiles—and awoke with him beside her. She was holding his hand, and the marvel of that distracted her from the dull, ceaseless throbbing in her back. She shifted slowly, carefully, and turned her head. He was asleep in a chair beside her. Not her chair. And this lumpy pallet wasn't her bed. Then she remembered: an assassin's arrow and

Pano's hurried flight to rebel territory. Waking up to discover that Kai had come, and it wasn't a dream and he had told her.

Tears trickled out before she could stop them. They dripped from her nose onto his hand, and he jerked awake. Even half asleep, he was alert for danger. She wondered what had happened to him in the last few months. His confusion cleared and they regarded each other silently. Those beautiful, malleable eyes had irises this morning, a blue as deep as her mandagah jewel.

"I didn't know if I'd see you again," she said.

He ran his fingers through her hair and then down her jaw. His expression was so tender her breath caught. "I would have come sooner," he said. "I was..." He looked away from her abruptly and his eyes turned nearly black. "Your Mo'i has a great deal to answer for."

Lana stared at him. "But you've just come to Essel. Were there other eruptions? Did something else happen?"

He frowned. "You haven't heard? The volcano unleashed great towering waves. Thousands of people have been swept out to sea. Crops were flooded. Fish stocks decimated. People are starving, Lana. I'm the water guardian, and there was almost nothing I could do about it."

For a moment, all she could hear was the blood rushing furiously past her ears, the crash of the ocean. She had seen bad storms on her island, before the floods came that destroyed everything. She had seen the way the winds and great waves could wash whole houses out to sea and leave the land so pristine you'd never know anyone had lived there. Involuntarily, her eyes drifted to the open window, and this time she saw the faint outline of the death spirit.

"Did you know of this?" she whispered to it. But of course it had. "Why didn't you tell me?"

"Does the jailer give the prisoner his key?" it said, its cryptic locution curiously reminiscent of a geas. She wondered what it could mean, but when she turned to Kai she saw he was staring at her as though she had gone insane.

"The death," she said, "outside the window. Didn't you hear it?"

He turned, but the death had vanished again.

In a torrent stemmed only by occasional moments of exhaustion, she told him of all that had happened since they parted—Ino giving her the book by the lake, the death and the eruption, her mother missing and Akua hidden from her, Nahoa and the machinations with the rebels. At that, she paused.

"I know there wasn't much choice, but I wish Pano hadn't taken me here. I'm in debt to him now."

Kai frowned. "Who else could have helped? If the Mo'i wants to kill you..."

"The Mo—Kohaku tried to kill me? I thought it was just some angry Esselan. They hate me, Kai, you know. They think I caused this. As though I could ever..." She shook her head violently. "Kohaku couldn't do this. It's impossible. Sure, he was angry, but try to kill me?" She thought of the self-important but kindhearted teacher who had so impressed her at thirteen. "He's the same one who taught me on the island, all those years ago. He isn't like that."

Kai was giving her that look again, as though he was thinking a hundred things he wasn't sure he should say aloud. "Men change, Lana. Some a great deal. He's already responsible for killing tens of thousands of souls. And from what I hear, imprisoning scores more. Do you really think he'd balk at killing you, just because of your old connection?"

"Is the black angel truly so naive?" said Eliki from the door. "I don't know if I should be horrified or charmed." Lana turned so she could face the door and winced. Kai helped her sit while Pano joined Eliki.

"Is it naiveté," Lana said, "to mistrust the word of the two people who have so much to benefit from putting me in this position?"

"We don't kill innocents," Pano said quickly, putting up a hand to forestall Eliki's response.

"Maybe you just wanted to hurt me. Threaten me with Kohaku and I'm suddenly in your power."

Lana knew that her theory wasn't terribly coherent even as she said it, but she didn't want to believe the other explanation.

Eliki looked contemptuous. "From what Pano tells me, you're only alive now thanks to Bloody One-hand's wife. Even if we would engage in the sort of ploy you're suggesting, the assassin's goal was clearly death, not injury. You think we want you dead, when you are so much more useful alive and inciting the populace?"

Lana found herself slumping against Kai, furiously biting her cheek to keep her exhausted, surprised, betrayed tears from seeping out. Even Kohaku? Would everyone she had loved betray her?

"She's hurt and tired," Kai said, giving Pano and Eliki the look that had quelled scores of defiant spirits. "Perhaps you two should leave."

Pano looked angrily at Eliki and walked closer to the bed. "I apologize, black angel," he said. "Eliki often forgets common courtesy in her dedication to the cause. But what she says is the truth. One-hand tried to kill you yesterday. It was a bow and arrow the assassin used, and your Kohaku is the only one who has them. Our craftsmen have been trying, but they haven't figured out how to make them fly true."

Lana nodded in quiet defeat. A bow and arrow. Even in the lawless age before the spirit bindings, they had been cruel, shocking weapons.

"And now I suppose you'll tell me that with Kohaku determined to kill me, I'm only safe here with you?"

Eliki smiled. "It would appear. Unless you want to quit Essel entirely, and something tells me you won't do that until you find some clue about your mother."

Kai's eyes were darkening, and just a glance told her he had finally understood her dismay at waking up in rebel territory. He said, "You do know what I am, right? She's under my protection. You won't like what happens here if you try to coerce her."

He would have said more, but Lana squeezed his hand and forced a cool smile to match Eliki's. "I'm sure our dear rebel leaders would never dream of making me do something I don't wish to do. I'm sure they want my participation in their civil war to be fully consensual. I'm sure they will offer me a great inducement for that consent."

Pano choked back a laugh, and even Eliki's smile grew a touch less frigid. "Inducement? Caring for you on our meager resources? Protecting you from the mad Mo'i?"

"And for that I'm sincerely grateful, though you understand if I don't want to endanger myself further by participating in your propaganda against the Mo'i. I have to find my mother, after all."

Kai was giving her a little sideways smile that made her stomach flip, despite everything. Perhaps after she had rested and the others had gone away, she and Kai could have a true reunion.

"Oh, how can you think of your mother at a time like this?" Eliki snapped, waving a pale hand as though she would slap her. "Twenty thousand dead! Half the city destroyed, and that despot still sits there in his fortress, dredging up horrors from before the great spirit bindings and destroying our freedoms daily with his edicts and abductions. And here you *dare* tell us that the tens of thousands of mothers who are dead or missing are nothing compared to yours? *You*, with the influence to make the whole city understand how their leader has betrayed them, you *dare* tell me you won't help because your stupid mother is missing?"

Lana's fingernails dug into her palms, though she hardly noticed. She was aware of a desperate fury and a cold, private fear that what Eliki had said was right. That she was truly the venal and selfish person who could place her own problems high above a sea of everyone else's misery. Perhaps everyone does that—but not everyone had, as she did, the power to help others. Faced with the moral choice, Lana wondered if her singular focus on Leilani and Akua meant she was making the wrong one. She glanced at Kai, and then quickly away. She knew he was thinking of the conflict that had driven them apart months ago, and the horror it had taken him so long to forgive: even knowing all she did about Pua and the effects of the geas, she couldn't regret the binding that had saved her mother.

"Your causes are not mine, Eliki," she said. "Do you realize what your rebellion is leading to? A civil war. And you ought to know precisely what war does to the spirit bindings."

"That's the Mo'i's burden. He's caused this. He's broken all the rules. So long as he keeps his power, no one will feel compelled to keep within the boundaries of the bindings."

Unexpectedly, Kai spoke. "He's destroyed the system, Lana. And without that, we might all destroy each other."

"We might all help free the spirits and commit mass suicide," Lana said.

Kai's eyes were ice pale and remote as a wind. "And so you let Essel bleed to death instead."

Lana threw up her hands and winced. "Oh, are you a radical now? The *water guardian*?"

"Well," he said, so softly she wondered if the others heard him, "at least your goals and desires can be relied upon, Lana." And now he was certainly speaking of Pua. She wiped her eyes and turned from him. Perhaps their relationship truly was impossible. But she couldn't bear to think of it just now.

"My mother is not more important than all the others in this city, but she is *mine*. You will help me, or I refuse to help you."

Eliki stared at her for a moment, and then turned away in disgust. In the end, Pano was the only one who would meet her eyes. At least he seemed understanding.

"I've told my people to look out for any information about a one-armed witch and an outer islander," Pano said. "I've heard nothing definite, but someone at the fire temple claims the head nun has started sending supplies to a house on the far edge of the city."

"What does that have to do with my mother?"

"Probably nothing. But he said there were two mandagah jewels in the package. He noticed because they're so rare these days. I thought your mother might have been a diver."

Lana could have stood up and danced, damn their disapproving expressions. *Mama*, she thought, *I'll find you. I'll stop Akua, whatever she's planning*. In her joy she turned to Kai, but he had gone cold and distant beside her. And so she found herself looking out the window again, to the death, opaque as a man against the ruined street. Its mask mouth stretched wide. She was dimly aware that even a few months ago, the sight would have disturbed her.

"Closer, Lana," it said.

She laughed. Beside her, Kai turned. The death vanished immediately. He looked back at her ecstatic face and shuddered.

6

L ANA HARDLY SAW KAI OVER THE NEXT TWO DAYS. He said that he was taking stock of the city and finding any clues he could about the state of the spirit bindings, but she knew that he was avoiding her. He hadn't said so, but he probably believed every one of the cruel accusations Eliki had hurled at her. And perhaps he was right. Perhaps that time on Okika had damaged her—made her too aware of parental sacrifice, too beholden to her mother's love. Kai, who had grown up almost entirely apart from any other humans, and often had difficulty interacting with them, seemed to drown in his capacity for empathy. It had led him to protect her, when she'd been about to die in front of an inn on the rice islands. He hadn't known a thing about her, but he cared anyway. Who was she to deserve someone like that? If she slept alone, at least she'd grown used to it.

Her wing was too sore to allow much movement, and so she distracted herself from her pain and loneliness by delving into the black book with a single-minded intensity. Though she was increasingly fascinated by the story of Aoi, Tulo, and Parech, she still didn't understand why Ino would have dared so much to give it to her. Aoi had lived and died more than a thousand years ago. The only possible connection was the spirit bindings. They had begun in Aoi's time, and now, in Lana's time, it seemed that they were unraveling. But surely any information about the great bindings would be better given to a guardian like Kai than to an ignorant witch's apprentice like Lana. Was it possible Akua had managed to interfere with one of the three original bindings? Lana groaned and put her hands over her head. She found it difficult to focus on anything else the longer her mother stayed missing.

"What is Akua doing?" she said aloud, just because she had been alone with these thoughts for so long.

The death laughed outside the window. But as she had thought many times before now, the emotion behind it seemed almost affectionate. She had bound it, once, with the knowledge that it suffered from petty human emotion. But affection?

"You are strange," she said to it.

"As are you, black angel."

And, even more oddly, the backhanded compliment relieved some of her misery. She puzzled a bit more over the black book. Aoi's method of making the boat invisible to their pursuers had made her gasp just a little. Binding the death was an incredibly risky geas, but Aoi seemed to have no knowledge of her recklessness. Humans imitate spirits at their peril—that was one of the lessons she had learned from the book of postulates Kai had given her in the water shrine. And yet Lana kept coming back to that geas.

She had never heard of any binding that conferred invisibility, let alone in such a dangerous way. Could she cast it now? She found her hand drifting to the bone flute. She hadn't used it since she came to Essel and played that one time with her father. Something about that performance had kept the death bound for the last few months. She could feel that binding pulling taut and knew she would need another geas soon to keep it from killing her, but she worried. A sufficient personal sacrifice would be painful and exhausting. And there was no other way to bind it without using Akua's flute. Sometimes she caught herself staring at the flute's yellowing, smooth surface, and thought: *perhaps it wouldn't hurt.* But she couldn't fool herself any longer. Akua had kidnapped her mother, had led Lana to kill another person, and had destroyed her life in some complex game where the bindings were so deep and strong she thought she must have sacrificed a village to forge them.

Or at least an arm.

No, Lana would just have to sacrifice. She wondered for a moment if perhaps, now that Kai was here, he could help her. But then she recalled the frozen, remote expression on his face when she first balked at helping the rebels. And after that, he treated her with courtesy that always seemed to avoid both intimacy and proximity. She wouldn't prey on his natural empathy by asking for his help now. She had that much pride.

She dozed on the splayed pages of the geas book, and when she awoke the streets had plunged into a misty twilight and her mouth was sticky with thirst. It seemed like too much trouble to call out. After a moment, she carefully levered herself upright on the pallet and then placed her feet on the floor. The drag on her damaged wing muscles was painful, but not unduly so. She stood and then gripped the wall when the room wobbled. She waited until she was absolutely sure she wouldn't fall down and then went downstairs to find something to eat.

Eliki was in the main meeting hall, eating by the fire with one hand and reading some loose, handwritten pages with the other.

"Lipa said you should stay abed for a week at least," said Eliki mildly.

"I think Lipa doesn't have much experience with wings."

Eliki shrugged, indicating her polite doubt even as she acceded the point. Lana pursed her lips. If only she could manage even a fraction of that poised assurance, that withering disdain. Even now, she so often felt like an untutored child in a room of adults.

"Would you like the rest of my meal? I find I don't have much of an appetite these days." Lana looked at Eliki's plate: some local fish and boiled leeks. She was a little surprised by the latter—rumors had it that the rebels could get very little produce, since their control of the first district didn't include access to any docks. Farmers in the decimated seventh district smuggled in what they could on foot. She thought to question Eliki's largesse, but hunger overcame her objections. Eliki was silent beside her, occasionally reading and then scribbling on the paper. The food was bland and lukewarm, but even this small meal was welcome. As the cold set in, more and more would go hungry in the city.

"Here," Eliki said abruptly, when Lana was finished eating, "how's this? 'The black angel herself, sent to us as a harbinger of the turbulent times to come, an avatar of the spirits who knows more of their ways than any other—"

"You can't say that."

Eliki paused. Her pale eyes flickered with the reflected firelight. "I believe we had an agreement?"

Lana sighed. "But that's not true. Plenty of others know more about spirits than I do. Kai, for one. Akua, for another."

"Akua the one-armed witch?" Lana nodded and Eliki shrugged. "Complete honesty, I have found, is not a particularly useful scruple in a campaign to rouse the populace, but fine. It works well enough without it." She continued: "'The black angel has confirmed what we have all suspected: the tyrannous bloody Mo'i lost his hand in a bargain made with the fire spirit. He sacrificed to loosen its bonds so he could come to power. And in so doing, he has destroyed this once great city and murdered several thousand of its citizens. Are we to swallow this betrayal when even now he imprisons and tortures us on no grounds, with no charges? The black angel has loaned her aid to the rebel movement, and who would know better than she the destruction of which Bloody One-hand is capable?'"

Eliki put the pages back down on the table and looked at Lana expectantly. "Well?"

If Eliki printed this, Lana's fate would be forever bound with the rebels. But if she refused and left, Kohaku might assassinate her and Eliki might print it anyway. She sighed. "If you must. When does it go out?"

"It takes two days to run the presses. We'll start tonight." She grinned, and for once the expression seemed to hold no calculation or malice. "Reluctant you may be, Lana, but you will help our cause immeasurably. And you must know we're in the right."

Lana looked away, into the fire. "Yes," she said quietly. But sometimes she felt that she would sacrifice "right" for "safe," if she could.

She never seemed to have that choice. And wasn't she a coward for even wanting it?

"There were waves," she found herself saying. "Great waves caused by the eruption. They flooded other islands. Thousands more died, and with the crop failures the toll might go much higher. Kohaku caused that too."

"Waves?" Eliki breathed, sounding dazed at the thought of the destruction. "Did he truly?"

She began to scribble furiously again. The night was growing frigid, so Lana sat on the floor, closer to the fire. She'd started to drowse when the flames guttered. She turned to see Pano, entering with the young rebel soldier who'd been scarred by fire.

"There's been fighting," he said, his face haggard and grim. "Refugees from the seventh district farms bringing us supplies. One-hand got wind of it somehow and ambushed them."

Eliki went unnaturally still. "Casualties?" she asked, her voice crisp and uninflected.

"Two of our own dead, three more shot with his arrows."

"The civilians?"

"I'm not sure, Eliki. It was dark. At least twenty bodies before we got them through." He seemed anguished.

"How much food did they bring?" Eliki's tone hadn't changed. Well, she certainly had the constitution for sustained violence.

"They'd raided what was left of the stores. Enough for at least two weeks."

Eliki nodded once and gathered up the loose sheets of paper. "This goes to the press immediately, Tope," she said, handing it to the soldier. He nodded and left. Eliki and Pano stared at each other for an almost interminable moment. Lana held her hands to the fire, forgotten and confused. What was the history between these two? Why did it seem as though they were having a conversation without speaking a word?

"This can't go on, Pano," she said softly. "We will lose this in a month, maybe two."

He shook his head with uncharacteristic violence and balled his left hand into a fist. "The people have already suffered—"

"And they will suffer more before One-hand is through with them! We need that port, Pano. You know that."

"He has bows."

Eliki drew herself up, so that in the low light her pale skin and blond hair seemed to glow like that of an angry spirit. "And we have the heart of the people. Wait until they read what One-hand has done to them, Pano. We can reach the old docks, even without arrows."

The old docks were the ancient ship port in the lesser bay at the top of the sixth district. Rebel territory ended at the northern border of the first district. Perhaps they could smuggle some shipments through, but how did they hope to control it? Lana gasped when her clouded mind finally made sense of their subtext. Eliki meant to conquer the sixth district with arms, and use Lana as a rallying point from which to do it.

"I never said you could use me to start a war!" The two of them turned to the fire, so startled she realized they both must have forgotten her presence.

"You agreed to help our cause," Eliki said, her voice shot through with venom. "We're in rebellion against a tyrannical government. How did you think we would use you? To weed the garden?"

Pano was slightly more diplomatic. "We've already fought with the Mo'i's forces, you know that, Lana. *If* we have to fight for the docks," he said, shooting a glance at Eliki, "we'll do everything we can to minimize the damage."

Lana wrapped her arms around her knees against her sudden shivering. Pano was right. She'd known this wary alliance with the rebels would involve some violence. But a full-blown civil war?

Still, Pano had told her of the mysterious house where Makaho had sent supplies and two mandagah jewels. He had access to dozens of people and institutions across this city that could help her find Akua and her mother. Was she willing to give that advantage up for an increasingly abstract principle? So that she could stay on the sidelines in a war that was almost certain to happen anyway? Surely if she had to choose a side, it was better to be here with the rebels than with Kohaku, who had already done so much damage. She wished that Kai were with her. He would be able to navigate this morass better than she. Sometimes she felt that her love for her mother was the only thing keeping her from sinking entirely.

"The longer you continue fighting, the greater the chance that the spirits will break free and take away all of our choices. You know that, right?"

Put so starkly, this seemed to startle Eliki. But Pano merely shrugged in that quiet way of his and Lana thought that he had spent much time dreading precisely that. "If we let One-hand win, after all he's done, because of the threat of the spirits—we may have imprisoned them, but we would still become their slaves."

Lana closed her eyes. She was exhausted and her back hurt. She would need to leave tomorrow and search out that house in the seventh district. She would need to find her mother and find Akua and bind the death. She was a black angel. She was the witness to the start of the first war in five hundred years. Kai could hardly bear to look her in the eye.

She did not notice when she slipped into sleep, or when Pano draped a blanket over her shoulders. Something roused her when the moon had set and the only light came from the embers of the dying fire. She saw him as a gray shadow, at first—his hair a mix of black and glowing orange. He had been staring at her, though she couldn't see his face or read his expression. She had to speak to him. It would be easier this way—deep in this twilight unreality, his face hidden in shadow. So she couldn't see his contempt or indifference.

"I know what I did to Pua was wrong," she said softly. "I don't think I'm a good person anymore. Maybe I never was. Maybe most people aren't, Kai, and their lives don't force them to realize it. I'm selfish and I care about some people's suffering more than others and I know all this, I just can't change it. I know..." Her voice caught. He still hadn't moved. "Won't you please say something? Say you don't hate me?"

Kai was still for several painful moments and then moved jerkily, like a doll brought to life. He lowered his head, shook it, and then knelt before her. His eyes were black and absorbed the dim firelight like a sponge. She felt the urge to caress his cheek and stopped herself.

"I don't hate you. You know that."

"But you don't love me?"

"Would I be here if I didn't, keika?"

"Maybe you're worried about me having sex with someone else. Maybe you've decided you need an heir so we can be rid of each other, maybe—"

He leaned forward and kissed her. She held still, surprised at first. Then what felt like a lifetime of desire crashed through her and she was a raft loosed upon it. She forgot her terror at losing him, the gnawing guilt that had prompted her confession, her mother, Akua, war, death. She forgot the earth had exploded and she'd become a black angel and that she'd killed the aunt of the man she loved for the sake of her mother. There was only this room, this fire, this half-charred floor. His hands in her hair, and his lips, and then his tongue in her mouth. A passion she'd all but forgotten she could feel.

The soldier cried when the news came back to the Mo'i's house that the black angel still lived. And was now an agent of the rebels, no less. "S-someone pushed her, your honor," the man said, his voice cracking on the honorific. "I couldn't get a clear shot...please, I have a family—"

"Who were the ones with her?" Kohaku interrupted, with a most uncharacteristic mildness.

"Who?" the soldier said, startled into coherence.

"Yes, who? Who does the city have to credit for saving the black angel's life? For allowing her to help the rebels with this?" He lifted the flimsy paper of the rebel pamphlet and let it flutter gently to the floor.

The soldier knelt so quickly that Kohaku thought he must have bruised his kneecaps. "Please your honor," he said again, "I have—"

"Who?" repeated the Mo'i.

And now the soldier appeared to grasp that his frightened babbling might be giving the Mo'i far greater cause to be displeased than his failed assassination attempt. "I don't know, sir. It was dark. There was a woman. In a hood. That's the one who pushed the black angel. And a man. That's the one who chased me away."

"A man. Perhaps you noticed what this man looked like?"

The soldier blinked, but, to Kohaku's relief, refrained from begging for his life again. "A bit taller than me. Dark hair, graying. His clothes were common and worn. A laborer of some kind."

Kohaku considered this. "Yet, I wonder what sort of common laborer would be on speaking terms with the black angel? Or daring enough to chase down a provincial soldier?"

Said provincial soldier opened his mouth and then closed it, belatedly recognizing both a rhetorical statement and a trap. It was just as well. Kohaku had long grown tired of the more brutal necessities of this job. What had started with Nahe had never truly seemed to end. The spirit of his murdered sister always spurred him on.

"Did you make out the man's face?" he asked the soldier, finally. "Well enough for someone else to draw it?"

The soldier, having finally decided he was unlikely to be killed or tortured, gave a shaky nod. "I believe so."

"Good. Consult with your commander for the details. I want a recognizable drawing by the end of the day."

The soldier stood. Kohaku looked back down at the sprawl of papers littering his desk. Maps, mostly. Areas of the city decimated by fires, streets rendered inaccessible by lava flows, neighborhoods full of people sickened due to contaminated water supply. Death and destruction everywhere. Why, then, would even his sister's relentless spirit desire even more?

"And the black angel? I mean, should I try again?"

Kohaku looked up, and something in his expression made the soldier take an involuntary backward step. "I'm sorry I—"

"No," Kohaku said, confused and unhappy with the sensation. "No, you're right to ask, and no, please refrain for now. The rebels have her. We'll gain no more benefit from trying to kill her." *Not after she's already accused me in public.* "Let's see if we can't devise a more useful strategy. Killing is very wasteful."

A pained smile froze on the soldier's face as he bowed and exited. Wasteful, indeed.

Kohaku suspected that the man the soldier had seen was one of the leaders of the rebel movement. If he could get a good enough likeness, this misadventure with Lana might bear some fruit after all. The thought, innocuous enough, brought back the same rush of sick dread he had felt ever since he gave the order to have her assassinated.

"You can't afford to let her live," said his sister—or at least, the fire spirit's tormented representation of her.

Kohaku had not seen her in several days, but he was unsurprised at the timing of this visit. He'd long ago resigned himself to the knowledge that she would never leave him. He had destroyed this city for the sake of his love and thirst for revenge—and yes, not least for power. He deserved to be haunted by the ghost of his dead and beloved sister.

She sat in a tall chair covered in cushions and near to the fire. His reading chair. He loved that chair. Now, with his sister's hair tumbling over the arm, he knew he'd never be able to relax there again. Her eyes were the only aspect of her appearance that gave away her true nature: instead of the green he had loved, they were a dense, flickering blue, like the flame at the heart of the fire temple. The fire with which he had made his now infamous bargain.

"I should never have ordered her killed," Kohaku said, with more energy than he intended. "You goaded me into it...to kill *Lana*..." He found himself shivering. He was glad Lana hadn't died.

His sister smiled sweetly. "I could never goad you into something, dear brother. You have all the power in this relationship."

"You torment—"

"You're *alive*. And the Mo'i besides. You could just ignore me."

And yet he found that to be the one thing he could not do. He could scream and rage and curse her in every ancient language he had studied at the Kulanui, he could kill a dozen people to placate her, he could reason and cajole and laugh, but he could not ignore. She was his sister. Even if she wasn't.

"It's too late, anyway," he said, pushing aside the pile of paper and standing. "She's gone public with everything she accused me of. If I kill her now, I'd just inflame the whole city against me."

His sister laughed. He had, by now, grown used to that laugh, though it was nothing like how she had laughed when she lived. His sister had been deaf since she was seven years old, after all, and though she could make sounds, they came from her throat as though down a long tunnel, distorted and made strange by distance and time. The spirit's laugh was clear and painfully close. "Far too late for that, dear brother. It might cause some temporary problems when she turns up murdered, but the people of this city have no great love for a black angel. They'll forget. For now. But who knows what she'll turn into if you let her live?"

Kohaku began to pace the room—four steps to the fireplace, ten to the other side of the room, and seven back to his desk. He had nearly killed Lana. Now Emea wanted him to try again. "I can't murder someone just on the suspicion of their potential!"

"But you can murder them on the suspicion of their thoughts?"

"You yourself told me I can't let subversive thinking propagate freely among the populace. They had to serve as examples."

"And I'd say a black angel would make a huge example."

Kohaku rubbed his knuckles into his temples. There was less hair there now than just a few months ago. He was balding, turning gray, getting stomach problems like his father and worry lines like his mother. Kohaku had always expected to get old. He remembered what he had been like on Lana's island all those years ago, teaching students and envisioning a career that had seemed assured: a meteoric rise through the Kulanui, a young rustic protégé who would blossom under his tutelage...

He had tried to kill *Lana*. She'd had a puppy crush on him. She would spend hours with that friend of hers, the one who died in the floods afterward, peeling oranges and giggling.

"No!" he said, pausing in sudden fury before his usurped chair. "I refuse. I will not stoop so low. Once, in self defense. No more. Besides, the soldier said the bolt went home. It's immoral to attack an injured enemy."

Emea raised her dark eyebrows. "And you imagine she could fight back before? Kill her, brother. The rebels will use her," she said. "They will fight you. You'd be safer with her dead."

"Then I will be less safe."

Something in his steadfast refusal must have been new, for she fell silent. Ghost-Emea was almost never silent.

"Can you imagine it?" Kohaku said after a moment. His voice was filled with bitter humor. "We should have a celebration."

Emea gave a quizzical stare. "Should we?"

"We have at last, dear sister, discovered a line that Bloody One-hand will not cross."

7

THE REBELS RECEIVED UNEXPECTED NEWS the next morning. The fire guardian, Senona Ahi, had sent word to the fire temple to expect his presence sometime in the coming weeks. The news had leaked almost as soon as it arrived, and shocked those who heard it. It was unprecedented—even for Essel—to receive even one diplomatic visitation in each generation from the guardians. Two different guardians arriving at one time was a sure indication of troubled times, even more so than the existence of a black angel.

Pano told them over their morning meal. Lana felt Kai stiffen against her and knew his eyes had gone hard and chilly even without looking up at him. She understood his concern, but all such emotions seemed separated from her by a hazy shroud of wonder. Kai had returned to her. Kai had forgiven her as much as he was able. Kai still loved her. Eventually, she knew, the old problems would start to encroach on this peace, but she would hold onto it for as long as she could.

"Is my presence known here?" Kai asked.

Pano shook his head. "A few rumors. Nothing credible."

"I suppose I'll have to confirm the rumors. Your fire temple is in for a shock."

"Don't underestimate them. The head nun acts harmless, but she's nothing but politics and intrigue. I don't know what her end-game is, but she's ruthless at playing it."

Pano's voice had taken on such an uncharacteristic edge as he said this that Lana sat up and took a good look at him. He seemed tired, as usual. He had spent nearly all night out, and clearly some of that had been at the fire temple.

"How are Nahoa and the baby?" she asked, and was rewarded by his sharp look of relief.

"Little Ahi is healthy as a fish. Getting fat, too. Only the lady and her maid are allowed to touch the baby now. They're all tired, and no wonder." He smiled, his eyes distant, and Lana wondered at the interest he had taken in those two.

"Will you meet him, Kai?" she asked.

He nodded. "It's time I learn what I can. Senona will have his own information. And perhaps we both can confront the Mo'i with it."

"One-hand is even more dangerous than the nun," Pano said. "At least Makaho is sane. You see what the Mo'i did to your black angel."

Kai shrugged. Lana realized that the past year had stripped much of the diffident, awkward gentleness from him. He had always known how to love, how to care; his aunt had taught him that. But his recent time among humans had taught him to fight, to distrust, to lie. He wasn't suited for it, but he had forced himself anyway. "I'm the water guardian," he said. "Short of a mob attack, there isn't much he can do to harm me."

Lana squeezed his hand, but he didn't seem to notice. He left a few minutes later, and Pano followed him. Lana allowed them both to think that she would spend the day resting, but as soon as she was alone she found a cloak and the paper upon which Pano had scrawled the location of the house in the seventh district. Kai had brought the cloak back from her apartment with a terse note from her father, wishing her a speedy recovery. Her father didn't mention Leilani, but she read the concern behind his words. Probably of far greater importance to him than Lana herself, she thought sadly. What would he think when he read the rebel broadsheets explicitly claiming Lana's support? He'd been careful to only lend his help in areas controlled by Kohaku's forces. He'd condemned the violence from both sides, but it seemed to her that he held the rebels more at fault. They were fighting against the legitimate government, after all. He already thought her some weird, freakish creature. Every time she called a geas, it seemed a little more of his affection slipped away. And yet she couldn't stop doing it, because how else would she find Leilani? It had seemed so simple when they first found each other. But without her mother as a bridge, they were strangers to each other.

With hardly a wince she plucked out a feather and muttered a quick geas to the wind spirit, binding it to disguise her appearance. She preferred to reserve her sacrifices for truly important things and not matters of convenience, but she couldn't afford to be remarked upon in the street. Kohaku might hear and try to kill her again. And she especially didn't want Makaho to have any idea she'd found the house. She knew her geas had worked when the people in the streets—some reinforcing the burned buildings, others clearing away debris—only gave her the briefest of glances. Anyone who stared too long would probably be able to see through it, but she was safe enough for now.

Lana didn't have much money—the utility of which was decreasing daily in any case—so she took her time and walked. The ash was so deep in some places that Lana had to walk around until she found a path someone had shoveled through. The drifts on either side were so high she couldn't even see the sun. She pulled the edge of her cloak over her mouth and nose so she wouldn't breathe too much of the acrid air. She had heard of what happened here in the weeks immediately after the eruption. Ten thousand deaths on impact, and then thousands more following as people died of their wounds or of exposure or starvation. First district residents got the last of the Mo'i's food and medicine—when they got it at all.

When the rebel forces had stepped in to fill the gap, they were welcomed by the people. In the chaos, no one noticed at first that this part of the city was now being controlled by a different, ad hoc government. It took three weeks for Kohaku to act. He armed his guards for the first time in living memory and sent them in to quell the insurrection. They failed, of course. It's very hard to fight a battle in a densely packed part of the city where everyone hates you. After the first skirmishes, the rebels armed themselves as best they could. They drew their line at Sea Street, using the mountainous lava flows as organic barriers. An uneasy ceasefire had held until now, but as Lana had gathered from listening to Eliki and Pano for the last several days, Kohaku's use of the ancient bows and arrows had changed the situation. With at-a-distance weapons, Kohaku could attack them at his leisure while his troops stayed out of harm's way. And now that the cold was setting in, food shortages threatened to starve everybody before they could find a way to fight back. It seemed likely that she had picked the losing side.

Only soldiers were walking the streets when she finally reached the massive pile of hardened lava that marked the border with the seventh district. This wasn't so heavily barricaded as the border on Sea Street. Compared to the rest of Essel, the seventh district was the provincial backwater, largely unchanged for the last thousand years. Back when the city of Essel had taken up only a fraction of the island, the area of this district had been distant farmland. Now it was nominally part of the city, but plants far outnumbered humans and buildings. And that was a good thing, because otherwise all of Essel might have starved to death in the weeks after Nui'ahi erupted.

Ash choked even the fields that hadn't been abandoned, and mixed with the dirt of the unpaved road into a hard gray sludge that smacked at her sandals and coated her ankles. Pano had said the house was near the western beaches, in an area of town known to the locals as the Rushes. With the noon sun shining down in a clear, cloudless sky, Lana finally felt warm enough to bunch the cloak under her arm. A breeze blew and she took a deep breath. As always, that unmistakable sharpness of ocean air, even from the saline waters that surrounded Essel, sliced through her heart like a serrated blade. If she closed her eyes, the rich earth from the nearby farms, the silence, the distant ocean, could almost make her believe that she was thirteen again and back home. That she and her mother were still divers, harvesting jewels from mandagah fish and following the path her ancestors had carved out for more than a thousand years.

"If I didn't know you better, I'd say you were about to cry."

Lana's eyes snapped open. The death was beside her on the deserted road, mask neutral, but its voice amused. "How do you know I'm not?" she asked. Her heart was certainly full enough.

"You haven't cried in months."

She stared at it. Months? But she realized it was right. She hadn't even known. She'd cried often enough in her life. It was just that, lately, there hadn't seemed to be a point. Or perhaps there was too much of one, and no relief to be had by indulging in it. "You sound as though you spend your days observing me," she said. "Am I so interesting?"

"All humans are so interesting."

"Then why not spy on another?"

"Oh, now you're playing innocent?"

She had to smile. "What should I play?"

"War," it said, "is a game of strategy. You may have heard that it is generally prudent to study one's opponent."

"This...between you and me. This is war?"

"The war isn't between you and me. But it's war nonetheless." Its voice, which had been hard and frightening, softened. "Don't forget that, Lana, if you hope to survive."

It vanished. She might have smiled at her burst of affection, if she had not been simultaneously aware that the death had once again reminded her of its duty to kill her. She should not have forgotten. It disturbed her that she had.

In the Rushes, abutting the western dunes, the buildings looked old enough to predate the spirit bindings. They were made of strong stone and wood from the long-depleted red acacia groves. Only the fire temple and the Kulanui still had buildings in these ancient architectural styles. The centuries had forgotten this section of the city. And even the greatest disaster Essel had seen in a thousand years had not done very much to damage it, aside from some dustings of ash from the latest gray rain. The air was chill, but not unbearably so, and Lana took her time as she walked past the squat buildings with their broad, flat roofs and raised foundations. Some of the windows held cloudy, rough-cut glass as old as the buildings themselves. The citizens looked less disaster-struck than elsewhere in the city. Children played in the streets and a few stores had opened for business. She offered one vendor a hair ribbon in exchange for a jackfruit pastry and it only took him a moment to judge the deal fair. A great deal of the city had begun to resort to a form of ad hoc barter. She asked after the street with the house and learned that it was this very one, just a mile further down the road.

"Right on the dunes," the man said. "But we don't go there much," he added, just as she was turning to leave. "It's real old, but no one's lived there in years. No one takes care of it, but it stays upright. Winds, floods—nothing cracks its foundation beams. No rot touches its timber. Anyone who's tried to stay there always leaves quickly. The last one claimed it was haunted."

The vendor's tone and face were still perfectly friendly, but she recognized a warning to an outsider when she heard it. "But it isn't haunted?" she said carefully.

He bent forward. "Nothing haunts the rushes but spirits, keika, and I suspect you know we've got plenty of those."

His gaze lingered a moment too long on the spread of her wings and Lana felt her breathing hitch and her cheeks flush. The disguising geas still held; she could feel its binding, but this man somehow suspected what she was anyway.

"After what happened to Nui'ahi," she said, "I'm sure we must all be swimming in spirits."

He gave a tiny shrug and laughed. "You're probably right at that. Why, we just had some delegation from the great fire temple itself up through here, and I'm sure our poor neighborhood hasn't seen their like since the days that old house was first built."

He was fishing for something. And yet, he still didn't seem very threatening. It made sense that an important man in a neighborhood like this would take note of any outsiders who passed through, whether fire temple representatives or a lone girl like Lana. "The fire temple? Truly? I'd heard they were hiding themselves in that great complex of theirs. Afraid of the angry hordes or something."

"We thought it strange, too. Most of the seventh is loyal to the rebels, and the Rushes are no exception. And even stranger, keika, they were seeking out the same ancient spirit house you are."

Lana found herself curiously steady. Her heart might be pounding, but it felt more like exhilaration than terror. *I'm the black angel*, she thought.

Ignoring the pain from her healing wound, she stretched out her wings until they splayed against the westerly sunlight and cast them both in shadow. He frowned. He could tell something was there, just not quite what. Then, deliberately as she could, she bit the corner of her tongue just hard enough to bleed.

"Let this one see," she muttered, and his eyes widened. She'd never manipulated a geas quite like that before, and so felt a distant, secondary pleasure at her growing mastery.

"I think," she said, over his quiet shock, "that we are probably going there for quite different reasons."

He grinned. "I don't doubt it, keika. I've read what they wrote about you. It means a lot to know the black angel believes in the cause."

Lana nearly grimaced. She couldn't tell him that her support was prompted far less by belief than by circumstances and expediency. So she forced a smile and said, "I trust you understand how dangerous it will be if the fire temple learns of my visit here."

He took an extra pastry from the warming coals and handed it to her. "We haven't survived so long without learning to keep our own counsel. We're as tired of One-hand as everyone else in this city."

There was something about the force of the statement—as often as she'd heard things like it for the past several months—that made

Lana feel nearly ashamed of her own ambivalence. She thanked him and went off quickly.

It wasn't that she didn't believe in the rebels' cause, but violence could bring an even greater disaster to Essel and the rest of the islands. The more she saw of what Kohaku had done to the city since the eruption, the more she sided with the rebels. But the fact was that secret imprisonment and occasional assassination, however unjust, would do nothing to disrupt the great spirit bindings. A full-fledged civil war certainly could. And as the rebels hadn't taken leave of their senses or their morals, she felt like they bore more responsibility for understanding this existential threat and ceasing hostilities. Was the nominal freedom of the island worth a hundred thousand more deaths?

And yet...she paused on the sandy, seashell-lined road. That didn't entirely explain her position, did it? Even if she didn't approve of the escalating violence, she could certainly use her newfound influence to curb it. She could help them organize. She could help them negotiate. She could do all in her power to aid their mission without war. And what was she doing instead? Desperately trying to find a one-armed witch and her mother, a situation of almost oppressing importance to her personally, and increasingly insignificant given the other crises confronting the world.

But it was just like with Pua, wasn't it? She knew what she *should* do, what she *should* feel. It did not stop her from feeling entirely the opposite. Saving Leilani still eclipsed every other consideration.

Dunes covered in pampas grass and twisted bushes stretched for a quarter mile from the road to the ocean. On her other side, goats nibbled the scrub brush, and if she squinted she could just make out a few jackfruit trees at the start of the farms. Only the occasional bird call and the comforting crash of the waves disturbed the quiet. Even her sandals crunching on the road seemed embarrassingly loud.

She began to feel the strain of her disguising geas and so let it go. At that instant, the death appeared beside her again. She glanced at it with mild curiosity, but it remained silent and she didn't feel compelled to speak first. Besides, she could just see the house, raised on stilts like all the other buildings in the Rushes, but made from acacia wood so well-cured it had turned an almost fiery red. Grass grew on the flat roof, but that was the only real indication of its abandonment. She wondered what she would find there. Pano's information had been vague enough that she didn't truly think she'd just walk in on her mother and Akua unexpectedly. But she still hoped that whoever had decided to move into this spirit-haunted place would be able to give her some clue, some guidepost on her quest.

Someone had left sandy footprints on the stairs. Lana paused for a long moment, straining to hear any noise besides the ocean and her own rapid breathing. But the house looked utterly abandoned, like the vendor back in town had insisted. Surely even temporary squatters would leave some sign of their residence? The windows were dark and soot-streaked. She wondered how the glass in them had survived through the centuries.

"Spirits?" she muttered.

"They're all around us, you know," the death said, and she had to laugh. But then, if she closed her eyes, she wondered if she could almost feel their presence. Some sort of power emanating from this strange, abandoned place. There were ancient geas here, palpable in their strength and longevity.

She shook her head to clear the image and climbed the stairs. The door opened easily on hinges that did not squeal or groan. But now she doubted that was a sign of recent repair. She stepped inside.

The air was cool, but not stale or musty. From the light that streamed in through the encrusted windows, she saw that the main room was entirely empty of any furniture, and the only thing that could be charitably interpreted as a sign of human habitation was the surprising lack of dust on any surface. The house was entirely open, though on either side of her she could see empty grooves where sliding screens might once have gone. A few steps further inside and she could have sworn she was being watched.

She whirled around, but it was only the death, waiting balefully at the threshold of the house.

"Mama?" she called, just to be sure. The waves crashed. An osprey sailed silently past the open doorway. There was no one here. "Akua?" she said, after a long moment, and then, "Damn you, Akua, what do you want with me!"

She made a cursory circuit of the house, but discovered nothing. Just as she was about to leave she noticed the package the fire temple had for some reason delivered to this house. It had been bundled into a basket of straw, and when Lana bent to open it she saw quickly that it hadn't been disturbed. Pano's information had been accurate: it contained some clothing, a few jars of preserved fruit, and dried grains, but no mandagah jewels that she could find, even when she upended the basket onto the floor. Did that mean that someone was living here? Or that Pano had been misinformed? Perhaps they'd even been stolen. Lana had heard that mandagah jewels now fetched nearly ten times the price they had when she'd been a diver. Finally, she gave up. Without even bothering to put away the package, she left the house and started back down the long road. She was exhausted already, and it would take until nightfall at least to go back to the rebel camp.

"I will find her," she said fiercely to the death floating serenely along beside her. "I will find them both. I will save my mother and I will make Akua explain herself."

"Will you now?" it said.

"And you can tell her so!"

It said nothing.

Halfway back to the rebel camp, a man in a burro-drawn cart drew up beside Lana and offered to give her a lift. Her feet had started to ache in earnest, so she accepted graciously. The sun was setting and a wind from the greater bay had turned the day frigid. Lana settled her wings for warmth and was grateful that the man seemed as little inclined to speak as she was. He started down the road that followed the seventh district border and intersected with Sea Street. On this new route, Lana saw several of the medical tents and food lines that Kohaku had established in the worst-hit parts of the city. He hadn't done a terrible job of responding to the crisis, Lana thought. And as he had access to far more resources than the rebels, he was in a far better position to give more help to more people. Yet he had caused this suffering in the first place. Does one forgive the murderer because he clothes the widow? Back in Okika, when she'd been apprenticed to Akua, she'd watched the witch cripple a man to save his wife and daughter's lives. Akua had also treated the man very well afterward. Lana knew that it hadn't lessened his hatred.

On a whim, she asked the man where his ultimate destination lay. The fourth district, it turned out, not far from where she lived with her father. It had been several days since they'd last seen each other. Perhaps she could even convince him to come back with her and help the rebels. After she and the man parted ways, she walked the remaining few blocks. Her father wasn't home yet, but there was food in the larder. As she ate, she looked around. Her father had barely disturbed the place since she had left. Her scrying materials were in the corner, already collecting a fine patina of dust. She wondered if she should take them with her. Perhaps the thirtieth try would give her something new. She sighed.

"I wish you'd at least talk to me, Akua," she said. The witch didn't answer. But her father did come home a few minutes later, humming a little tune to himself that Lana recognized as one he'd been working on for the last several weeks. She caught herself grinning and rose to meet him.

"Papa!" she said, rushing forward to embrace him, "It's good to see you."

He was clearly surprised to see her there, but he returned the embrace. "You're back? Are you okay? They said someone shot you."

"Kohaku sent an assassin. I know," she said, at his shocked expression, "I couldn't believe it either. But I'm fine. It missed everything important. I'm just a little sore."

Her father gave her an uncomfortable glance and then looked away. "I'm glad," he said gruffly. But he didn't look glad. He looked worried and upset. "Sabolu, that girl from the fire temple? She came here a few times looking for you. She said she had learned something about that witch."

"What did she say? Did she leave a message?"

"She said to tell you the witch asked after some disciples of the napulo. And the head nun gave her the information—I suppose the fire temple keeps tabs on those fringe groups? She says it must have been a few weeks ago, at least, but it was probably the tiny fire shrine in the fifth district."

Lana didn't understand why Akua would be involved with the napulo, but finally! Some clue that she hadn't just vanished with her mother like sea foam. She hugged her father again. "Oh, Papa! This is better than I'd hoped. I hope you paid Sabolu."

His smile was fleeting. "She'd never have left, otherwise. I played her a bit of music, since there's a new piece I'm working on."

"The tune you were singing just now?" she said. "Does it have words? Maybe I could play it with you sometime."

"That would be nice. I don't have any words yet. It's about the city, and all the lost and missing—" He cut himself off, as though all the air had left the room. Lana averted her gaze until he regained his composure, but her chest felt tight. *Oh, Papa.*

"She's still alive," she said. "I'm sure of it. And unharmed."

Her father nodded reflexively. "Yes," he said, though she wasn't sure he believed her anymore.

"I'll find her," she said.

But at this, instead of turning mute and shuffling away, her father raised his head. His lips had thinned to a white line. His eyes were wide. He's furious, she thought in amazement. She'd never seen her father angry before.

"And *how* will you find her, Lana? How? Because I hear rumors that the black angel has thrown her lot in with the rebels. That she's fighting with them now and is doing a good job of getting herself killed!"

She'd never explained to her father the nature of her bargain with the death. She'd never made it explicit that her mother would die if anything happened to her. But he understood it, regardless. If not in the particulars, in its general shape: she was his only link to Akua. Without Lana, he had no chance of finding his wife again.

"They saved my life," she said quietly, unsure how to meet his fury. She felt his accusation like a knife in her gut. She also had thought herself a bad, undutiful daughter for accepting other obligations while Akua still held her mother. But then, she had thought herself an amoral person for only caring about her mother's fate. What did that make her father? Maybe it was like she had said to Kai—most people aren't good; they just never have to make the decisions that would reveal their failings.

"They promised to help me if I allowed them to print what I said about Kohaku."

"What help are a bunch of starving laborers, Lana? You *know* Kohaku! If you had just stayed quiet, you could have had the help of the Mo'i of Essel."

Lana thought she might just vomit the food she'd bolted down so quickly, but part of her agitation was due to anger. How dare her own father judge her so harshly? "I don't want Kohaku's help. He's responsible for thousands and thousands of dead—"

"And you're responsible for your mother!"

They fell silent. He looked nearly as stunned as Lana felt. He'd never said it before. He'd always skirted around even the implication. Her mother's abduction, when it was spoken of at all, existed in a world devoid of all cause and effect. Stripped of all mention of Lana's relationship with Akua and the lost year she had spent away from them, being chased by the death.

"And you?" she said, her voice rising with fury. "You're so free from blame? I was your *child*, she was your *wife*, and you left us to come here on some mad dream that nearly killed us all! Build instruments in Essel? Why not find real work in Okika? Why not stay with us? Maybe then we'd still be a family and Mama would still be here with you and she wouldn't have nearly died and I wouldn't be a spirits-blighted *black angel,* with death always at my heels!"

"Lana." His voice cracked. "I didn't—"

But she laughed at him, her anger turned quickly to bitterness. "I am responsible," she said. "I am. I should have known what Akua was, but I pretended I didn't see. I will carry this in my ashes, Papa. I became a black angel for her. Do you understand? I gave up everything for her, and this is still my fault. But Kohaku has done something far worse. You know that, too. You spend all day caring for his victims, after all. Yes, Papa, I could have curbed my tongue and gone to him for help. I tried, you know. Knowing what he did, I asked for his help." She smiled suddenly. Her father seemed stricken into stillness a few feet away. "But you know what's funny? It turns out there's a line even the black angel won't cross."

She grabbed her cloak from the back of the chair and walked to the door. "I'll be in the rebel camp. You can come to me any time. They'll welcome you."

Her father didn't say anything when she left. Nor, she imagined, for a long time afterward.

· 8 ·

NAHOA SOMETIMES THOUGHT OF HERSELF as an apprentice, learning a trade as demanding and exact and, yes, occasionally dangerous as her first profession. She couldn't say that being a spy was more exciting than being a sailor, as both seemed to consist of long stretches of boredom punctuated by moments of heart-searing terror. In spying's favor, it required very little physical exertion. Caring for Ahi with only Malie to help was exhausting enough to make her blanch at the idea of days spent climbing rigging and securing sails. In sailing's favor, she recalled with some nostalgia the relaxation of never having to distrust people, and of never having secrets more damning than who she might invite for a tumble. Now, Nahoa had begun to keep a schedule in her head of the movements of the stewards, the maids, the cooks, and the minor temple officiants. She had made Malie show her all the tricks she knew of the temple, after sternly informing her that Ahi's life would be in danger if she ever betrayed Nahoa. She trusted Malie out of necessity, but it still didn't stop her from paying as close attention to her maid's movements as possible. Malie had informed on her once. She might do it again, though Nahoa hoped their shared love for Ahi would make that impossible.

Pano had contacted her several times in the weeks since Ahi's brush with death. He reported that the black angel was recovering well and, even more shockingly, that the water guardian himself was Lana's lover, and had come to find her just hours after the attack. Pano had just smiled at Nahoa's shock and said that he supposed such a legendary person as the black angel wouldn't be satisfied with a more mundane partner.

"Well I wouldn't know what to do with a half-spirit lover. Hell, just one Mo'i is more than I can handle," she'd said to him. And then Ahi had begun to giggle for no reason at all, and Pano played with her until he had to leave. Pano hadn't asked her for her help explicitly either time—in fact, it seemed he went out of his way to avoid discussion of rebel business—but he brought her a copy of the latest rebel tract.

The paper was flimsier than the pamphlet Pano had accidentally dropped in her lap those many months before in the Mo'i's kitchen, and the writing was more densely packed, but she recognized it immediately. It mostly consisted of one essay written by the rebel leader Eliki detailing Lana's allegations against Kohaku. Pano had touched her hand when she read the headline: "Incontrovertible evidence of Bloody One-hand's nefarious deal with the fire spirit to destroy our beloved city: Black Angel speaks out for freedom and justice." She seemed to be shivering, though she didn't know why; it wasn't as though she hadn't heard the servants whisper the same things a hundred times before. But Pano had to leave, and then she and Ahi were left alone.

"I wonder what you'll think of your father," Nahoa said to Ahi late one night, after the third time she had forced herself through the article. Eliki was right. Who in all the islands knew more about spirits and spirit bindings than the black angel herself? And now she learned that Lana had known Kohaku deep in her past, long before either of them had any inkling of their intertwined fates. Lana had met with Kohaku the day before the assassination attempt. She'd actually had the gall to accuse Kohaku to his face. Even Nahoa, the mother of his child, wouldn't have dared risk that. She'd seen too much of his mad, bloodthirsty temper to think anyone safe from it.

So Nahoa believed the accusation. What else could she do? She'd suspected it the moment she'd seen the volcano erupt, deep in the throes of her own labor. The hours Kohaku had spent in his aerie, speaking to thin air and staring balefully at Nui'ahi. The grisly charred claw of his left hand that he kept as some inexplicable token. The fact that he would never tell her how the fire spirit had come to choose him as Mo'i. But still, but still—she had married and loved the man who was responsible for the death and suffering of tens of thousands of souls. She had loved him even as he descended deeper into his insanity, kidnapping and torturing hundreds of people for nonexistent crimes. He was the father of her child. Ahi even had his reddish hair and wide nose.

Ahi smacked at her wet cheeks and gurgled in a questioning sort of way. Nahoa hushed her and went to find Malie. The maid was drowsing before an empty plate of food in their chambers.

"I'll be back soon," she said, handing Ahi over. Malie yawned and glanced at the closed door. Nahoa nodded once, briefly. She couldn't stand to read that pamphlet again or think about all it meant about her life for the past year. She had to do something or she'd go as crazy as her husband.

"It's good," Malie said, "that at least you can find some peace in prayer."

Nahoa was surprised into a grimace, and Malie covered her laugh with a cough. But Nahoa took her suggestion and brought the pamphlet with her to one of the many flame chapels scattered throughout the main temple building. She hesitated in the entranceway—looking around as though attempting to decide which way to go, but really observing the servants. She'd been awaiting the legendary fire guardian for weeks, ever since he sent that letter, and she had heard that he'd finally arrived. She thought of asking one of the servants if he stayed in the temple, but she didn't want reports of any undue interest getting back to Makaho. So she just lingered as long as she could until she noticed one kitchen servant heading down the eastern corridor bearing a formal luncheon for two. Certainly promising. She trailed at a sedate pace, careful to keep him in her sight. After a few turns she determined he must be headed to one of the meeting rooms that overlooked a hot spring, so she veered off into one of the flame chapels. It was empty, but she knelt and prayed just in case. She tossed the pamphlet into the tiny flame and watched until it had completely turned to ash before rising and exiting the room. Now for the tricky part. No chapels adjoined that particular meeting room, but on a mild day like today it was likely that the window would be open and she could overhear them if she lingered in the garden below. So long as she hid beneath the eaves of the temple, someone would have to either be watching from outside or looking straight down from the window to notice her. She took a quick stroll around the adjacent gardens for show and then pressed herself into the shadow of the wall when she was sure she was alone. She edged through the bushes and withered flower beds until she came close enough to the open window to overhear a conversation.

"I don't think it will." It was a man's voice, so deep and rough she had a hard time making out syllables.

"You *don't think*?" said another man. His voice was much lighter and very smooth.

"You know as well as I how difficult it is to gauge the great spirits, even in the best of times."

The other man sighed. "Yes, but I'll be bound, this is so much more critical than the best of times, Senona. We can't afford to know so little."

Nahoa allowed herself a small smile. So she had guessed correctly. Senona Ahi, the fire guardian, was speaking above her. But who was he speaking with, if not Makaho?

"The fire spirit schemes, I know that much. But it's become opaque to me. It has methods of hiding itself, and I'm buried in the rush of spirits freed from this disaster alone. It takes advantage. Even you must have felt it, right? Though, yes, I know you're the luckiest of us three. Water is quiescent."

"But for how much longer? Even this eruption caused waves like the islands haven't seen in five hundred years. With the other two spirits breaking their bounds, how much longer before even water follows suit? It's more docile, but perhaps all the more deadly, for that."

First the volcano, and now *tsunamis*? Nahoa wrapped her cloak more firmly around her shoulders and squatted in the dirt behind the bushes. So the second speaker was the black angel's half-spirit lover: the water guardian.

"We must confront him," the fire guardian said.

"What do we have to threaten him with? Even during the few weeks I've been in this city, it's quite clear to me the man has taken leave of his senses. He is paranoid and dangerous. He tried to kill...."

"Yes," the fire guardian said gently, after a moment. "I heard of that. And now she's proved to the populace exactly what he's done. I commend her bravery, I suppose, but you do know what that means?"

"War. Of course. She understands that, too. They gave her a hard choice."

For nearly a minute Nahoa heard nothing but the clatter of bamboo plates and the gurgling of the hot spring. She would have thought that they had left if not for the occasional sound of feet shuffling restlessly against floor mats.

"We must appeal to his humanity, then," the fire guardian said in a doleful rumble. "Whatever's left of it. He must be made to understand that none of what he unleashed can be rectified without a great sacrifice. And because he was the one who so benefited from the initial binding, he is the only one who can make that sacrifice."

Water's laugh was soft, but derisive. "Compel Bloody One-hand to sacrifice himself for the good of the people he slaughtered? We have a greater chance of convincing death to cancel burnings."

"Even so."

A pause. Then, "You're right, of course. Even if we will almost certainly fail."

"I must leave soon. There are many other volcanoes and calderas where I can sense fire's struggle. At least Nui'ahi has already erupted."

"This evening, then. If the Mo'i does not sacrifice himself, how much longer do you think we have before the bonds break. And which first? Fire or death?"

"I cannot speak to death. That we have heard nothing of El-emake seems ominous. Fire? It is difficult, Kai. The world has become more interconnected than it was in the age of the bindings. Just one more disturbance like this one in Essel, and every system of human civilization could fall apart."

Kai laughed. "Well, so long as we're staying positive," he said. Nahoa would never have thought to hear such bleak humor from one of the legendary guardians.

They left when the sun began to set behind the mountain, plunging the temple gardens into frigid shadow. Nahoa still sat where she was on the frozen earth in the garden, shivering and unable to move.

The end of everything. Death on a scale unimaginable. Worse than before the spirit bindings, worse than when the wind spirit broke free. There were so many more people in the world now, after all. And all this, as she knew from the painfully frank discussion she now wished she hadn't overheard, could be laid at the feet of her husband.

No, she thought fiercely, in his *hands*.

She had helped Pano once before. Recently, she'd tried to spy for him, but now it seemed that her efforts had been halfhearted at best. Whatever she could do to save this city—to save the world, perhaps—was her duty. In her own small way, Nahoa had enabled this atrocity. Kohaku had once implied that she had become his reason to live. His reason, perhaps, to bargain for his life with the fire spirit.

She should go back. It was freezing and her breasts were sore. Ahi would want to drink. But before she could coerce her stiff limbs to creep back along the shadowed wall, someone else entered the room above her.

"You're to make fifty by week's end," a man's voice said. Curt, like he was giving orders.

"These plans are rather crude." Makaho's reedy voice was un-mistakable, though it lacked the unctuous servility she usually employed with Nahoa.

"You've made them before."

"Yes, but this bow is twice as large as the others. It might be difficult for my craftsmen to calibrate in such short time."

"Well, try then. If it seems as though you can't do it soon enough, make the regular ones. The Mo'i feels the rebels are plan-ning something. You've seen their latest rags. They'll want to move while the populace still believes their lies."

"Of course. I understand. Tell the Mo'i that he has, as always, the fire temple's full support. Here, I'll show you out."

The door once again slid open and shut. Nahoa counted, very deliberately, to thirty. No one was there. Quickly she stood and used the rush of fearful energy to dig her feet into the raised stone on the outside of the building and then hook her arms over the ledge of the window. Since it was open, it didn't take much more ef-fort to push her torso through the lip and fall inside the room. Her thump sounded catastrophically loud to her ears, and she froze for a moment, wondering what excuse she could give to a servant opening the door. Nothing happened. She looked at the table, still covered in the remains of a barely touched luncheon. Beside it sat a stack of matched papers, covered in detailed plans for constructing the now-infamous bow and arrow, the very weapon that Pano and the rebels had tried and failed to imitate. Her breath came out in nervous stutters. If Makaho found her now she didn't know what she would say. She grabbed a few of the leftover bean cakes from the table—maybe she could claim she was hungry?—and studied the designs.

At first she thought to memorize the important parts, but she quickly realized that was impossible. She had a good spatial memory from her years of sailing and tying rigging, but it would take a genius to be able to recall all the measurements on these plans. And if she got it wrong, it wouldn't be of any help to them at all. She flipped through the pile. It appeared that they were copies of each other, but it only made sense that the craftsmen would need multiple plans if they were to fashion these in such a short time. Well, there was only one thing she could do. Saying a small prayer, Nahoa pulled one of the sheets from the middle of the pile, folded it up, and tucked it up the sleeve of her shirt. With any luck, Makaho would assume that Kohaku had given her one fewer than usual. Clerical errors like that were sure to be common. She thought she heard the sound of approaching footsteps in the hall outside, so she ran back to the window and rolled awkwardly onto the ledge. Before the door could open she dropped into the mulch and bushes and waited. Sixty long seconds and she started walking back around to the western entrance.

A long walk. That's all she had taken. There was no reason for anyone to suspect otherwise.

There had been some sort of battle. Not at Sea Street—that stretch of the border was too well defended—but further north near the sixth district, where the rebels had been pierced through with arrows while they smoked and cast bones to pass the time. Lana heard the shouts and screams from the next street over, and she walked alone toward the blackened heaps of volcanic slag that marked the border. Normally there was some commerce between the rebels and those who lived along their edge. Now, as Lana approached the Sea Street barrier, all she could see were tightly shuttered windows and the scuffling blur of someone rushing desperately to safety. The death accompanied her now, which she noted with grim curiosity. How many had died this time? How many would die if Eliki succeeded in her goal to gain more territory to the north and reach the old docks?

Lana approached the line slowly, with her hands up and her wings clearly visible. The rebels had no bows, but she didn't want to take a chance. They recognized her immediately and two rebel soldiers flanked her as she scrambled through their fortifications. Inside, all was chaos. She stood for a helpless moment, staring at the men and a few women being carried on crudely woven reed mats to the healer's building. She recognized the feather-fletched hafts of wood that sprouted from their bodies like some fearsome flower. Some of them screamed and others were eerily silent, but her body recalled the pain and she shivered. She wondered if there was something she could do, some sort of sacrifice that might save some of their lives. But the only item of use was the smooth haft of hollowed and polished bone in her pocket—Akua's arm bone flute. She hadn't used it in months, not since she first came here. She looked at the death beside her, holding itself with an uncanny stillness. She could sense its anticipation at the upcoming glut of souls. She would be doing those soldiers no favors by going among them with a death avatar, and even fewer by trying to heal their wounds with a geas tied to the same witch who had kidnapped her mother.

"How many will die?" she asked it, turning away from the bustle and walking toward the shadows.

"I'm not a soothsayer," it said.

She gave it a wry smile. "Fine. But you can tell who comes closest to the gate."

"All of you," it said, its voice as chillingly impassive as when they'd first met. "Whichever of you goes through, it's a difference of inches, not miles."

The meeting room was unguarded and empty. The last few weeks had been a constant struggle in the rebel camp. The Mo'i had restricted the flow of resources into the first district as best he could, starving the people inside in order to defeat them. And a rough sketch of Pano—imperfect, but still recognizable—had been circulating around the city, making it difficult for him to go anywhere anonymously. Lana had tried to keep out of their way, letting Kai help them when he would and otherwise searching out a geas that might find her mother. She'd tried the first shrine Sabolu had suggested, but none of the people there would even admit to being napulo, let alone seeing Akua.

She wondered where Kai was, but it wasn't hard to deduce Eliki and Pano's whereabouts. She sat on the steps outside, because the air was wet and not too cold. The rebels scurrying back and forth, living and dying, might as well have been actors on a stage. She felt distanced from them, like all those years ago when her best friend Kali had drowned in the floods. She had seen her entire island gather for Kali's funeral, but she had hardly felt a thing. That was why they had left. That was why Leilani had taken a job as a waitress and Lana had worked the vats in a laundry. She had renounced her family's legacy. Born to be a diver, she had instead become apprenticed to a witch. Like Ino had always said—Lana had been born for water, but taken by death.

She had escaped it for now, but one day she would have nowhere left to run.

"But not too soon," she muttered to herself. Not before she could save her mother.

She wasn't aware of having made the decision, but she found the arm bone flute in her palm and her mind was racing for the shape of the geas she could cast. She had perhaps been going about this the wrong way. The flute was the strongest connection she had to her former teacher. She had avoided it out of fear, but maybe the lesson of the black book and its strange, foreign story of Aoi, Tulo, and Parech was that she had to be braver. She had to risk more. Perhaps the spirits responded to timid geas with timid boons. After all, how else could Akua have made such a powerful object as the flute without an equally powerful sacrifice?

Akua had never taught her the base postulates that gave power to spirit bindings. She had never explained to Lana the true nature of the powers they manipulated. Kai had taught her that, in the long idyllic months in his water shrine. But perhaps Akua had given her a gift of sorts, after all—since Lana was not tied down to any classical education on the nature of geas, she was freer than most apprentice witches to imagine. Just like Aoi, she thought.

She needed to find Akua. But more than that, she needed to understand Akua. Her former teacher was vastly more skilled than Lana could hope to be. Her geas were subtle and powerful. It was ludicrous to imagine that Lana could ever find her by means of something so mundane as a scrying if Akua didn't wish it. So, Lana needed to approach the problem from another angle: communication. Akua clearly planned to use Lana for some purpose. It wasn't impossible to imagine that she might agree to talk with Lana, so long as the geas would reveal nothing of her location.

Yes. That had to be it. A first step. She brought the flute to her lips for the first time in months and began to play. She found herself reconstructing the tune her father had written for her mother, but adjusted to the higher register of the flute. She tapped her foot lightly to keep time and closed her eyes. She could feel the power swirling around her like a charged fog, feel the eyes of the spirits, the net of power from Akua's sacrifice reaching out and tying them to her. The rush of danger was immediate and intoxicating: if she did not have the strength to bend these spirits to her will, they would devour her. She thought again of Tulo in the black book, and the strange world of her spirit sight. Lana had only barely glimpsed the spirit world, but she imagined that right now a menagerie must surround her.

She put the flute down, but kept her eyes closed. "The geas binds the human with the spirit, the will with its pure effect." She paused. Now what? Her hands began to shake and she forced them still. It felt like she was throwing herself into an abyss. She hadn't recited a nonconforming geas in so long. She thought of Aoi, plunging herself and her friends into the spirit world on a whim. She'd survived long enough to write the book. And what someone as inexperienced as Aoi could do, Lana could do also. "I bind the sound of this flute, and the power therein, to the sound of its maker and her will. Carry my voice to the witch called Akua and bring her voice back to me."

The faint outside light that penetrated her eyelids was extinguished like a candle flame. She opened her eyes in panic, but she could see nothing but inky black. She could hear nothing but her own breathing, harsh and short, and the increasingly frantic pounding of her heart. What had she done? Had she tapped into some power she couldn't contain when she invoked Akua's flute itself?

But no, she had no sensation of overwhelming power, of angry spirits freed from bondage. Just this silence, and now, just at the edge of her hearing, the faintest of noises. Waves, perhaps, crashing against a forgotten shoreline. The creak of feet shuffling across ancient, water-shrunk boards. A ship? Unsurprising. And then Akua spoke.

"This is clever, Lana," she said.

Lana felt her cheeks flush in reflexive pleasure and then frowned. Akua had deliberately set out to ruin her life for reasons still obscure to her. So why was it still so hard to keep perspective while in the witch's presence? Why did she still feel like her eager student?

"I don't imagine I'd still be alive if I weren't clever," Lana said, with more venom than she'd intended. "Of course, you'd know more about that than I do."

"Perhaps," Akua said. Lana could almost see Akua's enigmatic half-smile, the complacent way she would lean back in her chair and wait for Lana to piece together some puzzle. "But I doubt you went through so much trouble, with such an unusual geas, to snipe at me. What do you want?"

"*My mother back!*" The words seemed to explode in the unnatural occlusion surrounding her. A burst of red fire in pitch black. She blinked in the darkness.

"I see you do," Akua said quietly. She seemed surprised as well. At least, that's how Lana interpreted the suddenly somber tone. "I'm afraid I'm not quite done with her yet."

"Have you—"

"She's safe. I enjoy her company, actually. What I'm doing won't harm her at all, Lana. That's not what this is about. It was an ancient, dangerous geas you cast that solstice. It's tilted my plans a little."

Lana opened her mouth and then forced it shut. In her own oblique, meandering way, Akua was revealing things about her true purpose. Lana couldn't afford to scream whatever insults sprang to her tongue and lose the chance to glean a few more hints.

"I've learned a lot in the past year, Akua. I have some idea of how powerful you must be. How much you must know. Give me leave to doubt that anything I'm capable of could tilt your plans in any way."

Akua was silent for so long Lana grew afraid that she'd closed the connection. But when she spoke, it was with the considered wryness Lana remembered so well. "You have learned a lot. I can see that. Perhaps you'll resent this, but I'm very proud. I don't think you understand, Lana. I would never have picked you...I *could* never have picked you if you weren't capable of tilting my plans. There was no other way to bind the geas, no other way to find the proper balance. It wouldn't accept anyone less than my equal."

Lana was startled into a denial. "But I'm not your equal," she said.

"You could be."

Lana heard her breathing grow harsh and ragged; sweat clung to her skin like the mist from a fog. Akua's equal? Master of spirits from every quadrant? And how had Akua become the greatest witch in the islands? She had tricked people into sacrifices—countless others just like Pua, agreeing to a sacrifice they didn't understand, and often paying for the mistake with their lives. And others, like a cobbler back in Okika, had agreed to Akua's demands, knowing precisely what that entailed. She had manipulated and murdered and sacrificed her way to an almost unimaginable level of control. Lana thought of Ino, who had collapsed with the agony of stretching his geas enough to give Lana the black book. A geas Akua had laid on him.

"I won't," Lana said, her voice trembling with such righteous anger she almost didn't recognize herself. "I'll die before I let myself become as cruel as you. I won't sacrifice my integrity for power."

"But haven't you already? What about your mother?"

And it was like she was at the water temple again, Kai confronting her over what she should have known about the linked mandagah jewels. Akua was right. Lana had already crossed that line.

She'd already sacrificed a life for her own desires. How was she to know that every sacrifice Akua had manipulated or forced hadn't been for something she cared about as deeply as Lana cared about her mother? If she could justify her own actions, why couldn't Akua?

Or if she had a line, shouldn't she draw it now?

"I love my mother," she said, her voice raw as a fresh wound. "More than you could possibly know. I've already become more like you than I'd ever have wanted. I've had to make choices no one should have to make. But if it comes to this, if I have to become you to defeat you, I will lose."

"Your mother—"

"*I will lose.*"

Akua's sigh floated through the darkness like the breeze from a lake. "Oh, Lana," she said. Pride and despair and maybe even hope.

"Akua," Lana said, "why are you—"

"The death!" Akua's voice was frantic, and then gone. Lana could see again, but the only thing in her vision was the death's mask, glowing and quivering with the anticipation she now understood.

No, not for the paltry harvest of souls killed in the most recent rebel skirmish.

Her geas had run out. No binding held back the death.

"I'm sorry for the necessity," it said, and she thought, *we are too much alike: the death, the witch, and I.*

The black book

The spirit sea held its own dangers. Invisible from the humans who pursued us, we were like beacons in a harbor for every creature of the spirit world. Flying fish battered the mast with their tails. A giant blue octopus poked a monstrous eye from the waters and watched us balefully; Parech noticed that in its eye swam a thousand glowing eels that gnawed and snapped at one another. Of us all, Parech was the best versed in the stars, but even he lacked the knowledge to guide us safely across the ocean all the way to Essel. And here in the mirror-world of the spirits, we could not trust the sky. The moon or the sun would rise, but it made no difference to the amount of light. The stars would blink in and out without warning, sometimes careening through the sky like torchlight on the wall of a cave, and sometimes seeming as static and unchanging as a painting. And only occasionally did they resemble the constellations I'd learned in my youth. Parech hunkered among the barkcloth and dried breadfruit in the hold and attempted not to look out much. I think the spirit world disturbed him. It invalidated too much of what he knew, and constantly caught him wrong-footed. I wasn't terribly happy in the spirit world either— because I realized I did not have a very clear idea of how to get us back—but my fascination with everything we saw made up for my unease.

And we both had that other, unexpected reason to appreciate the whim that had pushed me to take us here.

Here in the spirit world, Tulo could see.

"You're not so ugly, Aoi," she said to me and stroked my unraveling braid.

She bit her lip when she saw Parech, and didn't say anything at all.

When we were happy, the spirits would crowd around and watch. I could never see the slightest twitch of an expression on their alien faces. But their eyes (those that had them) would follow our movements. They would drift in the wake of our laughter like a child trying to catch blowflower seeds. At the second not-moonrise of our journey, Tulo started banging on one of the baskets of breadfruit and Parech sang and I found myself on my feet, clumsily going through a dance for a good harvest I remembered my mother teaching me when I could barely walk. Oh, the spirits glowed then, throwing multicolored light on our mundane skins like the sun filtering down to a reef.

At some point, they began to join in the music. Some hummed along with Parech in voices that rumbled like the sea, like a volcano's sleepy belching. Others pounded the rhythm against the waves and each other: *tat, tat tat, tat.* And still others floated around me as I danced, coming so close that I could breathe the resin and seaweed and tar of their skins, but never touching. I grew tired eventually and sprawled beside Parech. After I caught my breath, I added my voice as a counterpoint to his, and Tulo abandoned the breadfruit casks. She danced to the beat of the spirits and all of our mingled voices. It was like that time on the beach in Okika, but more primal, less human. Tulo could see them, but then, she'd always been able to see them. This was a foreign maze to us, a catalog of frightening wonders, but to her it was as familiar as a worn floor mat.

The spirits touched her. For a few moments, one and then another appeared to dance with her, mimicking her movements as best they could. A giant dragonfly lifted her into the air and she rose, shrieking and laughing until another one brought her back down again. Parech stood up, afraid that she would fall, but I stayed sitting. I knew by now that the spirits would do nothing to hurt her. She had no need of geas or binding for this. I was beginning to understand that there were other ways for humans to engage spirits.

The spirit sun of black and violet rose again, and most of the spirits departed. The three of us slept in the hold of the canoe, propped up against one another like flour sacks. After a few hours, I awoke to find Parech sitting beside me, soaking wet and naked except for a loosely draped loincloth.

"You went swimming?" I asked, my voice rough.

He grinned like he'd just won a fight. "Turns out it's mostly a real ocean. Just some strange things in it. To think, Ana, that Tulo sees this all the time! I don't know if I could. I think it'd drive me mad."

I didn't find it as disturbing as Parech did, but I silently agreed with him. The sooner I could devise a way for us to leave, the better. "I think we must be far past Maaram by now," I said to him. "It should be safe to take us back."

Parech turned his head and regarded me. He raised an eyebrow. "Don't tell me the great Ana doesn't know how?"

I sighed. "Or how to navigate back to Essel even if I could. I can barely walk north on a clear night. I can't get us there. Tulo can't. And you might have, if we were starting from Maaram."

He touched my hair, made into a frizzy halo by the constant saltwater spray. "Then we'll land someplace safe and hire someone to navigate. We'll be okay, Ana. You'll see."

But I remembered how, just before I found a way to save us, Parech had been planning to give himself up to save Tulo and me. Parech said "we," but he meant "you." I wondered when that had happened. Why it seemed almost gauche to remark upon it. Part of me didn't want to find a way out of the spirit world because I was terrified of that split.

"It's so dangerous," I heard myself saying. "But I don't think we can stay here. Maybe that isn't safe either."

"Everything's dangerous, Ana."

"You're a soldier. You would think that."

"Almost dying every day just makes it clearer. We're all of us inches from the gate. And every day, a few stumble through. We'll all have our turn. No sense in living otherwise."

He meant it as sort of pragmatic comfort, but I shivered and wrapped my arms tight around my sides. I didn't like to think of death. Not my own, much less his. I didn't understand why Tulo said the death spirits liked to be near me—I hated make'lai more than anything.

"I wish death would die," I said.

He laughed, like I'd hoped. That finally roused Tulo, who flopped onto her side and opened her eyes like she was unwrapping a piece of candy.

"You're both so beautiful," she said.

"You're not the first woman to tell me so, Princess."

He reclined against a sack of barkcloth with such a bright-eyed, smug expression that Tulo elbowed him in the ribs.

"I think we should go back today," I said, and told her of my discussion with Parech. Tulo's face grew still as I spoke, and when I finally prompted her for a response, she just shrugged and stood up. "Do whatever you like. You're the Ana. I'm going swimming."

She approached the railing at a dead run and leapt into the waves. The ocean here resembled dense, rippling clouds of impossible shades. But it splashed like water, and when I peered over the edge it seemed that Tulo wouldn't come to any harm. She mostly treaded, looking back at the spirits who had congregated to watch. She evinced no surprise at their macabre shapes. But though she could see the spirit world, she'd never been *in* it before. She could never interact with them the way she did now. Her spirit sight was only useful inasmuch as the spirit world mirrored the human one. I imagined having to reconcile the sight of the spirit ocean with the touch and feel and taste of our own.

"She doesn't want to go back," Parech said, coming up behind me.

I brushed his weapon-callused palm with my fingers. "Yes." Tulo took a deep breath and dove beneath the waves. "Would you?"

By the time the spirit sun had set, I'd devised a geas I thought might get us back home safely. I'd been raised believing in gods, I suppose, like most everyone else. My family had a household god—small and impotent though it seemed to me at the time—and my father would lead the rites at the start of each harvest and planting season. But that had been a small part of my life when the flood killed my parents. When my priest took me in, he taught me all the precepts of napulo, the spirits, and the great unknowing. In this age of bindings, the napulo philosophy has grown in popularity. I imagine it will only continue to do so in the future. But at the time, my priest belonged to a fringe sect that was regarded warily at best, and feared and reviled at worst.

Because what he taught disempowered all priests, all gods, all supplications without sacrifice. There are no gods, only spirits. All the gods we perceive are but sprites and avatars—manifestations of the great forces of nature: earth, fire, wind, water, and death. The only supplications one may make are through sacrifice. The only possible interaction is through binding. Some peoples, like Tulo's, could make geas with their "gods" through sacrifice, though this was largely unintentional. Others, like the Maaram Anas, had immediately embraced the napulo philosophy and done all they could to learn the methods of spirit binding. But what the napulo gained in power, they lost in certainty. The key tenet was unknowing: no one knows what lies beyond the gate. There were no ancestors, no afterlife, no ghosts. Just spirits and humans and nature imperfectly understood. I realized that if I wanted to become a true Ana—with that kind of power and reach—I needed to embrace everything my priest had ever taught me. I needed to understand the napulo philosophy that formed the root of geas techniques. Up until now, I'd been flying blind. When we reached Essel, I promised myself I would learn everything I could. I would become a force to reckon with, and then I'd be able to protect Tulo and Parech from anything. We'd finally be safe.

But for now, I knew enough to be careful. I planned to cast a reverse of the very same geas I had used to take us here. Parech offered himself for the sacrifice this time, but I refused. The cut on my arm was healing, but I thought it would simpler to reopen it.

Tulo seemed alarmed by the idea, though. "There's other things that bind them," she said, as I readied the knife on the deck.

"Just sacrifice," I said.

"Yes, but there's other sacrifices than blood. You think it means nothing when someone offers palm wine or a fish? Or when people spend the night in prayer?"

I sighed. "There are no gods, Tulo. Or ancestors. Just spirits. And the cleanest way to a spirit is—"

She smacked the knife out of my hand. It skittered nearly to the edge of the deck. "You think I don't know that?" she said. "You think I of all people don't know full well what sacrifice means? You don't have to cut yourself. It's dangerous, Aoi. Rot could set in. I've seen it happen. The poison snakes through your body until it reaches your heart. Parech, tell her!"

Her outburst had made Parech uncharacteristically serious. "I've seen dozens of soldiers die from shallow wounds. She's right."

I started to retrieve the knife, but looked at her face and relented. "Then what should I do? Get on my knees and pray until morning? Give them our breadfruit?"

Tulo smiled slowly. "Well, why not?"

So I returned Parech's knife to him and he used it to hack open two of the tight baskets of breadfruit. The aroma was heady and rich, so the three of us stole a few handfuls before depositing the rest at the prow of the canoe. At this point, the spirits were obviously curious, hovering around us in a dense cloud. Parech shivered and looked over his shoulder too frequently. He didn't complain, but I knew he'd be kissing the ocean when we finally returned to the human world. He hacked open a green coconut and we each drank from it. I hoped that would be enough to last us through the night, since I didn't think it would be politic to take a food break while we prayed. Later, I learned that disciples of the napulo called this sort of arrangement a sacrifice of time. Some spirits are more receptive to it than others—wind, especially. The three of us got down on our knees—"a sacrifice of our comfort, at least," Parech muttered—and when I was sure all was ready, I invoked the geas.

"I call on the death spirit," I said. A hush seemed to come over the menagerie of alien creatures hovering before us. They stilled, and then as one, parted. They gave the thing that came through a wide berth. *Everything*, I thought, *comes down to respect and fear. Even for them.*

It looked just as I had last seen it, when it first took me here. White robes, a key on a rope, and an impassive mask. Like, but unlike, any god-statue I'd ever seen. "And this time?" it said. "How would you bind me?"

I took a deep breath and hardened my gaze. "We offer our food, vital stores for our survival. And we offer our prayers until the stars set and the sun rises."

It sailed close, over the railing and inches from my face. "You can't bind us with that," it said, harsh but cruelly amused. "What do you think death is? One of your niche gods?"

My mouth went dry. I felt Tulo and Parech tense beside me, but all I could do was croak out a helpless, "I…"

"You're very young, Ana," it said. "Try one of these others." It turned its cruel mask to the still crowd of spirits and I understood what it meant. And then I realized what power I must have, in my ignorance, invoked.

"The death?" I whispered. "The godhead?"

"It's never so simple as you humans like to pretend. But, certainly, yes, more than I think you'd planned to call. A word of advice, Ana. Pay more attention to detail."

And then it was gone. No flashy exit, just vanished like a foam bubble atop a wave. I looked down at Tulo and Parech. They were staring up at me with wide eyes that caught the witchy light from the gathered spirits. But I could still feel power gathering around me, the bindings I could cast. Only now I needed a spirit I could hold.

"Wind," I said, pointing to a bird with silver wings and a beak like a polished mandagah jewel. And from my finger I could see, like ink on paper, a line sprouting from it to yoke the hapless wind sprite around its dainty neck.

"We give you all this," I said, "and in return you take us back aross the border into our own land, where you may see us, but we may not see you."

It glared at me and made one frantic attempt to fly away. But the glowing line from my finger was getting fatter by the second and the sprite was caught. It squawked, as though strangled, and then settled on the mast to watch us balefully.

Halfway through the night, it started to devour the breadfruit. By the time the morning came, I could feel the power we'd generated like the air before a storm.

"Take us home," I told the sprite.

The passage, this time, was frightening and rocky. The ship groaned as it was buffeted by winds from nowhere. The sea and sky dropped away, leaving the ship alone in an inky black. But I felt the binding hold, and knew we'd be safe. Soon enough, the real sun pressed against my eyelids and the real ocean lapped fiercely against the canoe. Above us, the sprite squawked and tore through the remainder of the binding.

"Good riddance," I thought I heard it say, though my spirit sight was fading.

Parech scrambled to his knees and kissed my forehead. I looked at Tulo, an expectant grin on my face, but she was staring straight ahead, right past my shoulder. I said her name, tentatively. She looked at me, but her eyes roamed and I realized with a shock so sudden it made me choke.

I'd taken her home and made her blind again.

We reached Essel three weeks later, after plying a navigator from a lonesome atoll with all of the reed mats we had on the ship. He didn't seem concerned about his return trip, and I certainly didn't pressure him. I'd want to get off of that island myself, had I the misfortune of being born there.

We managed to save the barkcloth and the remainder of the breadfruit we didn't eat. Parech was good at feeding us from the ocean. His Akane tribe, he said, had been coastal. It was easier to survive that way than fighting for prime river land in the interior. So he recognized when the waves changed in such a way that signaled a lagoon; he knew the best times for catching albacore and the best nights for tracking schools of humu. Sometimes he'd use a spear on a line, and sometimes he'd use last night's fish to bait a hook. Our navigator didn't speak much of the five languages at our command, but he understood the desire to eat. It didn't take long before he and Parech learned to communicate quite well about islands where we might load up on fresh water and coconuts and screw pines. And when the two of them started going on about differences in fishing lures, Tulo and I politely took ourselves to the other end of the canoe.

She had not forgiven me for taking us back. Once, I tried clumsily to justify my decision, but she just stood up and walked away. She grew listless, spending long hours by herself, staring out at the sea. Sometimes Parech or I would join her. She was a little gentler with him; I could see from her face that she opened up more. By the time we reached the barrier reefs that are the first marker of Essel's waters (though still far to the south of its main harbor) the three of us had gone nearly gray with the monotony and unrelieved tension. So I suggested that we sing together.

And with a fury made all the more frightening by its unflinching steadiness, she balled up her fist and punched me. I just stood there, shocked, while my mouth filled with blood and Parech belatedly took hold of her arms.

He led her away, though she didn't struggle or seem inclined to any more violence. I looked after them and then spat over the edge. My jaw ached and my mouth felt bloody and torn, like someone had raked across it with an asp. I had never been punched before, but I imagined that it would swell. Our navigator was perched on the mast, drinking from a green coconut. He caught my eye briefly and grimaced.

"Crazy," he said in heavily accented Maaram, pointing at Tulo. I pursed my lips, greatly inclined to agree with him. I understood her. I truly did. I'd seen her face when she realized she could see us, and I'd felt the constant strain of her blindness. The few days' reprieve must have made her reality all the harder to bear.

Yes, I understood. But that didn't mean I would silently bear her temperamental peevishness any longer. So I walked over to where she was sitting with Parech, holding his hand while her lips trembled. She looked up at my approach.

"I'm not pretending that this is as hard for us as it is for you," I said. "I'm not pretending that your grief isn't real. But Tulo—we've been walking on rockfish around you for the last two weeks. I don't deserve it, and neither does Parech. Pull yourself together. Are you a princess of the Kawadiri or not?"

She stiffened, her back straight as a mast and her chin turned haughtily up. "What would you know of it? You're just some wetland peasant."

"And you were blinded by your own people and then cast out like a shard of broken pottery!"

We stared at each other, both a little shocked that I had said it.

"Aoi..." Parech whispered hoarsely.

I felt myself trembling. "We're what we make of ourselves, Tulo," I said. "No one knows what lies beyond the gate."

"So you think I should forget what was done to me? Should I pretend that I can still see the scar on your right shoulder? Parech's two-toned hair?"

Tears burned in my eyes. Two-toned hair. Parech's roots had grown since he first bleached his hair with the juice of the salo fruit, and so the contrast between the black close to his scalp and the white-blond in the sun could well be called two-toned. I hadn't even noticed until she said so. I had everything she desired, and what a waste I had made of it.

"We can't undo your sacrifice."

She reached out. I guided her hand to my face so she could feel my tears. "I know," she said. "I know. I'm normally much better at this. Thank you for reminding me." She disengaged her fingers from mine. "Would you both...I just need some time."

Parech and I stared at each other for a moment and then silently withdrew as far as the small confines of the canoe would allow.

I took off my sandals and sat with my feet dangling in the clear blue water.

"You'll look like fish to a shark from below," he said in Ku-kichan, crossing his legs beneath him.

"Then you'll just have to save me, brave Akane warrior."

He yawned and leaned back on his elbows. "I was exiled, you know. They stripped me of my shells and cast me out without even a waterskin. I was meant to die. But you see, Ana, I've made a life out of cheating death."

I had always wondered why he left. "What did you do to make them renounce you?"

"I killed the chief's son. I challenged him and I won."

"But then it was fair!"

He laughed and leaned back on his elbows. "No. There are no death-challenges among my Akane tribe. The shaman forbade them, on pain of exile. And so you find me fighting for the Maaram pigs half a world away."

He seemed as easy and unconcerned as he always did, tipping his head back into the sunshine and sighing. I thought that he must have been at odds with his people for most of his life, even before they exiled him. He was too peculiar and unconcerned and stubborn to get along with many people. I splashed my feet in the water and smiled a secret smile. So of course he got along so well with us.

"Come on, Ana, aren't you going to ask why I killed him?" Parech said.

"You just want to shock me with it. What do you think I'm going to do, Akane? Renounce you for your sins? I've always known you have souls on your conscience."

"Ah yes, but this is the first soul. At least, apart from battle. I know you're curious."

I reached down and splashed him with some seawater. "Of course I'm curious. Please tell me, vile soldier, why would you kill some innocent boy and abandon your people for two vain and cruel girls?"

His eyes seemed deep with pleasure. He had dangled a lure and I had caught it: an ancient dance. "He raped my sister, and when the pregnancy showed, claimed she had seduced him. No one else would have her, so she became his concubine."

"They didn't punish her for what you did?"

His eyes grew distant, scanning the humps of atolls on the horizon. "No. Why else would I sacrifice so much, Ana? All of the boy's widows had to be cared for by the chief until they died, and never forced to marry again."

Instinctively, I leaned down and stroked back the thick mass of his bleached hair. "Well. We always knew you Akane were barbarians."

This startled him into a laugh. For a moment, when our eyes met, I wondered if he too felt that delicate flowering of heat, that desperate tingling of the lips, but then we heard Tulo's lithe footsteps walking across the boat.

"I thought we could sing," she said, her smile tentative and genuine.

Parech leapt up and hugged her. I took her hand, my heart warring with a loss precisely equal to its gain.

Essel was everything I could have wished and nothing like I imagined. After we passed through the chain of garrisoned atolls scattered along its southwestern waters—forward guard against any of the predations from their Maaram enemies—it was a mere two day's journey to the main harbor. The harbormaster demanded three hand-lengths of sennit braid just for one night's docking privileges, which made me choke and which Parech paid without even bargaining. I realized that left to his own devices Parech would bankrupt us before the week was out, so I took it upon myself to inquire among the locals as to the best and cheapest place to moor a small trader's canoe. The answer, I discovered, promised us a situation better than any of us had dared hope. Like Okika, Essel had its own farmland. Indeed, most of the rich soil south of the great sentinel of its volcano was nearly devoid of anyone but a few farmers. Certainly no one who would charge us for pushing our canoe onto the beach.

The area we finally selected was an idyll: a mile distant from a small farmers' town but otherwise utterly still, and half wild. Tulo could see here as though there weren't a city just a few miles inland, and the soil just past the dunes made every vegetable grow to the size of a baby. We used nearly all of Taak's extortion payment for lumber from the dwindling red acacia forests on the eastern side of the island. In the meantime, we draped oil-infused barkcloth over tall stakes and lived like happy peasants. The land here didn't seem to belong to anyone, and by Essel law, anyone living in a place for two years without someone else objecting had the right of ownership. When our resources started to run low despite our rationing, Parech had the idea to dig a deep pit and fill it with some of the fresh water used to irrigate a nearby farm.

"And what good to us is a mud pit?" I asked him.

Tulo grinned slyly. "You're smarter than you let on, aren't you, Parech? We'll seed it with fish, Aoi. Fresh fish all year long, and we'll always have money."

Money was the curious form of payment the Essel chiefs had devised to help pay for their constant wars of conquest. Instead of something useful like food or mats or pottery or sennit braid, they had devised a series of stone chits that were supposed to represent value. They claimed that anyone could go to the hall in the center of the island and redeem this money for a certain length of sennit braid, but I had my private doubts. They seemed to be issuing the stone chits faster than even an army of fleet-fingered women could weave the tough cordage.

But we used the rest of the cord Taak had given us to buy the fish, and Parech spent days combing the city for advice on methods of raising them. In the meantime, Tulo and I busied ourselves drying bundles of grass and weaving them into tight mats for the floor of our tent and—eventually—the floor of our house. What extra we could make, we used for exchange. We spent most days busy and hungry and most nights exhausted and full. But we were happy.

As the cold grew bitter and thick and the wind from the ocean made the three of us huddle together like worms under a log, we decided to do all we could to finish at least one room of the house. Tulo reprised her role as street-corner spirit talker, this time for the purer purpose of relieving the gullible of their sennit braid and money. Parech used those funds and the promise of more to hire a few strong men to cut the logs and hoist them into place above the earth. They notched the logs so they would support each other, and we caulked the spaces between them with red clay. The roof we thatched with leaves and tall grasses soaked in resin over the wooden frame, and then lashed down with what sennit we could afford. It wasn't a beautiful house, or perfectly made, but it was our own and we loved it immediately. We had plans to build one more room at least, but that would have to wait until our fortunes improved. The fish in the pond were slowly breeding. Soon, we might have enough to sell.

As the cold set in, and the frantic work on the house finally eased, I began to spend hours walking through the city, silently observing what I could. That Essel was preparing for war was obvious when I looked for the signs, but those were less overt than in Okika. I wondered if we should perhaps alert the chiefs to the upcoming Maaram raid, but I didn't feel particularly compelled. I couldn't imagine Essel had become so great a power by being careless about such matters. But there was something else brewing in the city—another sort of war, though this one had no leaders or armies. The napulo philosophy's influence in Essel shocked me. It seemed every third conversation I heard discussed the obscure creed my radical priest had taught me. And with its widespread acceptance came a curious new idea. If there were no gods but spirits, and if we humans could be sure of nothing save our current existence (so this line of reasoning went), then surely we could do no better for ourselves than to bind these spirits for our own benefit. As a woman selling cups of warm kava in the street told me one evening: "If we're all gonna die, then you bet I'd like to live in the meantime!"

This idea seemed to culminate in a notion so stark in its hubris that it left me breathless the first time I heard it: a final geas to bind the ultimate expressions of each spirit to humanity's will. How the nameless progenitors of this idea proposed to forge such an awesome geas I had no idea—my throat went dry at just the thought of summoning the death spirit again, let alone forging chains strong enough to keep it bound forever. And yet that very fear made me want to explore the idea more deeply, to seek out those women (and the few men) who understood something of spirit bindings. None of them had any more of an idea than I did about how such an ultimate binding might be accomplished, but in the smaller details they could teach me much. I became a student of geas, that ultimate practical expression of the napulo creed. When Parech called me Ana now, he never quite meant it as a jest.

I came home late one night in the deep cold—the longest night of the year, we all later learned—a little drunk on kava and amant. I had learned a dozen postulates from an old witch who lived by the great bay, and had scribbled them all down in a crabbed hand in my precious notebook (the paper inside being significantly more valuable than even the fish-leather cover). I had the giddy, free-wheeling sense of coming ever closer to an achievement I didn't even dare put into words. Almost as though I thought the spirits might be watching me.

Which, of course, they were.

Tulo and Parech were sleeping when I staggered inside the room that still smelled like freshly cut wood and drying clay. They had grown tangled in sleep—her hand on his chest, his leg straddling her dark thighs. I regarded them for a long moment and then wiped my eyes. I fell asleep quickly and was awakened not much later by a sound like a mountain groaning. Only a moment later did I realize that the ground was shaking. Our new house, our beautiful house, was creaking ominously on its new, unsettled foundations. Tulo was already awake, but glancing around the room in bleary-eyed panic. I wondered what she saw, but had no time to ask her. Parech slept like the dead, as usual.

"Wake up, you stupid fool!" I yelled, shaking his shoulders. The earth screamed again, so I could hear nothing else, and above us one of our precious new logs creaked. Parech shot to his feet and grabbed Tulo by the elbow.

"Get out!" I shouted. He hesitated for a moment and then turned. Tulo stumbled along behind him, her eyes dashing left and right at flitting ghosts. I scooped up our blankets and what mats I could hold. The ground shook again, tossing me to the floor while the logs snapped above me. I had no time. I gripped the bundle tighter in my arms and hurled myself out of the door. Our makeshift steps had collapsed, and so I smacked into the earth just as our house listed sideways. The second support cracked, and I might have been crushed under the inexorable force of our collapsing house if not for Parech, who gripped my forearms with bruising fingers and pulled me out just in time. He held me to him and I stayed there while the earth groaned and rocked around us. I could hear the fury of the waves now, even over the diminishing rumbles of the earth. I looked north, to Nui'ahi, and saw to my relief that this earthquake hadn't fully awakened the sentinel, though it belched more smoke than usual.

Parech gradually released me and we looked at each other in wordless, thoughtless shock. I nearly jumped when Tulo put her hand on my shoulder.

"Are you all right?" she said.

Her dark brown eyes darted less—indeed, they focused on me until I thought I might drown in them. I was shaking. So was she.

"What...what did you see, Tulo?"

"They were everywhere. They knew what was coming. They danced, Aoi. They danced like we did on the ship. I couldn't hear them, but I thought they sang, too."

My teeth started to chatter loudly. I couldn't tell if I was frightened or cold. The waves crashed against the shore, spraying high over the dunes. I wondered if the water might reach us, or if we'd be spared at least that disaster.

Parech took a long look at the two of us and shook his head. "Everything is in the house. We'll freeze to death out here. You two use the blanket. I'll go into the village and see what I can find."

He hugged us both fiercely before he went. I wondered if he would borrow or sell something, or if he would simply steal what he needed. I knew that for us, he would do whatever was necessary and hardly note the difference.

I guided Tulo over to the dunes, where we might shelter from the wind, and covered us both as best I could with one of the blankets I'd managed to save. We shivered together beneath it. She put her head on my shoulder.

"Is it gone?" she asked.

I looked at the house the three of us had built. "Flattened, I'd say, not precisely gone."

"Oh, Aoi."

Tulo reached up. She stroked my tightly braided hair and then began to unweave the thick plaited strands.

"You have beautiful hair," she said. "Mine goes everywhere. Yours...well, if I could see, I'd braid flowers into it with five strands and make it into a crown."

"If I could—"

Tulo put a finger over my lips. I stopped talking. I stopped breathing. We stared at each other. And then, as though falling in a pond, I inclined my head and kissed her.

We were warm, that longest night. Warm, and comforted, and filled like cups with painful pleasure. We lay tangled inside each other, beneath the blanket, and I thought unexpectedly, *I miss him.*

"He'll be here soon," Tulo said, nuzzling her face against my collarbone. She fell asleep and I listened to the waves.

I looked up when he approached, though he moved silently as always and the water boomed. I saw his face clear, clear in the moonlight: the knowing, the shock, the sad smile.

I missed you, I wanted to say, but he turned and left us alone.

PART IV

. . .

Desperate Men

· 9 ·

❦

WHEN LANA COULD SEE AND HEAR and touch and taste again, the only sensations she could quite make out were of closeness and warmth. She smelled something familiar and clean, like water from the ocean.

"Are you all right?" Kai asked.

She shivered and nodded against his chest. She didn't want to open her eyes. If she did, she would have to acknowledge what she'd promised. She'd have to deal with the damage she'd done. Nothing felt any different, which scared her even more.

"Lana?" Kai said, as though frightened by her silence.

"I was stupid. I forgot the binding would break."

"I thought it might. I should have warned you. I'm sorry."

Lana had to smile at this. "Perhaps next time you should worry less for my pride." She paused. "It almost had me."

Kai's shuddering breath tickled her scalp. "I thought it did have you. How did you bind it?"

She grew aware of a slow coil of terror, migrating from her stomach to her throat and curling there like an eel. "My wings," she said. "I gave it my wings."

Kai jerked back suddenly, his eyes turning clear violet in his shock. They were still seated on the steps just outside the main rebel headquarters. The cold air was filled with a fine haze of ashfall. Lana gripped her shoulders and ground her teeth, waiting for his indignation. This was, perhaps, her steepest sacrifice yet.

"But you still have them," he said.

Lana sat straight up. Slowly, hardly daring to believe it, she moved her hands behind her. They encountered, like they had every day since that morning in the ruins of the wind shrine, the smooth texture of her outer feathers and the downy nap beneath. She flexed her muscles—aside from the slight twinge from her almost-healed wound, her wings unfurled against the steps just as they ought.

"I still have them," she repeated, numbly.

She looked up, staring at the darkened landscape, searching for the death spirit. But it was gone—all she could see were the waning signs of the battle: people running from the apothecary house carrying bandages and water, speaking animatedly as they rushed to and from Sea Street, while soldiers hefted weapons that seemed ominously dull in the moonlight.

"With what could you bind me?" the death had asked her. Its key was not at its waist, but in its hand. She could smell something like blood on that key, but also cold. She had never known you could smell cold before that moment, but with the death inches from her face she knew instinctively that no human would be able to survive its touch. The infinite chill of death.

More than anything, she hated to be cold.

But what could she offer it? Too late to use Akua's flute, too late for a normal sort of sacrifice. The last time, in Kai's temple, she had bound it with a whim, a guess that it felt emotions as mundane as the fear even now constricting her heart and lungs. And it had let her go. This time she wouldn't get away so easily. It meant to take her—she could tell by its uncanny stillness and its voice, cold as the key. It had cut itself off from the passion she knew it could feel.

But then, it still waited for her answer. And so she had offered the first thing she could think of: the wind's gift, and the wind's curse.

"Take my wings," she said.

It stilled. The chill seemed, infinitesimally, to thaw. "Clever," it said, a smile in its voice, if not on its mask. "The sacrifice interferes with another spirit's power."

"That's not my concern."

"True," it said, and then Lana was back, shivering in Kai's arms.

They went inside and he built up the fire while she told him all she remembered. Kai was silent for a long time after, busying himself with taking the clay jug of palm wine from the fire.

"It seems you offered an impossible sacrifice. The wind is the equal of the death, so the death couldn't interfere with its gift."

"So then I got something without sacrifice? Isn't that impossible?"

Kai frowned and poured them both cups. "It should be. But no one really understands the rules of conflicting powers. *Someone* had to sacrifice. But not you, this time."

But then *who*? She couldn't quite shake the sensation that this time she'd been too lucky. That, perhaps not now, but eventually, this desperate sacrifice would come due. She took the mulled wine gratefully—though she knew that her body had never left the steps, she still felt the chill of the death's key deep in her joints, in the back of her throat. She thought there was a reason why the sensation reminded her of old age.

"I never knew that, about the lead key," he said into their silence.

Lana took another sip; a warm, slow burn rose in her stomach. "Neither did I. And I've read the death postulates three times through, so I know it's not there."

He rubbed the back of her hand and smiled. "Perhaps we should hire a printer to issue a corrected edition," he said.

"We can tell Eliki to put off next week's edition of the rebel pamphlet. She won't mind, will she?"

"And we can tell the death spirit to leave you alone for a time—"

"And Kohaku to resign—"

"And Akua to give your mother back!"

Lana's laugh stuck like a bone in her throat. A wave of nausea worse than what she had felt when the death spirit broke her geas washed over her. She put her head between her knees.

"Lana? I'm sorry, it was stupid of me to say it."

"I almost killed her, Kai! I just realized...I almost killed her. Again."

Kai froze. His hand on her back was rigid. "*You* almost died," he said.

Lana forgot her nausea. "That's what I mean. What else have I been doing this for, Kai? It's all for my mother. These wings, the death, Akua's damned arm bone flute...do you think any of this would have happened if not for my mother?"

"You'd kill yourself for her."

"Of course!" she said, noticing the curious atonality of his voice. Was he thinking of Pua again? She considered the conversation she'd had with Akua just before the death took her. She'd discovered her line, after all this time. What she had done to Pua before she didn't think she could do again, with full knowledge. Perhaps she should tell Kai that. Maybe then he wouldn't be staring at her now with stormy eyes.

"Haven't you ever thought that some of us would miss you?"

How did the world look through Kai's eyes? She didn't know. She had thought she did—she had thought she understood his anger over Pua—but she realized now that she'd only been looking at one half of everything. The other side of his anger had always been his love. She faced death every day; it had become commonplace to her, unremarkable. But she understood now that it had never been that way for Kai. He had always been afraid for her. He had always wondered if perhaps, this time, the death might win.

"Kai," she said, putting her arms around him. He didn't return the gesture, but he didn't break away. This close, she could feel his shoulders tremble. "We're all of us inches from the gate," she said slowly, remembering something Parech had said in Ino's black book. "And every day a few of us stumble through."

"Not all of us lean against its bars and dare them to open, Lana," he said, but he hugged her.

"I don't want to die," she said softly.

"But you're willing."

Nahoa kept the plans under her shirt and didn't tell even Malie what she'd seen and heard from her roost in the garden. Her maid suspected something, but was wise enough to keep silent. Ahi swatted at the bundle of paper near her mother's breast, but otherwise seemed content to keep the secret. Nahoa waited for two days, frantic that someone would discover the plans were missing and search the temple compound. But nothing of the sort happened—even if Makaho had noticed the loss, she could hardly proclaim that she was helping supply the Mo'i with advanced weapons against his own people. Even in the most loyal parts of the city, support for the Mo'i was grudging at best. She heard rumors of a battle the morning after she took the plans and was nearly frantic with her inability to contact Pano. He'd always come and gone as he pleased, and she imagined that he'd be busy now with the casualties. Kohaku's attacks on the rebel encampment had grown more frequent ever since he had sent that assassin to kill the black angel, ever since someone in the fire temple had nearly killed her child.

She did not intend to let Ahi's perfect health make her complacent about the ongoing danger. Someone had tried to kill her baby. Considering how much it would hurt Makaho's political position, she doubted it would be anyone loyal to the fire temple. And she could believe many things of her mad husband, but she knew in her bones he'd never hurt her or Ahi. Which left...who? A madman? The rebels? But Pano had saved Ahi's life by taking them to the black angel. She had seen his face. She knew him. Why poison Ahi and then heal her? To gain Nahoa's trust?

"But he'd already had that," Nahoa whispered onto Ahi's downy crown, as her child suckled. "He still has it. I wish I could find him."

So some other faction. Some piece of the political puzzle she didn't know about. Great Kai knew that in the aftermath of the eruption, politics in this island had fractured like a dropped plate. No one could keep track of all the rival gangs and interests scrambling to take advantage. But she would just have to find out, wouldn't she?

Since she had no way to contact Pano, Nahoa tried to forget the treasonous paper tucked under her shirt. The rebels needed the information, that much was certain. She was afraid of what would happen to them in a pitched battle if they had to fight with sticks and knives against bows and arrows. But in the meantime, she would keep her ears open. She wondered what Pano would think of her industriousness, and grinned.

"Well, if a gardener like Pano can start a war, I don't see why a sailor like me can't gather some information. Am I right, baby?" Ahi, finished with her meal, shook her head in a way that might be construed as agreement.

"Who do you think is loyal to the old hag?" Nahoa asked, pitching her voice low in case someone could overhear her at the door.

Malie looked up from the socks she'd been mending. "Are you speaking to yourself, your child, or your maid, my lady?" she asked, with some acid.

"Not many others to talk to, are there?" Nahoa said. "And some are better at conversation than others, ain't they, Ahi?" Ahi giggled.

Malie continued her careful stitches. "You seem to get on well enough with the gardener king."

Nahoa glared at her and stared at the door, though she supposed that Malie's voice had been quiet enough. "There's an antechamber and solid stone behind us, my lady. We're safe."

But Nahoa had grown wary since her foray in the garden. The few times since that she'd passed by Makaho, she'd been sure there was some glint of suspicion in the old hag's eyes, some careful appraisal. She knew Makaho looked at everyone like that, but that didn't stop Nahoa from being afraid. So she scooted close enough to Malie that they could converse in whispers.

"Pano saved Ahi's life," Nahoa said.

"He's also fighting a war against your husband." Nahoa glared at her and Malie looked down quickly. "You know Makaho thinks she can make you take him back on her terms."

"Then she'll have to make another wish."

Malie snorted. "No doubt. You want to know who's loyal to her? The whole temple is afraid of her, but that doesn't mean they haven't found other opportunities worth the risk—like we have."

Nahoa liked that "we." She trusted Malie out of necessity and what she judged were their mutual interests. But it was still hard to know where her true loyalties lay.

"So who should I suspect?" Nahoa asked.

Malie laughed again and plucked Ahi from the floor. "Well, how should I know? It's not like we go around wearing purple slashes and proclaiming death to the Mo'i. But you want to know who I suspect might keep secrets?"

Ahi reached out and grabbed a tuft of Malie's hair. "Ura, the one who brings supper most days. I think he must be one of the napulo—he has the ridges on his wrist from the prayer braids, and he's always making offerings. Little Sabolu in the stables seems eager for an opportunity at least. Hell, even the old hag herself. With Makaho, unfortunately, you never know which side she's truly playing."

"But she couldn't've—" Nahoa broke off. They both looked at Ahi, settling herself against Malie's shoulder.

"No," Malie said softly. "This one's too valuable to her alive."

"So Ura and Sabolu. I think both of them touched Ahi that day. I was going out to market."

But Malie shook her head. "Don't trust anybody. Make a list. It was *someone*, my lady. The black angel told you so. And what I know is little enough."

Nahoa nodded thoughtfully and went back as best she could through the two days before Ahi got sick. Ura the servant, Sabolu the stablegirl, Makaho, and two serving girls whose names she didn't know. No strangers. No one who made much sense.

She drew Ura into conversation that evening when he brought their food. Malie was right; he seemed nervous—his eyes constantly darting to the door, wiping his fire-scarred palms on his trousers. But though she played with Ahi ostentatiously enough, he seemed to regard her daughter with no more than polite interest. Nahoa wondered about the imprints of sennit braid on his wrists—why would someone who subscribed to a creed that so violently rejected the spirit bindings come to work in the fire temple itself? Could some of the napulo have aligned themselves against her? But if so, what good did it do to hurt her baby? Nahoa let him go, inexplicably worried. He might be a good actor, but his clear unease said otherwise. She doubted that whatever he was up to had anything to do with her daughter. After all, her husband had recently made being napulo punishable by death. Ura had more than enough reason to be nervous.

Having dismissed Makaho for political reasons, Nahoa sought out the two kitchen maids that night. She brought a sleepy Ahi with her, and asked for a glass of warm milk.

The girls were young and probably related; they had the same wide almond eyes, though one was a bit taller than the other.

"Oh!" said the taller one, after she had gotten over the shock of seeing the Mo'i's wife in the kitchens. "The baby keeping you up, lady? Our mama was always complaining when she had our brother."

Nahoa nodded, though it was unfair to Ahi, the sweetest, most agreeable child there ever was. It was an excuse.

"We're so glad she's doing well, miss," said the shorter one abruptly, as her sister busied herself with the milk. "We heard she was so sick those weeks ago. They said she might die, but we didn't believe it and look! Healthy as an eel. She's beautiful."

"She is, isn't she?" Nahoa said, beaming despite herself. She should be interrogating these girls, subtly ferreting out their secrets. But the longer she spent with them, the more absurd her suspicions felt. These girls—from somewhere deep out in the islands judging by their accents—were young and naive and trusting. She doubted they could even manage to steal salt from the larder, let alone poison an innocent baby. So she took her milk and walked back slowly to her apartments. On her way she passed by the doors to the main fire room and was surprised to see one of them still open. Makaho was seated alone inside, her naked back rashed with heat as she bowed repeatedly to the fire. She mumbled, but no words Nahoa could make out. Something about her seemed almost frenzied, but after a minute Nahoa shrugged and walked away.

The hag was crazy. Everyone knew it. Even after Nui'ahi, no one believed regular humans could pray to spirits. It took a sacrifice like Kohaku's, or a particular person like the black angel, to make them obey human will. Makaho bowing up and down like a string-puppet struck her as pathetic, absurd, laughable. So she chuckled, and Ahi burped against her chest.

The two guardians sat across from Kohaku, fire and water allied in righteous wrath. They had refused his polite offer of refreshment with an almost synchronized shake of their heads. Kohaku found himself possessed of an eerie conviction that he was staring at an ancient sculpture of a two-faced god. One pale as a white-capped river, the other dark as charcoal; one with eyes variable as the sea, the other with glowing orange embers set in his face like gems. For all their dramatic outward differences, Senona Ahi and Kaleakai looked like nothing so much as alien brothers.

Kohaku shifted in his backless chair, uncomfortable under their twin gazes. They said nothing, and Kohaku floundered for some method of breaking the tension. But growing terror slowed his thoughts.

"I'm afraid they might stay there forever unless you say something, brother."

Kohaku closed his eyes, but he could still hear her. "They think you're insane, you know," said the ghost of his dead sister. He opened his eyes and saw that she knelt between the two guardians, who seemed as oblivious to her presence as everyone else.

"Why are you here?" he said. The words seemed to drain the air from the room. Kohaku had to force himself to breathe.

"And you used to have such skill at diplomacy," Emea said. Kohaku glared at her. The fire and water guardians shared an enigmatic look.

"We have come to warn you," the fire guardian said. His voice was a deep rumble, like stones before they spit sparks. "The fire spirit still struggles against its bonds."

"Well, I hardly needed you to tell me that," Kohaku said.

The water guardian, Kaleakai, leaned forward. His eyes changed as he did so, losing their irises in favor of a storm-churned ocean. "You show remarkably little remorse, for a mass murderer."

"It looks like he knows you, brother."

"Quiet!" Kohaku yelled, before he could stop himself.

"You deny—" the water guardian began, but Senona Ahi raised a hand to silence him. Senona's nostrils flared, as though he could smell something. He turned his head. For a moment, he and Emea stared straight in each other's fire-filled eyes. Then Emea guttered out of existence and the fire guardian shook his shoulders, like a horse dislodging a fly.

The water guardian tilted his head. "Senona?"

"Nothing we didn't already know. This one thinks he can play with a great spirit."

The ghost of his sister might make him want to scream, but he felt as though he could hardly think without her. What did these two know? Would they kill him for what he'd done?

"Is this about the ramblings of that mad black angel? You can't prove anything. Leave before I call the guards." Each sentence came out fainter than the last.

Senona Ahi shook his head. "We have no time to play these games with you, Mo'i. You sacrificed your hand to weaken the bindings. We know this. I assure you the black angel has nothing to do with our knowledge. Indeed, I'm rather impressed she figured it out."

"Are you going to kill me?" Kohaku didn't mean to ask it. He certainly didn't intend the hint of longing that infused his words.

But the fire guardian laughed. "Of course not," he said.

"If that would solve the problem," said Kaleakai, "I promise we wouldn't be speaking to you right now."

Kohaku could think of no response to that.

"The trouble," said Senona Ahi, "is that you have unleashed something. You don't think the fire spirit has made that offer to thousands of other penitents over the years? People desperate with your particular combination of despair and thirst for revenge? And yet only you succeeded. That makes you a powerful person—the only person who can stop the fire spirit before it breaks its bonds entirely."

"Break? What do you mean?"

"He means," said the water guardian, whose eyes had turned ice-chip blue, "that if you don't agree to sacrifice yourself in the service of the fire spirit's binding, it will break free entirely."

Kohaku stared at them. They stared back, said nothing.

"You want me to kill myself."

"We want you to sacrifice yourself. The lip of Nui'ahi would be appropriate, considering. But any fire death would do, so long as you dedicate yourself appropriately—"

"Leave."

"You probably didn't know your sacrifice would murder—"

"*Leave*. Guardians or no, I will kill you."

Senona Ahi stopped in mid-speech. His gaping mouth might have been comical if not for the hint of fire in his throat.

"Do you doubt it?" Kohaku said.

Kaleakai stood, and dragged Senona Ahi up with him. His hand left pale blue imprints on the other man's elbow.

"No," said the water guardian. "I expected as much."

The woman kneeling on the floor of the tiny local fire shrine went quiet with shock when Lana walked inside. The sennit braid she had been carefully winding and unwinding with ritual fervor around her left wrist fell limply to the floor. By her lined face and slate-gray hair, Lana guessed her to be at least sixty. She'd been one of the women fighting off the Mo'i's guards in that hellish scene before the fire temple, when one of her fellow napulo disciples had burned herself alive in the public square. Lana spared herself a quiet moment of relief. This was the fifth supposed napulo enclave she'd visited in the last week. She'd begun to wonder if they'd all vanished in the wake of Kohaku's edict.

"I heard Bloody One-hand captured you," Lana said. "You escaped?"

The woman gathered the coils of worn sennit braid from the floor with trembling hands. Now that Lana looked, she could see bruises up and down her arms, faded to mottled yellow and green.

"He released me," she said quietly.

"I've never heard of him releasing someone."

The woman clutched reflexively at the rope in her hands. "I was lucky. I have influential friends."

Lana wondered about that. "And the other napulo?"

Her mouth pursed in what might have been anger or grief. "My friends were not in time for her. What brings you here, black angel? Did you want to lecture us for our unseemly spectacle? For wanting the bindings to weaken? And to think that we still mention Polonuku's name in our prayers."

"Who?"

The woman gripped the edge of the altar and hauled herself carefully upright. "You don't even know her name? Your predecessor. The black angel who sacrificed herself to remove the unholy binding."

"You honor *her*? And what of all those killed in the wars and disasters after? Even if you hate the bindings, how can you countenance..."

The woman's cheeks were flushed with anger; her knuckles pale where they gripped her worn prayer braid too tightly. "A necessary penance for the evil we committed. Make no mistake, black angel, all the bindings will come due. Whether we napulo exist or not, nothing as unnatural as the great bindings can last forever."

Lana sliced the air with her hand, furious, but wishing she could instead be cool and supercilious. The trouble was that she knew the nature of binding too well to dismiss this napulo woman's position. She might disagree with her conclusions, she might want to vomit at her blithe acceptance of mass death, but she understood.

She saw what bindings did to Ino. She had stood on the top of the ruins of the wind shrine and heard the spirit itself tell how it hated the bindings. But it had also said something else. Something she doubted the woman would believe.

"The wind spirit gave me these wings," she said. "Do you want to know why? Because something about keeping me alive helped reinforce the death spirit's binding. It said that it remembered the world before the death was bound, and afterward, and it preferred the world after. So does your philosophy have a place for that? A spirit that prefers the bound world?"

She had, Lana noticed with grim satisfaction, managed to shock the napulo disciple. The woman held herself so still that Lana had to count to see if she still breathed.

"You are not lying," she said finally.

"No," Lana said.

"What are you doing here? What do you want with us?"

"I'm looking for a one-armed witch."

"And you think we'd have anything to do with someone who binds the spirits for her livelihood?"

"If you had the same short-term interests, why not? Besides, she's not an ordinary witch. For all I know, she's as much a napulo as you."

The woman tossed her braid on the altar and walked closer to Lana. "What do you want this woman for?" she said. Her voice was very low. Lana wondered who she thought might overhear.

"She has taken my mother. I'm afraid of what might happen if I don't get her back."

"I never met her, but I heard of her. They said she came through two months ago, looking for ancient books and letters—accounts we kept of the age of bindings."

"But why would napulo have accounts of the bindings?"

For some reason, this made the other woman laugh. "Do you know what napulo means, black angel? It's the word for binding in the old Maaram tongue. Maaram is what Okika used to be. A thousand years ago, the napulo were a community dedicated to studying the spirits and the process of binding. Some thought to use the bindings for power. A few of the wiser ones knew that such bindings could only be a perversion. They were marginalized, and of course, you know who won that argument. Over the centuries, the only napulo who would claim the title were those wise ones who had opposed it from the beginning, and we inherited the wealth of knowledge amassed over that time. So you understand? Part of what we do is to atone for our own sins. It was a napulo disciple who bound each of the great spirits."

Lana took this in. "And you're saying the one-armed witch knew this?"

"She must have, to ask us. And I don't know why, but those she asked trusted her enough to give her some of our most cherished records."

Lana felt her wings shaking in her excitement and stilled them. Careful, now. This was more than she'd dared hope for, based on Sabolu's information. "Do you know what records she took?"

"Anything we had about life geas."

"You mean the death spirit?"

"Well, yes, but more specific than that. They were all methods of binding the death to extend life."

Lana felt the blood drain from her face. She had to remind herself to breathe. Binding the death to extend life. Like the binding she had used to save her mother. Could that be why Akua had kidnapped Leilani? To somehow disrupt Lana's life geas?

"Do you know anything else? Where she is now?"

The woman, clearly sensing her agitation, put a hand on Lana's shoulder. "I'm sorry, keika," she said. "But the woman vanished as she came. No one knows."

Lana had a dream. She couldn't remember the details, only the vaguest of impressions: scudding clouds, the calls of moa and other beach birds, the dry switching of tall grass on the dunes. And the waves, always the waves, crashing like a spirit's hammer on the shore. There were no people in this dream, not even Lana herself, but the impression of the place—like and utterly unlike the beaches she had known as a child—had been of a world deeply loved. She woke and gingerly moved herself from Kai's arms so she could reach the black book. It didn't take her long to place the vague dream connection. The beach she had dreamed of was the place where Aoi, Tulo, and Parech had decided to build their house.

Aoi hadn't called it the Rushes—maybe that name came later—but she had written that they had built on the western shore, deep in the farming country. Lana couldn't believe that it had taken her this long to associate their home with the strange house that Makaho had been sending supplies to. The house in the black book had been destroyed in an earthquake, and the house on the beach had been standing for centuries, but it was the first hint that the events in this strange book might relate to her problems now. For whatever reason, Akua hadn't wanted her to know this story.

Akua also didn't want her to know that she'd been associating with the napulo. Lana recalled with sick dread the possibility that Akua would attempt to break Lana's life geas. Lana knew that she had done something to disrupt Akua's plans when she recited that geas—Akua had as much as told her so. But she still didn't understand what good it would do to break it now, more than a year later. Akua meant to use *Lana* for something, but why Leilani?

"Something wrong?" Kai asked, yawning. She hadn't realized he was awake.

She laughed. "What isn't? When did you get back? How did the meeting go?" His hands trailed up her back, buried themselves deep in her black down, and gently worked out the knots in her muscles. "As well as we expected."

Lana stiffened. "He threatened to kill you."

"I'm the water guardian, Lana. He can certainly try."

She told him of her enlightening visit to the napulo woman, and her realization about the significance of the house in the rushes. "I thought I'd visit it again today," she said, and smiled when he offered to accompany her.

She went down ahead of him, only to find Pano and Eliki arguing in low, intense voices before their untouched morning meal. Eliki had pages and pages of scribbles in front of her, and her clothes were so rumpled and her face so haggard that Lana thought she must not have slept all night. Pano hardly looked any better.

They took no notice of her approach, and so Lana just tried to be discreet while she ate what they'd left out. Their voices were low enough that she couldn't catch every word, but she saw the map of Essel on the table and could easily guess the subject. Eliki wanted the northern docks. This was already the coldest winter Lana had ever experienced, and the worst months were still ahead. She remembered hearing of "volcano colds" in the days before the spirit bindings, but she hadn't really grasped what it meant. Volcanoes were hot, at least until their constant spray of ash and smoke choked the sky and brought a pall to everything beneath it. In this sort of weather, the food stores that their sympathizers in the seventh district could bring them would be severely limited. Without a port, the rebels would soon starve, and no war would be necessary. So, Eliki proposed to get the port—a compelling argument. But Lana sympathized with Pano, who understood the implications of such violent, uncoordinated conflict far better than Eliki, it seemed. And no one could overlook the threat posed by Kohaku's bows.

Lana could tell that they had been engaged in this argument for most of the night. And judging by Pano's bleak expression, he was losing. Lana put her finger over her lips when Kai came down. He took one look at the two rebel leaders and sighed. Neither of them had anything of use to offer this discussion.

To get to the Rushes more quickly, she and Kai hired a rickshaw, and she contemplated briefly what an odd, disturbing pair they must seem to the outside world. But they were both used to the stares and the reflexive spirit invocations by now. She bought two pastries from the vendor, using some coils of sennit braid she'd found in Kai's luggage. She'd had that idea after reading the black book. The ubiquitous cordage had been a type of currency in that long-ago time, and given the disaster they found themselves in, she thought they could all learn a few lessons from the previous age.

They had finished the pastries when they finally reached the ancient house at the end of the road, dark and unchanged. And just as before, she felt the power of the geas binding this house, of the spirits tied to its preservation. But she saw no signs of habitation. She and Kai looked at each other and mounted the steps.

The door was open a crack, as though someone had come inside and forgotten to latch it. But Lana was sure that she'd closed the door when she'd last left. She pushed it open. The air inside was warmer, despite the lack of any fire. The room was empty. Even the package that had been waiting by the door had vanished.

"No dust," said Kai behind her.

She shivered. "No. There wasn't any last time either. But someone's taken the package."

"Do you think maybe this is just a delivery location? Maybe the recipients live elsewhere."

Lana nodded slowly. "That would make more sense, wouldn't it? This place...I don't see how anyone could live here for long."

"It might be a geas that makes you feel that way."

Lana had to smile at that. "And when did Akua ever need artifice to frighten people?"

"You think this is her place?"

Lana walked a few steps deeper into the room and looked around. She hadn't realized it until she said so, but the geas she felt here reminded her of the ancient house by the lake in Okika. She wished for some of that mysterious "Maaram herb" mentioned in the black book. If she could view the spirit world, even partially, perhaps she could converse with the spirits bound here and learn more about Akua's intentions. But she had never heard of any such thing outside of the black book. The Esselans had destroyed a great deal of knowledge when they finally conquered Maaram in the great war.

"Some of it must be hers," Lana said. "The three in the black book built it, I think, but there must be something important about this house. Some reason she came here."

"You think the black book is that important?"

She shrugged, frustrated. "Ino nearly killed himself to give it to me. He wouldn't have done so without a reason."

"But you still have no idea what it is. And it's distracting you. What makes you think this house is anything other than what it seems? The book. And who gave it to you? One of Akua's creatures."

"You think Akua *meant* for Ino to give it to me?" She remembered the look of anguish on Ino's face as he collapsed into the mud at the lake's edge. "Impossible. You weren't there. You wouldn't understand."

"You don't think she's devious enough?"

"I don't think Ino is! That whole time, he was the only one who cared about me."

Kai put up his hands. "All right. I can understand friendship at least. But you have to acknowledge that Akua could have bound him in such a way he had no choice."

"But why this elaborate game? Why give me a book that means nothing to her?"

"We're here, aren't we? Chasing down mysteries a thousand years old."

"Makaho sent something here—"

"Makaho is a spider. She's involved in everything and strives to turn everything to her advantage. This house could be related to a dozen of her schemes. You want Akua, Lana? Then design a geas that can break through her defenses. Or better yet, Makaho's."

Lana looked at him, astonished. "I should have thought of that."

They left the house together, but on the threshold she paused and looked over her shoulder. Utterly empty, just as it had been before. But she was overcome with the sensation of watchful eyes, and she shivered as an oddly warm and gentle breeze briefly caressed her wings.

NAHOA FOUND SABOLU. The girl was lazing in the hay, fiddling with a cloth of intricately dyed red-and-blue barkcloth. She scrambled up when Nahoa approached, straw sticking out wildly from her hair like a fool's crown.

"Should I fetch a carriage, my lady?" she asked.

Nahoa shook her head and regarded the girl carefully. She seemed a bit guilty, but that was just as likely from being caught dawdling as anything more sinister.

"I just thought you might be able to help me," she said.

Sabolu nodded—maybe a bit too eagerly—and quickly tied the barkcloth in an inexpert knot around her tousled hair. How had she afforded such fine cloth, anyway? In these scarce times, it was hard enough to pay for a meal, let alone a frivolous luxury item. Surely the fire temple didn't pay her so well. She had to be running errands on the side.

"I can do plenty," said the girl, lowering her voice, "but I'll need something for it. And I don't like kala much no more."

Nahoa thought. "I have a barkcloth skirt. You could take it in with pins."

Sabolu grinned so wide Nahoa could see a gap in the back of her teeth. She was opportunistic, sure, but enough that she would deliberately murder a child? Nahoa felt sick just thinking about it. But *someone* had to be guilty.

"What d'you want, then?" Sabolu said.

"I want to make a geas. Something that will hurt a person without them knowing it."

The smile fell from Sabolu's face as fast as a ripe coconut. "What would I know about any of that? I look like a witch?"

Not really, Nahoa thought. But she said, "I just hear that you know people. The sort who might be able to find me a geas."

Sabolu hugged her elbows and looked around the deserted stables. "I might. But those things are dangerous, lady. You don't have enough trouble with that old hag? She knows about geas, too."

Nahoa was glad she hadn't brought Ahi. Sabolu's fear was infecting her—she checked the stables again and nearly jumped when a mouse scurried into a corner. "Not Makaho," Nahoa said. "Someone else."

She felt as though her heartbeat was loud enough to echo off the walls by the time Sabolu spoke again. "I can't...I don't work with geas no more. Why don't you ask the black angel? Word is she knows all about them."

Nahoa swallowed. Careful, now. "Where is the black angel, though?"

Sabolu seemed relieved, as though this were more comfortable territory. "With the rebels. I ain't seen her there, but that's where her papa said she went."

Sabolu clammed up after that, as though her relief had let her say too much, but Nahoa didn't mind. She was eager to leave anyway. Sabolu had done something wrong with a geas, and she didn't want to think that this eager girl had done anything to her daughter. But who else could it have been? Sabolu had warned her about Makaho, warned her about the geas, but then she'd also implied that she'd been in rebel territory. What business could even a precocious girl like Sabolu have west of Sea Street? Everything seemed to be leading her back to either Makaho or the rebels, but she couldn't believe that any of them would want to hurt Ahi. So perhaps that left a mysterious third party.

She sighed and took a long walk in the gardens before going back to her apartments.

She heard Ahi's squeals and giggles long before she slid open the door. She expected to see Malie, but there was someone else in the room. He was lying on the floor holding Ahi high above his head. One would think the child had never been so happy in her life.

"Oh what, sweet one? Should I put you down? Or should I tickle you...here!"

Ahi squealed again, and Nahoa felt something warm spreading from her stomach to her tender breasts, to her neck and cheeks and ears until she was overflowing with it.

"She loves you," Nahoa said, surprising herself.

Pano gently put Ahi down and let her play with one of his large, rough fingers. "I think this little one loves life."

Nahoa didn't argue. She didn't want to lose that sense of profound happiness she felt when she looked at the two of them. Malie was seated by the door, reading a book, but Nahoa could tell she wasn't paying it much attention.

"Is it safe?" Nahoa asked her. She didn't remember seeing anyone in the hallway on her way here.

"As safe as it may be. I hope that one knows enough to be careful."

Pano grimaced. "Malie seems to think it is impossible for a gardener to also be endowed with good sense."

Malie snapped her book shut. "Not when that gardener is fool enough to think he can win a war against the Mo'i himself."

"It doesn't matter what I think we can win. Eliki thinks we'll lose, and soon, without access to a harbor. And she might be right."

"If you're going to lose either way, then surely you're better off not killing so many in a pointless war first!"

Pano considered this carefully, but Nahoa felt as though her words had hurt him. "Do you think," he said finally, "that Bloody One-hand will let us off so easily if we surrender?"

Malie blanched and looked down. Nahoa rushed over to hold Ahi and remembered, though she wished she didn't, what the two guardians had said about her husband in their meeting the other day.

"If you're going to fight a war," Nahoa said, her voice a little thick but otherwise steady. "You might want these."

She undid the top buttons of her shirt and handed the plans, now slightly damp, to Pano. His gaze was blank and distant as he took them. He seemed exhausted. The preparations for this new battle had to be taking their toll on him. He looked at the plans for so long that Ahi fell asleep. His expression was one of wonder, tempered by bitter resignation. She realized with a flash that she had just guaranteed the war that he didn't want to fight.

"How did you find these, Nahoa?" It was the first time he had addressed her as an equal, by her name. It gave her enough courage to tell him what she had done.

"Eliki will be pleased," he said, when she finished. "You might have just saved our lives."

But many would die, she understood. She'd never seen a war— no one alive on the islands had—but she remembered that much from the stories.

"Why did you come here, Pano?" she asked, and then wished she hadn't because he suddenly seemed so worn down and sad.

"I thought that you might speak to your husband again. Ask him to do the right thing."

What right thing? Nahoa thought frantically. Kill himself? Had the two guardians told the rebels of their solution? But Pano was continuing, "Tell his troops to stand down. Promise to stop the secret detentions. Give those imprisoned a fair trial. Work with us to help the victims."

Nahoa's expression must have been wild, because Pano took her by her shoulders and made her meet his eyes. "It's okay if you're too afraid. He's unpredictable."

Of course he is, Nahoa thought. *Two of the spirit guardians told him he'd be better off dead!* But she knew that Kohaku had been unstable long before that. "I'll speak to him," she said. "He won't listen to me, but I'll try."

He rolled up the plans and slipped them in the band of his trousers. "If you need to reach me, ask the young one in your stables. She can get into our camp with a message."

Nahoa was momentarily speechless. "She's working for you?"

Pano laughed. "Among others, I imagine. The child has a head for business."

After he left, Malie gave her a speaking look and went off to find their dinner. Nahoa stroked Ahi's head and wondered at the anatomy of betrayal. It wasn't Pano. She wouldn't believe it. She'd believe Kohaku before Pano. And so that left Makaho, who had so much to lose by the death of this child that Nahoa thought she must either be insane, or playing a game that none of them could guess at.

There would be war. Lana would have guessed this from the quiet, determined industriousness that had engulfed the rebel camp in just the one day since Pano had returned from visiting Nahoa. But she heard more than she'd ever wanted from Eliki and Pano about the battle plans and strategy for pushing rebel territory north to the old piers. Kai helped them. He said that if there was going to be a battle, it should be done cleanly. Lana wasn't so sure. She thought that they should try harder to negotiate with Kohaku, no matter how fruitless it seemed. Surely anything was better than further destabilizing the spirit bindings?

But sometimes Lana thought that Eliki didn't believe in any spirits at all. To her, the only harm was political. The only solution was violence. Or, at least, violence was the primary option. Lana kept to the room Eliki had given her, for the whole of the first district had dedicated itself to making as many of the coveted bows and arrows as they could. Thanks to Nahoa's ingenuity. Lana wondered what it must have taken for her to break with her husband like that, to give his mortal enemies his most deadly secret. Kohaku had become notoriously cruel—she wondered how much of that cruelty Nahoa had witnessed firsthand.

The main hall of the rebel camp was now filled with ten or so soldiers, sanding down boughs of wood and fitting sharp triangles of alloyed copper onto notched hafts. Eliki and Pano spent a great deal of time huddled close to the fire, poring over maps and reports from their soldiers and spies, which came in at odd intervals. Late one evening, when Pano was out on one of his long errands, Lana even spotted Sabolu receiving whispered instructions from Eliki. Sabolu's eyes widened when she saw Lana observing her and she nearly fell on her face as she stumbled out the door.

Lana frowned and squatted by the fire. Her hands always felt frozen these days, so she held them up as close to the licking flames as she dared. "I hope you're not putting that one into danger," Lana said quietly to Eliki.

The rebel leader's cool, pink-eyed stare was unnerving. She managed to convey contempt without so much as a flicker in her expression. "And what makes you think I can choose that for her?"

"She's young. Too young to understand what might happen if she gets caught."

Eliki tilted her head and blew a derisive puff of air, as though she couldn't be bothered to laugh. "Oh, you're suddenly so concerned for her welfare? You paid the child to spy for you, too. She knows Makaho better than either of us. I think she understands precisely what she's risking."

Lana thought of the startled fear in Sabolu's eyes and wondered if Eliki might not be right. But still... "You're about to start a war," she said.

Eliki frowned; on her normally smooth and controlled features, it had the force of a snarl. "This has always been a war, black angel. Do not mistake that."

"And if you lose it?"

"Then I imagine the spirits whose disposition so concerns you will make all of our lives so miserable that Sabolu will have far greater problems."

Lana sighed, outmaneuvered but still uneasy. "Isn't there some third way? Something other than all this?" She gestured to the room, where one rebel soldier was testing the fit of an arrow into a newly made bow. It made her back ache just to look at it.

"Like what? Going to Bloody One-hand and hoping he won't massacre us all for believing we should have better governance?"

"Don't put it so—"

"Intelligently?"

"Like one of your damn pamphlets! Not everything stands or falls on principles. There are people—not just your rebel soldiers, but regular struggling people—who will die when you fight your way north."

"We're issuing a call for all in the area to leave or join us here."

"And you think everyone will? What about the old, the sick, the injured? Imagine them stuck in their half-burned homes, wondering if it will be the rebels' or Kohaku's arrows that kill them?"

Eliki's mouth thinned. Suddenly, her eyes seemed not so much pink as red, reflecting the fire. "We do what we must. There are no perfect solutions."

"You're playing with people's lives, as though they don't matter."

"We're saving them. Or have you forgotten why those people are sick and injured? Why their homes are half burned? Why there is no one in this city who hasn't lost someone they love to a painful, fiery death?" Lana's throat felt very dry. "So you'll become as bad as him to stop him?" she asked, though almost immediately she wished she hadn't.

Eliki leaned back in her chair; fire extinguished, suddenly exhausted. "If you're as naive as all that, then I don't know why you're here. Go back to your father. Help him tend the injured in One-hand's hospitals. Congratulate yourself on your benevolent good works. But leave us be, for we have work to do."

So Lana stood and left her, angry and wounded and inexplicably ashamed.

It was difficult to entice the head nun out of her temple, but Kohaku had done so that afternoon, much to Makaho's thinly veiled displeasure. The ash clouds filtered the sun into perpetual twilight, turning the winter air chill enough that even Makaho had deigned to drape her pendulous breasts in a swath of austere black barkcloth secured with a rope. Even so, her hands were red and chapped with cold. Kohaku ordered a tea service brought for them before she could object. The fire temple might be one of the most luxurious dwellings in Essel, but the head nun lived as simply as an outer island officiant. Kohaku had never seen any evidence that Makaho harbored the slightest religious conviction, and yet he had to admit that she held herself detached, as though all of these mundane politics in which she so forcefully engaged were only an ugly means to a higher purpose. She accumulated power and wealth like an urchin does a stench, and yet she seemed to use none of it for personal gain. She flaunted her ascetism and used it to her advantage. Kohaku sipped his tea and watched as Makaho leaned closer to the fire. What hair she had left was wiry, gray, and close-cropped. Her eyes were a small, hard brown and her skin was dark for an Esselan and liberally marked with old burns.

"Am I particularly beautiful today, Mo'i?" she asked, her thin lips twisting into habitual scorn.

Kohaku looked down quickly at his tea and grimaced. "Much the same as always," he said.

Makaho laughed. "Ah, neatly done. But I assume you did not call me here to admire my looks."

Kohaku stood abruptly, agitated as he had been for the last several days. "Of course not," he said, and was surprised to hear what sounded like a snarl.

"You could have come to the temple," Makaho said, unfazed. "It raises fewer questions."

He stared at her for a moment and then began to pace. "Your temple has leaks," he said, and was pleased that the effort to keep his voice steady had largely succeeded.

This didn't surprise her. "It's a large facility. As is the Mo'i's house. Nothing of importance has escaped."

Nothing? He wondered bleakly. Yet how long before he saw this headline in those damned rebel pamphlets: *Bloody One-hand can save the city—his self-sacrifice will put Nui'ahi to rest.* Kaleakai, the water guardian, was still walking free and helping the rebels. It had been five days since the two guardians had confronted him in the temple. If the public heard what they had said, Kohaku wondered if any army would be large enough to protect him then.

"Every day he stays free you're in greater danger," Emea said, appearing beside Makaho.

Kohaku ignored her. If he was insane, he couldn't afford to let anyone know it, especially not a ruthless player like the head nun.

"You know what you have to do," said his sister.

He glared at her, realized what he had done, and quickly shifted his gaze to Makaho. "I know what we must do," he said.

She inclined her head. "And what is that, Mo'i?"

"Lay a trap for him."

She tilted her head in polite confusion. "Who?"

Too late, Kohaku realized that he had been continuing his conversation with Emea. "The water guardian. Kaleakai," he said.

"I didn't realize he had become an ongoing concern. I take it your meeting didn't go well?"

Kohaku resisted the urge to scream. "He's a threat to the stability of my government. There's no other way. Something with a geas, but a trap, otherwise no one will be strong enough to overpower him. Do you know a witch we can trust enough for this?"

Makaho put down her tea. "Are you suggesting we kill the water guardian through treachery, Kohaku?"

Her tone was remarkably flat. She could have been asking him if he preferred amant or palm wine for all of her apparent interest in the answer. One could be lulled by her pretense of disinterest, but he had learned caution.

"No, I'm suggesting we capture him through treachery. He knows too much. I hear he's helping the rebels—"

"He's the black angel's lover, and *she's* helping the rebels."

That bit him more than it should have. "So then he's a danger," Makaho tilted her head slightly, a gesture that might have been appealing on a younger, beautiful woman but on her looked merely sinister. "So they both are. You've already tried to kill her once."

She'd heard about that? But better not to show his surprise. "He's more important. If we capture him, we'll have leverage over the rebels. Especially if he's with Lana."

"I see," she said, and he realized that she must have guessed some of it. But it didn't matter—she knew better than most how Kohaku's secrets drove him. He just needed to prevent her from knowing the details.

"I have some familiarity with geas," she said. "Nothing that could harm him in a direct confrontation, but a clever trap I think I could manage."

This surprised him. "I've never seen you lay a geas before."

She shrugged. "I prefer to leave the fire spirit to its business. There are still those, you know, who don't feel the spirit bindings were an entirely wise decision."

Kohaku could only stare. Makaho, the head of the largest monument to the spirits in all of Essel, had sympathies with the napulo fringe movement?

"Like the barbarians who live on the wind island?"

Makaho smiled with bloodless lips. "Like them. Like a few other, more civilized people. The spirits were bound by people, Kohaku. They can be unbound."

"With such marvelous results," he said, gesturing west without thinking.

"And to think, the napulo disciples have made you a hero."

The irony resonated a second later and he flushed. Of course. Who else would a representative of the fire spirit, a sympathizer with the anti–spirit-binding napulo, align herself with than the one who had helped weaken that very spirit's bonds?

"See, brother? You did a good thing. The times are changing."

Kohaku turned on his heel so he could avoid Emea's blue flame eyes. Everything had gone wrong since the fire spirit's temple, hadn't it? And no matter how he tried to smother the flames, ever more kept leaping up around him.

"So you'll help me with this?" he said, still turned away from her.

"When have I refused you, Mo'i?"

Indeed. Such was the nature of her hold over him, the nature of his utter dependence. "I heard my daughter was ill," he said. Around Makaho he didn't bother to mask the pain that entered his voice whenever he mentioned Nahoa or Lei'ahi. She knew so much that any subterfuge would be vanity.

"Yes," she said. There was a strange note in her voice—almost tentative—that made him turn around. She wouldn't meet his eyes. "It was very bad. I don't know what you heard."

He felt as though he'd been punched in the gut. He sank less than gracefully into his seat and took a long pull of his bitter, lukewarm tea.

"You should have sent for me."

"She wouldn't have let you in. You know that."

He supposed he did. "But there was no reason not to tell me after. Not unless you suspected something." He paused. "Something much worse than a leak."

Makaho placed her hands primly in her lap, but he knew he had finally hit upon something that disturbed her. "I have no evidence it was anything other than a natural illness. She's quite recovered. Children sicken all the time."

"But you suspect, don't you?"

"I have no evidence."

"Oh, since when do you need evidence, Makaho? I thought you could smell deception."

"You give me too much credit."

Kohaku leaned forward and lowered his voice. "I think I give you just enough. You know precisely how much you're worth to me if you can't guarantee the safety of my wife and daughter. Do we understand each other?"

Makaho's eyes were furious, but her voice was calm enough. "As always. I will protect them with my life."

"And you will tell me when you discover who is responsible?"

Makaho stood with a little less grace than normal and walked to the entrance. "Of course. I have business to attend to. You will hear from me when I have the ones you want."

He let her go and waited until he was quite sure he was alone before putting his head in his hand and letting out a long moan.

"Don't be so sad, brother."

Kohaku's teacup smashed against the wall.

· 11 ·

KAI SUGGESTED THAT LANA TRY A SCRYING on Makaho, but she encountered fragments of trivial conversations and vertiginous maelstroms through which no sane mind could pass. In other words, the predictable confusion generated by someone who knew how to manipulate spirits. She pulled back. It was naive to expect the head nun of the fire temple to be vulnerable to such a simple attack. So she took out the old postulate book and flipped through the pages for fire that she hadn't yet memorized. The dry list of postulates, "fire sucks life from air," "fire blows a killing wind," "the hottest flame is the one you can't see," made her eyes glaze over and her jaw crack before she was even halfway through. It was one thing to read through the death postulates; her sense of self-preservation, at least, kept her engaged. But fire, of the three bound spirits, had always seemed the least relevant to her life. She brushed some of the ash off of the pages and watched it sink onto the bed covers. Until now, she reflected, and applied herself with renewed focus. After an hour, however, she still hadn't found anything that seemed like a sound base for a geas to use on Makaho.

Her gaze caught on the black book, sandwiched between the bed and Kai's small stack of belongings. She almost picked it up to start reading again, but she resisted the temptation. She didn't believe Kai's theory that Ino had deliberately given her the black book to distract her. But still, it didn't hurt to have a reminder that she had more pressing goals. She spread her wings and lay down in a jumble of feathers on her pallet. The postulate book was a heavy, almost reassuring pressure on her chest. If she wanted to get around Makaho's defenses, she needed to be clever. What would Aoi do in this situation?

"Probably just find the nearest fire spirit and make it talk," she muttered. And then, "Damn." If her friendship with Ino had taught her anything, it should have reminded her that spirits are independent, intelligent agents with their own desires. She had joked to Akua once that Ino let her scry without a sacrifice because she'd given him her friendship. She would probably never befriend a fire spirit, but that was no reason why she couldn't compel one to tell her what it knew.

Excited, she flexed her wings and plucked out a small feather.

"A small flame may be devoured by a larger one, but it may also last much longer," she said. "I bind a spurt of flame. One that has watched the conflagrations of its masters."

She felt the power in the room, the anticipatory silence. But she realized that she had no extra way of seeing whatever spirit she had summoned.

"I bind you to speak to me," she added.

"The great fire isn't my master," said a disembodied voice from somewhere near her sandal. If she squinted, she thought she could just barely make out a distorted flicker by the floor, a heat shimmer and a lick from an angry flame.

"But the great fires can devour you," Lana said.

"So you call the shark your master?"

"Point taken."

"This is a strange binding, black angel."

"I want you to tell me all you know of Makaho," she said.

"We don't pay much heed to human politics."

Lana had to roll her eyes. "Only enough to manipulate a human into weakening your binding."

"That's the great fire. I'm just a lowly flame."

"You must at least know of the geas she uses. How does she bind you?"

"She binds us to serve her purposes."

Lana had a distinct urge to kick the flame. "*What* purposes?"

"We help the Ana. We lift bindings from one to put them on another. We see the Mo'i. We offer help to those who would release the foul binding."

Lana felt her breath stick in her throat. Release the foul binding? She knew where she'd heard language like that before. When she'd made the sacrifice to the wild wind that had made her a black angel, she'd requested aid from the lost wind tribes. And one of their number, a boy named Yechtak, had led her to the ruins and told her of his life without binding. His people called hers "binders" and thought what they had done was evil, much like the napulo did. And if she understood what the sprite was saying...

"*Makaho* is a napulo? She's against the spirit bindings?"

"I know nothing of your human allegiances."

Lana rather doubted this, but she let it go. This explained a great deal, after all. Her alliance with Kohaku. And this mysterious Ana—Lana wondered if, finally, she'd begun to glimpse the shape of Akua's inscrutable game. Could *Akua* want to release the great death spirit?

"And the Ana you help. Does she have one arm?"

She felt a warmth on her foot and the flame made a sound like fire crackling through kindling. Laughter? "She has spoken of you, as well."

"Where is she? Does she have another woman with her?"

"I cannot say. She does not bind us."

"No," Lana said slowly. "No, she wouldn't. Akua has always been death's creature, hasn't she?"

The sprite didn't answer her directly but said, "Death has its own plans, black angel. And Makaho lays her traps."

She squatted down on impulse. For a flickering moment, her vision of the true world dimmed and she had an impression of a tiny bird, like a starling, with wings of red flame. Then the fragile binding snapped and she was alone.

"What traps?" she said softly, to the empty room. So many schemes, and such a shadowed path through them.

Makaho schemed to break the fire spirit's binding. And if she was helping Akua—the most powerful Ana in the islands, after all, and one who had a disturbing affinity with death—then that must mean that the death spirit wasn't far behind. Hadn't Kai himself told her of his fears about the death spirit's instability? They had all thought that, in the end, it was fire that had succeeded in partially breaking free. But what if it were both? What if the eruption of Nui'ahi were both a goal and a feint, a way for one spirit to distract from the other's plots?

What if the death spirit were about to break free, and Akua had pledged herself to the task? She had bound Lana to something on that long-ago day in the small death shrine on her lake. She had made Lana a party to some aspect of her pact with the death. And then Lana had entered into another agreement of her own free will in order to save her mother's life. If Akua was manipulating everyone to help free the death spirit, then she was using Lana and her mother as her primary tools.

Shaking and furious, Lana sprinted down the stairs and out through the doors, ignoring the startled craftsmen busy in the main room. The air outside was empty of any specters.

"Death!" Lana yelled, her voice cracking. A few walking past gave her a sharp look and then hurried on. She scared them. She didn't care.

"Avatar!" she yelled again. "Show yourself!"

It appeared like a blink before her, serene and mildly curious. "Yes, Lana?" it said.

She could not get much closer without walking through it, but she leaned in so it could get the cleanest impression of her fury.

"I won't let her free you," she said, her voice shaking. "I'll keep you bound, I swear it."

Just the thought of the destruction that would follow in the wake of its release made her dizzy. Would anyone survive it?

"And your mother? Will you kill her for the sake of an unnatural binding?"

Lana opened her mouth and then closed it. To her shame, she couldn't answer, so she looked away—anywhere but that horribly familiar, placid mask—and saw something astonishing:

Large white flakes, like bleached chunks of ash or coconut shavings, falling from the cloudy, white-glow sky. She put out her hand. The chunks melted like ice on her skin and settled in the folds of her shirt. They caressed the edge of the death's robe, as though wondering whether to acknowledge its existence, before resting on the ground beneath it.

All around her, rebel soldiers and runners and ordinary people were stopping to stare. One young girl tilted her head back and opened her mouth wide. Lana licked her hand, where several of the flakes had melted. Water. Pure water.

Sky ice? "What is this?" she said to no one in particular.

"Snow," said a frustratingly familiar voice. Eliki had returned while she had been arguing with the death. Lana thought she would act dismissive of the wonder falling out of the sky, but she looked around with as much surprise as the rest of them. A smile surprisingly devoid of irony or derision tugged at the corners of her mouth.

"I saw snow once," she said. "When my daughter was born. It wasn't as much as this, but I saw the ice fall out of the sky."

"In Essel?" Lana asked, despite herself.

"No," Eliki said, her pale eyes still warm and distant with memory, "A small fishing community, but not much nearer the inner islands than here. They saw snow every few years, but we left soon after."

Lana looked at Eliki and tried to imagine it: a young mother, because Eliki for all her strangeness and ferocity could not be very old, living on a backwater island probably much like Lana's own. Her daughter would die far too young, but Eliki wouldn't have known that. Could she fish? Had she even dived beneath those frigid waves to bring up seaweed and clams and other treasures far more mundane than the mandagah jewels of Lana's youth?

Eliki caught Lana's stare and laughed softly. She brushed Lana's shoulder, releasing a powdery spray that blew away in the wind. "You look at me and what do you see? A spirit? A monster? We're all human, black angel."

And what did that mean? Humans *bound*—each other, spirits, it didn't matter, so long as something could be bent and manipulated. Lana did it as much as anyone else. She tried to imagine the life of the mandagah, solitary and unencumbered by all but the most basic needs. Impossible. She would have to cease to breathe before she ceased to bind.

"And isn't that the horror?" Lana said softly. Eliki raised her eyebrows, but before she could say anything a soldier ran forward, slipping on the ice-slick ground and breathing harshly. He shouted Eliki's name once and then fell to his knees.

An arrow, fletched with partridge feathers, protruded from his back. Lana blinked. People were shouting—pounding footsteps through the now-cursed snow, a distant scream. And the snow, falling like a thick, implacable blanket from the sky, muffled sound and isolated the horror that was all too clear before her. Eliki knelt, holding the gasping soldier up long enough for him to speak his news. His words were perfectly intelligible, and yet Lana found herself straining for their meaning: barricades breached and fires in the streets. Fighting, that she understood, and death. She turned to where the death still stood.

"Don't you have somewhere to be?" she whispered.

"Reaping my bleak harvest? Not just yet."

No, she thought frantically, perhaps not. Perhaps Akua wouldn't even have to go through the trouble of freeing the death spirit. Perhaps this war would destabilize the millennia-old bonds perfectly well on its own.

"Lana!"

Eliki's voice, sharp and urgent, dragged Lana back to the moment. She stared at the tableau of the too-pale rebel leader gripping the sagging body of a wounded soldier and thought, *it has come. Nothing I can do will stop this.*

Her legs were stiff with cold, but they ran quickly enough. "What should I do?" she asked.

Eliki was gracious enough not to do more than nod. "They've attacked Sea Street. Bloody One-hand must have gotten wind of our plans. He's trying to hem us in here before we can even think of pressing north."

But Lana didn't see resignation in Eliki's fierce smile. "But you're still going to try for the harbor?"

"He doesn't know we have bows. Pano can keep him tied up for days at Sea Street while our archers pick them off. Even Bloody One-hand doesn't have enough soldiers to besiege all of our borders. This might well work to our advantage after all. Take this one to the infirmary. And if you've overcome your squeamishness? Find Pano. I think he can use those wings to our advantage, black angel."

Lana nodded briefly and hauled the befuddled soldier to his feet as gently as possible, while Eliki sprinted away through a swirl of snow that swallowed her quickly.

"Can you walk a little?" Lana asked the soldier. He grunted and coughed a spray of blood, but he moved forward.

"Do you like the snow, Lana?" the death said, when she had finally gotten help for the now-insensate soldier.

Lana looked down at her hands, covered in icy water and blood. "It makes the world look clean."

The death seemed to consider this. "I won't take him," it said, and Lana knew it meant the soldier, so gravely wounded. "Not just yet."

It seemed to vanish in the snow, in the white swirl of the wind, and Lana realized her teeth were chattering hard enough to make her jaw ache. Her socks had long since soaked through with melting ice. She wondered if she should find a pair of covered shoes to borrow, but she didn't even know who owned a pair. Perhaps she could ask Kai to use a geas to dry her, but she doubted she could find him in this confusion. And in any case, he would need all of his strength for the war. She felt a momentary stirring of panic for him, and then quashed it. If anyone could keep safe in this mess, it would be Kai.

It was unfair to have to fight a war in this snow, this quiet miracle. But she would fight it. Just as everyone else here would. All of her other choices were so much worse. She ran to Sea Street for warmth and as a distraction from her terror. Hundreds of people hurried past the fortified barrier, heading north to Eliki and the sixth district border. A lone two dozen stayed behind here, huddled behind the barricades cobbled out of dismantled houses and fresh bamboo, aiming and shooting through narrow slits.

Those who saw her coming through the blinding snow gasped or cursed and stepped aside. It wouldn't be a very good omen to see a black angel during a war. She must look to them like a specter of death. No matter that she could tell them in precise detail how wrong their image of death must be.

She found Pano easily enough. He was behind the tallest barricades, shooting with seven other archers at the heart of the Mo'i's force.

"Pick off the ones who get too close, but don't waste arrows!" Pano shouted, before readying his own bow for another shot.

"It's a mess!" one of the archers, an older woman, yelled back. "Can't hardly make out anyone."

"Just make sure they're not ours and shoot," Pano said, with the air of a man who is thoroughly acquainted with an intractable problem.

She grumbled, but let loose another arrow that must have hit its mark, judging by her sudden, feral grin.

A nearby man let off a shot and cursed volubly as the bow cracked in his hand. Pano silently handed the man his own weapon.

"I'm sorry," the man stammered, "I didn't think I pulled back too hard—"

Pano just shook his head. "Just keep shooting and be more careful. If we fail here, everything is lost."

He finally saw Lana, standing in dumb silence before him.

"Black angel?" he said, a mild, weary query. "Are you looking for Kai?"

Lana shook her head and swallowed. "Eliki told me to find you."

"Is she—"

"No," Lana said quickly, to relieve Pano's panic. "No, she's fine. But she said you could find a use for my wings."

"Ah," Pano said. His smile was so pleased and reassuring Lana found it impossible to regret her decision. If there had to be war, she was glad to be on his side.

He directed her to fly over all the borders of the rebel territory, to see if the Mo'i had redirected any troops for stealth attacks and to relay any messages from the skeleton forces. And then, she was to fly to Eliki herself and relay any messages back to Pano.

It was exhilarating, even given the wet wind and lingering ache in her left wing. Her heavy wing strokes flicked off most of the moisture, and she became grateful for the obscuring snow, because it protected her from arrows. On the other hand, that also made her own visibility frustratingly poor, and she had to land at a central point on each of the borders just to see anything useful. The respites served a good purpose—her flying muscles weren't nearly as strong as they could be, and the air was so cold up high that she wondered if she would ever feel her toes and fingers again. The soldiers gave her blankets and access to their carefully tended fires until she was thawed enough to fly off again. Both the southern and northwestern borders were surprisingly quiet, given that a war was being fought in the northeast. Lana meant to ask Eliki for replacements of two of the archers' bows, which had cracked in half.

Lana took to the north almost eagerly, in the tense hope that at last, one way or another, Essel would know who ruled it. And if they were lucky, the rebels would win and avoid the level of bloodshed that might cause lasting damage to the bindings.

But all such hopeful thoughts were eradicated when she finally found the rebels battling north through the sixth district. They had covered a surprising amount of territory, she thought, given the brief time that had passed since the battle began. Nearly a quarter of the way to the old harbor already. But an updraft nearly sent her tumbling out of the sky when she flew overhead. As she approached the earth, she grew aware of the oppressive heat and choking smoke. It took her longer than it should have to realize what was happening. After all, Kohaku had always been remarkably intelligent, whether investigating the customs of a backwater outer island or waging war in the world's largest city.

The rebels were gaining territory. But every inch Kohaku had to cede, he burned to the ground.

The strategy would have been even more dangerous, she supposed, if it weren't for the snow that quickly banked the fires before they could spread. A small blessing. She could see people frantically fleeing into the rebel lines. To Eliki's credit, the soldiers let anyone who looked like a civilian through. But the careful rows of charred and blackened buildings told their own story. Even if the rebels won this battle, would it be worth the cost? Several thousand more hungry mouths to feed, and only the sympathizers in the seventh district able to provide food? And with every shelter and all of their belongings systematically destroyed, how long before the sixth district started blaming the rebels for the destruction they'd allowed to happen?

Lana rushed to find Eliki as soon as she landed. The rebel leader had called a temporary halt to their forward march. A wise strategy, Lana thought, but the only one she could reasonably pursue at this moment. Eliki was giving terse instructions to two small runners when she saw Lana approaching.

"Well," Eliki said sourly. Her face was nearly black with ash and her clothes soaked through. Lana wondered how she wasn't shivering or ill, but the war apparently agreed with her. She looked fierce and beautiful, for all her disconcerting paleness. "Your friend was born in the wrong age. He's ruthless enough for the Maaram, isn't he? He'd burn down the whole city just to save it."

"What will you do?"

Eliki shrugged. "Wait. Pretend that we're considering his patently fake truce. They won't want to fight at night, not in this weather. By that time everyone should have had time to flee." She paused and regarded Lana. "Might the spirits help? Lipa, the apothecary, said there's not much your witchery can do for us, but perhaps you'd know better."

Lana was surprised. "A geas? To fight a war? Eliki, the sacrifices I'd need in order to make even a bit of difference..."

She shook her head. "Lipa said as much. I understand now why there are so few witches. So much sacrifice for so little return."

Lana was inclined to agree with her, but she still had to smile. "And waging a rebellion in the heart of Essel?"

"Perfectly reasonable, of course." Eliki looked back out at the blackened remains of the sixth district houses. What fires still burned were even now being doused in a blanketing white. "If we're lucky, maybe the snow will make the houses so wet that he won't be able to burn them down even if he tried."

"And if the snow stops?"

She looked away. "There's nowhere we can go but forward."

Lana understood now how self-righteous she had been in their previous arguments, as though Eliki didn't precisely grasp the moral consequences of her actions, as though they didn't matter to her. They mattered very much. But there are sometimes only bad choices. If Eliki surrendered now, Kohaku would ruthlessly decimate the rebel forces. If she pressed on, Kohaku might turn the entire sixth district into a funeral pyre. She had nowhere to go but forward.

So Lana simply asked, "Do you have a message for Pano?"

"You can tell him what you've seen. He'll understand."

Lana nodded and gathered her tired muscles for one last flight.

"Oh, and ask him for more bows. My archers are clumsy with the shafts."

An amorphous worry nagged at Lana for a moment, but Eliki was soon distracted with further preparations and she shrugged it off. Pano took her news about the sixth district as calmly as he took everything, but she could tell that he was shaken. The bows here were not holding up much better than they were anywhere else. And Kohaku's tactics horrified her.

"I can't believe he's doing this," she said, shivering beneath the blanket that Pano had draped over her shoulders when she landed.

"He's very smart, Bloody One-hand. But you ought to know that." Pano flashed her a wry smile and checked again on the Mo'i soldiers. They had gathered warily just beyond the range of rebel arrows, waiting on a signal from Kohaku. And all around them the impossible snow continued to fall, thicker and even more implacable than ashfall. The wind blew it up into great dunes against the bulk of the fortifications and the burned-out buildings nearby.

Lana looked up at the uniform sky, curiously bright despite the twilight gloom. The few torches mounted on the wall at irregular intervals reflected orange in the falling snow. She was reminded of Kai. She hadn't seen him all day, but she knew he had been with Eliki for much of the battle.

"It doesn't look like it's going to stop, does it?" she asked.

"The war?"

"The snow. Eliki said the more snow we get, the better chance we have of winning."

"Well, at least it means that One-hand can't burn down half the city in spite. But it's just as hard for us to move on slick ground covered in knee-high ice as it is for them."

Since the snow and dark had effectively ended the fighting for the day, Pano accompanied Lana back to the northern front. Eliki was encamped under a tent just barely warmer than the outside air and in danger of collapsing under the heavy white drifts piled on top of the oilcloth. The soldiers here were an even more motley assortment than Lana was used to seeing around rebel territory. Women and men and some children who couldn't have been older than thirteen sat huddled around fires and in abandoned buildings, attempting to wait out the night and the snow. They wore no uniforms and carried makeshift weapons—indeed, this was the only characteristic that clearly distinguished them from Kohaku's soldiers, who were equipped with blades whose only purpose had ever been to kill. The rebel soldiers, such as they were, fought mostly with adzes and kitchen knives and makeshift spears. They guarded their skin with clothing padded with packed straw in the worst case, and haphazard greaves of bamboo in the best. They were not suited for fighting, nor practiced at it, but they had determined to do so anyway. Lana wondered at that. Up until the unexpected start of this war, refugees had steadily streamed into the rebel encampment. Why couldn't they be like her father and accept the brutalities of Kohaku's regime? Perhaps they had just been affected by it too directly.

The little remaining food from the stores had been passed out among the soldiers. The sight of even those meager meals made Lana's stomach rumble. Inside the tent, Eliki was writing a letter and ignoring the plate of food sitting on the table. She looked up sharply when the two of them came in and frowned.

"Sea Street—"

"Safe. It's the snow. I've never seen anything like it."

Eliki's smile was small, but satisfied. "I doubt you ever will again. It was a bright day when you brought the water guardian to us, Lana."

There was something so specific in her pleasure that Lana knew Kai had done something for them. "Where is he?" she asked.

Eliki waved her hand as though this hardly mattered. "He said he needed to get to the ocean, so I gave him a cloak to hide that hair of his. He should be back soon."

"The ocean?" Lana repeated. She remembered when they had lived together at the water shrine, how he would sometimes spend days among the water sprites, almost entirely losing that part of him that was human. She knew that he needed that sometimes, but to go to the ocean in this weather in the middle of a battle. It could only mean that he had been working some sort of powerful, draining geas. "What did you have him do?"

"You were just walking through it," Eliki said.

At this, even Pano was shocked. "The water guardian caused the snow?"

"Not at first. But he has persuaded enough water from up off the ocean to keep this snow going for at least two more days."

Lana hugged her elbows, not entirely against the cold. Two more days? He must be exhausted. She hoped he would come back soon. She hadn't seen him since this morning.

Pano pulled up two stools and gave Lana Eliki's untouched plate of food. She started to eat it, numbly, while the two rebel leaders argued about the implications of the weather.

"You know we can't fight as well as One-hand's army, in any case," he said. "If he decides to forge ahead in this snow..."

"He'd be mad to."

"Our Mo'i is not famed for his sanity."

"Well, his soldiers might just refuse. I think he won't risk it. Not while we offer him the chance of armistice."

"And when we renege? Even the water guardian can't make the snow vanish."

"No, perhaps not. But it will be easier for us to push ahead in the snow than it is for One-hand to defend it. And he won't be able to burn down the city."

Pano sighed and dropped his head into his hands. His dark, curly hair seemed to have turned half gray in the last few weeks. Lana wondered how much longer either of them could keep up this pace. "I've asked One-hand's wife to speak with him one more time. Perhaps she can convince him to end this."

Eliki considered Pano and shook her head as though in regret. "You are good to try, no matter how hopeless the errand."

Pano gave a brief, bitter laugh. "I miss orchids. At least they listen to reason."

Kai went to the seventh district, the rushes, because he knew he'd encounter the fewest people there. Even the water guardian reached his limit sometimes—inevitably during the Weeping ceremony, where each water guardian sacrifices his life for his son's power, but sometimes before. His connection to the waterbird of legend gave him access to a vast reservoir of sacrificial power, but even that was tied to his own well-being. He couldn't do something as drastic and extreme as what Eliki had asked of him today—piling enough water vapor into the clouds above Essel to cause the snow storm to continue for two more days—without risking his life.

And so, despite the cold and the snow he himself had caused, and the battle raging in half of the city, Kai needed to find water. He left his clothes on the dunes and walked naked through the snow-piled sand until he reached the foamy surf. The waves were high and ragged, disturbed by the storm and the semi-frequent murmurs of the earth that had occurred ever since the eruption. He was still human, so the frigid water made his skin turn blue and his teeth chatter until his jaw hurt. Then the first wave crashed over him and he dissolved.

It was a relief, after all this time, to give in to that aspect of his nature where his humanity became a memory so distant that it took him whole tide-turns to even remember his name. There were sprites near the shore, just as there were everywhere, but not so many as he would have thought. They regarded him with wary respect; they knew him immediately but had never seen his kind before. Water guardians are well known for their reluctance to venture beyond the waters of their shrine. He drifted on the top of the water like sentient sea foam, confident enough in even this dangerous form to not mind when a whale blasted him apart. He came back together languidly, his separated selves a curiosity. He remembered the first time he had taken this form: Lana had drowned, thanks to that horrible sprite who lived in his grand-mother's well. She hadn't been breathing when he re-formed in the water and dragged her back out. Even now, as far from his human thoughts and emotions as he could travel, he felt a chill shadow of the fear that had gripped him then, and every time since when Lana dealt with the death spirit. One day she would lose. He knew it. She had to know it, too, but she didn't seem to care.

He heard the moonrise like a lover's call, pulling him up toward the sky, pushing him further up the shore. He sighed with the tides, though the moon itself was entirely obscured by snow clouds. Slowly, some measure of his strength returned to him. Sprites of all kinds started to surround him, compelled by his connection to the waterbird and his own bright essence. As the tide came in, he fed on their power. It wasn't an arrangement like a geas, a straightforward binding of power based on sacrifice. This was a far murkier transfer, based on his spirit nature, not his human one. He was strange and powerful and yet like them; he was a creature of the greatest sprite of all and so they honored him for it.

Eventually, Kai realized that he was being swept farther out to sea and took shape again. Not his own, but that of a seal. He wouldn't be able to make powerful geas for several days without additional sacrifices, but at least he wasn't in danger of dissolution. Lana would be worried about him. He pushed through the water, exhilarated by his speed and agility. He had missed this. Soon enough, he washed ashore, fully human again. Now, the cold inevitably whipped at his naked body. He rushed to his pile of clothes, but stopped.

A sprite waited for him. It was fire, in the shape of a pure white horse, with torches for hooves and smudges of black ash for eyes. A silver tether tied awkwardly around its neck explained its clear irritability: it was geas-bound. A gust of wind, spraying Kai with snow and sea foam, reminded him that he had yet to clothe himself.

"You seek me?" Kai said, attempting to keep an eye on the fire sprite as he tied his pants and pulled his shirt over his head.

"She said the guardian swam here. She said you need to come."

Kai remembered Lana, on the front lines of a war. "Who?" he said, carefully.

"The Ana. The witch. The one you've been seeking."

If anything, this made Kai's stomach go even more hollow. Akua? After all this time, why would Akua reveal herself? And why to Kai, not Lana? It made no sense, but he couldn't refuse this fire sprite's summons. How could he face Lana again if he ignored this chance to find her mother? He was drained, true. Akua had sent for him at a time when he was least able to protect himself from her. But still...

"Where is she?" he asked.

"I'm to take you to her."

Kai decided this wasn't any more dangerous than agreeing to see her in the first place, and so he mounted the fire horse. He was not very surprised to pull up in front of the old house that so obsessed Lana.

"You were right, keika," he said softly. She would never let him hear the end of this when he told her. He dismounted the horse and watched as it walked up the stairs and inside, the fire of its hooves never marking the wood. He followed.

He had never seen Akua before, but he knew the face of the woman even now releasing the fire sprite from its bargain. Makaho smiled at him.

"The sprite meant you?" he said. "An Ana?"

"No," Makaho said. "I'm no binder." And Kai understood a few more things.

"Why did you bring me here?"

But the head nun did not answer him. Another voice did, disembodied, emanating from the shadows like the most powerful and terrifying of spirits.

"So I would bind you, water guardian."

He knew her, even before he saw her. Knew her from her power and the dry, private humor and the inexorable neatness of this plan. She would have known, even if no one else did, what had caused this unprecedented storm in Essel. And, knowing that, she would know how drained he was, how incapable of a geas that could effectively defend himself against her. She seemed to step from the shadows, though he knew that she had not been in the room a moment before. Akua. The woman truly responsible for his aunt's death.

"You should give her mother back," he said, having considered and discarded a dozen other defenses.

"Yes, poor Lana. But not quite yet. As the tide may push and pull water with its invisible force, I bind you stay with me until I let you leave, Kaleakai."

Akua was too nuanced a witch to leave a tangible sign of her binding, but he felt it nonetheless, like a noose around his neck. He had never been bound before. No one but this extraordinary, dangerous, terrifying woman would dare treat the water guardian like any other sprite.

Makaho remained seated on the floor, rigid and patently afraid. Kai was distantly amused to see the apparently imperturbable head nun so out of her depth.

"Your people had best learn to fight in the snow," he said to her. "Because we're getting a lot of it."

· 12 ·

NAHOA HELD AHI AGAINST HER chest long after she had stopped drinking. She couldn't bear to relinquish her. Not now, when it was distinctly possible that she might never see her daughter again. The war that had been looming like a thunderhead for the last three months had crashed around them. And Nahoa could no longer avoid the truth: she might be the only one with the power to stop it. No one had as much of a hold over Kohaku; no one else could convince him to stand down. Pano had asked her to speak with him, but that was before the war had begun.

"I don't think just speaking will do the trick, Ahi," she whispered. "You be good, promise? I'll be back soon enough. Your papa won't hurt me, no matter how crazy he's gone. Just be good for Auntie Malie, and I'll be back before you know."

Ahi burped, which Nahoa supposed was reassurance enough. She went to the pallet in the corner of the room and shook Malie gently awake. Her maid shot up immediately, as though someone had screamed.

"What is it? Is Ahi—"

"She's fine. I need you to take her for me."

Malie lifted Ahi and frowned. "Are you going somewhere, my lady?"

"Only to see Kohaku. He came a little while ago."

"Is this for Pano? What he's asking isn't safe."

"What is safe these days? And anyway, it's not for Pano. Or not just for him."

Ahi began to hiccup, and Malie absently held her over her shoulder, rocking to ease her discomfort.

"Nahoa. You're not going to...you can't go back to him."

"If it will stop this war? What right do I have to let all these people die for my own comfort?"

"Kohaku is unpredictable. What if you go back and the war doesn't stop? What if he hurts you?"

Nahoa shook her head. "He won't hurt me." But perhaps she said it with a little too much conviction?

"And what about Ahi?"

"You'll take care of her."

"And what if you die?"

Nahoa had to wipe her eyes, but she didn't waver. "You'll take care of her."

Malie sighed. "I could kill Pano. Truly, I could, for dragging you into this while my back was turned. He knew I'd never approve. That's why he found you alone."

This was news to Nahoa. "I never thought of you as the protective type," she said.

"Someone needs to be."

Ahi had fallen asleep, so Nahoa just kissed the crown of her head and left before Malie could make her change her mind. She knew she had to do this, but that didn't mean she had to be happy about it.

Kohaku had yet to finish his meeting with Makaho. Nahoa waited impatiently outside the secondary fire room, where he and the head nun conversed about their horrifying schemes in absolute privacy. She was too nervous to even want to spy on them. Pano hadn't contacted her since the battle started, and she was sick with worry for him. She had even gone to the stables to find Sabolu, but the girl had been gone on some errand that the other one, Uele'a, had been at a loss to explain.

Finally, frustrated past endurance, Nahoa nodded at the guard standing outside the door and pushed her way inside before he could stop her.

"And the other?" Kohaku was asking.

"I'll let you know as soon as I do. There's nothing definitive just yet."

And then they both noticed her. Kohaku's face lit up in a way that made her stomach clench, but Makaho just frowned. "We were just finishing, my lady. What's your business?"

It was unusual for Makaho to be so short with her, but Nahoa was too agitated to mark it. "I'd like to speak with my husband," she said.

Makaho narrowed her eyes at the both of them and then shrugged. "You may use this room, in that case. I will contact you soon, Mo'i."

The head nun left the fire room and then the two of them were alone. Kohaku looked at her and took a few tentative steps closer. "How is Ahi?" he asked.

"Good. Happy as ever. She can suck on a screwpine wedge for hours."

This seemed to make him miserable, though he still smiled. "I'm glad. Makaho tells me she was sick."

"She's fine now," Nahoa said, made terse by her confusion. Of course Kohaku couldn't be responsible. She felt horrible for even suspecting him.

"Nahoa..." He cleared his throat. "Do you think you might come back. Eventually? I miss you. Both of you."

Great Kai. Nahoa couldn't even speak. She knelt with shin-jarring force on the marble floor and turned her head away from him. She could not cry. Not on top of everything else.

"I'll do it," she said. Her throat was dry—her voice was barely a whisper—but Kohaku still heard her.

"Nahoa? You and Ahi..."

She coughed and forced some strength into her words. "I've got conditions."

He had been about to embrace her, but he stopped now, confused. And perhaps a bit angry.

"Not Ahi. She stays here. Just me. And you have to call off this war. And the disappearances. All of it."

He stared at her for so long she had to fight just to breathe. Her heart pounded so hard it would have woken Ahi. Great Kai, please let this work.

Her husband stood with frightening speed and knocked plates and remnants of food from the table. A flush was livid on his cheeks. "*They're* the ones fighting a war against me! What am I supposed to do? Let them take over the Mo'i's house and start passing laws?"

"Yes! If that's what it takes to end the violence. Haven't you made us suffer enough?"

"Nahoa, you can't, not even you..."

"Everyone knows," she said mercilessly. "It's no secret now. Not with the black angel and the guardians."

That last made Kohaku dash forward and grip her face between his hands with enough force to make her tremble. She wasn't really afraid—not even now—but she had never seen him so furious before. Not with her. "What do you know about the blasted guardians?"

"*Everything!* I know what they said you should do. I think you're a coward for refusing them."

Always afterward, she would wonder what made her say it, when she had never once thought such a thing. Why had she lashed out at him with such cruelty? They stared at each other in shock. He sat back on his heels. His eyes were wet.

"Oh, sister," he said. And again, "Oh."

She had started this, and she would finish it. "My conditions, Kohaku."

"It's too late. I wish you could see that, Nahoa. The war is started. I must finish it. If I could give all this up, I would. But I'm the Mo'i and I have obligations. You wouldn't understand. You're just a sailor."

That hurt, like she supposed he intended it to. "You don't want me back?"

The tears flowed freely down his face. "More than anything."

"But not more than war."

He raised his chin, his face the mask of blind stubbornness she knew so well. "I will win this, Nahoa. And there will be peace in Essel, and you and Ahi will come back to me. I promise."

There was such self-delusion in his gaze, so much fear. She wondered how long he had been out of her reach—if perhaps she should have made this offer sooner.

"Goodbye, Kohaku," she said, and fled the room.

The corridors of the fire temple were eerily silent, given the hell Nahoa knew must be exploding outside. Makaho had agreed to care for some of the wounded in the dilapidated southern half of the complex, but the casualties so far had not been half as large as they'd all feared. Nahoa understood why when she looked outside: the snow that she had marked as a curiosity a few hours prior had turned into an awesome white blanket, falling over the charred city and softening its hard edges. She had only ever seen snow on her trips as a sailor to the inner islands, and even then, nothing like this. A true inner-island winter made it far too dangerous to sail, though she had heard from those who lived there of these piles of frozen water. It looked like a spirit-borne ashfall to Nahoa, something entirely otherworldly. She huddled, chilled, before the clear glass windows overlooking some of the better-kept gardens and pagodas. The snow obscured all but the tallest plants and weighed down the trees, but it melted before it reached the steaming hot springs. She knew the pools were much too hot for bathing, but they still looked inviting against the backdrop of so much cold.

This snow had to have stopped the fighting for now. Perhaps it could stop it forever? Or perhaps Kohaku, better equipped and far more ruthless, would merely wait for the rebels to starve and freeze to death before going in and killing the rest of them. Perhaps Pano would get a special, public execution to honor the occasion.

She shuddered. "He wouldn't do that. He wouldn't." But it was like Malie had said—she wasn't sure of anything anymore. Only Ahi made sense to her, and even she would grow inscrutable as she got older.

She heard the familiar smack of Makaho's calloused, scarred feet on the floor, but she didn't turn around. Nahoa wished she would just go away. But she wouldn't, any more than Kohaku or his war would.

"What do you want?" Nahoa said, and almost winced at her own rudeness.

"I was worried for you," she said mildly. "The Mo'i was quite upset when he left."

Nahoa could imagine. "Well, I'm safe," she said, still looking out at the snow. She could see Makaho's distorted reflection in the glass, though she tried not to focus on it. Makaho's expression was diffident and obsequious as always. As though that fooled anyone. She seemed disinclined to leave and so finally Nahoa sighed and turned around. She attempted to walk straight past her, but Makaho took a discreet step to one side so as to block her passage.

"I thought I should tell you, my lady," she said. "With the state of affairs outside being what it is, I've taken the liberty of assigning a guard. Your husband agrees with me. I don't expect any harm to come to you while you're here in the temple, but still, we can't be too careful about you and the baby."

The way she said "baby" was so pointed that Nahoa blanched. What did she know about Ahi's illness? Was she implying that she knew its geas origins? And if so, did that mean she had caused it? But then why threaten her with it now? Nahoa's head hurt with the puzzle that no piece of information seemed capable of teasing out.

"I wish you wouldn't," Nahoa said. "It's hard enough around here without some soldier following me around all day. I'm sure Ahi won't like him." Actually, her daughter was far more likely to love the new face, but no need to admit it. A guard would make it much harder to hear from Pano safely.

Though perhaps that was Makaho's true purpose?

Makaho shrugged apologetically. "I understand the inconvenience, truly. But we only have your well being in mind. I hope you'll bear with it?"

Pretend I have a choice. "Of course." She attempted to move forward, but Makaho still blocked her way. She gave Nahoa an appraising look.

"I trust Ahi is well?" the head nun asked.

"Yes. Fine. Perfect. And she's probably very hungry by now, so if you don't mind..."

Makaho smiled and moved aside with a little bow. Nahoa walked away, her pace a hair short of a run. The guard was already stationed outside the antechamber doors when she arrived, and Malie was arguing with him in a whisper.

"This is absurd," she was saying, with the air of one who is repeating herself. "We have no need for further protection here in the bowels of the fire temple."

"There's a war on, miss," he said, also with an air of repetition. "The head nun wants you to be safe."

"Does she imagine the rebel hordes are going to storm the gates?"

The guard pursed his lips, as there was no safe answer to this question. Nahoa shook her head and grabbed Malie by the elbow.

"Come on, he won't move, and you know it. The old bag sent him."

The man lowered his eyes and seemed about to stammer out some sort of apology or introduction before Nahoa slid the door shut. They walked into the inner chamber, shut that door, and knelt against the far wall.

"I don't think he'll be able to avoid a guard," Malie whispered.

"I know. Do you think we should warn him?"

She rolled her eyes. "Please. Pano's been sneaking around where he doesn't belong since you were sucking on screw pines. Don't worry about him."

But Nahoa did worry. She worried if he was safe, if the rebels had actually made the bows and arrows she'd given them the plans for, if he'd eaten, if he'd come back. But now he couldn't.

"My lady, " Malie paused, her eyes as wary as the guard's. "Do you know why she's guarding us, after all this time?"

Nahoa thought back to her strange conversation with Makaho. "I think she's worried. About Ahi. Like she knows something about what happened and she's afraid for her."

Malie took this in. "You don't think she did it."

"I don't know."

"I think you're right. I think she has too much to lose, and she must have learned something that made her afraid for you." Malie paused, and then said pointedly, "Something about the people you've been consorting with?"

"About...but Pano would never—"

Malie held up her hands in preemptive surrender. "I know, I know. You trust the gardener."

Nahoa had never understood Malie's consistent distrust. She'd just attributed it to her generally wary and sour nature toward other people. But now, so closely echoing Nahoa's own private worries, it made her furious. "What's so damn wrong with the gardener, Malie?"

"He used to work for the old bag, you know. Not when you first met him. A few years before that. Half the gardens you see on the bayside are his."

No wonder he could sneak through the temple so easily. Nahoa had never even wondered. Her stomach felt curiously tight. She reached for Ahi, but the child was sleeping. "So?" she said. Her voice was small.

"Well, isn't it funny, my lady? That he used to work for Makaho herself and then he worked in the Mo'i's house, and now suddenly he's some flaming revolutionary?" Malie spoke as quietly as ever, but her words seemed to fall from her lips like embers.

"Not suddenly," Nahoa said, remembering. "He was writing pamphlets against the Mo'i when I was there."

Malie rolled her eyes. "Yes. Pamphlets. Not wars."

"Well, things have changed, haven't they? Half the world blew up! It's not as though he could have kept tending the Mo'i's orchids while half the city starved, and my own bloody husband responsible!"

Malie froze. She seemed surprised. "It never was just about Pano, was it? Why you agreed to help."

"About Pano?"

"I've seen how you look when you think he can't see."

"Ahi likes him," she said, though this seemed inadequate.

"Ahi likes everybody."

"He likes Ahi. He'd never—" Nahoa stopped herself because she seemed to be trembling. Her throat felt tight, like she might cry. "He'd *never.*"

Malie's expression—previously so hard and cold—melted like a handful of the snow outside. She embraced Nahoa, a gesture so unexpected she could only submit to it. The tears began not soon after. "Shh," she said softly. "I'm sorry. I'm sorry. I hope you're right."

THE SNOW FELL AND FELL UNTIL the afflicted citizens of Essel likened the blanketing white to a shroud. Even the children were admonished not to play in the towering drifts, lest they lose themselves in the powdered ice. What little food had been available vanished for all but the wealthiest, those with servants to pay or admonish into braving the weather with armfuls of sennit braid. People disappeared and were discovered hours or days later, frozen, eyes closed and bodies gently curled as though they had simply lain down for a nap. Some claimed the water spirit was punishing them for giving too much to fire. Essel's solitary water temple—never well kept and in recent years close to collapse from disuse—drew crowds so large they had to line up in the street.

There was a war on. The Mo'i's soldiers had marched through the streets some days before, when the snowfall had just been a pleasant novelty and not a sure sign of the apocalypse. For the first time since the eruption, no one could see Nui'ahi. Bereft of their sentinel, the citizens of Essel watched the low-grade war being fought in the heart of the city with apocalyptic fatalism. The northern borders of the rebel encampment were slowly expanding, largely by dint of the fact that the Mo'i's army had unwisely chosen to burn the buildings that might otherwise have provided them with cover.

But who could have guessed that the ragged rebel forces—largely composed, it seemed, of seventh-district farmers and first-district beggars—would have found some way to arm themselves with Bloody One-hand's most deadly weapon? It had to be that black angel, the soldiers whispered, as did the townspeople nearby. That strange girl who had come to their city and never left. The harbinger of the great sentinel's fire now seemed to carry the snow like a mantle over her great black wings. She flew over the city, silent as a nightmare. A shadow was all the warning anyone had through the enshrouding whiteout of the snowfall. And looking up, the black angel's face was never quite visible, though her eyes seemed to glow like embers.

On the third night the snow fell, the angel circled thrice overhead, sending those of the Mo'i's soldiers who saw her plunging to their knees, heads bent, palms out in supplication. Edere kept his head tilted up, and for a moment it seemed she held his gaze before vanishing into the misted night. His unnatural calm gave way to unnatural terror. He clutched the ax the Mo'i had given him and muttered, "Ancestors grant our souls mercy," a half-remembered prayer whose meaning he only dimly understood. His grandmother had said it sometimes in extremity. But she was from a deeply rural island on the outskirts of Okika and prone to rustic superstition. He'd heard that the black angel made any man she touched shrivel like a withered vine. He'd heard that she'd been seen cavorting naked with the fire spirit on the rim of Nui'ahi. He'd heard that she used to be a girl, a diver who had traveled from one end of the earth to the other in search of a spirit to give her wings. He didn't believe any of the stories. He didn't care who she had been or what she did or said—she was the black angel, and her presence meant death on a scale his rustic grandmother could never have imagined.

She was lucky to have died all those years ago. The home her father built had burned down in the second wave of fires. Edere had joined Bloody One-hand's army to save his mother and sister from starvation. And it hadn't been such a bad job so far. Edere and his cadre of the Mo'i's soldiers had been waiting in uneasy truce for days. Sometimes a stray rebel arrow would land perilously close to their front line and sporadic fighting would break out until cooler heads prevailed on both sides. Two of Edere's friends had been wounded that way—medical runners took them both to the tents, but he privately wondered if he'd see either of them alive again. Wounds festered, particularly the deep punctures made by the arrows.

It was nighttime and snowing and the black angel had silently watched their camp for days. No one expected that the next rebel arrow to land among them would presage more than the minor skirmishes they'd already encountered. But the arrow that punched through his neighbor's neck heralded a volley that found marks throughout the lines, judging by the shouts and curses and screams he heard like ghosts from the snow.

"Weapons out!" came the frantic cry of his group's chief, seemingly unaware of the arrow shaft poking out of his left forearm. "Forward! Forward!"

But there was no need for them to meet the rebel enemy. They'd already come, silent as the black angel under cover of night, to finish this unholy war once and for all.

Edere fought them with his ax, which he had only recently learned to use. He was tall and unusually large; his opponents were even less familiar with their weapons than he. It would have been easy work to dispatch them—they were in so close now that their archers didn't dare fire for fear of hitting their own. But every time his sharp blade connected, he could feel muscle and bone parting from the force of the blow. He could hear their screams and see the blood that sprayed in the wavering light from the fires. He slipped on the now slick, steaming snow, but his opponent was already lying there, groaning and begging for mercy.

"Back! Fall back!" came the cry up the line, and Edere realized that he was almost alone here by his campfire. The rebels rushed forward to claim the land. His erstwhile opponent—a woman, he saw now, and almost as young as his sister—lay still and moaning in her own blood. Edere stared. Her intestines spilled onto the snow like straw in a badly packed mattress. Had he done that? He realized that he might even know this woman, in another world, another life. He might have bought breadfruit from her; he might have seen her playing with her friends on the street corner or fishing off the pier. She was just another Esselan, devastated by the eruption. Just like him. He knelt, though rebel soldiers swarmed closer.

She still breathed. Blood dribbled from her lips into the snow. She locked her gaze with his and he could see her terror and her pain so clearly he wanted to vomit. He had done this. The ax fell from his numb hand.

"What's your name?" he asked. Someone was yelling at him—not a rebel, one of their own, one of the medical runners braving the conflict to pick up wounded stragglers. Edere pushed him off.

"What's your name?" he said again to the girl, bending his head so that he might hear her better. He couldn't save her. Nothing could. But he couldn't let her pass beyond the gate like this, anonymous and unmourned and transient as a snowflake.

She lowered her lids. Her breathing was hard and labored.

"Come! There's nothing we can do for her! You have to come!" the runner was shouting. Edere ignored him.

"I have a sister," he said. "Her name is Uele'a, she's your age."

The girl coughed. "I don't know...anyone. Like that. Everyone's dead."

Everyone's dead. For a hysterical moment, it seemed as though she meant it literally, that they were the only two left alive in all of Essel, in all of the islands.

"I'm Edere," he told her, dimly aware that something had happened to the frantic medical runner.

"Leipaluka," she said. He held her hand. The fear in her eyes receded like a tide. She smiled a little. He watched as her eyelids drooped and her breathing grew more and more shallow. He was almost sure she had died by the time one of the rebel soldiers yanked him to his feet.

The medical runner had also been captured and Edere regretted that he had been the cause of another man's misfortune. He was half-gray and looked unspeakably weary—Edere wondered how such an old man had taken a job ferrying wounded soldiers out of the battle. Perhaps he too had lost everyone, like Leipaluka. Or perhaps there was someone in his life he wanted to protect.

"You couldn't just leave like the rest?" the man whispered while the soldiers debated what to do with the two of them. "The girl was dying!"

There seemed to be something missing from this statement. "But you stayed," Edere said.

The man shrugged, his fury a short-lived flame. "You were alive." He looked up at the approaching soldiers, their faces shrouded until they were just a few feet away. "But not for long."

"Eliki says we're pressing on," the rebel soldier said. Freshly healed burns puckered one side of his face and, unlike most of his companions, he carried a real war blade and wore metal greaves that looked ancient enough to have actually been constructed for battle. "We don't have time to bring them back as captives. Slit their throats and let's go."

Edere had known he might die in this war, but he hadn't imagined it would be quite like this. Slaughtered like a ritual sacrifice for some dark witch? He thought about struggling. He stood taller than most of these men. But his weapon lay on the ground a few feet away. They'd overpower him quickly.

"I'm the black angel's father," the man beside him said.

Everyone stared. Edere felt a hysterical giggle tickling his throat like an itch.

But at least this did make the rebel soldier hesitate. "She's the black angel," he said, as though this made the impossibility clear.

"She wasn't always. Her name is Iolana bei'Leilani. She's nineteen years old. She was born as a mandagah diver in the outer islands by the death shrine. She became the black angel like you became a rebel soldier. Choice and circumstance."

The soldier in question seemed to find this situation too bizarre to ignore. "She grew wings by choice and circumstance?" he said, smiling a little.

The man, the black angel's father, shrugged. "I suppose she did."

The soldier bent his head until he was eye to eye with the man. They stared at each other for a long moment, but eventually the soldier stood up and clapped the man on his shoulder.

"Nice try," he said. "But we have a war to win."

Edere realized that the men would kill them both at precisely the moment the scarred rebel soldier turned his back and the man holding him loosened his grip. *Her name was Leipaluka*, Edere thought, and drove his elbow hard into his captor's stomach. He whirled around, grabbing the old man and yanking the adze stuck through the band of the doubled-over soldier's belt in the same move.

"Run!" he yelled at the old man while he kept the soldiers at bay with the adze. "Her name was Leipaluka," he said, pointing to the body. "Remember. Someone has to remember. Tell your daughter."

The old man didn't waste unnecessary words. Within his weariness Edere could see understanding. "And yours?" he said.

Edere told him. The old man nodded, squeezed his hand and turned to sprint away. He moved fast for a gray-hair. Edere, feeling the sting of a blade connecting with his shoulder, focused on the battle. He made his way closer to Leipaluka's body and hefted his other ax. He was wounded. He could see the blood from his shoulder dripping into the snow, but he couldn't feel it. He couldn't feel the weariness in his limbs or the grief he knew was there at never seeing his mother or his sister again. Was Leipaluka now reunited with the ones she had lost?

"*Se maloka selama ua ola, ipa nui!*" he shouted, turning the ancient prayer into a battle cry—

"—What lies beyond the gate, I do not know!"

Kapa paused when he heard the man's roar. He turned around as though compelled to by an unseen spirit and so bore witness to Edere's death. At least three others lay bleeding around him. The arm holding the ax had been hacked off. It was this—only this— that allowed the scarred soldier to pierce his heart through. If Kapa stayed he might get caught again, and so render Edere's sacrifice meaningless. *Sacrifice*, Kapa thought, turning again and running, though his throat burned and his lungs ached with cold and grief. *I've heard enough of that word for my lifetime.*

The rebels would have murdered him in cold blood to keep the battle moving forward. Those were the people his daughter had decided to support. A different sort of bitterness clawed at him now, but he was finally safe behind the front lines and so allowed the immediate needs of his body to distract him. In the apothecary tent, someone draped a blanket over his shoulders and gave him a mug of warm palm wine to drink. It was weak and watered down, but it eased his shivering. He was half-soaked and covered in blood. Aside from a perfunctory question to see if any of it was his, no one noticed. There had been all too much blood in Essel of late.

Kapa fell asleep in the tent and awoke when the first glimmerings of dawn were pushing at the cloud cover. Left to his own devices, he probably would have slept longer, but someone was insistently shaking his shoulder and so he opened his eyes.

"Sabolu?" he said, still groggy, and so surprised to see the young stablehand here, of all places, he wondered if he might be dreaming.

She beamed. "That's right. Glad to see you still alive, Papa." She called him that. Short for Black Angel Papa, but perhaps also just because she liked him. After Lana went to the rebels, Sabolu had come to their flat several times looking for her. He'd given her dinner and a few kala, when those were still worth something. She was young and bubbly and oddly full of secrets. He thought that whatever she was doing for Lana couldn't possibly be the end of her information-gathering activities. He worried for her, but she laughed him off.

"You should go back to the fire temple. Quickly, Sabolu. It isn't safe here." The medical tents were located safely east of the rebel's activities, but given what he had seen earlier there was no telling what might happen.

She shrugged, as though a few thousand soldiers armed with deadly weapons were of as little concern to her as an unruly horse.

"Black angel sent me. She wanted to make sure you were alive. Said she heard something from the soldiers about them trying to kill you."

Kapa had to turn away. Any mention of his daughter, however offhand, tended to overwhelm him. But now, oh great Kai, how he missed Leilani. Surely she would know what to do. Lana had heard about what the soldiers had done. She'd been afraid for him, just as he'd worried about Mo'i arrows when he'd seen her flying high above the battle.

"Well, I'm fine," Kapa said, when he could speak again. "As you can well see. Now go back to the temple and stay there."

Sabolu pouted. "But what about the black angel? I promised I'd let her know."

"Did she say to meet her back in the rebel camp?"

"Well, she said to send a message."

Kapa suppressed a sigh of relief. It was good to know Lana wasn't that thoughtless. "Then I'll pass the message. Go back, Sabolu. You don't want to get caught up in this."

Sabolu, to his relief, finally seemed to come around to this idea. "All right, then," she said. "I'll see you, Papa." She hesitated, and then lowered her voice. "I don't think I like the smell of blood."

"I don't much like it either, Sabolu," he said, equally softly. Leilani would love this child. "And if you see the black angel later," Later, later, so vague and useless. Sabolu had to know what that meant, but she didn't say. "Give her this name: Leipaluka."

"Leipaluka? I had a dog named that once. Who's that?"

"A dead rebel soldier. A Mo'i soldier named Edere didn't want her forgotten."

Sabolu frowned at this and he would have tried to explain— though he wondered if there was any explanation that wouldn't confuse her more—when six new wounded soldiers were carried into the tent along with frantic message-bearers.

"There's a new force helping the rebels. They've come into the old docks by ship and are fighting their way south!"

"We're open on two fronts?"

"Quickly, I need bandages!"

Sabolu looked around, her eyes wide and suddenly afraid. Kapa stood quickly and walked her to the door.

"Back. Now, Sabolu."

"I'll see you again, right?"

"Of course. Don't forget to tell Lana that name."

"Lana?"

Great Kai, how had he gotten so old? He remembered when his parents drowned in the storm. He remembered when Leilani's mother had been murdered and she proposed to him at the burning. He had been as young as this little girl once. So had his daughter, free and eager and utterly ignorant of the ways of the wind.

"The black angel," he said. "My black angel," and pushed Sabolu away—

—away from the crowd chattering in such a fascinating yet indecipherable way around the medical tents and toward the army-guarded road that led back to the fire temple. The Black Angel Papa hugged Sabolu tight before she went off, which reminded her of her own papa. She hated to see him leave, to go back to that tent filled with the metal and rust and rot smell of dried blood and sick bodies. What if one of the soldiers pierced him through with those awful, great knives? Or bashed his head in with a stick? What if he caught the cold-sickness she'd seen on her way here: the blackened fingers and toes that could only be cut off? She didn't like this nagging fear, this new worry for someone else. Her parents had died years ago. She'd learned to take care of herself. She had her own barkcloth now and a nice store of sennit braid hidden in the barn in case she needed it for an emergency. She knew the old hag's secrets and she knew the pale one's secrets and she knew the black angel's secrets. She could trade them forever and get rich, rich, rich, like a chief of ancient Essela. But now that she knew

Black Angel Papa, she had to wonder what might happen if she told the old bag everything the pale one planned. Or if the black angel discovered what the pale one had made Sabolu do to that jolly, fat baby. What would Black Angel Papa think if he knew that she had almost killed a baby? He'd probably hate her. She didn't want that. And she hadn't wanted to kill a baby either; it was just that the pale one never quite said what the bundle of feather and bone in her pocket would do once it touched the crown of the kid's head and Sabolu hadn't asked, now had she?

"But she's fine now," Sabolu said aloud, for the hundredth time. No one else knew. She was safe. After this war was over she'd find even more secrets and sell those until she could buy a nice house on the ocean like her father had always wanted. And Papa could come and live there with her and the black angel could visit if she wanted, too. Lana. She had a name, his black angel. She thought of that other one he had given her, Leipaluka, and shook her head. Old men could be funny sometimes. Who cared about the name of some dead rebel girl? Besides, there probably wasn't anyone alive who remembered her.

Unless it meant something else. She paused, nearly on the threshold of the fire temple. Yes, of course, Papa had been around a dozen other people, and any of them might have overheard him. He'd probably been speaking in code. A code that she needed to tell the rebels. She'd wondered why Papa and the black angel were fighting on opposite sides, but it made sense if he were spying for her. Sabolu grinned, pleased with herself. She went around the back of the temple, through the gardens to an entrance she'd discovered years ago that led to the kitchens. She snuck here often, because it was a good place to overhear conversation and also to get warm in the heat that spilled from the great ovens. She pushed aside the vines and opened the door, but didn't get much farther than that. There was already someone inside. Sitting down, his head on his knees. She smelled blood, but she couldn't see it. His clothes were too dark and wet with melted snow.

"Are you dead?" she said.

"I don't think so," he said.

She shut the door. "Oh, Pano. It's you. I heard the old bag put a guard on the wife, if you wanted to see her."

Pano grimaced. "So I have noticed."

"You're still here."

"I was hoping to discover a plan."

"By acting dead?"

"You're much too clever for me, Sabolu. Do you think you could get the guard to come away? Give them orders from Makaho?"

Sabolu rolled her eyes. "You think they'd believe me?" She paused and looked at Pano more carefully. "You're hurt?"

"Arrow in the leg."

"You can give me something?"

He seemed amused by this, which Sabolu chalked up to perversity. Pano and Eliki both were the oddest people. "I think we could arrange remuneration."

Sabolu had learned what that meant a few weeks ago, because Eliki liked big words and Sabolu liked any words that had to do with money. "How much?" she asked.

"Ten loops of sennit braid and a feast on rebel territory."

"You think you're gonna win?"

Pano didn't quite smile, but some tension left his face. "We've had reinforcements," he said, the same way someone else might say, "We've seen the spirits."

"Good. I'll be right back."

Sabolu didn't try to hide or anything when she walked through the temple to the wife's quarters. They all knew her here, and her business often took her all over the complex. The guard was from the Mo'i, though, so he eyed her suspiciously until Malie told him to let her in.

"You have a message from Pano?" the wife said, so eagerly that her fat baby actually removed its mouth from her nipple to protest.

Sabolu thought she was speaking mighty loud, and Malie—always sensible—apparently thought so too, because she glared.

"I thought you two might like to see some horses," she said.

Sabolu took an involuntary step back when the wife stood. She didn't want to get any closer to that kid. For all she knew, whatever spirit geas the pale one had given her would still work if she touched it again. And Pano wouldn't like that at all. The guard trailed them while they walked at a maddeningly slow pace through the halls, though Sabolu knew that was safer. Outside, they hurried. The path between the temple and the stables had been kept clear, and Malie glared at the guard when he tried to follow them inside. Uele'a had gone, for some reason, but that was easier for her purposes anyway. No need to pretend to admire the horses. She gave Malie directions on how to find the secret entrance and handed them some bandages and liniment they used when the horses had chilblains. The wife looked like she might faint. She was a bundle of nervous energy, that wife. Sabolu didn't understand how she had come to be at the center of so many political webs. She'd be better off in a fishing village in the outer islands.

"Oh," she said, remembering Black Angel Papa and his strange message. "Do you know a Leipaluka? She's a dead rebel soldier. And there's another, one of the Mo'i's, called Edere. I think it's a code for the black angel."

Malie frowned. "I'm not sure. A rebel and a Mo'i soldier?" And then the wife tugged on her sleeve and the two of them left. Sabolu leaned against one of the horses for warmth. She thought of how much money she'd earned in promises this day and smiled. It was good. This war was treating her very well, for all she didn't like the smell of blood. She and Papa would get their house in less than a year at this rate. And then she'd be out of the stables forever.

"Though I might miss you, Sweetstraw," she said, burying her face in the gentle mare's mane. She didn't mind horses, really. Manure smelled miles better than blood.

The stable doors always creaked and groaned when they opened. "Uele'a?" she called. "That you?"

But no, the owner of the footsteps came into view a moment later, though he was still silhouetted against the open door.

She recognized the graying ginger hair, even if she had never seen his face very close before.

"The old—I mean, the head nun ain't here, if that's what you want."

"That's not what I want," he said, and his voice was very still, like a film of ice over a spring—

—frozen, but with something powerful bubbling up beneath. *That's not what I want.* The girl was so young. It made him angrier, it made him want to lock her up with the others, hang her from the ceiling like Nahe for daring to do what she did to his child, to his baby, how could anyone be so depraved it made him want to spit and so he leaned back for a moment, back into the snow and the cold morning air and spat with remarkable violence into the white drifts. He turned back. The girl was babbling at him, something about a rebel soldier called Leipaluka and one of his own called Edere, he didn't understand a word, only that she didn't know enough to be afraid just yet. He stepped forward—

—and closed the door. Malie had wanted to ask Sabolu for a knife or a pair of shears, because Pano's pants had stuck to the wound, but she didn't dare interrupt the Mo'i, whatever secret business he might have inside the barn. She heard Sabolu mention that soldier's name, Leipaluka, and thought perhaps it had something to do with her spying for the war. So she turned back to the gardens. Inside, Nahoa was doing her best, but Malie winced at how her hands trembled when they attempted to pull the cloth away from the wound. Someone—possibly Pano himself—had already wrested out the arrow itself.

"Flaming night, my lady, you'd think you were dressing a chest wound."

She knelt and pushed Nahoa gently aside. Pano was holding Ahi, which Malie didn't think was quite the best idea, all things considered, but she was aware of the futility of questioning the gardener's trustworthiness with my lady.

She looked up at Pano, but he was gazing at Nahoa with the sort of expression that made Malie's stomach sink. Had this war made everyone insane? The gardener loves the crazy Mo'i's wife. And the wife? Well, she hid her emotions about as well as a macaque in mating season.

"My lady?" Malie said, her tone, as usual, betraying none of her inner frustration. "Could you go to the kitchens and fetch some water and a cloth? And a knife, if one won't be missed?"

Nahoa, apparently grateful to be given this simple task, stood on shaky legs and practically fled down the passageway. Malie waited until her footsteps had receded before rounding on Pano.

"Her husband will kill you," she hissed, and though Pano looked mildly surprised, he did not seem confused. So she was right. Until this moment there had been some sliver of hope, some remote possibility that he had shown so much partiality to Nahoa for a different reason. Now she saw the doom they were both walking so blithely toward, and she could strangle them.

"I've done nothing," he said, and she had to admire how even his tone was, given how much she expected the wound must be hurting him.

"Thank the spirits. And for how long will you do nothing?"

He shrugged. "I'm a gardener. She's the wife of the most powerful man in the world. What could I do?"

Malie crossed her arms. "A little more than a year ago she was a sailor. And now she's at the center of a dozen political conflicts, not to mention a war, estranged from her husband, who has gone insane, and caring for his baby alone. In you dance, as calm and caring as you please. You think it hasn't gone to her head?"

"Gone to her head?" Pano repeated, sounding the syllables out as though they were in some ancient language whose meaning he might eventually parse.

"Yes, you bloody fool, and if you don't do something to stop it, you both are going to—"

But Nahoa's footsteps in the hall cut her off and she had to settle on glaring meaningfully at Pano while he stared back at her, dazed and abstracted and a little in awe.

"Sorry," Nahoa said. "I had to chat before I could get away."

Malie got to work, efficiently cutting through the pants leg and then soaking the wound in water until the cloth could pull away cleanly. The puncture wound looked nasty and deep to her, but Pano told Nahoa it wasn't as bad as it could be.

"Perhaps not," was all Malie said, before she rubbed in the horse liniment and bound his thigh in yards of hemp.

"This might be over by tomorrow," he told Nahoa, while Ahi slept peacefully against his neck. Malie had to admit that the child did seem particularly fond of him. But she was a baby who loved the world and this could in no way be construed as evidence.

"There really are people fighting for you from the north? Who are they?"

Pano shrugged, his face full of the same wonder that Malie had seen when he looked at Nahoa. "No one knows. There are rumors that they're a diplomatic delegation from Okika. Of course, there're also rumors they're barbarian warriors from the wind island, so anything's possible."

"Okika?" Malie said. "You know what that means, don't you? The Maaram wars, a thousand years later."

"Maaram?" Nahoa repeated, and Malie refrained from rolling her eyes. Honestly, she'd grown to love Nahoa, but sometimes it was galling to be reminded how low Malie had fallen and how high this former sailor had flown.

"The Maaram empire. It used to be centered on Okika. There was a war here, right around the time of the first spirit bindings. Essel defeated them and colonized all the islands."

"But the islands aren't colonies of Essel. Not anymore."

Pano smiled at her, his indulgence far more gentle than Malie's. "No, that changed after the spirit bindings. Slowly. No one could fight wars, so all the islands got their autonomy in the end. Trade agreements, different systems of government. Essel always at the center, of course."

"And now you think they want to change that? By fighting against the Mo'i?"

Pano's face went as blank as a wall, and even Malie felt too sobered to do more than twist her lips in disgust. So Nahoa understood the implications. Eliki and Pano had unleashed a monster, just as Malie had known they would. If a war could be fought in the heart of Essel, then a war could be fought anywhere. Okika might help the rebels now, but perhaps it wouldn't be very long before they decided they could be much better managers of the city than the Esselans.

Pano said he had to leave. She hoped it was to rush straight back to that unnaturally pale rebel leader and plead for an immediate truce, but she had even less faith in Eliki's judgment than Pano's. Malie made a few quick stitches to close the gap in his pants leg and he wrapped his deep-hooded cloak around himself once more. Ahi started to scream as soon as he handed her back to Malie, which made her look nervously down the passageway. Luckily, Ahi's screams gave way to more gentle whines.

Nahoa and Pano took their leave of each other without once touching. It seemed to Malie that they might as well have kissed for all the longing looks they gave each other. Great Kai, but she hoped Pano was smart enough not to confess his feelings to Nahoa. Pano left without a backward glance and Malie dragged Nahoa away before she could stare feelingly at the shut door. They approached the stables but turned back when they saw their guard had vanished. Had he noticed their escape? Or perhaps the Mo'i had sent him elsewhere. The temple itself was a scene of orchestrated chaos. Wounded soldiers poured in—some on their own feet, some on litters—and even the hallways were being used to accommodate them. Ahi seemed confused and upset by the chatter and the moans and the strange smells. She started to cry again and Malie bounced her up and down, whispering nonsense.

The main entrance and the offshooting fire room were still clear of the war traffic. In fact, the hall was eerily silent, empty except for the three of them.

"My lady."

The four of them. They both turned. Makaho was sitting on the floor in the doorway to the main fire room. Her body was streaked with ash for some reason, and she had never looked older. Her face sagged as though drawn down by invisible weights. All the years Malie had worked in Makaho's orbit, she had never learned what truly drove the head nun. It couldn't just be power. Her disdain for her own wealth had never been for show. But what other reasons could she have? Obscure revenge? Immortality? Piety? That last would have made Malie laugh in other circumstances.

"May I speak with you alone, my lady?" Makaho said, all obsequiousness. Nahoa looked uncomfortable, like she always did in the head nun's presence. It said a lot that she had chosen to come here rather than stay with her husband those many months ago. But then, Malie knew some of what she had discovered in that room in Kohaku's cellar.

"Those wounded soldiers," Malie said, remembering Sabolu's odd message. "Is one of them called Edere?"

Makaho shrugged, a gesture of such weariness Malie was surprised. "How should I know their names? We have two hundred at least, and more dead. Why?"

"Oh," Malie said, wondering if she should say and then deciding it couldn't hurt. "Sabolu was asking after someone named Leipaluka. A dead soldier with some connection to Edere. But I'll go," Malie said. She could do nothing more to delay Nahoa's conversation with the head nun. Makaho gave her a tired smile, full of the peculiar sort of fondness—

—that perhaps Makaho had always felt for her. Malie had been born a pampered merchant's daughter in Ialo, Okika. She had traveled the world on a private ship, had taken lessons from private tutors, and might have even attended the Kulanui if not for the unfortunately spectacular downfall of her father's business. With his wife and two daughters in penury, he had thrown himself over the edge of the great waterfall. Makaho, sensing an opportunity, had offered the oldest daughter a job that paid well enough to support her family. She had accepted.

Nahoa watched Malie leave with a particularly bleak expression.

"Come inside," Makaho said, levering her stiff limbs from the heated floor. "I promise not to eat you."

Nahoa had the grace to look embarrassed. Makaho allowed herself a moment of regret for how she was about to further burden this girl. It was too much that all of these responsibilities had been placed on her shoulders, just as it was too much for the black angel, herself even younger than Nahoa. Makaho had become the head nun of the fire temple when she was just a few years older than them. She'd risen above those older and better qualified. She'd schemed and stolen and even poisoned to become the first elected supreme head of the fire temple who harbored napulo sympathies. She hid herself well, but the few napulo scattered throughout the city had known, and she had felt the pressure of their approval like a lead chain all her fifty years in office. She was so close now. Kohaku, that fool of a Mo'i who had only undertaken the holy action to get revenge, had done so much of the hard work for them all. Now, with this great Ana, a napulo disciple for the death spirit, Makaho had a chance to see two great unbindings in her own lifetime. It was a prospect that kept her up late at night, bowing and feverish before the great fire.

"Your rebels are going to win," Makaho said. Nahoa looked at her sharply—as well she might, Makaho thought with grim amusement.

"They're not—"

"They would have lost, you understand. Even with this snow the water guardian nearly killed himself over. The rebels fought because someone gave them plans for the one weapon they could not build on their own. And so they followed these plans exactly— as of course they would. But nobody there knew that the strength of a bow is fatally compromised when the wide middle isn't shaved nearly flat. Nobody would have known until firing four or five arrows—perhaps the precise number one might fire to test it, just to see if it works, yes? But after that, snap! The bow falls apart. Useless. But they didn't know, and their army is already engaged. And the snow may fall, but it can't fall forever. And when it stops, their bows will still snap and our bows will still shoot true. And *they would have lost.*"

"But now...now they won't." Nahoa seemed very frightened.

"Yes," Makaho said, more gently now. "A new player has entered the ring. I didn't foresee that this might spill outside our borders. That sort of thing hasn't happened in a thousand years."

Nahoa stared into the fire and kept her gaze there when she spoke. "The plans were fakes."

"Yes," Makaho said.

"You meant to trap me into sabotaging the rebels."

"Not you in particular. Just their informant. I didn't realize it was you until you took them. I was surprised."

"But you didn't give me the guard until three days ago. You must've known about the plans for weeks!"

"I didn't give you the guard because of your disloyalty, Nahoa. I told you—he was for your and Ahi's safety." Makaho shook her head, remembering her conversation with Kohaku less than an hour before. She had told him what he demanded to know. Oh, great fire forgive her, but she had told him. "I told him to attend to his other duties. There's no more need for him now."

"You...tell me what you mean."

Makaho had to admire her directness. "I know who laid the geas that poisoned your daughter."

Nahoa waited, her face a picture of silent anguish. Makaho relented. "Sabolu," she said. "Though not of her own volition. The orders, the geas, and the object it was tied to, came from a mind far more calculating."

"Yours?" Nahoa said, though Makaho could see in her eyes she was flailing.

"Of course not, my lady. Even were I not an essentially decent human being who would never harm a child for political gain, I have absolutely nothing to gain by killing Ahi. And everything to lose."

"Where is she?" he had asked, his face a mask of rage and his voice as calm as still waters. Great flame, great flame, what have I done?

"Then who?"

"The rebels."

"Not Pano!"

Makaho shrugged. "I don't know who among them."

This information shocked Nahoa into tears, which told Makaho all she needed to know about the depth of her loyalty to them. She had thought that perhaps she'd informed occasionally out of spite, but it seemed the ties went deeper than that.

"You will not follow me," he had said. And she did not. She waited, but she did not follow.

"There's something else," Makaho said, though the girl was still struggling to control her sobs. Was her worldview cracking? Had she imagined herself to be some flaming revolutionary? "Your husband wanted me to discover who tried to kill Ahi. I gave my word to tell him what I knew."

Nahoa's head snapped up. She wiped her eyes. "You told him about Sabolu."

What could she say in the face of that horror? It was just a mirror. "Yes."

Without a word, Nahoa stood and walked out. She went straight down the main temple steps and around the front to the stables. This time, Makaho followed. The door had not been latched. It swung wide in the wind. From the outside, they could hear the horses snorting in some kind of agitation, but nothing else.

"Sabolu!" Nahoa called, before she stepped over the threshold. A name like some sort of talisman, a light held before her to banish the darkness. Makaho stood half naked in the snow, hesitant as a little girl, until she heard the sound of Nahoa retching onto straw.

Great flame, great flame, what have I done?

Makaho walked inside. As if in a dream, she saw what Nahoa must have, before she turned away for her sloppy grieving. There was a great deal of blood all over the dirt and straw floor, and the smell seemed to be agitating the horses, particularly a tawny mare who kept nosing the body as though to push it awake.

The body. Kohaku had cut her throat. No, that wasn't accurate. He had ripped out her throat, vocal box and all. He had stabbed her in the chest, though it was unclear if that had happened before or after he killed her. Her expression was slack, her eyes closed, and yet she still gave an impression of agony Makaho knew she would never forget.

"So many dead already," Nahoa whispered. "So many dead. And you told him."

Great flame. "She almost killed your daughter."

"She was a child! She couldn't have known what she was do-ing."

"And if she did?"

"You think she deserved this?"

Makaho accepted the withering scorn as her due. She should not have asked that.

"Leipaluka," Nahoa whispered.

"The dead soldier?" Makaho asked.

"Sabolu gave us the name. She was trying to find anyone who knew her. Now they're both past the gate."

"*Se maloka selama ua ola,*" Makaho began—

—"*ipa nui,*" finished the one called Nahoa, and the death spirit gathered the little soul like fruit from a tree.

"I have to go," Nahoa said, and the old witch let her leave. The little soul wanted to look at her own freshly dead body. The death let her. She was unhappy about something, but they were all un-happy, and it paid her little mind. *Black angel,* it heard her say, and then it drew the soul from within its robes and let it speak. The avatar is the death, but death is not its avatar. This spar of the godhead had inconvenient feelings.

"You have to tell the black angel," the little soul was saying. "You have to tell her to remember Leipaluka. She's a rebel soldier. She died."

"So did you."

Like most little souls, this seemed to sadden her. "No one knows who she is," she offered.

"Maybe you will ask her," it said.

"Can't you tell me now," she said, like so many before her. "What lies beyond the gate?" Like Lana herself had, back when this game was fresh.

It shook its head and flew high above the city, so the little soul would delight in the view and feel some pleasure before it fulfilled its duty and opened the gate. Before the game, it had never done this. If the godhead did not delight in death, it did not likewise regret its necessity. The little soul laughed and so he took her higher.

"This must be what the black angel feels like all the time!" she said.

And the avatar thought, *no*, but did not say so. It expanded its consciousness; it saw the world. The young woman who had been with the little soul's body hurried through the streets now, her face covered by a cloak. In the homes still standing, people huddled around fires for warmth. Outside, it was much the same, though they held each other closer. It saw the dead everywhere, great souls and small souls, wise souls and wicked ones, all rising from the earth like mist. It harvested every one, and yet it was still alone with the little soul, flying high above the city. The avatar might be bound by petty emotion, but it is not even passingly human.

"Will you tell Papa I am sorry?" she said.

"Your father is dead," it said, because it knows such things.

"No, not my father. The black angel's father. Lana's father. He works in the apothecary tent for the Mo'i."

"Then I must already be there," said the death, and then it was.

The transition did not disorient the little spirit. It thought she must be very hardy.

A man with graying hair and callused, wiry hands tied a tourniquet. The death knew those hands like it knew its key. They had played a melody once, and if the death could be said to dream of anything, it dreamed of that lament played in the ashes of a once-great city.

"I know him," was all it said.

"He plays music," she told it.

"Yes."

"I wish he would play for me," she said, and it put her back inside its robe, because it could not think of any way to grant this request. It could not bear the little soul; death, who had borne the world.

As it always did when it felt this way, overwhelmed with the petty emotions with which she had taxed it, it found the girl. She had become a black angel, but she would always be the girl to it, the one who had bargained her life for her mother's. The one the old woman had done everything to manipulate, yet still confounded her expectations.

She was near the battle but behind the main line. The dying souls flew at it like sea foam; it bifurcated itself to deal with them. She was arguing with the other woman, the one from the stables, who had also mentioned the name of that dead soldier.

"It wasn't Pano!" the woman was saying. "I know it."

But Lana looked as though the woman had punched her in the stomach. "What am I supposed to do? Call them both in and demand they tell me which of them ordered a little girl to murder a baby! How could Pano not have known?"

"Do you think Eliki tells him everything? You know they don't always agree. Maybe she knew he wouldn't like the plan and kept it from him."

"But what plan, Nahoa? How does this make sense? Eliki isn't cruel. She isn't insane."

"If you're implying—"

"He ripped an eleven-year-old's throat out!"

They were silent for a few seconds, breathing heavily as though they'd been running. "All right," Nahoa said finally. "All right. He's crazy. I know he is, believe me. But he ripped her throat out because of how much he cares about our daughter. Okay? Makaho wasn't lying. She was terrified. Maybe...maybe Eliki knew that. Maybe she knew that if Makaho couldn't protect me or Ahi, Kohaku would go nuts and cut off ties. Maybe she thought that if the fire temple and the Mo'i weren't united, they'd be easier to defeat."

"That does sound like Eliki. But there's no way to be sure." She shuddered. "I can't accuse her unless I'm sure."

"It wasn't Pano," the woman said stubbornly. "So it had to be Eliki."

The two stared at each other, at a bleak impasse. The death, wearily, opened its robe and found again the little spirit.

"I don't like it in there," she said. "It's dark and your key smells of blood."

"Which of the rebels gave you the geas for the little baby?" it asked.

"Oh, the pale one," she said.

"Did the other one know?"

"Nah, everyone knows he's in love with the wife. He'd never hurt her. The pale one made me promise not to tell."

"Pano didn't know," said the death spirit to Lana. She looked up, startled. It would have seemed to her that it just appeared.

"How do you know that?" she asked and then her face fell. "Oh. Oh. Poor Sabolu."

"She wants you to play a song," it said, though it knew that anything she played on the old woman's flute would bind it. It did not mind so much, being bound in this way. It did not want to kill her. It had come to find its duty onerous, and so sought out ways to avoid it.

The other woman was round-eyed when Lana took the arm bone flute from her pocket and put it to her lips. She played that new melody, the one her father had written.

"I like this song," said the little spirit. "I didn't think so before, but she's like her papa."

The fighting up ahead had come to an abrupt stop. A thousand muffled thuds of weapons hitting the ground became a roar. The flood of souls slowed to a trickle. The death grew curious about this abrupt cessation of hostilities and so followed Lana and the pale one, Eliki, and another limping man forward through the rebel lines and the sandwiched remnants of the Mo'i army. They met the mysterious northern force almost precisely in the middle. The army commander was there, but he waited for one other who was a bit slower in coming. The death sensed him long before he saw his face. It could smell the wind spirit on him like desert air. It recalled the fight above the ruined temple on the mesa and wondered if enough of the wind spirit was present here to fight again. The boy had been younger then. He had witnessed the birth of the black angel, and the wind spirit had marked him as surely as it had marked Lana.

"Yechtak!" said Lana.

"I have come," said the boy, now man. "I trust not too late?"

The death was reminded of the little soul by its side. Of the key that smelled of cold and blood and the gate past which no knowledge returns. "Come," it said. "Let's away. This world is not yours any longer."

"Tell Lana about Leipaluka," the little soul said, so it whispered the name in her ear.

"Who's Leipaluka?" Lana said—

—as though she were speaking to someone else entirely. Yechtak remembered that Iolana often did that. But the pale one, the one with the hard, wary, fire eyes to her left, answered the question. "She decided to fight yesterday, but she made our meals sometimes."

The black angel grimaced. "I think she's dead," she said. The pale one looked at her in horror. Yechtak thought it strange that of these three, only the hard one knew the name of the woman who made their meals. Among the wind tribes, the privilege to bring the evening meal to the chief was a highly coveted honor. And no chief would ever dare not know and respect the one who performed this service for him. Binders, as he had often realized these past months, had no end to their strangeness.

"I come as the black angel's ambassador," he said, reciting the words he had learned by heart on the journey, "with a pledge of support and reinforcements from the people of Okika, who sympathize with the plight of the brutalized Esselans."

"Okika?" she said. And then, more softly, "...and the Maaram army invades." Yechtak didn't know what to make of this, so he didn't respond.

"We are at your service, black angel."

The pale one spoke up. "I thank you for your help so far, ambassador, commander. But I should make it clear that I lead the rebels in all matters. Lana is an adviser."

Yechtak blinked and struggled to keep his composure. He hadn't planned for this contingency. How could the black angel herself not be the leader of her own army? "Do you agree to this?" he said, finally.

Iolana looked as though a bone had lodged in her throat. She glanced back at another young woman who seemed so tired and worn that she might faint into the snow. What had happened between those two? What were these strange, tense undercurrents? Behind Yechtak, his own army was growing restless. All the weeks he had envisioned this reunion, himself at the head of a victorious army swooping in to save the day, he had never thought it might end like this: tense and potentially self-destructing.

"Well?" the pale one snapped, but she was nervous as well.

"Lana?" said the other one, the quiet man on her left side. "What is it?"

"Sabolu is dead, Eliki," Iolana said, her voice scraping. "One-hand ripped her throat out."

"Not here, Lana," said the pale one, with quiet urgency.

"And she is dead," continued Iolana, "because you devised a

crude geas and gave it to Sabolu so she could murder Nahoa's infant daughter in the hopes of breaking up a political alliance."

The quiet man seemed as sickened and shocked by this as the other two. He stared at the pale one, but he didn't speak. She went very still. She denied nothing. Yechtak had to admire her grace.

"I'm glad it didn't work," she said. "I didn't want to do it."

"Spirits bound, Eliki," said the quiet one.

Iolana looked Yechtak right in the eyes. His heart started to pound. "Arrest this woman, Yechtak. *I* am in charge of the rebel army."

The black book

Nothing changed, because everything did. We lived for a time in a corner of a local farmer's house spared by the earthquake while we rebuilt our own. Tulo and I found our joy in each other whenever we could—which wasn't often, given the lack of privacy. Parech said nothing. Tulo and I hardly referred to the new dimension of our relationship. In truth, we didn't need to. It seemed so natural, so right, that I only thought about it as something new when I noticed the occasional reserve in Parech's demeanor. Sometimes I felt the distance between us like a block of ice. I knew that we had hurt him and I knew that he felt angry with himself for being hurt. Perhaps Tulo knew as well, but if so she said nothing. I watched Parech, like I always did. I wondered, like I always had. Only now, I had something of my own.

In the aftermath of the earthquake, Tulo's fortune-telling act proved particularly lucrative. Everyone in Essel plunged into religious frenzy, sure they had done something to anger the gods or the spirits or their ancestors. She spent long hours past sunset touching people's foreheads and pretending the spirits cared about their problems. Though her Essela was excellent, she affected tortured syllables and half-Kawadiri phrases to aid her reputation. After all, her primary appeal was her exotic appearance once she decked herself in pelts and feathers. In the meantime, I helped Parech salvage what materials we could from the collapsed house, and we began to build again. I couldn't stand the thought of losing another house, and so in the evenings I redoubled my studies of the napulo philosophy and spirits and geas. I was determined to become an Ana so powerful I could keep everything I loved from destruction and decay. I had high ambitions. But I would start with a house.

After we spent the day driving the piles for our foundation deep into the ground (so deep, we hoped, that this time the earth would have to split apart to dislodge them), I forced Parech to stop and give me the metal knife he had purchased soon after we landed. The blade was almost supernaturally sharp, which was to my purpose.

"Ana," he said, keeping a wary hand on the corded grip while I attempted to take it from him. Our fingers touched and lingered. "The spirits are so fond of your blood, are they?"

He smiled, he always smiled, but I felt like I had that night when he saw Tulo and me tangled beneath the blankets: punched in the gut and unable to breathe. Something in the clear quiet of his gaze. Something about the care he had always shown us, shown me, that I understood was extraordinary. And so I treated it as ordinary as the wind. "Would you rather spend all night on your knees?" I asked, my voice high and thready.

"Rather than watch you cut your arms like stripping barkcloth? I think we could all manage."

I shook my head. "It's no good, Parech. Those sacrifices aren't nearly as strong as blood."

"And what use does some wandering Kukichan farm girl have for that sort of strength?"

"You can't bait me, Akane. I couldn't bear to see this destroyed again."

Parech let go of the blade abruptly. It fell onto the upturned earth. He turned away from me, toward the grassy dunes and the unseen ocean. The day had been unseasonably warm, but the sun was sinking now and the ocean wind was brisk. "I saw you before she did," he said. "The first day we met."

I was so astonished that I said, unthinking, "But she couldn't see me."

He smiled but still didn't turn back. "Well. Obviously. She was the first thing you noticed, right? Not the poor soldier bleeding to death by her feet. But I knew you were there, even before you stepped into the grove."

"How?"

"I felt you. I felt lots of things. Dying is a curious sort of procedure, I think. You felt powerful and hungry and watchful. I thought you might be my death, until I saw you."

"And what did you think then?"

He grinned and leaned against one of the new foundation piles. "That I was lucky to die in the presence of such formidable women."

I blushed, but it was a warm and friendly sensation, like the gentle pressure I felt when Tulo kissed me.

"When I saw you..." he began, but he shook his head and reached down to pick up the fallen blade. He wiped it on his loincloth. "Will the spirits disdain some Akane blood, then?"

I grabbed the knife. This time he let me take it. "Haven't you spilled enough already?"

"Haven't you? Just this once, Ana. It's *our* house, after all."

I let him. It wasn't so much blood, I reasoned. And I wanted, I confess, to test the theories of some napulo philosophers about the relative merits of self-sacrifice versus the willing sacrifices of others. He seemed pleased and grim all at once, which reminded me of how he had been at the tensest moments of our grift back in Okika. Perhaps this side of Parech was the one he showed in battle: focused yet subtly joyous. I knew I loved him then. Like a fool, I thought his shedding blood might prove he loved me, too.

I invoked the geas I had devised for the task, one of water and earth, because I had not yet learned how to master more than two of the great spirit manifestations within one binding. I did not want to risk this going badly for the sake of experiment.

"I bind you for protection, to keep this house from decay and destruction so long as there are those with the ties to sustain it."

The sun had set, but the stars and moon provided enough light for our task. I wondered if Tulo would return soon, and what her spirit sight might make of these proceedings.

"I bind you as well," Parech said, and I felt the redoubled tension in the geas like a bath of ice water on my skin. I glared at him, but he just smirked. Nothing for it, now.

"I offer you his sacrifice," I said.

"I offer you my sacrifice," he said, and I threw up my hands and told him to get on with it. He cut beneath his collarbone, since he determined anywhere else would prove difficult while building the house. He walked to each of the six sheared tree trunks, orphaned upright in the earth. He allowed some of his blood to drip on each of them, an expression on his face of such solemnity I found myself comforted. This felt right and proper. This felt powerful, as though whatever else Parech had given the spirits with his sacrifice had been worth more than his blood. When he finished, I knew they were bound so tightly it would take all three of our deaths to release them. The house would be safe. Parech looked at me when we had finished.

"Was that fine, Ana?"

I grabbed a handful of switch grass and pressed it against his collarbone to stop the bleeding. His eyes and his two-toned hair. The laughter in his voice. The house we would build together.

I laid my head on his chest, not speaking, and he held me until Tulo came home.

The first Maaram ships were spotted a week later by soldiers on outposts deep in the northeast coral atolls. The Esselan army was already on high alert, having been warned of the impending Maaram attack by their numerous spies in Okika. As we'd noted at the time, the Maaram had done a very poor job of hiding their intentions. The first battles were minor and deep out at sea. They affected no aspect of life on the mainland, and so we only noted their existence as a curiosity, a topic of conversation late at night when we spoke to each other in contented exhaustion. Progress on the house proceeded. Tulo knew of the geas I was binding into the very cords and timber and wattle of the building, but she seemed disinclined to ask questions. Perhaps she knew everything I could have told her—she could actually see the spirits I had bound to the preservation of our home. After the first night, Parech silently brought home small animals—macaques and pigeons and once even a rat—that I could use as minor, unwilling animal sacrifices. It was enough for our purposes, though I hated the sensation of their screams and their squirming bodies before I gave their souls to the spirits. Parech didn't seem to care one way or another. He ate their flesh, after all, when most Esselans followed the custom of avoiding meat.

Three weeks after the quake, after enough work to make the three of us want to sleep for days in exhaustion, we raised a rudimentary roof over the first room of our new home. We paid the farmer who had been kind enough to let us stay with her and relished our newfound privacy. Parech tactfully went to collect food for our evening meal so Tulo and I could give the house a proper welcome. If it was cold, that only made our pleasure that much more urgent. Parech gave us a lopsided smile when he returned with breadfruit slung over his shoulders and found us seated side by side, naked to the waist, sweaty and grinning like two little girls.

"Have fun?" he said.

"Think you want to join?" said Tulo, giggling. The two of us stared at her, as though we didn't quite know what to say.

A storm blew in the next day, making us grateful for the rudimentary straw thatch we'd put over our heads that kept out most of the water. I didn't fear for the structure of the house, but the leaks were uncomfortable, so Parech and I spent a wet, miserable day thatching what we could with large pandanus leaves coated in thick resin. The rains provided plenty of fresh water for our barrels, but unfortunately the winds and rain compounded the effects of the earthquake, devastating the irrigation ditches and reservoirs deeper in the city. They overflowed with muddy streetwater that brought a pestilence to all who drank it. It spread through all of the city. Essel's chiefs might have taken their boats to Okika and finished this war once and for all, if not for the fire sickness that devastated their people.

The symptoms began with a deep flush, as though one had smoked too much amant, followed by violent vomiting and watery stools. A rash bloomed at the throat and, in the worst cases, spread down the body to the arms and torso. At least half of those who contracted it were dead within a week; others lasted a month. By the time the storms abated and the pestilence passed, one in ten Esselans had died. Bodies piled in the streets and every stretch of beach reeked with the scent of charred flesh and blackened bones. Tulo told me later that the death spirits swarmed there like flies. She said that for a time they crowded my shape so thickly she could only see me for the darkness. I asked her for whatever details she could remember about them and wrote them down in a book.

But this was all later, because I was among the earliest victims of the pestilence.

Parech got sick first, but it was so mild we didn't mark it. He went into the city and came back with a fever that lasted just a few days. We only realized it must have been the fire sickness when it caught me. That day there was a break in the seemingly relentless storms. I sat out on the beach with Tulo and Parech in a comparatively refreshing drizzle on a mild, humid day. We were bundled into the Esselan long pants and sleeved tops and nursed a fire that we'd built in the shelter of the dunes. Parech was hip deep in the waves, casting a fishing line with a hook whose design he'd learned from our navigator. He claimed it was guaranteed to catch coastal grouper, an assertion Tulo and I vocally doubted, but we were happy enough to watch and see. I'd been shivery and achy all day, but the light mist was excuse enough for that and I didn't want to ruin our day together by complaining.

"Those waves are getting taller," I said to Tulo, conversationally. "You think he might drown?"

"It's Parech," she said, as though that explained everything. "Worry about eels, not waves."

"There aren't any eels this close to the inner islands."

"Well, then." Tulo turned her head in Parech's general direction and cupped her hands over her mouth. "Hey, soldier boy! When do you think we might eat?"

"You want to come and ask this grouper to stay on the line, Princess?"

Tulo's smile was bright. Her eyes narrowed like she was facing battle. "That prize fishing hook not working out for you, then?"

"Just give it a little more time. You'll see."

I would have stayed to listen to more of their banter; I loved it almost more than anything in life. But my chills gave way to oppressive nausea and I shot to my feet. Tulo glanced up at me, but I mumbled something and staggered to the waves. I started to vomit as the rising tide brushed against my ankles. I knelt in the wet sand, nearly doubled over, and emptied myself of every morsel of food I'd eaten. I felt Parech's hands on my shoulders.

"Ana?" he said. "Did you eat something rotten?"

I tried to speak but bent over instead, until the only thing that could come from my mouth was pale and foamy and burned my throat like fire. I groaned. The chill and aches had redoubled in the intervening few minutes. I felt light-headed enough to faint. I shivered despite the relative warmth.

Parech dropped his fishing rod and picked me up. He said nothing, but I could feel the tension in his arms.

"Parech?" Tulo said, when he reached her. "Is she...I see...it's as though..."

Parech froze. "What do you see, Princess?" he said softly. I'd never heard him so serious before. It almost made me want to laugh.

"I think it's the fire sickness," she said. "Death spirits are clinging to her like leeches. I can hardly see her light."

"Will she die?" he asked, in a voice so expressionless I wondered if he cared at all.

"I don't know."

"I can still hear you," I muttered, and Tulo let out a sound halfway between a laugh and a sob.

"We'll go back to the house," she said. "I won't let them get you, Aoi. I promise."

I don't remember very much of the days that followed. I was always cold, despite the blankets they kept piled upon me. It seemed as though some constant wind howled like a mad dog outside the walls, begging to be let in. I was afraid often, particularly when I escaped from the nightmarish dreamscapes of my fever. I felt death right in front of me, its breath like saltwater down my throat. I did not want to die; more than anything, I did not want to die.

Either Tulo or Parech was always there to feed me whatever I could get down and to clean up whatever I couldn't. Their presence was a constant, hazy comfort. I saw Tulo more than I saw Parech—neither of us knew what he did with his time, but he'd return sometimes with herbs for tea or feathers that he'd hang around the house. I heard him and Tulo argue about some of these odd trophies but could never focus for long enough to parse their meanings. The illness made me stupid, filled with the most brutish desires for comfort and survival. So long as they were near, I didn't care how they fought. Tulo was afraid for me. I knew because she would sometimes smear her tears on my face as she lay beside my pallet. When things got very bad—when I could hardly breathe and my skin felt as though it were burning and the air itself seemed to grow a shimmering haze and I could almost see the death spirits that hung in my every painful exhale—she sat on her heels and sang. It sounded more like the plaintive keening of a gull than anything that ought to come from a human throat. It was an eerie, ululating chant that she repeated until she grew hoarse and could hardly speak. I lost consciousness sometime in the middle, obscurely comforted and frightened in a different sort of way.

When I awoke again, painfully thirsty, Tulo was curled by herself in a corner and Parech was sitting by my head, staring blankly at the wall.

"*Se maloka selama—*"

"Don't, Aoi."

He used my name so infrequently that it stopped even this pitiful attempt at humor. His face seemed so bland and disinterested. So how did his voice sound like someone had stabbed him in the gut?

"I've asked everyone for help. Even those women you keep company with. All those sewer-side witches."

I frowned. "They know more than you...wait. Parech, how do you know the women I keep company with?"

His cheeks trembled like he might smile, but in the end couldn't quite summon the energy. He brushed my sweaty, damp hair from my forehead. "I asked Tulo."

"And how does she know?"

Now he smiled. "Was it a great secret, Ana? She followed you. I suppose you have a jealous lover."

This made me glance at her sleeping form and I was overcome with a sense of contented love so profound that I momentarily forgot the illness that appeared to be killing me.

"How is she?" I asked.

He sighed. "How are any of us? How are you?"

"Dying?" I couldn't help but turn it into a question.

"That's what they said. Those useless witches of yours. They said if you were already close enough to the gate to need a geas, none would dare say it. So there. That's the measure of your endless studies. Cowardice and weakness and death."

"Parech," I said, so disconcerted by this bitter, grim side to him that I wasn't sure what to say. "The witch has to be equal to the spirit to control the binding. Not many are equal to death."

"Am I?"

I pushed through the weakness that gripped me and turned so I could hold his hand. "No," I said, shivering with fear. "You would die, and I'd follow you. Would you leave Tulo alone?"

He shook his head and smiled—dark and bitter and furious, but a smile nonetheless. "You're clever, Ana. Always making me do just what you want. Even when I'd do anything..."

"I know." I hadn't before, but I did now. And now, looking at him, I felt that same peace, that same desperate contentedness that somehow merged with longing at its end.

He shook his head and stroked my hair until I slept.

I grew worse. There were moments when I felt as though some monster were sitting on my chest, forcing the breath from my lungs. There were moments when I coughed and coughed until I could taste the metallic tang of blood and the sour bile spilling from my lips. I burned with a fever that felt as cold as the bottom of a river during winter.

I saw so much, only a fraction of which I understood. I knew I was dying, because the ever-present light of the spirit world permeated everything when I opened my eyes. I could see its inhabitants. There were spirits tied to the feathers and other objects Parech had brought into the house: giant beetles with crystal wings; a single ball of flame with uncanny, twisting images at its heart; a clam that clattered around the floor on its mouth and swiped at the air with its giant, glittering tongue. There were tiny, hunched creatures dressed in white and black that hopped around my body like waterbugs. Their heads swung back and forth, as though someone had tied them to their bodies with a careless knot of sennit braid. In their light, I could sometimes see a greater shadow—a tall, robed figure I recognized even before I could make out the frigid outline of its key, the severe cut of its mask.

The earth and water sprites bound to the feathers Parech had bought tried to keep it away from me, but eventually it blasted away those minor bindings and knelt beside me. I was sitting up to regard it, though I was dimly aware that my body was in fact still sweating and groaning on the ground behind me. I felt healthy and alive in my terror and utter fascination. It had been many months since I'd seen this full manifestation of the death. I wondered if this would be the last time we met.

"I don't want to know," I said to it. My voice spilled from my lips like sand. The little deaths swarmed and gobbled up that glowing dust. They laughed.

The gaping hole the death had for a mouth turned upward. "What don't you want to know?" it asked. That voice! My non-body shivered with something akin to pleasure. It sounded like no human ever could, and yet like the bleakest ideal a human could ever hope to achieve. I thought, for a moment, that I might love the death in its aspect, if not in its act.

"What lies beyond the gate," I said.

"Don't you? Most humans long to know."

"They long to die?"

The hole stretched wider. "Clever, my Ana. Most humans long to cheat me. They demand knowledge without the final passage."

"I only wish to know about you," I said recklessly. "The gate —that's your domain. But beyond it?"

The death sprites abruptly ceased their feeding. The other spirits, the strong, silent ones I had bound to the very beams of our house, pushed their ponderous heads through the floorboards and stared. The me on the floor shuddered and choked, like she could hardly take a breath. The me staring at the death began to shiver. I had touched on something important without knowing. Perhaps there was a way to avoid this final knowledge even now.

"What do you think, my Ana?" said the death spirit, its voice beautiful as a shattered geode.

"That nothing is omniscient," I said. "Not even the godhead of a great spirit."

I had heard this thought whispered occasionally as an example of the wild fringe of napulo philosophy. I had not believed in its truth until that very movement, when speaking those words made a great spirit flinch, as though a dying human could hurt it.

"That sounds like a binding," it said finally. "But what sacrifice gives it power? You must know, Ana, that it needs be a truly great one."

And I had no means of making it. My body was so weak and sick any trauma might kill me. And I would not risk Tulo or Parech for something so dangerous and possibly futile. It knew this. That's why it still smiled.

"Time, knowledge, desire, need," I said.

"Nothing," it said.

"Don't open the gate."

It looked down at my body, uncharacteristically relaxed and breathing deeply. The tiny deaths had faded away, for reasons I suppose I still don't understand. I could dimly make out Tulo feeling my neck and laughing.

"It looks like I might not need to," it said.

When I tried to look up at it again, it was with my own aching neck and through my own hazy, fever-dried eyes. But I could tell even then that the worst was finally over. I lay in a tangled jumble of covers soaked in my sweat, and I felt properly hot for the first time in weeks.

"Aoi?" said Tulo. "Oh, Aoi, love..."

"I think it's okay," I said.

Tulo kissed me, long and hard, though I'm sure my mouth tasted none too pleasant. "If you ever leave me, I swear I'll never forgive you," she whispered. "I'll find a shaman and curse your bones, Aoi. I swear it. You and Parech both."

"Everyone has to die," I said, laughing, but even then I suppose I was thinking otherwise.

I recovered. Tulo and Parech both spent more time at home than I thought was wise, given how much money I knew we must have spent when I fell ill. But in their joy at my improbable survival, no argument could move them. Even after the last of my death-induced spirit sight left me, the world seemed to glow. Its real cause, I suppose, was almost embarrassing in its utter mundanity: I was happy to be alive and astonished to be so deeply loved. That I could have found such happiness when my parents spent most of their lives eking out the most miserable of existences made me sad when I thought on it. Whatever lay beyond the gate, I hoped it was something better than this world, or nothing at all. I could imagine no worse fate than being condemned to farm rice for all of eternity.

The first wave of Esselan soldiers had returned from the Maaram battle while I lay insensate. But the fever had laid waste to the city in the meantime, and with no one to challenge them, the Maaram regrouped and launched a new offensive during the rains that marked the start of the warm. "Only madmen or Maaram would fight in this," the saying went. Tired, depleted, but better equipped, the Esselan army took to their canoes and fought back the invading fleet. This time, the Maaram got as far as the southeast shore of the mainland before turning back.

Parech related these developments in absurdist pantomime, mimicking Taak's affected aristocratic accent when he wanted to portray the Maaram and a ruthless nasal drawl when portraying the Esselans. I never mentioned it but was grateful that he never evinced the slightest temptation to rejoin the army on this side. They would have taken him—questions that might otherwise have been asked were overlooked during wartime. Unlike in Okika, the Esselans paid their soldiers very well. But I don't know how Tulo or I could have lived with that constant stress, and I suppose he must have known. Instead, he spent most of his days out back, fortifying the rows of deep ponds he had dug for the fish, as his first too-shallow attempt had been destroyed in the earthquake. I had my doubts about this plan, but he swore he'd seen such fish farms before and I held my peace.

I spent the days braiding sennit from the raw strands of bark that Tulo would bring home from the market, and when my fingers cramped and turned orange from the staining, I would read the precious letters the other napulo disciples circulated among themselves, all with the goal of gaining the knowledge needed to harness the power of the spirits. Some merely wanted the wisdom, and argued against using these postulates to bind spirits, but they were by far in the minority. I considered their arguments more than most, I imagine. I was unusual in having actually spoken to minor sprites and one major spirit. I understood that while not by any means human, these creatures were capable of thought and rational action and emotion. To then bind them to our will must be a form of slavery. But on the other hand, perhaps it was wrong in the same way killing a fish for food might be. Unfortunate for the other living creature, but inevitable and in some natural way correct, because we had to do so to survive.

Humans had been binding spirits long before we had any idea what we did. Every knelt prayer to the ancestors, every jungle fowl sacrificed at the full moon to the gods both invoked something and bound it to that request. That we understood the process far better than those ancient tribes didn't negate its ultimately natural provenance. Who was I to gainsay millennia of human history? I didn't have the hubris to claim that bindings were morally wrong when the sweep of human civilization would hardly be possible without them. No. I sympathized with those fringe napulo, but I didn't agree with them.

I wrote circumspectly to my fellow disciples about my experiences with death. I focused on what I saw as the trivial details— the shape of the little death sprites, the precise dimensions of its mask—and glossed over the critical moment. Knowledge, and the lack of knowledge. I still didn't quite know what the death was so afraid of, but I knew that once I found out I would have access to more power than perhaps anyone else on the islands. But I needn't have bothered. The disciples were mostly afraid of the death spirit and evinced only the mildest curiosity about my report. Here on Essel, with the constant smoking reminder of Nui'ahi, it was fire that consumed most attention. Water as well was the subject of some mutterings, though those seemed centered elsewhere in the islands.

I was poring over some of these reports late one evening when I heard Tulo and Parech talking and laughing outside, near the fish ponds. I tried to concentrate again on the words, but it was no good. I suddenly felt as though I'd been trapped inside this house for years, not just a little over a month. Surely by now I was well enough to walk around outside! So I wrapped one of the blankets tightly around my shoulders and made my slow, careful way down the stairs and around the back. I had to pause several times to catch my breath, but it worked out well enough. I didn't even mind the cold. Water from a diverted irrigation ditch was filling the first pond. Tulo and Parech ran around it, laughing and screaming like five-year-olds. I smiled and watched them, too out of breath to even let them know I was there. Eventually, Tulo leapt over the pond and tackled Parech to the ground. They rolled over into the pile of upturned dirt. He rubbed some into her hair while she grabbed whatever object he'd stolen from her. Their laughter gave way to something quieter. I wanted to say something, but it was too late. I could only watch.

He kissed her. My own lips parted, as though it were me on the ground beneath him. She put her hand around the back of his head and pulled him in closer. Oh, I could imagine that first moment, the shock and happiness when his lips finally touched hers. I sat on the ground and closed my eyes.

I don't know when they finally saw me. But eventually Parech tapped my shoulder, obviously concerned in a way I knew was not strictly for my health. I looked between the two of them; they were holding hands. Everything seemed to glow again. I felt so happy, yet I thought I might cry. What was so wrong with me that Parech never did more than peck my forehead? Tulo said I was beautiful, but then Tulo spent her days staring at creatures with feet for ears.

"I brought a scarf back for you," Tulo said.

Parech just looked at me, his gaze unreadable yet almost piercing me through.

I staggered to my feet and hugged them both. It was the only thing I could do.

The day Yaela bound the great water spirit, the wind turned a human into an angel. I suppose no one but the spirits knew this on the actual day. But slowly, as the astonishing news filtered through the city (first as rumor, then as fact), we pieced the events together. Yaela, a napulo disciple who had discovered the teachings in Okika but lived primarily on an obscure outer island as a diver of some sort, had made the ultimate self-sacrifice on one of the three ice-bound inner islands, dedicating it forever to the service of the great binding. At the moment of her sacrifice, she had turned another man into a creature the napulo were calling a guardian—a half-spirit, half-human creature connected to the binding and capable of reining in the worst depredations of the water spirit. Now there would be no more tidal waves that could suck entire villages into the ocean without a trace, no more great floods. I thought of my parents and almost wept.

The wind spirit—sensing, perhaps that its time was not long behind—created its own peculiar hybrid creature. Not as much of a spirit as Yaela's guardian, but still more than human, wind's black angel was a girl who swept through the skies like a great crow. She had no power aside from her wings, but she marked the wind spirit's stance against what was happening. Her very presence prophesied conflict. No one paid much attention—the war was far more interesting than what must have seemed to the jaded populace of Essel like an endless parade of spirit-creatures. Having recovered from the fever, the Esselan army took advantage of the dry weather and launched a sneak attack on Maaram soil. They conquered several outlying islands and Okika City itself before calling most of the troops back for the planting season.

The council of chiefs sponsored an official celebration near the fire temple and the Kulanui, and the three of us went for the dancing and free-flowing palm wine. We lasted until the sun came up, getting drunker and giddier and more exhausted until we finally collapsed inside one of the more decrepit pagodas behind the fire temple. Tulo twined her hand in my hair while Parech seemed to fall immediately asleep.

"Do you think he's dead?" I said, staring at the war canoes still silhouetted in the hundreds against the rising sun.

"Who?"

"Taak, of course."

"Oh, the Maaram pig?" She shrugged. "How would I know? He was stupid enough."

This didn't seem adequate, but I knew better than to press Tulo on the subject of her most hated enemy. No one had cheered harder at the news that the Esselans had conquered Okika, despite the fact that Essel was hardly likely to be any kinder to her tribe than the Maaram were. An occupying force is an occupying force, no matter what language it speaks.

We fell asleep and were only roused when an officiant from the fire temple hit us lightly with her broom and told us to be on our way. Tulo and I stood, but Parech stayed on the floor, moving so slowly you'd think he'd just now gotten drunk.

"Pick him up if you have to," said the officiant, now truly annoyed.

I bent down to shake his shoulders and gasped aloud. His skin was burning to the touch. The officiant, having finally understood the situation, set off at a dead sprint back to the main hall. Tulo and I managed to lift Parech between us, but we had to hire someone to carry him back to the house. He regained consciousness somewhere along the way and looked hazily up at me.

"Maybe the death is angry you slipped from its grasp, Ana," he said.

"You're not going to die," said Tulo, with such morbid determination that it surprised a laugh from both of us.

"Well, in that case," said Parech.

It seemed to me that nothing could be worse than his illness, but Tulo gave me her word it was not half so bad as my own. The little death sprites settled for crowding the door, she said, and none seemed inclined to open the gate. We ventured into the city infrequently, though we were fairly sure that his was a relapse of the old fever, not evidence of a new contagion. While Parech slowly recovered, I took charge of his fish ponds. He told me the name of the dealer from whom he'd arranged to buy the stocks of baby fish and I purchased them myself.

"Feed fish?" I repeated to Parech in disbelief, when he'd recovered enough to give me instructions. "You eat fish, you don't feed them."

This made him smile. "Well, you do if you want to eat them later."

"Technicalities. You *hunt* fish. This farming business is decadent and newfangled."

"Oh-ho, the great Ana is now lecturing me about my modern ideas?"

"Spirit binding is as old as the moon."

"Not your kind of spirit binding."

"Ah, you've defeated me. I'll feed your fish."

A month after the celebrations, when the weather had finally turned warm enough for long evenings on the beach, Parech declared himself better. Tulo and I didn't believe him—he was still uncomfortably thin and his skin seemed somehow ashen beneath its natural brown-red hue. But he could walk around, and there wasn't much either of us could do but watch him carefully.

The fish in his ponds, quite improbably, grew fat and healthy. He made tentative arrangements with a fishmonger in the village to sell the first harvest. Tulo, relieved of the necessity to perform her fake fortune-telling, spent many hours helping Parech and decorating our house. I let them be. Neither my happiness nor my grief was anything I felt I could burden them with.

We spent a great deal of time on the beach in the evenings, sometimes by ourselves and sometimes with the other residents of the nearby village. A few weeks after Parech recovered, one such evening had turned positively balmy. Tulo and I discarded our bulky barkcloth shirts and danced together by the cookfire, much to the amusement of Parech and the other village residents. After we had dined on a feast of our very own farmed eels, roasted over the fire, Parech left the two of us to discuss supplies with the fishmonger. Tulo followed his easy movements with a frown that made me reach for her hand.

"They haven't left, you know," she said softly. "The little death creatures with those horrible bobble heads."

I had to force myself to suck in a breath. "You mean..."

"I don't know. I think he's still sick. I think it hasn't left him."

He hid it well, but I could believe that. But I didn't know what either of us could do. He'd get better eventually. He had to. There couldn't be a worse time for this to happen. I'd been meaning to mention a certain issue to Tulo for a week now, but I'd found reasons to put it off. I didn't think I could any longer.

"Tulo, you know that you're pregnant, right? You haven't had your period in two months."

She didn't look at me. "Of course I know."

"Why didn't you tell us?"

She shrugged. "Parech was sick...and you, I didn't know what you would think. I thought about finding hea berry."

"But you haven't, have you?"

"No." She sighed. "What sort of mother would I be, Aoi?"

"A princess," I said.

She told Parech. He was overjoyed, swinging her around the house until I grew dizzy. He immediately started working on building the second room, in a dedicated frenzy that belied his continued pallor and the worried looks Tulo gave him. Tulo took over caring for the fishes. I spent more time away from home, studying with the napulo and learning every scrap I could about the death spirit. Parech was about to become a father. I couldn't just let this illness eat him alive. Yet nothing I found seemed to fit.

In the meantime, a student I had known from Essel attempted to bind the earth spirit and died when he couldn't control the geas. No one attempted in his place—the earth spirit was very ill-understood and not nearly so important as the fire or wind spirits. There were rumors that a napulo from my own Kukicha was about to attempt a wind-spirit binding. He had different ideas from Yaela— wind would have no guardian, and he would establish the physical location of the prison deep in the outer rim, among the fringes of the Akane tribes. It sounded like a fool's dream to me, but I was curious to see if it worked.

Tulo's waist thickened, though she didn't look pregnant to anyone but us. Parech relapsed, with a fever not so high as the second time he fell ill. We made him rest for a week and he recovered enough to flaunt our concern. I did not ask Tulo if she still saw the death sprites. Just a look at her face was enough to tell me that. Finally, frustrated and terrified, I made up an excuse and accompanied him on the long walk into the city.

"Should I be honored the Ana has dignified me with her presence?" he said.

"You see me all the time."

"Those witches who wouldn't bother to help you on your deathbed see you all the time."

"You can't blame them, Parech. People die who lose control of geas. Who am I to them that they would risk it?"

"You sound so cold, Ana. Weren't you afraid to die?"

I turned to him and stopped. "Aren't you?"

He grimaced. "Ah. I see what this is. You and Tulo want me to lie in bed all day, is that it?"

"No, but you should take care of yourself. She says the death spirits haven't left you. The fever is clinging."

And I hadn't said this to even Tulo, but if the fever lasted much longer, it would never leave him. It might take years, but the death would dog him, making him sick again and again until finally he succumbed. The thought of losing Parech like that made me want to scream.

"I know that, Aoi. It's been a year now since we met. A year since I escaped a death that should have had me. You might have forgotten what you did then, but I haven't. Every day I have is a gift you've given me. So even if I die tomorrow, what right do I have to complain?"

"And us? What about us?" My voice was hollow as a reed.

"You have each other. That's more than most. Ana—listen, I don't want to die. But there's no sense in me railing against it. I should already be dead. I'm luckier than a hundred men I knew back in Okika. Do you understand?"

I did. But I wouldn't accept it.

My studies of the death spirit had hit an impassable wall, and its name was the southwest atolls. I'd known of the legends surrounding the natives' death worship for months, but it had seemed relatively insignificant until all my other leads proved fruitless. No one knew very much about them, despite their proximity to Essel. The atolls were so barren and harsh that Essel had never bothered to do more than set up a few military outposts on the coral. But the natives managed to eke out their living on coconuts and screwpines and a rigorous system of year-round fishing. I decided that I needed to take the two-day trip and learn for myself what they might know about death. I told Tulo and she agreed to go with me. To Parech we lied, using long glances and innuendo to imply we wouldn't mind some time alone with each other. He barely said anything, just shrugged and went back to building the house. So Tulo and I hired a boat. We promised him we'd be back in a week. He smiled and told us to enjoy ourselves. This made Tulo bite her lip and me look away and we could hardly bear to speak to each other for the rest of the day.

We had booked passage on a supply canoe to the military outposts. I had only the vaguest idea of where to go, so I asked the navigator where I was most likely to find the locals' religious leader.

"There's only one island with a bit of soil. Most of the pierced ones live on that when they're not on the water," he said. "You two sure you want to go there? The natives aren't very civilized."

He gave me and Tulo the sort of look that made me sure I'd rather be among the pierced natives than the men of the Esselan army. He dropped us off on an ominously deserted shoreline and said he'd come back in four days if we wanted to go back to the city.

Tulo held my elbow to guide her even though we were far from any human population. I wondered about this. She'd been sure-footed as a deer in the Maaram forest, and even at our house on the shore she rarely needed help to get around.

"Aren't there spirits here?" I asked.

"Yes," she said. Her lips were drawn and her face flushed.

"Is it morning sickness? Should we sit down?"

Tulo shook her head violently and then said, in a rush, "Oh, just hurry up, you stupid witch!"

I was so astonished that I followed her orders. She seemed to relax once we cleared the immediate shoreline and climbed a shallow ridge that afforded me a clear view of some of the island. I could see the faint outline of a settlement around a lagoon perhaps a mile distant. I said as much to Tulo in a carefully neutral tone and she grimaced.

"I'm sorry," she said.

"I remember my mother could be awful when she was pregnant."

"You have siblings?"

"No," I said, and wished I hadn't mentioned it. "The babies both died."

Tulo put her hand over her slightly swollen belly, as though that could protect her child from the same fate. "That's not it. The spirits here—they're all for the death. It sucks in all the light. Everything is so silent. I can't see anything. It's worse than Okika."

I knew how much Tulo hated that final denial of her senses, so I put my arm around her shoulders and waited until she had steadied herself. "I'm here," I said. "And we'll be back in a few days."

She kissed me and we lay back on the rocks. "I know," she said.

We lingered a little longer and then set out again for the tiny settlement. It consisted of little more than three long houses thatched with grass and pandanus leaves and perhaps a dozen small, traditional sea canoes settled in the waters of the lagoon. A few women were outside doing chores—some pulping long strips of bark and others cleaning basketfuls of sea worms. I didn't see any children or any men. I saw immediately why the Esselan navigator had called them pierced—on an older woman, it seemed every inch of available skin had been first tattooed and then pierced through with a sliver of whittled bone or coral. Her eyebrows, her nose, her lips, her ears all proudly attested to her status. As she was the only one not actively engaged in work, she noticed the two of us first. She spoke to us sharply in her own language, which sounded like a twisted, high-pitched version of Essela I couldn't quite understand. The general meaning, however, seemed clear enough: What do you want?

"Do you speak Essela?" I said, carefully spreading my hands to show we meant no harm.

She rolled her eyes and spat, as though to show what she thought of the language, but she didn't deny it.

"We're looking for a shaman or an elder. Someone who knows about the death spirit."

This made half the women—who had been studiously ignoring us—look up in shock. The old woman's eyes narrowed, drawing together the piercings in her eyebrows. "What does a city girl need with the key bearer? It comes to us all in time."

"I'm an Ana," I said, and was grateful that this word also held meaning for them. "I mean to learn everything I can about the great death. I've heard that your people call death a friend."

She snorted. "A friend? Only a city girl would say that. What would you sacrifice for this knowledge, so-called Ana?"

"Whatever I need to."

"Do you mean that?"

"So long as it's mine to sacrifice."

She stood up, a wary amusement in her eyes, and I saw that in the folds of her comfortably flabby belly, a crude bone key had been pierced through the skin. Despite the rough edges, I recognized it immediately as a replica of the key the death wore around its waist. If I had doubted their familiarity with the death before, this would have satisfied me.

"There's an island just a little ways from here. Any who wish to know the death can sit vigil in the sacred caves. And if you survive it? You might know what you wish to."

I wondered if she thought I would back down at her casual reference to the danger, but I handed her a long coil of sennit braid and asked if someone could show me the way.

"I'll go as well," said Tulo, surprising me, because she'd been so silent.

The woman looked at her and then again, and I saw her take in Tulo's directionless gaze and bulging stomach. "I don't think you'd want to risk it, fair one," she said gently. "You may stay with us while your Ana has her vigil."

"She's right," I said. "Something might happen to me."

"Then I could face the death spirit."

"The death knows me, Tulo. It's dangerous, but at least I know some of its ways. You'd stand no chance."

"I see the spirits every day! How dare you tell me I don't know them? I could probably do this a thousand times better than you."

"And if you fail?"

"What about you?"

I could have slapped her. "At least," I bit out, "I'm not pregnant."

This made her pause and turn away from me. I could tell the only thing preventing her from entering one of her rages was the watchful presence of the other women. Tulo didn't like to be left out of anything, let alone something so dangerous and vital to our future. But finally she shrugged and walked several steps away, toward the lagoon.

"Fine. Do what you will. I'll tell Parech if it kills you."

Tulo didn't give me any more of a goodbye than a sullen stare, and even turned her back on the canoe when I tried to wave. I bit my lip. I would see her again. I had to. The old woman herself took me out on the water, maneuvering the one-masted boat with calm efficiency.

"She's blind," I said, as though that hadn't been perfectly obvious. "If I don't come back, she'll need to go to Essel. Could you make sure someone takes her?"

She nodded. "I could arrange that. Though we don't often venture to the big island."

"She can give you barkcloth and more sennit braid once she gets there."

The woman waved her hand and turned back to the water, as though a payment hardly mattered. I would have thought these people would be grateful for whatever luxuries they could get from the "big island," but then, what did I know of such a remote, hard-scrabble life?

The sacred caves were located on what looked to me more like a sharply jutting hunk of oversized rock than anything that could reasonably be called an island. There were worn steps carved into one side. She told me to climb them and follow the path into the caves. I didn't imagine I could easily get lost. I thanked her again and grabbed one of the handholds.

"That baby she has," the woman said, as I swung my weight from the boat and onto the rock. I looked back at her. "You're not jealous of the father?"

I felt as confused as if she had asked me if I were jealous of the air. "He's the reason why I'm here."

She smiled. "Some advice, Ana: don't leave the caves before the death. No matter what. I'll return here in three days."

I climbed the steep rock face and watched her nimble little boat vanish in the ocean haze. The path here wound around the other side of the tiny rock and then dipped into a narrow, damp cave. I peered inside and took a deep breath. I couldn't stop this once I started. The lightless passage wound around for what felt like an impossibly long time, given the size of the island. Finally, it emerged into a much wider space, lit with sunlight that streamed through high gaps in the ceiling. The walls were decorated in ancient, deceptively simple paintings. A crude, spindly death with its mask and key and a star on its chest. Hunters spearing a great fish as it tried to swim away. A wooden mask hanging high on the wall, shadowed in such a way that for a horrified moment I thought the death had arrived even before I invoked it.

I started to tremble and forced myself to stillness. The old woman had led me through the formal preparations for the ritual on the way here. Carefully, I removed my clothes and shoes and stepped into the spring bubbling beneath the death's mask. It smelled like tree resin with just a hint of something thin and astringent, like blood. I bathed myself thoroughly and then took the plain earthenware bowl waiting on the edge of the pool. I filled

it to the brim and then carefully drank half. My skin prickled. The
light in the room began to change in a way that was by now quite
familiar. Naked and shivering, I walked again to the center of the
room and knelt. To my surprise, no blood sacrifice was involved in
this summoning. There would be no binding in any of the ways in
which I was familiar. This ritual was more ancient, more primal,
and therefore more dangerous. I had entered the death's space an
uninvited guest. I would offer my truest self to it, and in return it
would share with me as spirits so rarely shared with humans. We
would acknowledge each other as equals, not as powers warring
for dominance.

I looked up at the death's mask and said, in a voice too loud to
shake, "Mask, heart, and key. Won't you share my drink?"

I said this in the language of the pierced woman, though she'd
assured me that any language would do. And it appeared, stepping
out of the wall as though from another room, the cold key swinging at its waist. It acknowledged me with just a nod and, to my
surprise, knelt and lifted my half-drunk bowl of spring water with
scaly, spindly fingers that unrolled like a lizard's tongue.

"So you wish to cheat death after all," it said, when the water
from the bowl had somehow vanished beyond its mask.

"He's too young to die."

"And when has that ever mattered to death?"

"Then what *does* matter to it?"

"You truly want to know?"

"Why else have I come?"

It acknowledged this with a shrug. "Remember," it said. "You
have invited me inside." It touched my forehead and I fell, dazed,
upon the rock.

Dreams and memories and reality all jumbled up between them.
Which are the death's, which are mine? It is as if my younger self
is a ghost screaming a warning across time. *Don't leave home to
sneak into the forest,* she says, *don't leave your mother to care for
your father so that neither of them can escape that tiny house.* She

could have gotten out, I was told afterward, but she tried to save my sickly father and so they both drowned instead.

You have killed your parents, says the younger me, the angry ghost.

I killed my parents, I say to the death.

But then, "No," it says, "I did."

I see the flood sideways and upside down. My parents frightened and confused by the rapidly rising water. My mother screams my name.

"Aoi," she calls, over and over again, until my father promises I've already left.

"It's that boy," he says, and I can't believe that even as the water is rushing in through the door like a tidal wave my father is attempting to remember the name of a boy I played with in the forest. "She'll be fine," he says.

My mother tries to carry him, but my father's been sick for weeks and his legs can't struggle against the rushing water. It's up to their chests now. I see, through the death's eyes, how the entrance is about to collapse, trapping them inside. I see, through the death's eyes, that my father knows as well.

"Leave me, leave me," he sobs and begs for what seems like an eternity. My mother just screams at him to "move, please move," though I can see in her face that she knows it's useless. She looks at the door and back at her husband. Her daughter is on one side, her death on the other. The door collapses inward. She chooses death.

Living killed my parents, I think.

"Good," says the death, plucking their souls from their bodies like ripe fruit. "Why don't you ever think of them?" it asks.

"I wanted to forget." My parents are floating, dead in the muddy water. "Do you remember all your dead?"

"Yes. Yes. Yes." Each repetition is shot through with a different sensation: first hunger, then satisfaction, then grief. I think, is that how the death feels? Everything all contradicted, all at once? I think, is that any different from a human?

"Good," says the death.

I am lying on the floor of the cave again and the death is beside me. The world glows with spirit light; it is dark outside.

"How can I save him?" I ask.

"You're asking how you can overcome death."

"Am I?"

"And you know, young napulo; you know there's only one way to do that."

"You want me to bind you?"

Its mask is an inch from my face. The holes of its eyes burn with a dark, charred flame. I recall this burning chill from when I nearly died. It scares me more now. "I would make your life a misery if you tried and lived. Your every breath would be shadowed by my key. I would crawl through your dreams and poison your love and destroy what you touched until you would beg to know what lies beyond the gate."

I think of Parech. I think of his bemused resignation in the face of this monster that now threatens me. "I wish death would die," I say, an echo of a moment far removed from this and yet intimately related. I am reckless in my terror. I'm not like Parech, I'm not like my parents. I cannot accept this masked thing, this scourge of everyone I have loved.

Its mask touches my face, then pushes through. I cannot move my limbs. I cannot feel myself for the cold. I am dying. I have lost already, and Parech will not be long behind me. I stand at the gate. I can see no walls, but the air is like that of the cave: dank and humid. The light is dim, as though filtering through clouded stars. The death puts its key in the lock.

I try frantically to think of a way to fight it and remember the only time I ever saw the death disconcerted.

"How much do you really know," I say, "about the domain you claim to rule?"

It pauses, removes the key. "Watch," it says, and then we are somewhere else—a beach at sunset beneath a receding tide. A fire burns, and by its size and the unmistakable scent of roasting flesh I know it for a pyre. A small group of people stand upwind. They are short and oddly bent, as though suffering under an invisible load. Their hair is tangled and unkempt, they wear nothing but the crudest draping of undyed barkcloth over their genitals. A woman with a face as scarred and pitted as the skin of an orange is weeping. A support on the pyre collapses in a cascade of sparks. The smell momentarily intensifies. The woman drops to her knees, tilts back her head, and starts to keen, a ululating wail that so powerfully reminds me of Tulo that I gasp. I wonder where we are. I wonder who this woman has lost. No matter how strange and foreign their appearance or their clothes might be, her grief has connected us.

The man beside her, who has also been crying, touches her shoulder gently. He says something. I hear the words, but they're so unlike any language I've ever heard, I can't even determine the region.

"What is this?" I say to the death beside me.

"That which you profess to hate."

Though the death is beside me, it is also beside the funeral pyre. Its mask is longer and more angular. Around its waist is not so much a key as a rounded, whittled stick jutting upward. It reaches inside the flames and pulls out a little girl, hardly older than three.

"Who are these people?"

"Your ancestors."

It seems nothing so much as amused by my disbelief.

"Thousands of years ago," it says. "The world was different then. But some things always remain. Children killed by fevers. Women killed by childbirth. Men killed by men. Death may be inevitable, young napulo, but not the manner of it. I may reap the dead, but you give me the grisly harvest."

The woman attempts to run into the fire. The man drags her back only after she has burned her hand. I wonder if the wound will kill her, if she will get her wish, and become another soul for death to reap.

"But why?" The question bursts from me, like the juice of an overripe fruit. "Why must you? What about death says you must take Parech's soul though he's so young?"

"I take many souls his age."

"That's not an answer."

"No," it agrees.

The world goes black. No, there is a little light, like that from the glowing embers of a fading fire. A man sits before it, and he makes the hunchbacked people from a moment before seem like models of good posture. His face hangs in so many folds and wrinkles it's difficult to make out his eyes. His nose seems to have collapsed inward. His skin is the brown of rotting paper, his movements slow and painfully enfeebled.

"Were I to take his soul," says the death, invisible now, "would you call that evil?"

"He's old. He's had his time."

"But look how he struggles to live. If death is wrong, how does old age make it better?"

"He's suffering!"

I don't see the death act, but the old man slumps forward. What little I can see of his face relaxes, and I know his soul has left.

"Would you see suffering?" asks the death, and though I'm thinking *no, no more,* I say nothing. But it's not a moment of unspeakable age or unspeakable grief it makes me look upon, rather, one of familiarity and comfort. It's our house on the beach, and I see that Parech has finished the foundations and floor for the new room. I grin and almost call out to him before I hear the sound of someone retching. It's Parech, a little ways from the house, gripping his stomach. I call his name, but he doesn't hear me. He sinks to his knees, not quite groaning but with a look on his face like he wants to scream.

"Stop," I tell the death, "stop this. I don't want to see this. That's why I'm here. To help him."

"But he's suffering," says the death, precisely mimicking my intonation of a moment before.

"He's young!"

"So which is it that makes death immoral? Age or suffering?"

Parech staggers to his feet, though I wish I could make him sit down and rest. How many times has he hidden this from us? "Why do we have either?" I whisper. "Why can't we end both?"

The death gives me a small mercy; Parech vanishes and we are once again in the cave. The sun has risen.

"All bindings are between a human and a spirit, but without age and suffering there is no such thing as a human."

The truth of its words deflate me. I see that what I have been secretly hoping for—a way for the three of us to be young and happy forever—is impossible.

"Are we nothing else?"

"*You* would ask me that?"

I think of Tulo's dancing, Parech's constant laughter. I think of the year we have had together and I know what the death means: I have been happier than most.

"How long have you known the world?" I ask.

"As long as humans have."

"Forever?"

It laughs. This is first time I have heard the death laugh; it echoes in the hollow of my throat and makes me want to vomit. "Not so long as that. There were other deaths, for other things. Some things so far apart from human you might not recognize them as living."

"So how can there yet be things you don't know?" I say.

"No one can know everything."

"No human, perhaps."

"No *thing*."

"But what you don't know," I say, thinking aloud, "is that which can bind you."

It moves slowly, as though through water. Its fingers glide to caress my cheek. "Careful, Aoi," it says. "I may still yet take you."

But while it did not, I would ask what I could. "They say the sacrifice of wind is time and pain. Water is memory. Fire is freedom. But what is the sacrifice of death?"

It is silent, and very still, for a very long time. I cannot tell quite how long, but the cave goes dark again and I begin to shiver with cold and forgotten hunger. I long to move, I long to stand and run back through that passageway and into glorious open air, but I recall the pierced woman's warning and remain. If the death means to avoid its obligation by waiting me out, it will be disappointed. But the effort at remaining still takes its toll as the hours continue to slide by. My throat is parched, but I don't dare get another drink from the spring. My eyes flutter. I grow terrified that it might take my soul in my sleep. My arms grow a line of red spots from incessant pinches. And then, finally, the sun rises again.

"Life."

It vanishes and I fall back against the rock.

The old woman took us both home, though she had to sail through a war to get there. The remnants of the Maaram army had hidden themselves deep in the atolls, including her own island. In the midst of my death vigil, they had launched their sneak attack, injuring some villagers in the process of commandeering their boats. We didn't imagine they'd get very far, though, so the woman offered to sail around the main harbor and drop us off.

Tulo was very apologetic in her own way. When I first climbed inside the boat she hugged me and buried her face in my neck, breathing deeply as though she'd never thought to smell me again. I silently forgave her. Who understood her temper better than I?

I felt curiously calm, given the intensity of what I'd just experienced. The world of insurmountable worries and impossible hopes I'd left still seemed very far away. I'd seen the funeral of a girl ten thousand years dead and felt that mother's grief as though it were my own. I'd finally understood that Parech and Tulo would have to die, just as I would. I could only influence the manner of their passing. The death's sacrifice is life, it had told me, and wasn't that the ultimate paradox? For no one could live forever and remain human. And only a human could bind the death. So the sacrifice to bind the death spirit was inherently finite. And yet, perhaps, still worth trying.

To our surprise, the Maaram army had managed to bring their fight into the southern harbor. The waters had turned a vibrant red and the air was heavy with smoke and ash. Half of the fire temple had burned to the ground, along with several ships. The old woman didn't dare get very close. The Esselan bows, after all, would not discriminate between her boat and that of a Maaram soldier. We sailed west, past the bloody water and the burning city. Signs of the Maaram eased until they vanished altogether. Just our small boat, hugging a lonely shore. Tulo recognized our stretch of dunes even before I did—I'm not sure how, but she jumped up and pointed and, sure enough, there was the barely visible top of our house.

Parech was waiting for us by the time we pulled ashore. He looked healthier than I remembered—nothing at all like the pain-wracked figure the death had tortured me with in the caves. Tulo leapt out of the boat first and he lifted her up for a kiss. The old woman looked at me, curious, and I just shrugged. We pulled the canoe clear of the waves and then walked over the dunes to the house. Since we had left, Parech had managed to put up the foundations and half the walls for the new section. The old woman was particularly curious about the building style. The atolls didn't have nearly enough wood to build an entire structure from it. She seemed to like our cozy room even more. Parech generously offered her the first pick of the food we had left and then we settled down, him beside me.

"I take it that wasn't really a pleasure trip," he said softly, in Kukichan.

I sighed. "No. Parech, I think I know how to save you."

"Turn widdershins three times on a full moon? Sacrifice half of Essel to the ancestors?" He was joking, but I could see the glint of anger behind it.

"Bind the death spirit."

This startled him even out of the semblance of humor. He took my hand and I shivered. "That would kill you, Ana."

"No, that's just it." I explained some of what the death had told me. "All I need to do is discover that which it doesn't know. And I can bind it and save you."

"Aoi," he said. "You can't. How can you even think of it? Become a spirit binder? All to stave off a death that should have caught me a year ago? It will twist you. It will...you can't mean this. Even you can't mean it."

I straightened my shoulders, flaunting his concern as he so often flaunted mine. "You weren't so high minded about spirit binding when it helped us escape Okika," I said. "Or when it stops our house from falling down in an earthquake. You're the one who brought those geas-charms when I was sick."

"You know that's different. The great bindings. They're abominations."

Tulo drowsed in the corner, but the old woman was staring at us quite openly, though I doubted she could understand a word. I forced myself to lower my voice, though it nearly pulsed with my fury. "Now that sounds like the Akane barbarian I picked up on a battlefield. Would you have preferred I left you there? So your ignorant sensibilities wouldn't be offended by progress?"

Parech was not often angry, but when he was, he turned incandescent. He moved his face so close his clove-scented breath warmed my cheek. "This isn't progress, wetlander. It's the peevishness of a little girl, stomping her foot at the wind that dares blow, at the rains that dare fall and destroy her fun. We are alive and so we die. That is the beginning and end of it. If you subvert that, of all things, what do you think will happen?"

"I'll save countless people. I'll save you."

"And you'll destroy yourself."

"I don't care."

"What about Tulo?"

"She'll have you."

He closed his eyes and leaned in so his forehead touched mine. "And me?" His voice was barely audible. I gulped down an unexpected sob.

"I matter so much?"

He didn't even answer, just stood up and walked outside. Tulo looked up and yawned. "What are you two arguing over, now? Didn't you tell him you found a way to save him?"

"I think she did," the old woman said slowly. "But I think he didn't like it."

Tulo pulled a blanket over her shoulders and settled down on the floor. "Well, don't worry. He'll come around."

The woman and I looked at each other, and I realized that, in this instance, she understood Parech far better than Tulo ever would.

The pierced woman enjoyed our hospitality for the next three days, until the last of the Maaram army had been thoroughly defeated and the few survivors imprisoned. A few hundred Esselan civilians had been killed in the fighting, as well, and the city's jubilation at the victory was more subdued than after the last battle. I helped her pull the boat back into the ocean and wished her luck.

"There aren't many who have braved the death vigil," she said to me as she hauled the provisions inside. "But those who do use the knowledge in different ways. If you're an Ana, I imagine you want to bind it."

I just nodded, since it was clear she'd already deduced the truth.

"That man of yours is very wise. Sometimes death is the easier fate than living at any cost."

I clenched my jaw, but she was our guest and I wouldn't violate propriety enough to argue with her. She seemed to read this struggle like it was scrawled on a piece of paper, and laughed. "But, do what you will. You were strong enough for the death, so perhaps you're strong enough for this. He's sick, is he not? I've seen those sorts of lingering illnesses before. Can last for years, if that's any consolation. You might try blue vervain, if you can find any. It would ease him, at least."

I thanked her profusely for the latter, grudgingly for the former, and sat by myself for a long time after her tiny canoe had vanished over the horizon. There was no hurry. If this sickness would kill

Parech, it wouldn't be fast. I had time to convince him. And if I couldn't...

Somehow, I'd find a way.

Tulo gave birth to a boy we named Ileopo at the start of the cold season. He was turned the wrong way in her stomach and so she labored in agony for a full day. I realized she would die with him still unborn if I didn't do something. The midwife told me that she knew of a way to get a living baby from the womb of a dead mother. I asked her why she could not try on a living mother and she stared at me, as if I had asked her to stab herself. She refused to do it, calling it butchery. She called me names and said she had heard I was an evil witch who practiced heinous rituals, but she had come anyway. She left us alone and Parech watched her go, his eyes wide and flat with weariness and grief. He thought Tulo would die.

"Bring her back," I said, the only possible way appearing clear in my head. Tulo groaned and twisted, half-conscious on the floor. Her belly seemed large enough to pop. "Go and bring the midwife back. Tie her up if you have to."

He didn't even ask why, just slid open the door and went out into the cold wearing not so much as a shirt. He came back soon after with a squirming, breathless midwife who was red with indignation.

"I won't do it! I won't condone any of your heathen rituals, everyone knows what you do here—"

Parech covered her mouth with his hand and I flashed him a grateful smile. "You have to do nothing," I said, "but tell me where to cut. And if you think you should lie, contemplate that this girl's death and her baby's will be your responsibility. Am I clear?"

Parech removed his hand. The woman stared at me and then nodded once. She began to tremble and muttered a stream of words under her breath that at first I thought were curses and then realized were prayers. I didn't hear those very often in my napulo circles.

Parech gave me his sharp metal blade and told me to wash it in the ocean, because that's what the Maaram shamans had always done. When I came back, Tulo had revived enough to stare at the blade in open terror.

I stroked her hair and murmured something comforting while I steadied myself. I'd only heard of what I was planning to do to Tulo. In some ways, I understood the midwife's fear. I just had no other choice.

"We're going to cut the baby out," I told her softly. Her eyes, so bloodshot they looked red, widened.

"Aoi, you can't," she whispered. "You'll kill the baby. You'll kill me."

"Do you think I'd let that happen?" I said, hearing the cool confidence in my voice and marveling at it. "Don't you trust me?"

I felt her relax, felt her muscles go slack and her face turn into my palm. She smiled and I didn't think I would survive it if this didn't work.

"The death is afraid of you," she whispered. "You keep it away."

I didn't know what to say to that.

The midwife refused to do the cuts, but she described the procedure with what seemed like clear accuracy. Parech held Tulo's hand while I cut. She clenched her teeth and only screamed once, when I first put my hands inside her womb and began to turn the baby ever so gently in the right direction. There was a great deal of blood. Added to what she had lost already, I feared for her safety. But eventually I pulled the child head first from the opening in her stomach. I slapped his bloody back and he took a hiccuping gulp before screaming. The midwife, apparently astonished to see Tulo still breathing, helped me stitch her stomach back together and bind the wound. She stayed with her when Parech and I went outside with the baby.

He was grinning, staring at the baby like it was some wondrous spirit and not a shriveled up, squalling human creature. We bathed him in the ocean and cut the birthing cord with an obsidian blade.

"He has your nose," I said, and Parech laughed so hard he had to wipe his tears away.

We wrapped the baby in a spare barkcloth and carried him back into the house.

"I sometimes envy her faith in you," he said, just before he opened the door.

I touched his hair, which was now nearly all black again. "I love even your doubt," I said.

Ileopo is strong like his father and agile like his mother. He learned to walk before he was a full year old and never crawled again, preferring to stumble after some hapless seabirds on the beach, shrieking with laughter. It was nearly a year before we realized he was deaf. He naturally learned to gauge our expressions and perhaps even read our lips, so that he always seemed to respond to what we said. But the closest he ever came to saying our names was shaping the words with his mouth. If I called his name on the beach, I could bellow until I was hoarse, but he'd never notice until he turned around. I think Tulo might have known before Parech or I, but the prospect scared her so much she couldn't bring herself to say it aloud.

The problem, we all knew, wasn't so much that Ileopo was deaf. After all, there were other deaf people in the city and they seemed to speak to each other well enough using a system of language gestures. The problem was that Tulo would never be able to see her son speak. She, who should have been the closest to him of all of us, was now isolated from him as though by miles of water. She never complained, and learned what hand gestures she could from the two of us. Ileopo spoke the way he walked, with headlong, rushed enthusiasm. It made us laugh to follow his conversations, but he could never talk like that with his own mother. With Tulo, he showed the sort of insistent, loving patience that unnerved me in how much it resembled Parech. Unaided by visual cues, her hand speech remained tentative and garbled, but he always waited for her to finish and one of us to relay his words back to her. It was a slow, grinding system. More often than not, their companionship was silent.

Parech confessed that his uncle had been born deaf, along with three of his cousins. He hadn't thought about it before Ileopo was born. He hadn't realized he could pass on the taint. Tulo wouldn't speak to him for three days after he told her. And then she kissed him and never mentioned it again.

We've had four years together, all told. I love Ileopo like my own son and spend a great deal of time with him. Sometimes being with Tulo frustrated them both, and Parech was often weak or ill, more frequently as the years went by. The tincture of blue vervain the old woman suggested had helped, but Tulo could see just as well as I could that he was slowly losing the battle. Every summer for the past two years there has been a steady stream of plague deaths in the city. And always, I would see people still alive but drained and wan in that particular, painfully familiar way, and I knew that they too were dying. Ileopo seemed to know as well, though none of us ever explained it to him.

One evening, not too long ago, when I was teaching Ileopo to swim in the ocean, he pointed to the old tattoo on my right arm, the one that Parech had given me as part of our escape from Okika.

"Parech has them too," he signed. At the beginning, I'd chosen the symbol "irreverent" for Parech, which made him even more likely to laugh in any conversation with his son than he would be otherwise. "Do they protect you from the spirits? Tulo says there are always spirits around him. Bad ones. Maybe he should have a mark like yours to keep them away."

Had Parech translated Ileopo's speech back to Tulo, then? Or perhaps sometimes she spoke to him alone, when no one could tell her his responses.

"There are spirits all around us," I tried.

"No, not these bad ones. Tulo told me. And I can tell. He has bad ones."

I sighed. "He does."

"Can't you get rid of them? Everyone says you're a great witch. All the kids in the village are afraid of you, Aoi."

They were? I'd been so focused on Ileopo and the death spirit for so long that sometimes it was hard to remember the wider world. "Do you mind?"

He laughed. "They're afraid of me, too. But, Aoi, won't you save him?"

I hugged him very close, but I was done with crying.

Parech and Ileopo had a game where one would write something down and hide the note in the house; if the other one found that note, he would get whatever was written on the paper. At first, this was just our way of encouraging Ileopo to learn to read, but then it continued for its own sake. If Ileopo had been begging one of us for candied screw pine, Parech would write it down and hide it somewhere, and only take Ileopo once he found it. Sometimes both of them would forget that they'd started the game, and so every once in a while I would discover messages like little notes from the past—forgotten desires, passed over promises.

"See Nui'ahi," said one of Ileopo's notes that I found one evening, alone with Tulo. I didn't think they had ever gone. The smoke from the lip of the volcano would exhaust Parech too much these days.

"It's happening," I said to her. She stiffened and turned her uncanny gaze in my direction. We had been conspicuously not having this conversation since Ileopo's birth. She knew what I meant. "He'll die if he has another attack."

"I see the great spirit sometimes, near him. It watches Parech like a merchant would a tasty fish."

"The great death wears a mask, Tulo."

She glowered at me. "A hungry mask."

"Ile told me to save him."

"He knows?"

"I think he's guessed. The son is as perceptive as the mother."

"And the father. Parech will know if you try to do something."

I took a deep breath. I had been planning this for years. It scared me more than even death itself, and I had not thought that was possible. But there was nothing left for us but to try.

"A little girl stomping her foot at the wind," I said.

"What?"

"That's what Parech said this crusade of mine really is, when I first told him. He might be right. It might be better to let him die than disturb so much for his sake."

Tulo gripped my shoulders hard enough to leave a bruise. The years had not mellowed her, nor had motherhood, but they had subtly turned the planes of her face from that of a girl to a woman. They had given her an understanding and a sense of self the younger, hotter, more angular Tulo of five years ago never possessed. I loved her as much as I ever had.

"You don't mean that," she said.

"No. I don't."

I told her my plan.

"So you figured it out?" she asked. "What the death doesn't know?"

I told her I had, though I was by no means sure. She believed me, as always. Hadn't Parech told me he envied her trust? I went to find Ileopo and tell him. He's almost too young, but the calm, clear-eyed way he took the news tells me that he can do his part. Oh, when he looks at me like that, as though he can't quite make out what I'm thinking and his very impotence amuses him, I feel his father in my heart like a scar. I could not bear Parech's absence. Perhaps even less than I could bear Tulo's. At least she has shared herself with me. Her heart has always been cruel and harsh, but never closed like Parech's. We have been with each other for nearly six years and not once has he ever said what he feels for me. I think, now, that neither of us dare.

And so his son will conspire with his lover to deceive this man who has given up so much for all of us. He will hate them for it, but he will forgive them. I do not know that he will ever forgive me. I recall his fury when I first told him the outlines of this plan.

I recall his horror at the thought of me entering the select ranks of great spirit binders. The Akane hate all such things, and he still shares their essential prejudices.

And they might not be wrong, at that.

Spirits above, what am I doing? Will it be enough to save him?

Tomorrow I will go to Parech and tell him that his son is dying. He has caught the fire sickness, I will say, and it's ravaging this body. If he helps me bind the death spirit, I will say, we can save him. Parech will not believe me, of course he won't, and so I will propose to use an old geas, one of my very first, and take us all temporarily into the spirit world. For the first time, Tulo will see her son. And Parech will see, because I have arranged it to be so, a careful convocation of death sprites, apparently attached to his son. And he will agree, because it will never occur to him that I would do so much to manipulate him.

Tulo and Ile will stay here. Parech and I will travel to the inner islands, one of the ones not taken up by the fire or water bindings. I will sharpen his metal blade, because such a huge binding will require a like sacrifice. He will not know what that sacrifice is until his refusing would kill us both. And then, in the event, the death spirit will be bound, his life will be saved, and he will know how I've deceived him.

Then he will remember what we did in Okika to that poor Maaram soldier, almost certainly dead. He will remember that he taught me all I've ever needed to know about using others to get what one wants. Some may say Parech is immoral because he does this without qualms to those he does not know. But I know I am the worse person, because I am doing this to a man I love more than my own life.

A man I love.

I love.

Aoi is dead.

PART V

. . .

Ipa Nui

· 14 ·

H IS SISTER HAD BEEN JOINED BY A NEW GHOST, but at least this one didn't speak. How could she, when he had ripped out her throat with his own hand? Emea regarded the bloodless, voiceless ghost of the stablegirl with distaste.

"Was that truly necessary, brother?" she had said, when he staggered back into his rooms, his hair and clothes still wet with blood. His servants had taken one look at him and ordered several baths drawn. It always took that many when he got like this.

"You told me to do it," he said, running his hand through his hair long after all the blood had been rinsed away. Before, with Nahe, it had never been this hard. Even after Nahoa left, his deeds had never seemed to cling to him. His nightmares were of losing his wife and child, not of the horrors revenge had driven him to deep in the bowels of the house. But now he saw that sad little girl everywhere he went, and he felt her blood on his skin long after he had scrubbed it all away.

"You told me to do it," he said again, when Emea didn't respond.

Her blue-flame eyes had never seemed more inhuman. "No one told you to tear out her throat like some animal."

"She nearly killed my child."

"She was how old? Ten, eleven? The old nun told you she didn't act alone."

"I'll get the one truly responsible. I will win this war, and I will punish the ones who have hurt my daughter and then this nightmare will be over and Nahoa will come back to me."

Emea snorted. "Come back? You truly believe that, brother?"

"She will. She said she would, once I stopped all this. And I will stop all this as soon as I win the war."

The little girl's ghost shook her head and began to cry. Her lips shaped words, but he didn't try very hard to read them. Emea turned and pushed her aside, but her hands went straight through. She clucked her tongue.

"Win the war, will you?" she said. "Better get on with that, dear brother. Because it looks to me like you're losing. Funny, those Okikans seem to have long memories."

"This isn't the Maaram war."

"Not yet."

Neither of them would leave him alone, so he fell silent and scowled into the heat of his hearth fire. The old harbor had been well and thoroughly lost. He still had the superior army, superior weapons, and control of the majority of the island. But the fact that the rebels had managed to carve out even a sixth of the city for themselves filled him with baffled rage. He ought to be discussing plans with his chiefs or fielding parlay requests from whoever styled themselves the leader of the rebels these days. He ought to be combing his list of prisoners for informants and spies he could send back out into the shockingly porous rebel army. Instead he sat and brooded, alone save for his ghosts.

She had screamed, but not very loud. She had offered him secrets and said something about sennit braid, which had gone utterly unremarked at the time but kept coming back to him now. A stablehand had offered the Mo'i her entire life's savings, and it amounted to little more than a few ropes of cord.

Why did I kill her? he wondered now, far too late. What was that incoherent rage that had come over him, blotting out even the semblance of rational thought? Why not just imprison her like he had the others who crossed him? And if he had to kill her, why like that? Why like some mad animal in need of a mercy killing?

He recalled Senona Ahi and Kaleakai, the two guardians who had told him so starkly that he needed to kill himself to secure the great fire. He would have assassinated them, too, if it weren't for their power and influence. The stablehand had been his to kill, because she meant nothing to anyone.

He shivered. He reminded himself of Nahe, coolly calculating the misery he could inflict on people by virtue of the power they held. Emea had meant nothing, and so Nahe had treated her like nothing for all their years together.

"How did this happen?" he said aloud, though not to his ghosts. "When did I become like him?"

"Don't flinch now, brother," said the apparition who was certainly, absolutely not his sister.

"You aren't real," he said.

Her blue flames crackled. "Real enough to kill for. Real enough to die."

"But what can we do with her?"

This was not the first time this question had been asked this night, among these three. And, Lana thought, each set of answers seemed more tepid and unworkable than the last. She and Nahoa and Pano sat close to the fire, with the table Eliki always used for her work pushed aside. As the night wore on, Lana kept expecting their erstwhile leader to put in an acerbic, cool-headed suggestion that they would all argue with and then agree to. But now two of Yechtak's soldiers guarded her in a house one street away while she stared with a stern, unnerving distance at the wall. No one had thought to restrain her. It had seemed unlikely she could overcome the guards.

"Can't you just let her go?" Nahoa said wearily. "What can she do now, anyway? There's three armies in this damn city and she doesn't control any of them."

Pano, who had hardly spoken since the rebels had secured the old docks, regarded Nahoa with bleak intensity. "You don't know Eliki," he said. "We could turn her out with just the clothes on her back, and she'd return with an army in a year."

"But why would she want to?" Lana asked.

"She doesn't trust anyone else to win."

"Haven't you already won?" Nahoa said.

"You think your husband will just let us stay in the heart of his city?"

Nahoa bit her lip and fell silent. Pano added another log to the fire, though it seemed to Lana that the flames were plenty bright. *Some rebel leaders we make.* She wanted to sleep. She wanted to cry. She still didn't understand how all this had happened.

"What would Eliki do?" Lana said, in a creaky attempt at humor.

Pano didn't even bother to smile. "She'd kill her," he said. "And if I objected, she'd lie and do it anyway. Eliki is fond of elegant solutions."

"Like with Ahi," Nahoa said, and then they both fell silent.

"We have to tell Yechtak *something* in the morning," Lana said finally. This was also not the first time she had said this. As before, they both glanced up and then away, incapable of speech, let alone finding a solution. She couldn't stand it. She stood up and started to pace.

"We can exile her," she said. "Some place far away and hard to reach from Essel. The Kalakoas. We'll give her likeness to all ship's captains so they won't take her back here. We will publicly condemn her actions and prove that we are not just another version of Bloody One-hand. And we will send a message to the Mo'i and Makaho to negotiate a truce."

They both stared at her. As well they might. Lana felt as she had earlier that day, when she declared herself the commander of the rebel forces. As though she were on a precipice, staring down at her certain death. Like casting a geas, really. She felt for the red mandagah jewel beneath her shirt, so much a part of her now she hardly noticed its warm presence on her skin. She had been given responsibility once and had done all she could to avoid it. Perhaps this would work better. It could hardly turn out worse.

"Why would Kohaku agree to a truce? Pano just said he'll keep fighting."

Lana glanced at Pano, and it was clear from the intent way he watched Nahoa that he had already guessed Lana's solution. "Ahi is no longer at the fire temple, right?" she said.

Nahoa frowned. "I told you, Malie took her to her mother's house in the fourth district."

"So you—" Lana began, but Pano shot her a warning look and took Nahoa's hand.

"If you agree to help us, my lady," he said, "we could end this."

Nahoa blushed from the roots of her hair to her neck. Pano controlled himself better, but there was a certain quality in his stillness, like he might explode if he didn't move very carefully. Lana finally realized what should have been obvious from the moment they sat down together in this room.

"You want to use me with Kohaku just like Makaho did," Nahoa said.

Pano flinched, but he just said, "Yes."

"But he'll know you'd never hurt me."

"And what if one of his soldiers' arrows does?"

Nahoa opened her mouth, yanked her hand from his, and started to curse roundly and fluently. "Damn it, Pano! Why does it always have to be like this? Everyone twisting me any way they damn want for their own stupid reasons? Even you! Why can't you all just leave me and Ahi in peace? I wish you'd all go away forever."

Lana started to speak and then thought better of it. Pano looked as though Nahoa had stabbed him through the chest. He took a few gulping breaths.

"We can," he said, "if that's your wish. You only have to ask. We'd never...I'd never..."

Nahoa's fury, so immediately potent, vanished in the face of this. She took both of his hands in hers. "I know," she said. "I'm sorry. It's just hard sometimes. It seems like it will never end."

"Everything does eventually."

"I'll help you. Of course I will."

They were staring into each other's eyes and neither had made any move to separate their hands. Lana backed away abruptly and mumbled some excuse about needing to tell Yechtak their decision. They didn't acknowledge her. She almost ran outside, her eyes stinging. No one had seen Kai in four days. She'd gone through the stacks of dead bodies slated for the pyres, but there was no sign of him. She didn't think he was dead—he was the water guardian, after all, and surely his premature death would cause more havoc than this constant, barely tolerable constriction in her chest. But where could he have gone? The snow had stopped, as Eliki had promised it would, but the powdery drifts still towered above the cleared roads. She couldn't imagine how much of a sacrifice it must have taken for Kai to bring that much snow. Maybe he had gone to the ocean and drowned? But that was ridiculous. Kai *was* water.

Shivering, Lana walked over to the house where they had temporarily sequestered Eliki, Yechtak, and the Okikan commander. The guards posted outside the door let her in after a moment of surprise. This house was small and all on one level. Eliki was under guard in the small private room, while Yechtak and the commander slept on pallets in the common area. In theory, anyway. The commander slept, but Yechtak knelt in front of his pallet, his arms raised. He didn't seem to hear her when she came in, so she called his name gently.

He whirled around and fell back against the sheets. "Iolana," he said. He was the only person besides Okilani, the head elder on her native island, who used her full name. And he always used it as though he were naming a treasure.

"I thought I would speak with Eliki," she said.

His eyes widened but then he nodded. "Of course. Wait here. I will wake her."

Lana thought about letting her sleep, but then shrugged. She was responsible for this disaster. She could deal with the consequences. Knowing Eliki, she would only be expecting it.

Yechtak entered the other room and then beckoned for her to follow. It seemed that Eliki was having as sleepless a night as the rest of them. She sat in her solitary chair, staring at the pages of a book but not, Lana thought, actually reading it.

"The black angel would like to speak with you," Yechtak said.

Eliki raised her eyebrows but did not look up. Yechtak frowned.

"It's fine," Lana said. "You can leave us."

He hesitated, but then just bowed his head and left. Yechtak had told her some of what had happened in the year since they last saw each other. Apparently, the wind spirit itself had named him her ambassador. Lana had never heard of anyone like that in the legends of the other black angels, but given the almost worshipful way Yechtak regarded her, she could believe it.

"I take it you have judged my fate," Eliki said, almost amiably. She shut the book without marking her place and coolly met Lana's eyes.

"I didn't want this," she said.

Eliki waved her hand. "Of course you didn't. You couldn't have made your reluctance to serve our cause more clear if you'd thrown a tantrum. And since I can't blame ambition for our sudden reversal of fortune, I suppose I can only blame fate."

"You chose to kill Ahi."

"Choice," Eliki said, "is overrated. Sometimes the other choice is too unbearable to contemplate."

"A baby, Eliki."

"Is that what you came here for? To prick my conscience? You'll have to try harder than that. I've had to make mine stronger than iron to get this far."

"Maybe you shouldn't have."

"I suppose you think that was a choice, too."

They stared at each other, silent and calculating, two enemies far out on a narrow ledge. Who would push first?

"Have you thought," Eliki said finally, "about what it really means for you to do this? I helped start this war. I armed our people and developed the strategy and launched them against the far superior force of our tyrannous Mo'i, utterly sure in the knowledge that hundreds of them would die and we might not even win with their sacrifice. And when I realized that our bows were breaking and might destroy us before we even began, I convinced your lover to take the wonder of a snowfall and turn it into a deadly weapon. You have flown over the city, black angel. You must have seen the bodies of those frozen in the snow. I have almost destroyed this city so that I might save it. I believe utterly in the choices I have made, because they are the only ones I could have made. And if you disagree with me, if you feel that I have crossed a line that should not have been crossed, if you think I am like Bloody One-hand, mad with violence and all unknowing, then disagree with *that*, with those hundreds dead who should not be, and not some babe I did not even succeed in killing."

Lana leaned against the wall because she was trembling and did not wish to show it. What masochistic impulse had made her come to Eliki this night? She should have known what moral labyrinth she was inviting herself into. And now, how to get out?

"I saved her," Lana said, and then more loudly, "Ahi is only alive because I used a stronger geas to break your own."

Eliki's lips twisted. "Yes, I know. For a conscience, Pano has always been remarkably active. But, fine, my intentions were clear. If it were up to me, the child would be dead by now. Tell me, black angel, why her death weighs so much more than these other hundreds you have witnessed? Why not lock your lover in here with me for the innocents he killed with his blanketing snow?"

Lana swallowed carefully. She hated Eliki more than she had hated anyone in her life right now, even Akua. At least Akua's sins were unmitigated by this awful, twisting self-justification. Kai was gone, spirits knew where, and here this woman claimed, with horrifying accuracy, that they all shared the blame for innocent deaths.

"You ordered it."

"But *you're* the one who believes in the primacy of choice. He should have known what would happen."

But Lana considered how briefly Kai had been in this city, how little of his life had been spent around humans, let alone in a place packed with hundreds of thousands of them, and wondered how he would feel when he discovered what had come of his sacrifice.

Lana wrapped her arms around her shoulders. She felt helpless, like when she was very young and her mother had yelled at her for forgetting to take off her sandals before she came inside. "Eliki, I can't argue with you. You're smarter than me and you know it. But killing a baby for political gain is wrong. You have to know that."

"Sometimes there are only wrong choices. But there, at last, we agree—there's no use arguing this. I have finally done something even Pano cannot forgive, and so you must do something about me. Knowing you both, I very much doubt it will be an execution, though perhaps One-hand's young wife is feeling particularly vengeful?"

"She wanted to let you go."

Eliki laughed. "Did she? Well then, we have three fools at the head of this army. You should kill me."

"Pano said that's what you'd do. He said you preferred elegant solutions."

"Ah, Pano. He should have stayed with his plants. I never should have sent him to co-opt the Mo'i's wife. The oldest lesson in the world, and I forgot it: beware handsome men and young women. So what is it, then? Keep me in this room and hope I die quietly? Don't tell me you're actually going to let me leave?"

"You'll be on the next ship to the Kalakoas. Every captain will find it in their interest to never give you passage to our shores. You can try to disguise yourself, but I think it will be difficult."

"Yes," Eliki agreed, but absently. She turned back to face the wall. Her throat worked, but no sound came out. "Yes. That will work quite well." Now Eliki was shaking, though Lana could think of no reason why. She'd sounded positively sanguine at the discussion of her death or permanent imprisonment. "If you have the woman and the baby, you know you can use them to defang the Mo'i. He's reliably protective of them. It would be touching, in other circumstances. Be careful with the Okikans. I'm not sure what they want, but you can be sure it's not the liberation of Essel. If you can negotiate a steady enough truce with One-hand, try to make them leave. No one would survive an inter-island war. You've at least convinced me of that. Our greatest weapon is our cause. No one likes the Mo'i, Lana. Some are just more afraid of him than others. It might take years, but eventually the people will all be on our side, so long as we behave like the just and equable government he'll never be. Don't...no matter what, don't underestimate Kohaku's danger. He is smart and he is mad, and he has no empathy for those he hurts. Whatever follows him will be even worse. You should kill him, if you can."

"Eliki..."

She still wouldn't meet Lana's eyes. "Oh, I know you won't. Pano might."

"I'm sorry."

"Are you?"

"More than I should be."

"Yes. But how efficiently you dispose of your enemy."

Lana didn't realize until she stepped away from the wall that Eliki was crying. Not a trace of the tears had shown in her voice, or even in her posture, aside from the trembling.

"Are you my enemy?" Lana asked, softly.

"When you exile me, I know you will say it's for the baby. But promise me that you will say it's for Leipaluka and Sabolu and the ones who died in the snow. Promise me that it's for every innocent killed in the Mo'i's fires, and I'll be no one's enemy but my own."

"I promise."

Eliki sighed and dropped her head to her hands. "My daughter loved this city," she said in a voice Lana didn't recognize at all—tired and defeated. "She loved Nui'ahi and the temple, she loved the colored robes of the Kulanui, she loved the spring festival in the bay. I'd pay so she could catch her own worms and they'd roast them for her by the water. This city is everything I've ever loved."

"We will save it," she said, but Eliki's sobs had overtaken her words. Lana rubbed furiously at her own eyes and left.

15

Bound as a sprite, Kai's water self naturally dominated his human self. And as the spirit world became clear to him, like a filmy veil slowly pulled back from his eyes, he saw what Akua had done. She and Leilani had been living in this house all along it seemed, a simple sidestep from the human world. Even Kai hadn't noticed when he visited this place with Lana, which made him furious with himself even while he admired Akua's deft skill. They seemed as at home here as the ancient sprites, crotchety and torpid, bound to its very foundations and beams. This was certainly the house from Lana's black book. Perhaps Akua had found it just as Lana had, deducing the clues from the thousand-year-old diary. It was a good place to hide: near the city, but far enough away that no one would notice strange comings and goings. A house protected by spirits and so well guarded that even a guardian like Kai wouldn't notice it.

He didn't know what Akua wanted with him. He gathered that she had bound him on Makaho's behalf, but his grasp of the twisted human politics of this sprawling city was shaky at best. When Akua was present in the house, she stayed mostly silent, wrapped in a cocoon of contemplation too intense to even be called brooding. She was often away. He tried once to push against the binding and was repelled with enough force to send him crashing against the sturdy walls of the room. Akua had left earlier, and so only Leilani witnessed that last humiliation. Kai had never met Lana's mother before, but after a few minutes in her presence he understood many things that had never made much sense to him before.

"She must think you're very powerful," Leilani had said when he pulled himself painfully upright.

"And yet not nearly powerful enough," he said, and then smiled to leaven the bitterness he heard in his voice.

Leilani did not understand much more than he about the reason for her imprisonment. She had not suffered, but she was clearly lonely. She knew of the events happening in the city, but Akua was a lackluster storyteller and so often distracted that it had been difficult to get a complete picture. She knew that Lana had become the black angel, but she hadn't known of her role in the current war. Of her husband she had known nothing at all and turned away when Kai was able to tell her that he was safe. She did not cry, but the expression on her face was vulnerable and raw. He ached for her.

"He and Lana shared a home at first..." He trailed off when he realized he was entering uncomfortable territory, but Leilani sensed this.

"At first?"

"They...he was helping victims in the Mo'i's tents. She was helping the rebels. It caused problems."

She sighed. "Oh, Kapa. It was hard on him, maybe even harder than it was on me, not to see Lana grow up. In his heart she's still the girl we watched climb from the ocean with a mandagah jewel when she was thirteen."

Kai stared at her and then realized how much she still didn't know. It took a long time to tell the whole story—the bits before Kai knew Lana and everything after. Leilani smiled at him when he stumbled over seeing Lana for the first time. Too late, he wondered if he should gloss over the circumstances of Pua's death, but the words tumbled out of him.

"So you two..."

"We are fine," he said. "We understand each other." In the presence of the woman for whom his aunt had died, he felt the buried embers of his resentment cool and crumble away. Leilani was alive and Pua was dead. Nothing he did could change that. Now, he found his sadness made clear by the thought that if someone had to be alive in Pua's place, he was glad it could be her.

"I lost my mother," Leilani said, "when I was Lana's age now. It was the hardest thing I've ever gone through, except perhaps giving Lana away. And I can't tell you how sorry I am."

Kai could hardly meet her earnest gaze. He looked at her hands, instead. "Some things are never simple. Sometimes everyone is wrong and everyone is hurt. Lana and I have forgiven each other. And you have nothing to be sorry for."

Akua returned an hour or so later with a bag full of food and a piece of paper in her hand.

"You might be interested," was all she said before it dropping it in his lap. Leilani looked over his shoulder as he opened it.

The water guardian is at our mercy, read the plain, evenly spaced script. *You will cease all hostilities immediately and discuss options at our leisure.*

Kai looked up at Akua, who was watching his reaction with a certain grim amusement. "I hope you enjoy being at the center of Essel's great civil war. Makaho just had that delivered to the rebels."

Lana stared at the note for nearly a minute and when she finally shut her eyes, it was almost entirely out of anger, not fear or grief. Yechtak, who had come with the soldier that delivered it, put a tentative hand on her shoulder.

"I cannot read the binder language," he said softly. "What does it say?"

She told him. The letter was brief enough, after all. And Kai was not dead. At least she knew that. How the head nun had managed to capture a water guardian she had no idea, but at least he was not dead.

"The water guardian?" he said, frowning. "I do not...he is a legend of your binder mythology?"

This made Lana smile. "He's very real, for a legend. All the bound spirits have guardians. It's part of the cycle."

"An unnatural cycle," he said, and though Lana would just have dismissed him before, she now stayed silent. The more she read Ino's book, the more she wondered about the bindings. They seemed so inevitable and necessary, and yet humans had lived for thousands of years without them.

"What will you do?" he asked.

"Cease all hostilities, I guess. Not like I wanted hostilities in the first place. If they could capture him, then they could probably hurt him. We can't just surrender. But we have Nahoa and Ahi at least. That's a sort of stalemate."

"So it is all right?"

She shook her head violently and sank to the floor. "No. Not all right. Not at all."

"Iolana, is this water guardian, is he someone—"

"Yes."

Yechtak had grown up in the year since she'd last seen him. It wasn't just his height or his subtly thinner features. It was his carriage and grace and his quiet absorption of ways that must seem endlessly foreign to him. But in the instant of her admission he looked away, and she thought he seemed very young again. She remembered the strange night when she had woken up to him kissing her.

"Yechtak..."

"I also have a wife," he said. "She would have had my child by now."

A father? So quickly? Time truly changed everything. "You must miss her," she said.

"I hardly know her. She was my mother's choice."

He was giving her the sort of speaking look that she remembered from their journey alone to the wind shrine. But she had grown as well, and she understood what it meant. "I don't feel for you that way," she said. "You must know that."

The old Yechtak would have blushed with embarrassment and misery, but this one merely nodded. "I have known since I saw you again. It's all right. You are a black angel."

She smiled at him and they were companionably silent for several long minutes before the Okikan chief stormed in, bringing the cold with him. His name was Arai, a holdover from the ancient Maaram tongue. Only the oldest lineages on Okika retained the traditional names.

"There was a message?" he said, walking brusquely over to her. "Show me."

She raised her eyebrows—much, she thought, as Eliki would have—and handed him the note.

"You mean those rumors were true? The water guardian?" He shook his head. "The black angel and the water guardian. You Esselans don't do half measures, do you?"

Lana could have pointed out that she was probably more Okikan than Esselan, but just shrugged. Arai was tall and unattractively skinny, with a blustering, intrusive demeanor that she supposed had been counted on to achieve whatever bargain the Okikan council thought to wrest in return for their help. What that might be, he had yet to inform them, but she knew Eliki was right to expect it.

"Well, we must discuss this. It causes difficulties. Where's Pano and the woman?"

"Nahoa is getting her baby and Pano is with her. What sort of difficulties?"

He gave her a withering look. "What do you think? We need to press our advantage and conquer the rest of the city before your Mo'i can regroup. The council has an interest in a governing arrangement more amenable to both your people and mine."

Lana had a sudden, fierce wish for Eliki's advice. But she'd been escorted to a ship that morning and the soldiers were even now printing the pamphlet celebrating their victory and listing her sins. As Eliki had asked, it tasked her with the deaths of Sabolu and Leipaluka and those who died in the snow, in addition to the plot to kill Nahoa's child. Pano had written it and Lana wondered, given the bleak look in his eyes, if he wished that they might have kept Eliki's treachery secret. If she hadn't exposed the rebel leader so hastily in front of the crowd, perhaps they'd still have the benefit of her counsel. And yet, how could she trust anyone who was willing to go so far for her cause?

"We'll discuss it when they return," was all Lana said.

Arai gave her a long look that wasn't quite a glare and left. He forgot to shut the door.

"Yechtak," she said. "How on earth did you convince them to come here?"

"Everyone knew the black angel had joined the Esselan war."

"But still, how did they believe you represented me?"

He smiled. "I called a wind."

Nahoa, Ahi, and Pano returned a few hours later and they held their meeting with Yechtak and Arai. Yechtak stayed mostly silent, but Arai interrupted nearly everyone's speech with the pressing needs of his council. Pano's tone grew so even and steady that Lana knew he was furious enough to spit. Nahoa seemed to realize this as well—she handed him the baby in the middle of the meeting and Lana could almost see his calm returning.

"Your Mo'i wouldn't dare kill the water guardian," Arai repeated. "We should press on."

"I wouldn't be so sure of that," Pano said. "There's a reason we call him 'Bloody.'"

"Even he can't be so mad!"

Nahoa, Pano, and Lana shared a silent moment. Then Nahoa cleared her throat. "He might be," was all she said.

For once, Arai didn't argue. Scowling, he agreed to send a carefully worded reply to the fire temple. They agreed to the truce, they reminded them of the presence of Nahoa and Ahi in their camp, and they suggested that both parties meet in a neutral location some days hence to determine if a peaceful arrangement might be made.

Lana didn't think Arai was particularly happy about discussions of peaceful arrangements—for a man who had never witnessed a war in his life, he was remarkably martial. However, he held his peace. Perhaps he was just waiting for a better moment to strike at the Mo'i. Lana knew they'd have to keep a careful eye on him.

"The fire temple messenger brought a body, too," Arai said, after they gave the note to a courier. "Didn't you know? Some girl. At least it's cold out. Why don't you Esselans burn bodies with some decent speed?"

"Our burnings will be tonight," Pano said grimly. "Along with the rest of Essel."

Nahoa begged off, grabbing Ahi and almost running away before she would have to see the body again. And even Lana, who had seen a great deal of death in the preceding days, nearly vomited into the lingering snow when she saw the bloody hollow of the girl's throat and her pale, bruised face.

Arai, for once, found himself speechless. The soldiers covered her body again, averting their eyes. Makaho had sent a note. It read: "I would have her burned with honor."

"Your Mo'i did this?" Arai said finally. His voice was hoarse.

She and Pano just looked at him. Arai turned away.

They held the burning by the water, as dictated by long-standing Esselan tradition. The old harbor hadn't seen such a conflagration in centuries—there weren't often so many to burn at once, after all. Lana herself put Sabolu's body on the pyre, unable to shake the memory of another funeral for another dead girl. Her best friend had drowned in a flood because Lana had been too late to save her. Lana still dreamed sometimes of a certain shade of red, dark and fiery—the color of Kali's hair as it shone in sharp sunlight. Now Sabolu, as well, had gone past the gate.

By the time the bodies had all been prepared, the gathered crowd had swelled into the thousands. They were eerily silent save for the occasional ritual wail and muffled sob. Many held fresh copies of the latest rebel pamphlet, and Lana wondered what they thought about Eliki's absence. Lana did not know much about Esselan funeral traditions and, besides, the thought of standing before such a crowd terrified her. It was Pano who climbed atop a stack of boxes started to speak.

"*Se maloka selama ua ola, ipa nui,*" he said, his voice deep and carrying. For all those words were associated with death, it was unusual to hear them at a burning. Mostly, the grieving did not wish to be reminded of death's immutability. The only sound now was the delicate susurrus of the crowd's quiet shifting, the smack of the waves against the wooden docks.

"They have gone past our knowledge, but not our affections. With their sacrifices, we have won a victory that few among us believed possible. They have given their lives so that our great city might go another way, might move from cruelty and injustice and the arbitrary whim of a madman and toward peace and a voice for all its citizens. That they will not be able to see this new world they helped create is a grief we will always feel. But honor and remembrance are all any of us can give them now." He held the torch aloft and for a moment its fiery hues blended with the sunset behind him. The crowd gasped. Lana thought he would light the pyres, but instead he walked over to her and handed her the flame.

"I think they would see you do it," he whispered.

I didn't want this. She never had. But finally, she had learned to accept it. She lit Sabolu's pyre first, and the flames quickly spread to the others. She spread her wings to fan them. As bodies sometimes do, Sabolu's shifted as though alive on her bed of flames. Lana watched impassively until the fire covered Sabolu's face. She turned around. Deep in the crowd, a few people had begun to sing. At first, she assumed it was a traditional funeral chant, but as the chorused voices grew stronger, she realized their choice was far more unusual. The song had quietly gained popularity in the city ever since she and her father had played it in the aftermath of the eruption, but she'd never expected the force it could have when thousands turned its melancholic beauty into a ballad of palpable rage and grief. She faced them alone. "But within my heart, hope battles fear," she sang, and they answered:

"For I do not know what lies beyond the gate."

The fires burned all night, and though the crowd thinned it did not fully disperse. The grieving made a steady procession past the high, bright flames. A west wind thankfully blew the ash toward the sea, and the heat of several hundred burning bodies kept her warmer than she had been for a month. Ahi loved the flames. She reached out her chubby hands and laughed when the pyres blew off sparks. Nahoa grinned and played with her until she fell asleep. Looking at them, Lana felt an unexpected pang. But surely someday she'd have children of her own? If she could get Kai back. If she could rescue her mother. Leilani would love to be a grandmother.

Someone called her name, a voice familiar and comforting and dearly missed. She looked up. Her father had been watching the flames, but now he approached her, awkward and diffident.

"I asked at the fire temple when I didn't hear from Sabolu. They said she was dead. They said..." He shook his head. "I can't believe what they said. I thought she was safe."

"Kohaku is mad, Papa. You have to know that."

"I know. The whole city knows. But still, I thought he was better than a war, than....I was wrong. I'm sorry, Lana. I missed your mother so much I think I almost lost our child."

"No," she said. They were both crying. "Papa, I'm right here."

16

Nahoa slept in Pano's bed while Pano slept on the floor outside. Malie stayed in the room with her. Nahoa had attempted to argue about this arrangement, but they'd both refused to even entertain the other possibility. Malie because she suspected something had happened between the two of them, and Pano because he loved her. She knew this because he had told her so, very late in the night after the battle.

"You should know," he had said, "that I'll do everything in my power to keep you and Ahi safe." And she had asked why and he had said, "I think I've loved you since we first met."

And that was it. They hadn't so much as kissed. He refused to speak of it again. But still Nahoa felt her face flush when she saw him looking at her, and her denials were not very forceful when Malie asked her what Pano had done. After the burnings Ahi fell asleep right away, but it took Nahoa longer. She couldn't close her eyes without seeing Sabolu's blood on the straw, hearing the horse's panicked snorts as it nudged her shoulder. It was worse, in its own way, than seeing what Kohaku had done to Nahe in the cellar. Nahe had been in unspeakable agony; she had given him poison so he could die. And yet Nahe had been a grown man who had aided an innocent girl's death in as callous and cruel a manner as possible. What Kohaku had done was unspeakable. It was why she had left, pregnant and alone save for Malie. But at least Nahe had truly wronged him. At least she could understand the impulse that had driven Kohaku to those horrors. He had been, she realized, still recognizably a man she loved.

But the intervening months had truly made him as mad as they all said. Mad enough to rip out the throat of an eleven-year-old girl when all she had done was unwittingly carry out the orders of another. Mad enough to stab her corpse and leave his bloody footprints in the snow. She didn't know Kohaku at all anymore. She didn't want to. Sacrificing his hand to that fire hadn't just made Nui'ahi erupt. It had destroyed his soul. A part of her so small she couldn't even voice the thought aloud wished that he would listen to Senona Ahi and Kai. She wished that he would sacrifice himself so this city could live again, without the threat of the smoking sentinel, without the threat of his endless, senseless violence. But how could she wish the father of her child dead?

She started to cry. She thought it was soft enough, but Malie woke and held her until she quieted.

"Whatever Pano has said," Malie whispered, "you know you must do nothing. There is no way to tell what your husband will do if he thinks you love another."

"But I do."

"I know. I know. But no one else can guess."

The next morning, Lana woke them before the sun was quite up. They needed to speak without that Okikan general breathing down their necks about "amenable governments" and "equitable trade agreements." You'd think they'd already deposed the Mo'i, the way he went on.

"Makaho sent her reply," she said. Nahoa noted the absent way she wrapped her wings around herself to stave off the early-morning chill and thought they must be very convenient. "They agree to meet with us on the grounds of the Kulanui in six days."

"The Kulanui is neutral territory?" Nahoa asked. "It's right next to the temple!"

"She's right," Pano said. "If they try to sabotage us, it's a good location."

Lana shrugged. "We can try to negotiate, if you can think of some place better."

Malie, who had been playing with Ahi quietly on the other side of the room, looked up. "Why not on the water? You can go out in a boat with all of your guards on the shore. Not much they can do then."

Nahoa grinned at her. Honestly, it was reassuring, how smart Malie could be. Lana was nodding slowly. "That's good," she said. "They can't object to it."

"In the meantime," Pano said, "it would be good to consolidate our position. We have the old harbor and Nahoa, but I think Arai could just as easily turn on us as help us."

Lana looked away. "That's what Eliki said."

Nahoa wished that it weren't so clear how much these two missed Eliki. Nahoa hadn't wanted her killed, but it galled her to know how much even Pano still loved the woman who had tried to kill her daughter. If Eliki hadn't already been sent away, Nahoa would have slapped her. *If you're so damn smart,* she would say, *how come you thought it was a good idea to murder a baby? How come you think you're any better than my mad husband?*

But Eliki remained a living ghost, and Pano and Lana were discussing ways to remove Arai's Okikan army.

"Why not just ask him to leave?" Lana said.

"Are you serious?" Pano said.

Lana shrugged. "Well, if he doesn't agree, it's no harm done. Maybe we can offer him something as an inducement?"

"Because we are so clearly in possession of the sort of material wealth that would change the mind of a rich Okikan merchant?"

"Well, no," Lana allowed. "Not at the moment. But we'll have all of Essel, damaged as it is, once we've won. He claims this is all about trade, so let's make sure that it is. He leaves, he gets special tariffs, open markets, reduced docking fees..."

Pano paused mid-pace and looked at her very carefully. "That might work. But what's to stop him from staying with his army and forcing us to do whatever he wants?"

At this Nahoa had to interrupt. "But do you really think he wants a war? I mean a real one, between the islands, like before the spirit bindings? I think probably the Okikans are still scared of it getting that far."

Lana nodded. "She's right. He might be willing to fight if it comes to that, but no one makes a kala if the spirits break free. If we can subtly threaten a full-on war while offering him such a generous alternative..."

"And if he calls your bluff?" Malie said.

Pano frowned at her. "They're your people, Malie. What do you think? Will the rich Okikans be willing to fight a war a thousand years late for the jewel of Essel?"

Malie kept her voice calm, but Nahoa suspected it was only for Ahi's sake. "The question, gardener, is whether you are."

Pano opened his mouth to speak, but Lana put her hand on his shoulder. "I think it's worth the risk," she said. "The longer the army stays here, the harder it will be to make them leave. I'll go speak to Arai."

"You're sure?"

Lana nodded, and Nahoa wondered if she could really feel as confident as she looked. Their position still seemed so precarious to her. But what did she know? As Kohaku was so fond of saying, she was only a sailor.

Lana left. Pano forgot himself enough that he didn't even flinch when Nahoa held his hand. Malie just rocked Ahi against her chest and clucked her tongue, a sound more fond than scolding.

Before Lana spoke to Arai, she sent a messenger to the Rushes. As she suspected, the local leaders there were happy enough to agree to give their formal support to the victorious rebels. As Pano would say, success attracted friends. She suspected that the always-sympathetic eighth and fifth districts might fall into line soon. Armed with this increased territory, she entered the house where Arai and Yechtak had been quartered. Yechtak beamed at the sight of her, but Arai barely glanced up from the sheaf of papers he had been studying when she entered.

"And have you Esselans considered my terms?" he said.

At least he didn't waste time on pleasantries. "We have a counteroffer."

Now he looked at her, surprise emphasizing the gaunt lines of his face. "Do you? You recall how I saved your side from certain defeat not two days ago?"

"A favor for which we are suitably grateful."

"You'd best be more than that."

Lana wondered when she had ceased to be afraid of men and women like Arai, adults who wore their authority like a barbed headdress and cloaked any self-doubt in anger. Arai had come here at the head of an army and seemed prepared for bloodshed, but she was inclined to agree with Nahoa: he couldn't possibly be so complacent about the prospect of full-scale war as he pretended. And if she had declared herself the head of the rebel army, it was high time she acted like it. At least she knew that Yechtak would be on her side.

"We will offer you very favorable trading terms. Reduced tariffs, docking privileges, monopolies on certain goods."

Arai leaned back in his chair. "A good start." Lana allowed herself to smile. She could be as cool as he, if she chose. *She* was the black angel, after all. "A good *end*. In return for this, you and your forces leave within the week."

This startled Yechtak, who until this point had watched their exchange with baffled intensity. "But, Iolana," he said, "we are *your* army."

"I think Arai might have given you the wrong impression, Yechtak."

Arai cracked his knuckles. He seemed agitated. "They will obey me, as you said. You really wish to threaten us like this? With all—"

"There's no threat," Lana said, far more calmly than she felt. "Only an offer of mutual benefit. You don't really wish to fight this war. You don't want what it will unleash. No one wins if the great spirits break free, remember that."

"So you can fight your own civil war here in Essel and the spirits stay quiescent, but Okika gets involved and you threaten *us*?"

"Not quiescent," Lana said. "I didn't want this war to start at all, and now that it has we must end it quickly. The fire spirit is already slipping its bonds. I don't know how much more it will take before it breaks away entirely. Essel might have Nui'ahi, but Okika has its share of volcanoes, does it not? Do you really want to see a world without the great bindings, Arai? If you think very carefully, I think you'll see how this arrangement is the best for us all."

Arai stood up so abruptly that his papers fell to the floor. "You bloody Esselans." His voice was nearly a whine. He stalked to the door as though he would storm out, but at the last minute, he turned on her.

"Fine," he said. "You win. But *very* favorable trade agreements, black angel. Else I might be tempted to test the bindings further."

Lana's father hadn't settled in rebel territory. She didn't blame him—their apartment in the fourth district was far more comfortable. But two days after the burnings, Lana visited him. The meal they shared was the most companionable she could recall since they had reunited. It seemed that Kapa truly had decided not to judge her.

"I haven't forgotten about Mama, you know," she said, when they had polished off the last of the pan bread. "I'm not...I don't know what to do. There's so much more I'm responsible for now, but I haven't forgotten about her."

"Lana, I..."

"I know you think it sometimes. It's okay. But she's my mother, and I swear I'll get her back. Whatever Akua is doing, whatever she wants with Mama...I think one way or another, we'll know soon."

"How can you be so sure?"

Lana shrugged, and resisted the urge to look out the window and see if the death still hovered there. It had been mostly absent since Sabolu's death. "The spirits, they feel restless." The death had been so watchful lately, so silent. Especially whenever she asked about Akua. "A geas like the one she's making, something this complicated, it breaks if she takes too long. And she's been working it for *years*, Papa. I just think we won't have much longer to wait, one way or another." Lana took a swallow of water to attempt to quell the rush of dread in her stomach. But how was she supposed to uncover Akua's plan now, when all her other efforts had failed so spectacularly?

Her father started to speak, then shook his head and stood. "Do you want to play, Lana?" he asked. He held his lute, the old one that he had made so many years ago on their home island.

Lana smiled. "I shouldn't use my flute. It's…"

"I know. Do you want to try this? I just finished it. No geas involved, I promise." He handed her an acacia wood recorder, carved with delicate impressions of feathers and still redolent of the kukui resin finish. Her father had made a new instrument?

"It's yours," he said diffidently. "If you want it."

Lana could have cried. Instead, she put the recorder to her lips. They played together for hours, until the sun went down. The death stayed at the window, watching them both with such impassivity it felt like rapt adoration. She wondered how the music could hold it when she played with nothing more powerful than a recorder made of fresh-cut wood.

When she left late that night, it stayed by her shoulder, so close she imagined she could feel its insubstantial robes brushing her forehead.

Finally, she turned. "What is it?" she snapped. "Is this how you try to take me now?"

The death seemed to freeze. Through its translucent mask, she could see the main harbor, still glowing with laggard funeral pyres. Or perhaps that was merely the reflection of its memories.

"Have you thought about Parech?" it said.

Lana felt the bottom drop from her stomach. "Great Kai. The black book."

She stared at the last page for a very long time. The final three words seemed to be in a different handwriting. Parech's? Not Tulo's— Lana didn't think she'd been literate. It seemed that Aoi was the mysterious final binder, the one who had bound the death spirit. But that great Ana was rumored to have survived the binding. She must have. Isn't that what the death said? The great sacrifice is life. So who had died, and how? What was the final postulate, the one thing the death didn't know?

This was the knowledge she needed to defeat Akua. It had always been about the death, hadn't it? It was just so hard to remember when she spent her days surrounded by fire.

17

THE CORAL ATOLLS HAD BEEN MOSTLY FLOODED in the storms after the wind spirit broke free. A few scattered islands remained, but as she flew over their scorched, bleached remains, Lana thought it unlikely that any of Aoi's pierced people still lived here. She wondered if the sacred island might have vanished, but then stopped the thought. It had to be there. She had no other options. The death glided serenely beneath her. It did not speak once in the long day it took her to reach the first of the atolls. She didn't mind. Once she landed she took out the chart she and Nahoa had cobbled together out of what was known about the coral atolls and what Aoi had described in the book. The area most likely to hold the death island was southeast of her. She took out candied jackfruit and began to eat it, though she wasn't particularly hungry.

"I don't suppose you'd just tell me where the sacred island is," she said to it.

"Have you ever thought you might learn things you don't want to know?"

"It's the only way I can defeat her."

"You prove the point."

She didn't quite know what to make of that, so she pushed the map closer to its startlingly corporeal form. "Where is it?" she asked again.

And to her surprise, it unfurled a scaled, multi-jointed finger and pointed. They'd mapped no islands at all in that area, a bit to the north of where she'd thought to look.

She stared at it. "Why did you do that?"

"The avatar is not the death," it said, so reflexively it sounded like a prayer. "And you are about to meet the godhead."

The next morning, she filled two waterskins with fresh water and set out for the blank stretch of ocean the death spirit had claimed held its sacred cave. She couldn't dismiss the idea that it regarded her with a weary, inexpressible sadness. And yet she knew it would try to kill her the moment her binding broke.

The water had risen several feet in the intervening millennium between Aoi's visit and Lana's. She found the jutting lump of volcanic rock just where the death had said she might, but it now rose a mere seven feet above the ocean. She didn't immediately follow the still-clear path into the cave. She drank her water—one for now, and one for when she left—and contemplated. The last time she had sat vigil for a spirit, she had emerged a black angel. She hoped the death would grant her no such surprises, but she couldn't be sure. The nature of a vigil was to place oneself at the mercy of the spirits. But she would do it for her mother.

"Do you wait for me in there?" she asked the death. The avatar.

And again, she sensed that sadness. It shook its head. "The godhead awaits."

"But you're part of the godhead."

"I soon will be, I think."

She stood and fought off a strange urge to make some sort of farewell. But you can't hold the death's hand. Or hug its robes.

"Goodbye, then," she said.

It inclined its head. "You are worthy of us."

Inside the cave, seawater had pooled in the sloped bottom, but the spring still ran clear and she could make out the faintest traces of the ancient cave paintings on the walls. Even the death's mask remained, grim and timeless. She had made her decision and so she did not hesitate. The cave was chill, but she hardly noted it on her bare skin. She bathed even her wings, though it was awkward in the confines of the small spring. She took a bowl of water to the center of the cave and drank half.

"Mask, heart, and key," she said, perhaps the first person to invoke the joining in five hundred years. "Won't you share my drink?"

"So you have come," it said, and she finally understood all the ways in which the avatar was not the death.

The death that finds her is bright and primitive, with a mask that's little more than three crude holes in wood and a key that juts in an oblong thrust from its waist, like a fertility god. Its voice is deeper than the earth, harder than the rock they sit upon.

"The old woman," it says, "has played this very, very well. But this might just undo you both."

"I care nothing for her," Lana says, biting back a fear so primal and irrational she knows that alone could kill her. "I only want my mother."

"Then you are dead already."

Lana takes a breath and feels as though she is drowning. The water at the bottom of the cave has risen above her eyes and she's pulling its salt deep into her lungs. She is going to die. She is going to die. She thinks of nothing; she dreams of no one. She is an animal, a bird struggling frantically as it's doused again and again by the waves. For a moment, there is no one that she loves and nothing that she desires. Just to live, just to live, and for no good reason at all.

"What will you give us?" says this horror, this godhead who now longs for her extinction. "What will you give us for your life? Your mind? Your love? Your choice?"

Mask, heart, and key. It is a tiny thought, nearly lost in the maelstrom of inchoate fear. And yet it grows, calming the panic, subsuming the animal terror. She recalls her loves: Leilani, Kapa, Kai. She holds again her desires: peace and her mother safe and children of her own.

"Still yet you think," she says, her voice clear and more powerful than she's ever heard it. "Still yet you love. Still yet you choose."

The water vanishes as though it never was, because it never was.

"I give you nothing for my life," she says, in the hollow silence of the cave. "Because you are bound not to take it."

"The splinter of our thought might be."

"The avatar is the death," she says, and she sees just a hint of the surprise and amusement that mark the death she knows so well.

"What would you see, black angel?"

She has thought very carefully on this. If she asks about Akua's intentions directly, it might show her any number of misleading answers. But everything she has learned seems to come back to one central event: the great spirit bindings. If she understands that, she thinks, she will understand it all.

"A thousand years ago, there was one named Aoi. She went with another, Parech, to bind the great death. I would see what happened."

The death stretches wider and wider until there are two and then three expanding and expanding until the white robes surround her. Each wears a mask and key, but each is subtly different. The oblong fertility rod morphs gradually into a tablet and then a key. The mask is smoothed and grows longer, painted white and then decorated with the markings she recognizes. The deaths take a step toward her, then another. She understands that they will overtake her, and there is nothing she can do to escape. She looks at the entrance to the cave. She could try. She could run away. The deaths approach. The terror returns with their every step. She will die, she will die, she will—

"You can do nothing to me," she says. There it is again, that powerful voice, that unlooked-for assurance. The deaths pause.

"What will you give us?" they chorus.

"No," she says. "You will show me what I asked."

And they do.

It is very cold here, and she is still naked. She sees two people. They are in a different cave, standing near a rock with their backs to her. One turns and she sees it is a young man covered in tattoos. He is beautiful and has thick, kinky hair, bleached blond. She recognizes Parech like she might recognize Pano or Yechtak or her own father. The other woman must be Aoi. She is taller than Lana imagined she'd be. Her skin is lighter and her hair is long and beautiful, just like Tulo said. She wishes that Tulo could be in this vision, as well. Aoi speaks, but Lana can't understand her. She realizes that they must be speaking Kukichan, the ancient language of the rice islands that died centuries ago. She turns to the death, frantically.

"You must tell me what they say!"

"What will you give us?"

Mask, heart, and key. "A memory," she says.

She understands their words. "Do you want to save him or not?" Aoi says. She sounds desperate. Lana knows that she's deceiving him to save his life.

"If you do this, Ana, you can't ever go back."

"He's your son, Parech."

Parech turns away so that he's facing Lana, but he looks right through her. "Why would you make me choose between you?" he says.

Aoi slams her fist against the rock, hard enough that Lana winces, even from behind. "What am *I*? You stupid barbarian Akane, what am *I* compared to your child?"

It hurts Lana to hear the hatred and self-loathing in her voice. She wants to look away, but Parech makes Aoi face him.

"You still don't know," he says, and he smiles and there is laughter in his eyes. Lana remembers how Aoi first met him, a dying soldier laughing at his own death. "I told you once, and you didn't listen. I wrote it and you never found the note."

She turns her face toward him a little more, and Lana feels a tingling in her throat, a panicked constriction in her chest that has nothing and everything to do with the scene unfolding before her. She recognizes that profile. Great Kai, but she could go blind and still know that long, straight nose, those thin lips, those broad cheekbones.

"What did you tell me, Parech?" says Aoi, now Akua. Lana hadn't recognized her voice because it was too young and clear. A millennia had roughened Akua, like sand weathers stone.

"I said I saw you first."

"You can't love me."

"You've doubted it?"

"Not the way you love Tulo."

He kisses her forehead and then, as if he can hardly believe what he does, her lips. Lana shivers as she watches. *Have you ever thought you might learn things you don't want to know?* The avatar asked her, melancholic. And *yes*, she answers now. *Yes.*

He releases her and Aoi gasps.

"Love is not like that, Ana," he says. "To be parceled out and measured. I love you. I love Tulo. Surely, in all this time you've come to love me? At least a little."

Aoi is nodding, a puppet with tangled strings. "At least a little," she repeats. Parech has the countenance of a starving man who finds himself in a breadfruit grove. He laughs and lifts her up, but not for very long. His skin pales with the effort.

"More than a little," he says.

"You've doubted it?"

"I am a stupid, barbarian Akane."

They have sex against the rock. Lana does not look away. She wants this to be over and she wishes that she couldn't guess how very badly this will end. Akua had two loves and now she has no one. Eventually, they prepare for the binding. Parech holds the blade and Aoi kneels on the raised stone.

"No matter what I say, you must do it," she says, her voice trembling. Parech nods, too dazed perhaps to understand what her words imply.

"Save him, Ana."

"Mask, heart, and key," she says, in a language Lana recognizes as different. "I know the answer. That which the death does not know."

Lana steps forward, eager to at last learn the secret that might free her mother. But the death of the vision does not speak to Aoi. It enters her body and she slumps quietly against the stone. Parech is frantic until he feels her pulse, and then he looks around, as though the death might appear from the walls. The stone begins to glow, like metal before it melts in a forge. Aoi, still unconscious, starts to float. The red light turns white and misty, swirling around her like fog. Parech backs away. The light punches a hole in the roof of the cave. It seems to go on forever. Aoi floats to the top and then sinks again. She opens her eyes slowly and looks around.

Still within the confines of the white, roiling mist, she calls out to Parech.

"Your knife," she says. "Take my arm with it."

He understands what she means. He knows that she will die if he refuses her. He doesn't speak, but even Lana can see his grief and impotent fury as he looks up.

He will forgive them, Aoi had written. *I doubt he will forgive me.*

Lana doubts it as well. She can't bear to watch anymore, but when she asks the death to stop it just laughs. So she covers her eyes. She still hears the sickening thunk of metal into flesh, the screams that echo endlessly off the rocks. They don't stop for a very long time.

"The bone," Aoi says, her hoarse voice so clearly Akua's that Lana chokes back a sob. She doesn't look, but she hears something rip, something crack.

"*Make'lai*," Aoi says, raising her voice again with strength Lana can't even begin to understand. "Parech, I bind you as one. With this sacrifice, with my very bones, I make you the guardian of this death's binding and the founder of your line."

And now Lana must look, because she never guessed this end to the story. There's blood over both of them, so much that Lana doesn't understand how Aoi is still standing. She staggers forward, her left arm aloft and wreathed in white light. Parech himself is frozen. His eyes and mouth are filling with mist. Aoi slams the bone into the rock, and the sound reminds Lana of an earthquake.

The light from the rock solidifies into a column of air. Lana recognizes it from its cousin inside Akua's death shrine on the lake. The death stands imprisoned inside. Aoi lies beside it, insensate and bleeding. Parech's eyes are made of smoke. It drifts from his mouth as he speaks.

"Ana," he says. Where before his voice was young and filled with humor, now it aches like time. "Oh, Aoi," he says again, and Lana wonders how it is that he still loves her.

"Her name is Akua," Lana says. "Aoi is dead."

The death beside Lana touches her forehead. They are back inside the atoll's cave and she shivers uncontrollably.

"What memory will you give us?" it asks eager. "And it must be precious, else we'll take another."

Lana has no more defenses. The cold of the cave has seeped into her mind. She gives the death the first thing she can remember: she and Kali eating oranges in the top of a tree, tossing the peels to the floor and giggling.

"Let's make a pact," young-Lana says. "To go away together. To see all sorts of things we could never see on this island and then come back and tell everyone about it."

And Kali, as old as she ever will be, says, "You're the kind of person who can do things the rest of us can't, but assumes that there's nothing special about you."

The memory dwindles until all Lana knows is that there's something missing, something precious that she'll never have again.

The death sits across from her in the cave, satisfied. "What is it that you do not know?" Lana asks.

"Many things."

"What did Akua bind you with?"

"Akua did not bind me."

Lana grits her chattering teeth. "What is it that you do not know? What is the knowledge we all seek that even the death doesn't have? What about death is past death?"

The death waits. She stares at it. Clear, now. She almost stumbled upon this once before, when she bound it with the nature of its leaden key, a symbol of its ties to the earth. The death is a creature of the earth, of humans, of their finity. It guards the gate, *but just the gate.*

"*Se maloka selama ua ola,*" she whispers.

"*Ipa nui,*" it says, and she knows she is right.

18

THE EARTHQUAKE WAS MILD, BUT POWERFUL enough for an already decimated city. Several more buildings collapsed. A few fires broke out and were quickly controlled. Thousands of citizens, without the slightest encouragement, poured into the third district, before the gates of the Mo'i's house and the courtyards of the fire temple. Others lined Sea Street, putting down symbolic pandanus leaves and fruits and dune grass, chanting love songs. Rumors spread quickly, most false. The Mo'i had killed himself, the black angel had run away, the old nun in the fire temple had declared herself the ruler of Essel. Twelve hours passed, and the crowds did not disperse. Indeed, they swelled until an intrepid thief might have had the best year of his life among the abandoned homes of the fifth and fourth districts. Much of the city's sentiment still lay with the rebels, particularly after people learned of how they had so quickly meted out justice to that pale, demon-eyed woman who had tried to kill a baby. Still, they had all had enough of war.

And clearly the spirits had, as well.

Some people kept a wary eye on Nui'ahi, but most just turned away. If it would blow again, there was nothing they could do. Arai, the Okikan chief, abided by his agreement with the black angel. He and his army left a day after the quake. Perhaps he was hastened by the sight of his army's lines of attack choked, and sentiment in the city turned so firmly against his presence. He had come here to exploit the finest trade opportunity in a century. He had not counted on the Esselans being madder than a crate of eels.

Pano and Nahoa, aware that this unprecedented, peaceful demonstration held the seeds of a rebirth, made the arranged date and manner of their parlay with the Mo'i widely known. A day after the demonstrations began, they changed from a silent vigil into something closer to a solstice feast. The weather warmed— the three days of snow, it seemed, had finally cleared the sky of the choking ash. The farmers of the seventh and fourth districts carted their stores into the crowds, spurred by some impulse of magnanimity that would not be seen again. Flutes trilled and any surface at all turned into drums. Laughter was heard again on the streets of Essel, the sort of free and hopeful sound that the city had not known since its sentinel rained fire and ash. Owners of hookah lounges tossed amant onto the crowds like fragrant, dried flowers. Palm wine and kava kept them warm at night, when they weren't warmed by each other. Nine months later, the babies born would be called *kelala ua*, sparks of peace.

The day of the talks, a dozen new songs floated like flowers on the sea of people. They were mostly long, in the style of the old epics, with calls and responses and pauses for dancing. They told of the evil Mo'i, mad as a boar, who would kill anyone he looked upon. They told of the rebels, each one eight feet tall and more beautiful than the sun. Nahoa was a tragic figure, tied to her mad husband but in love with another (how the city had so accurately guessed this, Malie would never know, though she would eventually ascribe it to the animal wisdom of crowds). Pano grew flowers as large as palm trees and fought with a trowel. And the black angel? She was an enigma, a spirit but yet a girl, and whenever she entered a scene a melancholy strain would follow, a hint of "Yaela's Lament."

The cheers echoed across the island when the rebels marched through the city to the greater bay. Nahoa waved, Pano nodded with sage dignity. They hadn't wanted to start this without Lana, but they didn't even know if she was still alive. Right before he boarded the ship, a rebel soldier gave Pano a note. It was brief, but Nahoa couldn't read it. He closed his eyes for a moment. The crowd, seeing this, thought perhaps that he was overcome with the possibility of peace and plenty returning to his beloved city. Nahoa knew that something had happened, but she could not ask in front of all these people. The soldier, who had read the note and so understood Pano's grief, said something low and regretful to his friend.

Less than an hour later, the whole city knew what news the note contained. A new strain was summarily added to the songs for a new tragic figure, far more pitiable than Nahoa, who still had that fat baby, after all.

Eliki, the city mourned in its own fashion, imagining a woman ten feet tall with fire for eyes and a mane of white hair, who had dedicated her life to the city and drowned herself in the ocean when her folly took her from it. They did not know of her daughter, drowned so many years past, but they weren't far from wrong, all the same.

Kohaku was the leader of all Essel, but he stayed silent as Makaho led the talks. Much as he had all week. Even the increasingly pointed barbs from the false ghost of his sister elicited no more than a grunt. Makaho did not mind this state of affairs. He wondered, bleakly, if she even noticed.

"I have drafted a power-sharing agreement," she said, without preamble, when the ship had cast off and all four were present at the table. Lana was missing. He wondered if that meant the rumors were right, and she had run away. It did not seem like her.

"Perhaps you missed the crowd outside," Pano said.

"Perhaps you missed our superior army and resources. The crowd just wants peace. They don't care how they get it. I wouldn't mind some myself."

"I think you'd be surprised at how little love is left for Bloody One-hand in this city."

Kohaku hardly heard the epithet, but Nahoa winced, which was a little gratifying. She had not brought Lei'ahi. He wished she had, but he supposed that she didn't trust him any more than anyone else did. They said that she'd found the little girl's body. He couldn't even bring himself to speak with her.

"The ignorance of the commons will never surprise me," Makaho said. "That still doesn't mean you can win a war."

"We might," said Nahoa, and Kohaku heard more than enough in that "we" to make his misery complete.

"How loyal do you think that crowd will be if you decide to keep fighting instead of accepting our very generous offer? When the next earthquake comes? If Nui'ahi erupts again? Who do you think they'll side with, then?"

Nahoa glanced at Pano, her face as expressive as ever. They did not touch. He did not even look at her. And yet Kohaku knew. He had thought that he might win her back if he won this war. He saw now that he had a greater chance of learning to fly. She was lost, more permanently than he had ever suspected. Nahoa was not merely sympathetic to the rebels. He knew her well enough to recognize the signs: she was in love with Pano, the rebel gardener.

It did not matter what happened to him now, if it ever had.

"What are the terms?" Pano asked.

"You reaffirm the authority of the Mo'i and the selection by the fire spirit. In return, we form a city council along the lines of Okika, with Kohaku at its head and seats for representatives of the temples."

"Kohaku has to go."

Makaho narrowed her eyes. "I believe that would violate the principle of a power-*sharing* agreement."

"Why do you care so much, anyway?" Nahoa said. "No one's proposing to get rid of the fire temple."

"The Mo'i is selected by the great fire itself, my lady. You can hardly imagine I'd stand idly by while the rabble tries to dismantle the ancient tradition."

They glared at each other. How was it that his wife had spent so long in Makaho's care, given how much they disliked each other? But he knew why. What he'd done to Nahe had so horrified her that anything would have seemed preferable.

"I think you're flinching, brother," said Emea. Though lately, he thought, she did not even pretend to affect the mannerisms of his long-dead sister. He sometimes remembered the real Emea now. Her green eyes had been very kind, but she thought of him as stuck up and silly and he didn't think she'd been wrong. He'd loved her. Great Kai, how he'd loved his sister. He'd destroyed an entire city in his grief.

He'd ripped out a little girl's throat.

The ghost of the stablegirl dogged him now, as always. "I'm sorry," he said to her. She didn't respond. She couldn't.

"Did you say something, my lord?"

Pano and Nahoa were both looking at him like they'd just noticed he was in the room. "I'm sorry," he said again. "I surrender. Tell me what plan you have for the new government and I'll instate it as my last act. Whatever it is, I hope you at least improve on the Okikans. Another generation and the great families will declare themselves royalty."

Makaho stared at him in voiceless fury. Pano didn't seem to have understood what he said. Only Nahoa registered the slightest sadness.

"But Kohaku, what will you do? Go back to the Kulanui?"

This seemed so absurd that he laughed. Imagine, old Bopa forced to accept his research on the outer islands six years late. "No," he said. "I will follow my sister, I think."

Nahoa put her hands over her mouth. Makaho finally found her voice. "What does that mean, Mo'i?"

But he didn't have to answer. "He's going to sacrifice himself," Nahoa said. She was crying. "He's going to throw himself in the damn volcano."

He almost smiled.

Halfway up Nui'ahi, its namesake began to cry. As Ahi was a robust baby, her wails seemed louder than the wind of a high storm. Malie took the noisy bundle without complaint and started back down the mountain. Nahoa wanted to call her to come back, to let Kohaku have a chance at one last goodbye, but he just shook his head. Makaho had threatened to arrest them all when Kohaku proposed to help bind the fire spirit again. But he had coolly informed her that the news of his capitulation would be circulated to the crowd outside the moment they stepped off the ship, and did she care to have her fire temple overrun by a mob? Nahoa would never have guessed that the head nun was secretly one of those napulo kooks who thought the spirit bindings were evil, but it did make sense. Three quarters of the way to the lip, Pano started to cough and Nahoa told him to go back down. He tried to refuse, and she realized that he was afraid for her safety.

"Kohaku won't do anything," she shouted. No matter what else had happened between them, she'd always been very sure of his love. And that, she supposed, was why she'd felt like sobbing every time she looked at him. He had been her first love. She couldn't forget that or dismiss it, no matter what he had become.

Pano touched her shoulder before he left. The last few yards to the lip were slippery with brittle pumice stone that seemed to crumble wherever she put her feet. Kohaku pulled her up when she fell, but otherwise he stared at the lip of the volcano like he was meeting his lover. By the time they reached the top, the smoke made it difficult to see him, so she held his hand. She looked inside, just to say she had, but she could only make out a hint of a perfectly smooth orange surface, like a giant piece of glass. That was it? She'd at least expected some bubbles, like a stew. Maybe a hiss and scream of shearing rock.

"The fire shrine is more exciting than this," Nahoa said before she remembered why she was here, and when she had last seen the fire shrine, and all the million choices that led her to this place. Kohaku looked back at her and smiled.

"Do you regret it?" he asked.

"Regret..." Regret what? She had Ahi. Perhaps in another time, another way, they could have kept their happiness.

"No," she said.

She started to cough and Kohaku stepped away from her. He looked, not at the quiescent pool of magma, but up into the dense haze of smoke.

"You were never real," he said to no one. He laughed bitterly. "I offer myself as a sacrifice. A binding for my unbinding of the great fire."

He stepped off the edge. Nahoa screamed his name. She couldn't see him through the smoke; it was as if he'd never existed. She hadn't even said goodbye.

The house appeared as empty as ever, but now Lana guessed why. She didn't immediately recite the geas that would let her see the two for whom she'd spent the past three months searching. Instead, she looked around the tiny house, so well loved that Akua had kept it countless centuries after the deaths of Tulo and Parech. She imagined that if she checked, she'd find notes left by a father to his son, by a man to the woman with whom he'd shared so much and yet never quite enough. Had he ever forgiven her? To think that Aoi had turned Parech, of all people, into a guardian. Could any solution have been more against his nature?

"What were you thinking, Aoi?" she whispered, but no one responded.

Lana understood many things now. She had so much knowledge she ached with it. Far from wanting to crack the death's binding, as Lana had once suspected, Akua herself had bound the death a millennia ago. But now it was breaking free. She had known this for years. Decades, even. She'd devised a plan so ingenious it had taken Lana all the hours of her flight back from the atolls to decipher it, even though she'd been a central part of the plan for most of her life.

Akua had found a girl powerful enough to be her surrogate, but young and malleable enough to be kept ignorant of her role and the more arcane ways of geas. She had trained her to learn geas by heart, and yet conspicuously had not taught her the bases upon which they were formed. She had done this *not* to keep her powerless, but to make her as much like the Aoi of the black book as possible. In those days, no one knew much about the spirits, still less about bindings. Akua had needed to trust that Lana would be clever enough when the time came, but not so clever that she learned the truth too early. And the moment when the plan had crystallized, when Lana had agreed to the horrifying scheme without even knowing? The night she spent in Akua's death shrine, accepting the death sacrifices of hundreds of matched pendants. That night she had accepted the weight of Akua's lifetime of desperate measures as her own. She had bound *herself* inextricably into Akua's plan, and she should have known better. Ino had tried to stop her, she remembered. He had known what Akua was doing, even if he was geas-bound not to say.

Akua had sacrificed others to keep herself alive, because *life* was the requirement of the binding. But those deaths must have paradoxically strengthened the death against her. Until now, when it finally threatened to break free. Now those deaths were Lana's, and their expiation her responsibility. If she did not sacrifice herself on the altar of Akua's binding, she would be responsible for letting the death spirit go free.

But if Lana died, then so would her mother.

Lana had disturbed Akua's plans. She had learned something she was not supposed to know, and had prevented something she should have let happen. She had saved her mother's life with an ancient geas, and so invoked the death spirit earlier and in an entirely different manner than Akua had planned. And because Lana had tied Leilani's fate so inexorably with her own, Akua had kidnapped her mother. Lana could only assume that Akua thought her so depraved that she'd consider allowing the deaths of tens of thousands to save her own mother's life.

Not so long ago, Akua might have been right. Now, she'd make the hard choice if she had to. But that wouldn't stop her from using however much time she had left to think of any geas that might save her mother. But how much time remained in Akua's original binding?

That was the question she still could not answer. She doubted Akua could, either. The terms of her binding with the death obviously prohibited her from helping Lana in any way.

It was time. She took the flute from her pocket, Aoi's arm bone flute, and played a brief tune. The death, so invited over the threshold, gazed at her. It was her familiar death, not the terrifying all-death of the cave. And yet it looked different. So translucent and wispy as to be almost a shadow.

"How are you finding knowledge, Lana?" it asked.

"It's as you said. Death, what's happened to you?"

"I am being subsumed. The godhead tasks me with excess emotion. We want me dissolved and made again, different and unalloyed."

Dissolved and made again. "Is that...you're dying?"

"You could call it that."

"Are you afraid?"

"I'm not human."

Which was not, Lana realized much later, an answer. "I must bind you, death. One last time."

It inclined its head and she recited, with that perfect memory Akua had insisted she develop, the geas Aoi had first made to escape the Maaram army. "As you are out of the world's sight, so make me. Let me travel in the spirit world for a time, so I am invisible to the real one."

The world glowed, familiar in its shape and terrifying in its composition. Spirits were tied to the foundations, but the death dissolved before her, its mask lingering like a final farewell.

There were three people here, not just two.

"Kai?" she said. He was so pale, it seemed his skin had turned to water. His eyes held an ocean. He turned to her, but she couldn't read his face. She had never seen him look so inhuman, so much like the sprites he bound. She realized that this must be how Akua had captured him.

Akua. Not Makaho.

"You're working with the old nun?" Lana said. "She thinks you're napulo?"

Akua smiled. "I'm aware of the irony. It's good to see you, Lana."

But the one she truly sought stood behind Akua. "Mama," Lana said, and then forgot her words altogether.

"I've missed you," Leilani said.

She sounded so calm. She looked well. It surprised Lana. She hadn't expected Akua to take good care of her mother.

"You'll let them go," Lana said. "Now."

Akua frowned, not with anger so much as sadness. "I thought you understood this better by now. I can't let your mother leave. You have to know that."

Lana grit her teeth, nearly overwhelmed by the nearness of her mother and the seemingly unstoppable strength of Akua's will. "I do not care," she said. "I will take my mother back. I will keep her safe."

"Do you realize what's at stake, Lana? Truly? There's a reason I need your mother. One that goes beyond our own dispute."

Lana took a step closer to Akua. She'd forgotten how much taller the other woman stood—it had always intimidated her, but at least now she was too angry to care.

"I will keep my mother safe first. Then I will deal with whatever obligations I have because of your cursed geas."

"You agreed to it, Lana."

"And I should have known better."

"I let Ino warn you."

Lana paused, looking past Akua and her mother and her lover, and imagined the house as it had been when it was built. She imagined Akua as she had been, young and joyous and in love.

"He said it would twist you," Lana said.

Akua just smiled. It reminded Lana of Parech. "He was wise, for a barbarian."

"And Tulo?"

"She stayed with Parech, though she hated the death. We saw each other sometimes. It...he was wise, for a barbarian. Ileopo stayed with me in the death shrine. His descendants still serve there." She said this with perfect steadiness, and yet Lana still heard an ancient pain. How hard must grief grow, aged a thousand years?

"How much longer before your binding runs out, Akua? How much longer do I have?"

She shook her head. "If you've deduced that much, you must know I can't tell you."

"Yes," Lana said.

"You've done well."

"Only because you forced me."

"Yes," Akua said.

With a speed she guessed might be her only advantage, she whipped the small knife from her belt and held its sharp edge at Akua's throat.

"Lana!" That was Kai. Her mother only let out a strangled gasp. They did not move—they were bound, she was not.

Akua regarded her with a coolness that reminded Lana of Eliki, but only in how much farther Akua had traveled down that path of ruthless desperation.

"Will you kill me?" Akua asked.

"Release my mother."

"You know I will not."

"Release my mother, you bloody witch!"

Akua took a sudden, hitching breath. Her throat touched the sharp blade, releasing a thin line of crimson.

"Lana...Lana, don't you think I would end this if I could?"

Lana had to see the saltwater beading the polished metal blade before she realized they were not her own tears.

"Akua…" Lana's hand shook. If Akua pushed at her right now, she would fall to the floor like a solstice doll. Neither of them moved.

"Can't you trust me? Just this once?"

"Isn't that what you told Parech?"

And Akua leaned forward, pressing her neck into the blade with the grace of a bird diving for fish. She muttered a geas even as the blood dribbled down her neck and mixed with her tears. Several things happened at once, but all Lana understood at the time was how thoroughly she had been played, how great an Ana she had set herself against.

Kai stumbled forward. With the binding released, his body reverted to its normal, mostly human state. Her mother caught her up in a tight embrace and whispered, "There's so little time, Lana. You must hurry." All the while, Akua stared at them all, her neck bleeding and her eyes still unaccountably wet.

Lana felt Kai's hand on her back, smelled her mother's hair by her cheek, but she only had eyes for Akua. Everything had gone so wrong. She had come to rescue her mother, and now she had nothing left but Akua's struggle. Her mother's arms seemed to be fading, even as they pulled her closer. She knew that Akua was sending her back, and that a geas laid by this woman would be impossible for Lana to overcome.

"Where did you get your name?" Lana asked, as the room wavered. She knew almost everything about how Aoi had become Akua. Everything but this.

To her surprise, Akua looked away. "I heard it," she said very softly. "In those moments right after. I heard the name and I knew."

"Aoi is dead," Lana said, the same involuntary whisper that she'd uttered in the vision of the cave.

Her mother vanished, and Akua with her. Lana fell to her knees on the floor of the mundane, abandoned house that love had built and her tears seemed to scorch her face.

Eventually, she grew aware of Kai, his arms around her shoulders, his lips in her hair.

"I'm sorry," she said.

"I was wondering when you'd come," Kai said.

"I had to take a detour with the death spirit."

"Don't you always?"

She looked up at him. "If I have to die," she said, "then let me, Kai. Some things are worse than death."

And Kai promised, though he could not have known what she'd seen.

Leilani watched her daughter and her daughter's lover vanish from the house. She wanted to cry for what still might happen to them, but Leilani never cried. She missed Kapa. Great Kai, she missed him. To know he was alive and yet still so far away. Would any of them survive this great game of Akua's? Leilani knew why Akua couldn't let her go. However Lana had bound their fates together, Akua meant to undo it. But the powerfully complicated geas had been trickier than she expected. It seemed there were things that even a great Ana like Akua didn't know.

"If she finds a way to get me before you unravel her binding, what will happen?" Leilani asked.

Akua was staring at the walls again. "You know you can tell her nothing of what I say to you, right? If you break the binding now, everything is lost."

"I know," Leilani said impatiently. "You've said so enough. Though my daughter is a genius to have learned as much as she has."

Now Akua smiled, though she did not look at her. "That's certainly true. I'd never have picked her if she wasn't."

"I think Lana would call that a compliment she could do without."

"She would, at that. If I can't unravel the binding, she may die before she finishes, and you with her. A geas like that only plays to the death's strengths in this fight."

Carefully, Leilani voiced the option that she knew Akua must have considered. "You could kill me," she said. "It would solve the problem."

Akua turned to her slowly. "It would solve the problem."

"But you won't do it. Why? You tried to once before."

"I didn't know you then."

"That makes it okay?"

Akua smiled. After these many months, Leilani knew it meant she was thinking about the past. And her past, as Akua had gradually revealed, spanned a great many more years anyone else's. "No," she said. "It just makes it acceptable to me."

"Were Parech and Tulo the other ones who lived in this house?"

"Ever perceptive, Lei."

"How else would I get through the day?"

They smiled at each other, wearied and knowing. "Parech stole Tulo's spirit sight," Akua said. "Or thought he did. And after, when she asked him how he could have done such a cruel thing, he told her he'd never do it now. It's just that she was a stranger, and there was too much suffering in the world for him to care for those he didn't know."

"Maybe you shouldn't have believed him."

Akua shook her head. "You don't understand the way the world was, then. He was right. I've lived too long to care about everyone I meet. Eventually, you all start to seem like the river nits on Okika—too beautiful to look upon, and then rotting on the shores."

"Except for me?"

"You and Lana."

Leilani leaned back against the mat. Spirits shimmered above her; delicate, ghostly stalks of switch grass to hobble her feet if she tried to leave. Akua was nothing if not conscientious.

"How long does she have left?"

"Not long. I haven't been back there in many years..."

"Back where?"

"The death shrine. One way or another, that's where this ends,

Leilani. The rock at the heart of my binding, the column of smoke."
Akua touched her hand.

"We leave tomorrow. In fifteen days, we'll know if the death breaks
free."

END

Note on Pronunciation

THE LANGUAGE OF THE ISLANDS IN *THE SPIRIT BINDERS* trilogy is based mainly on Hawaiian, with some Japanese and a dash of invention. The use of an apostrophe (') in a proper noun (for anything besides a possessive) denotes a glottal stop—the sound one makes between the first and second syllables of "uh-oh," for example. Otherwise, names generally sound the way they look, with each syllable pronounced and no "silent e," as in English. For example, "kale" would *not* rhyme with "quail" but with "ballet." The letter combination of "ei" rhymes with "hay." The combination of "ai" rhymes with "sky." Below is a list of the pronunciations a few representative names and places.

Iolana – "EE-oh-LAH-nah"
Leilani – "lay-LAH-knee"
Mandagah – "mahn-DAH-gah"
Nui'ahi – "new-ee ' AH-hee"
Emea – "eh-MAY-ah"
Ino – "EE-no"
Pua – "POO-ah"
Malie – "MAH-lee-eh"
Kalakoa – "KAH-lah-coe-ah"
Ali'ikai – "AH-lee ' EE-kah-ee"
Kaleakai – "kah-LEH-ah-kah-ee"

Acknowledgments

I THANK MY FAMILY, AS ALWAYS, FOR BEING MY BIGGEST fans and best supporters. My writing group, Altered Fluid, for letting me moan about this novel and then helping me whip it into shape. My other pre-readers: Tamar Bihari, Rachel Lenz, Lauren Johnson, Fleur Beckwith, and Bill Steinmetz. T. S. Abe, for giving me such beautiful illustrations to help promote it. Scott, for everything. My literary manager, Ken Atchity, and my publisher extraordinaire, Doug Seibold. And finally, I thank everyone who has read *Racing the Dark* and emailed me or talked to me or just commented online about how you enjoyed it. I promise, this book wouldn't be here if not for you.

About the Author

ALAYA DAWN JOHNSON WAS BORN IN 1982 IN WASHINGTON, DC and graduated from Columbia University, where she studied East Asian languages and cultures. She has published short fiction in several magazines, and two of her stories were republished in the anthologies *Year's Best SF 11* and *Year's Best Fantasy 6*. She is also the author of the novels *Moonshine* (2010) and *Racing the Dark*, the first book in the trilogy *The Spirit Binders*, published by Agate Bolden in 2007.